A Touch of Mercy

by Regina Jeffers

Regency Solutions

ISBN: 9780615813820

A Touch of Mercy

(Book 5 of the Realm Series)

Regency Solutions

Mercy impatiently waited for Lord Lexford's appearance. She held an inkling of the viscount's handsome countenance for she observed two renderings of the man in the gallery. In the first, Aidan Kimbolt was no more than five or six years of age. He was the youngest of the three children, and Mercy suspected he presented his nurse a case of the vapors. An impish good nature played in his brownish-black eyes. Surely the portrait painter erred in the color for she never knew one with such richness. The second portrait was one of the viscount, his brother, and their father. Likely, the current Lord Lexford was fifteen or sixteen at the time, while his brother was in his early twenties. Compared to his brother Andrew, Aidan Kimbolt appeared lanky and boyish, while Lord Andrew possessed well-defined shoulders and a trim waist. All three men were exceedingly handsome, even the former viscount, whose age lines only added to his well turned out appearance. Yet, Mercy spent her time searching the countenance of the boy, the one not like the other two in his appearance. The one with the softer lines to his face and the more welcoming slant to his shoulders.

The sound of approaching footsteps warned Mercy of the viscount's arrival, and she stood to greet him. She had second and third thoughts on Mr. Hill's plan to present her as Lord Lexford's relative, but it was too late to change her mind. Mercy squared her shoulders and prepared to meet the man who would decide her fate. She found herself strangely unnerved by the possibility.

He entered in obvious irritation, and Mercy's heart leapt into her throat. The artist did not err. The viscount's eyes were mesmerizing. All she could say was they were more blackish brown. The color of the coffee beans she saw on sale in the marketplace. Absurdly long lashes. A wide brow over which a sandy blond curl dropped. Chiseled cheekbones. And a mouth that likely felled countless women. Her sister Grace erred: Viscount Lexford must be the most handsome man at the Prince Regent's party.

***

Aidan led the way to the study. He wanted to be done with whatever foolishness Hill concocted. Likely, the man wanted to plead for a return to Linton Park and to Hannah. If Aidan did not feel so vulnerable, he would drive his friend from the estate with a stick. Unfortunately, he held no doubt Henry Hill would remain his salvation.

However, after witnessing Mrs. Babcock's display of showiness, Aidan wondered if he made a mistake in returning to Lexington Arms to face his demons.

"Now what is of such great importance?" he began before coming to a stumbling halt barely five feet inside the room.

Aidan gave his head a little shake as if to clear his vision, but the image remained: A fairy goddess in a forest green gown. Red golden locks framed her heart shaped face. A compelling vibrancy surrounded her, and Aidan half expected her to take flight. His blood heated when he gazed into her eyes: The color of melted chocolate. She was dangerous. This woman was a perfect sin, and Aidan had to remind himself to breathe.

"Pardon...pardon me," he said on a rasp. "I was unaware we had guests." Without removing his eyes from the girl, he instructed, "Mr. Hill, would you be so kind as to make the proper introductions?"

Aidan could hear the smile in Hill's tone.

"Lord Lexford, permit me to bring to your acquaintance, Miss Mary Purefoy." His man paused for emphasis, and Aidan wondered what perfidy Hill practiced. "Miss Purefoy is your sister, my lord."

Cast of Characters

Members of the Realm and Their Ladies

James Daniel Kerrington, Viscount Worthing (Future Earl of Linworth) – the group's "unofficial" leader (resides at Linton Park in Derbyshire)

Lady Eleanor Agatha (Fowler) Kerrington, Viscountess Worthing – Kerrington's wife; Brantley Fowler's sister

Brantley William Fowler, the Duke of Thornhill (resides at Thorn Hall in Kent)

Velvet Elaine (Aldridge) Fowler, the Duchess of Thornhill – Brantley's wife and cousin

Marcus Alexander Wellston, the Earl of Berwick (Lord Yardley) - resides at Tweed Hall in Northumberland

Cashémere (Aldridge) Wellston, the Countess of Berwick (Lady Yardley) – Velvet's younger sister; twin to Miss Satiné Aldridge

Gabriel Luis Crowden, the Marquis of Godown - resides in Staffordshire

Grace Anne (Nelson) Crowden, the Marquise of Godown – Crowden's wife; a former governess

Aidan Colin Kimbolt, Viscount Lexford - resides at Lexington Arms in Cheshire

Mercy Elizabeth Nelson – Grace's younger sister

Johnathan Swenton – a baron (resides in York)

Sir Carter Stephan Lowery – a baronet - resides in London and Kent

Other Characters Important to the Story Line

Aristotle Pennington – the Realm's leader; the group refers to him as "Shepherd"

Murhad Jamot – a Baloch warrior who has been sent to England by the tribal leader, Shaheed Mir, to recover a missing emerald, which Mir claims the Realm has stolen from him

Rhamut Talpur – Jamot's partner

Sonali Fowler – Brantley Fowler's daughter by his first wife, Ashmita

Henry "Lucifer" Hill – Aidan Kimbolt's "man of all means";

Hannah's love interest; was rescued by Kimbolt during the war and pledged himself for 10 years of service to the viscount

Hannah Tolliver – Lady Eleanor's long time maid; Lucifer Hill's love interest

Baron Charles Ashton – the maternal uncle to the Aldridge daughters; Satiné Aldridge's guardian (resides at Chesterfield Manor outside of Manchester)

Satiné Aldridge – Cashémere Aldridge's twin sister

Lachlan Charters – a Scotsman who kidnapped Miss Satiné, thinking her to be Cashémere; struck Aidan Kimbolt a mighty blow, causing the viscount to lose his memory

Richard Breeson – Marcus Wellston's former batman; Ashton's steward

Baron Geoffrey Nelson – Grace and Mercy's wastrel brother

Sir Lesley Trent – a baronet and widower, who wishes to marry Mercy Nelson

Mathias Trent – the baronet's oldest son and heir

Squire Holton – Aidan Kimbolt's neighbor and the local squire

Prologue

"Nothing can make injustice just but mercy."
- Robert Frost

"YOU ARE A FOOL," he groused under his breath. Aidan Kimbolt shuffled the cards again, but his mind was far from the game of Patience he spread out upon a low table. His thoughts remained on the letter he received from his father. In fact, the letter's contents haunted both Aidan's waking and sleeping hours for the past week. From the moment Worthing placed the viscount's closely written message into Aidan's hands, Aidan regretted receiving it. *Not as if your refusal to read it would change the facts*, he silently chastised his foolish heart. *Susan means to have Andrew and a title.*

Aidan flipped the cards with more vigor than he intended. Instinctively, he glanced to where Worthing watched him. Very little escaped the man Aidan's small group of seven called, "The Captain." Aidan offered his friend an unobtrusive nod to permit the future Earl of Linworth the freedom of no censure.

According to Shepherd's orders, Aidan's particular unit of the British covert operations, known as the Realm, was to infiltrate Shaheed Mir's stronghold. The British government sought Mir's cooperation in protecting the English supply routes into this part of Persia, but in Aidan's opinion, Mir claimed funds for protection from both the British government and the mountain bandits, who plagued English outposts in the hilly terrain.

A shift in Worthing's shoulders warned Aidan something changed. They learned to read one another quite well over the three years they served together. With downcast eyes, Aidan surreptitiously watched as their leader whispered something private to Gabriel Crowden, the future Marquis of Godown, before having a brief word with Brantley Fowler. Fowler was infamous among the Realm for his foolish need to battle the image his father, the Duke of Thornhill, held among the *ton*. The current duke possessed a lusty reputation for debauchery, and Fowler often made it his business to save damsels, fair or not. It was an obsession, which usually resulted in their group needing to extricate themselves from an altercation, and it appeared Fowler meant to play the role of dashing knight once more.

For eight and forty hours, Fowler stewed over a bit of tribal law. Shaheed Mir declared one of the women a *quean*. Actually claimed the girl, who could be no more than fifteen or sixteen, worth no more than a rupee. As a result, the Baloch warriors took turns with her in a tent in which the girl was being held prisoner. In the three days the Realm courted the Baloch leader, the young woman's cries regularly split the air. Each time she called out, Fowler's fists clenched and unclenched in anger.

"Zounds," Aidan grumbled as Fowler suddenly stood. Aidan quickly gathered the cards to stuff them in an inside pocket before rolling to his knees to stand.

"I believe I will take a walk. Stretch my legs," Fowler announced as he moved toward the tent's opening. Without a doubt, Thornhill's heir meant to breech the girl's quarters and to silence her current anguish.

When a Baloch guard motioned Fowler away, Crowden stepped before the future duke to dissuade him, but Aidan knew Fowler's stubborn singularity would prevail over Crowden's warning. A quick glance about the tent announced the cautious preparedness with which their companions anticipated the upcoming confrontation. With a flick of his wrist, Crowden motioned Aidan to flank Fowler's right, and Aidan nodded his understanding. John Swenton and Marcus Wellston assumed an alert slant to their stances, while Carter Lowery palmed a double-edged knife, as he swung his legs over a low-slung chaise.

Raising his hands in an act of submission, Fowler smiled largely and casually turned in place. Obviously, the future duke inspected *his troops*. Only a raised eyebrow warned them what would follow.

"Forgive me," Fowler mumbled as if he meant to back away, but, instead, his friend wound up to strike the guard with an upper cut, sending the Baloch reeling with a broken nose.

A heartbeat later, a melee broke loose. Nearby, Wellston shot one of the charging Balochs in the knee, filling the tent with gray smoke, while Aidan fought off two of the tribesmen. He elbowed one in the throat to send his attacker gasping for air. With a knife Aidan retrieved from a small pouch at his side, he sliced the air before the charging mountain warrior. The cut left a deep red trail across his enemy's chest and took a nick from the man's chin.

However, before Aidan could turn to meet the next attack, one of Mir's warriors, literally, jumped upon his back. With an arm across Aidan's throat, the Baloch bent him backward, stretching Aidan as if he were a bowstring. He fought for breath, clutching at the guard's meaty hand. Then, just as suddenly, he was free. Crowden dislodged the man before delivering a perfectly placed dagger in the Baloch's throat.

Aidan rubbed his neck, but managed a raspy "Many thanks" before rejoining the fight. He used a large pitcher across an attacker's head to waylay another assailant, who pinned Lowery under a broken table.

"Now!" Worthing's voice rose above the battle's clamor, and Aidan knew without looking that Fowler rescued the girl. Along with his friends, he landed several strategically placed blows to quiet the last of those in the tent, but the sound of running feet announced the arrival of reinforcements. He followed Lowery and Wellston to the waiting horses.

Worthing motioned Lowery to accompany Crowden before he and Swenton headed off in the opposite direction. Aidan understood without being told he was responsible for providing Fowler and the girl protection in their escape. The others would draw the Balochs away from the trail the extra weight on Fowler's horse would leave behind. Aidan, as the group's best horseman, automatically crisscrossed the line in the sand, which led to the mountain pass.

As he watched Fowler's retreat from a proper distance to guard against another attack, he noted how the girl clung to the future duke's waist. The gesture reminded Aidan of Susan. He and Susan Rhodes were childhood friends, and, eventually, young lovers. She would often catch him about his back or neck, after Aidan teased her unmercifully, and then her arms would come about his waist, and Susan's chin would rest upon his chest. He would gently kiss the top of her head and plan their life together.

"Can you hear my heart?" he would say in that special way of those who hold a strong affection. "It speaks of my love."

Aidan shook his head in anger. In his distraction, he slowed his pace. Kicking the horse's flanks, he doubled his efforts to catch the disappearing Brantley Fowler.

"No more," he growled as he leaned across the horse's neck to make himself a smaller target. "My heart forgot its rhythm," Aidan said the words aloud to harden his resolve. "Susan Rhodes means to have Andrew." *Andrew Kimbolt, the future Viscount Lexford, my brother.* The thought sent bile to the base of Aidan's throat. He might as well hitch his hopes to the sun rising in the east. They could not sizzle any more quickly into nothingness. "It is why my father bought my commission and sent me to fight Britain's wars. Not to make me a man. Nor was it as he promised as a means to earn my fortune. Nothing more than a ploy to remove me from Lexington Arms, leaving an open door for Andrew to claim the woman I love."

Chapter 1

"IT WAS A MISTAKE coming to Linton Park for the Festive Days," Aidan silently told his image as he looked out upon the celebratory markings of the upcoming Christmastide. He had been gone from his home for months: Since early October when he thought to court Cashémere Aldridge and finally claim a bride, who would bring life, rather than death to Lexington Arms.

Death haunted his manor for more years than Aidan cared to recall. When he was but ten, Aidan's mother and his sister Aylene succumbed to consumption and influenza after being caught in an icy storm. He and Andrew were away at school at the time and missed the worst of the disease, as well as his mother's funeral. Aidan always carried the shame of not saying a proper farewell.

While he was away in service to his country, Andrew died in a duel over his mistress, and a second letter arrived in Bombay to announce Aidan was Lexford's new heir; and so he asked Shepherd to release him from his duties, and Aidan made his way home. He was not in attendance for Andrew's funeral either. That occurred some three years prior. Aidan arrived on Lexington Arms' threshold to find a devastated father, a grieving household, a pregnant widow, and a devious plan for him to marry Lady

Susan Kimbolt. But Death was not finished with him.

"Word came from the gatehouse that Godown's carriage approaches." Aidan turned his gaze from the window to his friend James Kerrington, Viscount Worthing.

"Godown? On Advent Sunday? The marquis would not travel on the Sabbath unless something of import occurred." Aidan abandoned his self-possessed misery and purposefully followed Worthing toward the main foyer.

Lord Worthing's pace quickened as he led the way through Linton Park's halls.

"I pray no other attempt on the marquis's life occurred."

Aidan lengthened his stride to keep apace of Worthing. He last saw Gabriel Crowden, the Marquis of Godown, less than a month prior in London. Aidan escaped the "care" of the Duke and Duchess of Thornhill and joined most of the Realm, including Godown, for London's Short Season.

In October, Aidan sustained a crippling blow to the back of his head during a kidnapping debacle of the wrong Aldridge twin. He thought he was wooing Miss Cashémere, but the lady and her sister, Miss Satiné, switched places. He should have known sprightly Cashémere Aldridge required a heavier hand than was his customary nature, but before Aidan could discover the truth, a crazy Scot ruthlessly attacked him. In retrospect, Aidan convinced himself if Lachlan Charters did not deliver the near fatal blow that rendered Aidan incapable of remembering major events from the past few years, he would have sniffed out the deception. Even if his personal life remained in shambles, Aidan would like to think himself capable of efficient detective work.

Instead of claiming a wife, after the attack, he spent a month recuperating at Thorn Hall under the care of Brantley Fowler's personal physician. Every time Aidan thought of the duke's attempt at charity he smiled.

"At least, Fowler keeps an excellent wine cellar," he told Worthing upon his arrival at Linton Park.

As he waited on the main entrance steps for Godown's

coach to maneuver the rough road leading to the manor, Aidan thought of those few brief encounters in London, which assured him, it was time to return to Cheshire.

At Lord Graham's ball, he and Godown shared cheroots on the balcony. They played their parts in bringing Sir Carter Lowery's older brother, Lawrence, to toe the line. The future Baron Blakehell made a very public proposal of marriage to an American girl named Miss Arabella Tilney. It was quite the spectacle with Lawrence Lowery dropping to a knee before the girl on a crowded dance floor. Sir Carter orchestrated the events, and Aidan's friend was more than pleased with the outcome.

"A bit dramatic," Aidan observed when he and Godown secured the privacy of a shadowed corner of the balcony. "Shoot me if I act so foolishly."

Godown's eyebrow rose in a taunt.

"You are not a believer in love? When came the change?"

His friend's words stung more than Aidan cared to reveal. He stiffened, unprepared for the marquis's question. Among his Realm associates, Aidan held the reputation of wearing his heart on his sleeve. It seemed he continually looked for love where none could be found. As he stared off in the darkness to compose his thoughts, he announced, "Maybe once. A long time ago."

Had he meant to convince the marquis or himself? Aidan followed his declaration with a smile: Feigned frivolity. Such gestures were his shield against the loneliness.

"Needless to say, that was before Thornhill invited me to Kent."

The deflection worked its magic. Any curiosity the marquis held evaporated.

"You cannot fathom the number of times I stumbled upon the duke and duchess in an intimate embrace. I swear, Godown, it is enough to make one wish for blindness. Has the man never heard of a locked door?"

The marquis laughed lightly. Aidan understood perfectly: Godown and Thornhill held a healthy competition waged privately in the most devious ways. To Aidan's relief, Godown dropped the subject of Aidan's personal life being in disarray.

"At least, the duke's lack of propriety sped your recovery."

Aidan shrugged noncommittally. His devils were his own, and some things were best left unsaid.

"Not completely, but the physician assured me my memory will return."

It was at that moment Aidan realized he must return to Lexington Arms to set his life aright. If he did not know his past, how could he find a future? So despite receiving an invitation to return to Thorn Hall for Christmastide, Aidan chose to accept the one from Lord Worthing. Fundamentally, Derbyshire was so much closer to Cheshire than was Kent.

"Do you suppose either of us will ever find what the others have?" Aidan ventured when his conversation with the marquis lulled.

Aidan longed for the peace of family since the day the headmaster unceremoniously announced his mother's passing.

Not surprisingly, the marquis possessed no more of an answer than did he, and in some ways that particular fact comforted Aidan. To know he was not the only one to dodge when he should run straight into love's embrace eased his pain.

"Unfortunately, I have no time for pursuing love," Godown confessed. "I must marry soon, but it will only be from duty, not from affection."

Three of the seven with whom Aidan served married for love, and although Aidan celebrated his friends' marriages, with each, he saw his own prospects dim. How could God grant all seven true happiness?

"Where is your mind, Lexford?" Worthing asked as Godown's carriage rolled to a halt.

Aidan gave himself a mental shake.

"Just wondering how I might extricate Mr. Hill from Linton Park now that my man owns Lady Worthing's maid's heart."

Worthing chuckled.

"I suspect with Hill's growing ardor, I must soon employ another lady's maid for my wife."

As Lord Worthing stepped away to greet the marquis, Aidan murmured, "Even my servant found true regard. Yet, Lady Love does not look kindly on me."

"Ah, Godown. It is you." Worthing called as he descended the steps. "When word came from the gatehouse of your arrival, I thought Ole Taylor lost his reason."

The marquis nodded to Aidan, but his friend appeared nervous, a characteristic rarely associated with Gabriel Crowden.

Aidan descended the steps to greet the man.

"You do realize this is Advent Sunday?"

Crowden's lips twitched in mock amusement.

"I told John Coachman to travel the back roads. I found it necessary to escape Lord Brant's house party. I will explain in more detail later."

Aidan's heart clenched. Only moments before, he assumed Crowden would know failure in marriage, but something of the marquis's stature spoke of anticipation. Resignation departed Lord Godown's shoulders to be replaced by eagerness. *Not nerves, after all,* Aidan thought.

"Let us go inside." Worthing gestured to the still open door. "Out of the cold."

When Crowden paused awkwardly, Aidan knew everything changed for his friend.

"I have someone with me," the marquis said matter-of-factly.

Aidan stifled the sigh of regret and plastered a smile upon his lips. Good-naturedly, he slapped Crowden on the back.

"You sly fox. You and Miss Haverty decided to elope, and you require our assistance to outrun the lady's relatives."

Something inside Aidan cracked. Needless to say, he was aware the marquis meant to marry Miss Alice Haverty, but Crowden's marriage was not one of true regard. His friend said as much in London. It was meant simply to save the man's title.

Yet, an undeniable peacefulness lodged itself squarely upon the marquis's countenance. Did Crowden find love with Miss Haverty? Aidan could not imagine how it was so. Personally, he found the girl an insipid twit, but an elopement would speak of passion.

Godown halted Aidan's steps.

"It is not what you think, Lexford," the marquis cautioned.

Aidan wished to scream that none of them knew what he thought. They never knew what he thought–only what he permitted them to see. Shepherd and the Realm saw him as a man who could make others believe he wished to be their truest acquaintance. That was the role Aidan played in saving Eleanor Fowler from Louis Levering. The amiable friend. Yet, that was certainly not he. They knew nothing of his deepest fears and longings. Bloody Hell! Even he possessed no idea who he once was. Lachlan Charters' blow scrambled Aidan's emotions, along with his mind.

Turning to the carriage, Godown extended his hand into the darkness.

"Come, my dear, we have explanations to make."

The marquis delivered a hard stare to Aidan and Worthing, daring either man to comment on the marquis's companion, the former governess Miss Grace Nelson.

Aidan understood immediately. Despite the evidence, which spoke of Miss Nelson's involvement in several attempts on the marquis's life, Crowden held a strong affection for the woman. *The peaceful countenance,* Aidan considered. *Lord Godown loves the woman. He may not realize it, but he does.* The thought saddened Aidan. He would wish his friend well, but if what he expected proved true, then the odds against his own happiness increased exponentially.

"Worthing. Lexford. You previously hold Miss Nelson's acquaintance."

Worthing found his voice first. The viscount bowed stiffly.

"Certainly, Miss Nelson, welcome to Linton Park."

To assure them of what Aidan instinctively knew, Godown

announce,

"Miss Nelson agreed to make me the happiest of men. We hoped Linworth's offer of Linton Chapel might extend to our joining."

⌒⌒⌒

Dutifully, Aidan sat with Worthing and Godown after Lady Worthing took Miss Nelson under her care. He even argued the point that the marquis should not consider marrying a woman who they suspected of extensive duplicity, but Aidan knew the futility of such reasoning. He wasted his voice. Every gesture. Every facial expression said the marquis's heart was engaged.

Later that evening when Aidan escaped the loving couple, he sneaked from the house and made his way to the folly overlooking the first of the lakes on Linworth's property. The conversation between Lord and Lady Worthing, Lord Godown, Miss Nelson, and the Countess of Linworth naturally turned to the wedding, and for the first time ever Aidan suddenly felt uncomfortable with his friends. Stepping inside the structure, he sat upon the cold cement bench. Instinctively, he pulled his great coat closer about him and donned his gloves. The December chill crept into his bones, but Aidan never considered returning to the warmth of his chambers. He required time to decide what was best for his future, and a deep cold matched his heart.

"God! What a quagmire!" he groaned aloud.

He scrubbed his face with his hands to clear his thinking: Physically, he was strong enough to resume his duties as Viscount Lexford of Lexington Arms, Cheshire, but mentally and emotionally, Aidan was less certain of his success. His injury, literally, shook him to his core. Until that incident, he thought himself well aware of his role in life. He was the dutiful second son of Viscount Arlen Kimbolt, Lord Lexford. He abandoned the woman he loved when his father pressed Aidan to do so, and he returned to Cheshire to marry a woman who did not love him, again at his father's insistence.

"Ironic that both women were one in the same," he reasoned.

Aidan braced his arms on his knees and dropped his head into his hands. His temples throbbed with the pain of remembering.

"Susan," he whispered her name into the night. "Why?"

From the day he woke from his injury in a room with Lady Worthing as his caretaker, Aidan repeated his wife's name and the question of *why* she chose his brother over him at least a thousand times. When Susan was alive, Aidan never possessed the courage to ask her.

"She was so overcome by Andrew's death, I could not drag an answer from her."

Now, she was gone, and no opportunities remained.

Aidan rubbed his temples roughly, making tight circles with his fingers.

"The bastard died in defense of another woman, for Christ's sake," Aidan protested. "I would have never deserted you. Could you not see that?" he asked his wife's image.

"Damn her!" He leaned his head against one of the white washed columns and closed his eyes. "We were doomed from the beginning," he murmured to the stillness. "How could we make a marriage from the shambles of Andrew's insensibilities?"

Aidan placed his heart and soul into making the former Susan Rhodes happy, but his brother's ghost replaced the easy closeness he and Susan once shared. Susan recoiled from Aidan's every gesture of tenderness. Where she once readily sought his embrace, after their marriage, his wife avoided him. They existed as strangers in Lexington Arm's many passages and rooms.

"Even with all the chaos between us, I never wanted you to follow Andrew," he said as his throat tightened. "We could have found a means to come together. We were friends once. I would have given you and the child my devotion."

Aidan could see her. See Susan swaying from side to side. Her arms wrapped about her waist, and her eyes closed dreamily upon the world. Could she see the flames grow higher. See his feeble attempts to save her.

"Forgive me," he whispered as tears formed behind his

lids.

"You require assistance, my lord?"

Aidan opened his eyes to find Lucifer Hill standing in the folly's opening.

"Do I appear in distress?" Aidan said with a bit more sarcasm than he intended. "I no longer require a nurse maid, Mr. Hill."

His man of all jobs frowned.

"Considering you sat on a cold bench for nigh onto two hours, you will likely be requiring some sort of nurse. If you wish to sleep in the cold, permit me to fetch you a blanket or two."

Aidan unfurled his stiff legs.

"No need to be practical. I will seek my bed." He rotated his shoulders and neck. "Despite the poor conditions, the sleep was restorative."

"Lord Worthing noted your unusual mood. Asked me to check on you," Hill confessed.

"Inform the viscount I am well. The physician allowed me to return to my duties."

He heaved a sigh of exasperation. Everyone thought him an invalid.

Hill nodded. "But your heart has not."

Aidan hated how well the man knew him.

"On the contrary," he said despite Hill's scowl. "I was considering how long I have been removed from Lexington Arms."

"You mean to return to Cheshire?"

Aidan stepped around Hill.

"There is nothing for me at Thorn Hall nor at Linton Park," he asserted baldly.

"Nothing but the best friends you ever knew," Hill countered.

Aidan turned to stare hard at the man he rescued from a trumped-up execution. He spoke in earnest.

"The best friends a man can possess, *along with their ladies*." He emphasized the last four words to make his point. "Men who take roots no longer have time for those who fly free as an autumn leaf."

Hill shook his head in disapproval.

"You know that is not true. Those men would lay down their lives for you."

Aidan shrugged his answer. How did one argue against the truth?

"I need to refill the holes in my memory, and I must start from the beginning. From my home. From Lexington Arms."

Hill nodded his understanding.

"When do we leave?"

Aidan noted the sad resignation on Hill's countenance.

"You may remain with Lord Worthing if you wish."

Hill's lips formed a tight line.

"I promised you ten years of service, and three years remain."

"It is not necessary…"

Hill interrupted Aidan's release.

"A man's pride is necessary, Your Lordship," he said flatly.

"And what of Hannah?" Aidan protested.

Hill smiled easily. "Hannah is a good girl. She will wait for my time to pass. We spoke on it." He started off toward the house, and Aidan fell in step beside his friend. "I ask again when we leave."

Aidan sighed deeply.

"I was thinking after Lord Godown's nuptials. At week's end."

"I will see to the arrangements. Leave the details to me, Sir."

Mercy wished she knew her sister Grace planned her escape from Foresthill Hall. If so, Mercy would have begged Grace to permit Mercy to accompany her. Instead, it took Mercy until the early days of November before she made her own exit from her brother's household.

She did not know how long she traveled the roads of the western midlands. Some five weeks. Possibly six. Mercy long since gave up counting the days. When she sneaked from her brother's house in the dead of night, Mercy thought to be in London by now. Thought she would find gainful employment. Likely, she would if she did not accept the aid of the Foyles. Mr. and Mrs. Foyle, if that was truly their names, offered Mercy a ride in their wagon and a place to spend the night, an offer, which filled Mercy with genuine hope for the future.

"I was such a simpleton," she groaned as she rolled straw into a tight bundle and laced one of her hair ribbons about it to make a pillow of sorts. Her time on the road taught her several hard lessons.

First, the Foyles dashed Mercy's dreams when they bound her with a rope and stole her purse, as well as the locket her mother presented Mercy on her tenth birthday. The memory of her assailants' laughter as they rode away into the dusk still haunted Mercy.

"If God is just, some day we shall meet again, and it shall be my turn to laugh," she declared.

Mercy also learned when to beg a bite to eat and when to seek out what she could find in the fields and orchards. Even when she was hungry, she refused to steal from those who barely scraped by. She knew from the way her dress hung loosely upon her frame that she lost more weight than she thought possible. A result of too many missed meals. Yet, as a genteel woman, she knew the value of charity, and she would not take from those with less than she.

"Less than me," she said with an ironic chuckle.

Mercy wrapped her cloak about her. She found a deserted barn, one which would likely fall down about her head, but one which was dry and relatively safe from others on the road. Since the famine of 1816, more and more of the populace took to the road– to look for a brighter future. Needless to say, Mercy was blindly ignorant of that particular fact when she set out from Lancashire.

Even with the poverty she observed among her brother's poorest tenants, Mercy never considered how widespread the unemployment in England had grown.

"Men be lookin' fer work everywhere," a soldier, who lost his legs in the war, told her when Mercy accepted a wedge of dark bread from the man.

She kept her eyes downcast but wary; yet, she had no reason for concern. Mr. Peet offered his protection from several unscrupulous-looking beggars, who meant to steal the soldier's meager meal. Mr. Peet, however, met their plans with one of his making. The man flashed a gun, which sent his assailants looking for another victim. Witnessing their ready retreat, Mercy spent a good portion of the day with Peet, who, obviously, relished her company. He gallantly kissed her gloved hand in parting when she decided it was best if she covered more miles before nightfall.

After her error in judgment with the Foyles, Mercy made a conscious decision to travel the back roads. In doing so, she found less offers of assistance, but she felt safer.

Some days as she trudged the dusty shire roads, Mercy chided herself for her naïveté. She thought this a great adventure. On balance, although Grace served as a governess, her sister met dukes and earls. Grace even attended a party hosted by the Prince Regent, but there was nothing "great" about the drudgery Mercy encountered. Yet, even on her worst day, she never considered returning to Foresthill Hall. All that awaited her under her brother's roof was a fate worse than the one her sister Grace knew. The thought of her poor sister dead upon the road to London brought a profound grief to Mercy's heart.

"Where is Grace?" she demanded when her brother Geoffrey returned to the house without their sister in tow.

Still reeking of the cheap ale he consumed the previous evening, Geoffrey swayed in place.

"Dead!" Her brother spat the word with contempt.

In disbelief, Mercy, too, struggled to keep her knees from buckling. *Grace*, she pleaded silently. Grace: The one person, who stood between Mercy and Geoffrey's baseness. When Grace returned to Lancashire, Mercy hoped she and her sister could mount a united front against their brother's ruination of everything for which their father, Baron Thomas Nelson, stood. Or if worse came, she and Grace could escape Foresthill Hall together. Perhaps, they could find a small cottage to share and mayhap, even gentlemen farmers to wed. A step down socially for a baron's daughter, but Mercy saw it as a superior choice to what Geoffrey planned for her.

"What do you mean *dead*?" her voice sounded hollow, even to her ears. "It cannot be. How can Grace be dead? She departed this house to stop your friend Lord Spectre from taking her under your alcohol-induced nose, but she is not dead! I refuse to believe it!"

Mercy and Grace regularly barricaded themselves in their rooms at night. Geoffrey's cohorts robbed the estate of everything of value and were determined to steal away both Mercy's and Grace's innocence.

In his angry response, Geoffrey threw a miniature of their father toward the fire. It was a customary gesture when her brother took on his "woe is me" attitude, the one where Geoffrey blamed his rapscallion ways on the late baron.

"Our sister is dead, I tell you!" Geoffrey fumed. "Dead to you and to me. We will never look upon Grace's countenance again. The road to London and our sister's own obstinacy robbed us of Grace's presence in our lives," Geoffrey declared. "That is what happens when a woman takes it upon herself to know what is best. Such decisions are a man's domain."

Mercy's hands fisted at her waist.

"That premise could be true if said woman had a man who would protect her," Mercy accused.

"I will tolerate none of your shrewish tongue," Geoffrey adamantly warned. "You may save your quarrelsome ways for Sir Lesley." Sir Lesley Trent made Geoffrey an offer for Mercy's hand. A baronet who outlived two wives, Trent had five legitimate children between the nursery and maturity and another family with his mistress in a nearby village. Trent thought to marry Grace some five years prior, but the baronet was in mourning for his second wife, and by the time the grieving period ended, Grace accepted employment with Viscount Averette outside of Edinburgh. The baronet then set his sights on Mercy. Sir Lesley waited impatiently for Mercy to come of age. The thought of tolerating the baronet's intimacies always turned Mercy's stomach. No future awaited Mercy as Trent's wife; for when Sir Lesley passed, his son Mathias would send Mercy away. The eldest of the Trent clan held a deep allegiance for his late mother. Mercy would be responsible for Sir Lesley's children, but would not be afforded even a small cottage on her late husband's land.

Mercy fought back the tears forming in her eyes' corners. Her lips trembled as she delivered her pronouncement.

"I shall offer my prayers for our sister. At least, Grace found her escape from the madness this house holds."

Mercy thought to say more, but her words would be wasted on the likes of her brother. Instead, she stormed from the room. That evening, she made the decision to pack a small bag with her most serviceable gowns and waited patiently for her opportunity to escape. Mercy held doubts her brother would grieve for either her or Grace.

She left Geoffrey one last note: "I shall follow Grace to Heaven or to Hell."

Aidan watched Godown and Worthing ride off together. The marquis required a special license in order to marry Miss Nelson in a timely manner. Evidently, from Crowden's tale, time was of the essence. Through a twist of fate, Gabriel Crowden required an heir before his next birthday or the marquis would lose a significant portion of his inheritance.

"First the bride and then the babe," Aidan muttered to the quickly retreating figures. Immediately, Aidan's thoughts turned to Susan and his brother's heir. "A child who should have been mine," he said with true regret.

"Your Lordship," a soft voice spoke from behind him.

Aidan turned slowly to find a red-cheeked maid. "Yes."

"Lady Worthing requested your presence in the morning room."

Aidan swallowed the groan, which fought to escape his lips. He certainly did not wish to spend the day listening to women twittering on about marriage clothes and what to serve for the wedding breakfast, but he promised Worthing he would secure the safety of Lady Worthing, who was heavy with child, and the Earl of Linworth, who suffered from heart troubles for the past four years.

"I entrust my most precious possessions to your capable hands," Worthing declared as he waited for a groom to saddle his horse. "Make certain both my wife and my father seek their beds for recuperative rests."

At that moment, Aidan "despised" James Kerrington. The man Aidan revered as his *Captain* and friend achieved it all: parents who doted upon him, a wife who expressed her devotion with every glance and touch, an heir, and another child on the way. Everything Aidan envisioned for his own life. Everything he lost.

"Inform Her Ladyship I will join her shortly."

The shy maid nodded and disappeared.

Aidan returned his gaze to the rolling lawns. He missed his home.

"At least, Lexington Arms is something of which I require no reminder. My home and that kiss."

Despite the inappropriateness of his musings, Aidan could not wipe the smile from his lips. When he awoke from the long sleep caused by his injury, he could recall nothing of the past two years, but a kiss. A kiss that made him hungry for "things he never knew." A kiss, which wiped away the deceit he discovered upon his initial return to Cheshire.

For some time Aidan assumed the kiss came from Miss

Satiné Aldridge. According to Lady Worthing, her brother Brantley Fowler, and Sir Carter Lowery, Aidan courted Cashémere Aldridge, but the lady and her twin Satiné exchanged places. Evidently, he wooed the wrong lady, a truth that ate at Aidan's pride. But he accepted the fact the "kiss" was the most important aspect of his brief encounter with Miss Satiné. It was the kiss, not the lady, which gave him hope.

His memory of his time under Wellington and his service to the Realm remained in tact. It was the time since his return to England some two plus years prior, which he could not recall. Aidan was aware of the majority of the details. Needless to say, his friends spent countless hours relating every feature of which they were aware. He learned of his sexual conquests, his continued role as a Realm member, and the innovations he put into place as the master of Lexington Arms, innovations, which eased the impact of the war and climatic devastation upon his land.

However, it was when Fowler arrived at Chesterfield Manor to assist his sister in Aidan's care that Aidan discovered the truth of the kiss, which haunted his subconscious mind. He asked specifically of the duke's knowledge of Susan's demise.

"I think I know, but I require someone to confirm my suspicions. Did I cause Susan's death?"

An array of emotions raced across Fowler's countenance, and for a few brief moments, Aidan feared his friend would offer a prevarication. At length, the duke said, "Not directly." And his friend's rendition of the event paralleled Aidan's remembrance. Later, Mr. Hill confirmed much of Fowler's tale. Neither witnessed Susan's death, but both heard Aidan's tale soon after the event. In fact, Fowler rushed from Brittany to Aidan's side.

And Aidan fully recalled his reaction to Marcus Wellston's appearance in Aidan's sick room. They held a bond not known among the other members of the Realm. The earl was the only one to fully comprehend the extent of Aidan's grief at not being able to save Susan from the fire his wife started for Wellston turned to the Realm as atonement for the earl's inability to rescue his twin sister

Maggie. But a chasm reared high between them.

"I plan to marry Miss Aldridge tomorrow morning in the Linton Park chapel," his friend awkwardly announced.

Lying in his recovery bed at Chesterfield Manor, Aidan searched his memory for actual images of Cashémere Aldridge. Sadly, none appeared. He knew from what Worthing shared that Aidan thought to claim Miss Aldridge, but the lady chose the earl instead. Although it was not in his nature, Aidan snipped, "And what do you wish of me, Berwick? My blessings?"

His friend swallowed hard, and Aidan immediately regretted his terseness.

"I never meant to fall in love with Cashémere. I told myself you were my friend, and I would not come between you if you were serious about Cashé."

Hearing the lady's familiar name spoken so tenderly rubbed raw against Aidan's usual amiability. His world imploded, and someone needed to pay for his misery.

"But I proved myself otherwise by kissing Miss Satiné," he accused. "Is that it, Berwick? It was a ruse, perpetrated by the young ladies."

The earl flinched.

"It is not that way, and you know it."

Then his friend spoke the truth of Aidan's life.

"You viewed Cashémere as a safe choice–someone you enjoyed–someone with whom you could dull the memories of what happened with Susan, but I never observed in you what I observed in Kerrington's and Fowler's countenances when they looked upon the women they affect. I suspect if true love existed for you, that if you held a soul-cleansing devotion to Miss Cashémere, you would never forget it–no matter what Charters did to you. Do you recall such a love, Lexford? If you say you love Cashémere in that manner, I will cancel the wedding; I will permit you the opportunity to make Miss Aldridge love you in return."

Aidan hesitated. He and the earl stared at each other for several seconds before Aidan surrendered to Berwick's demand for an answer. Aidan searched his memory and his heart. In neither did Miss Aldridge exist. Berwick had the right of it, and Aidan could not deny his friend's happiness? Dutifully, Aidan rejected his hopes and dreams in favor of his friend.

"No. I do not remember such a love. Surprisingly, I remember kissing Lady Eleanor during the farce involving Louis Levering," he declared baldly.

The certainty of the memory startled Aidan, but it did not displease him.

Aidan continued earnestly, "And I remember feeling clean afterwards. I also recall passionately kissing someone whom I suppose was Miss Satiné."

That particular memory was less clear than the one of Lady Eleanor, and Aidan quickly come to the conclusion he held no true memory of the event, only what his friends shared of the incident. It was in that moment Aidan realized his life skewed in the oddest of manners.

"But I possess no recollections of love. Miss Cashémere is not part of my memories," he finished.

"And yet, I cannot breath unless Cashémere is near," the earl confessed.

Another long silence ensued. Finally, Aidan mustered up the necessary words.

"Then I suppose you should marry the lady. I would not wish to be the cause of your demise." He reached out his hand to the earl. "We are brothers, Berwick, and brothers never stand in the way of the other's happiness. You have my blessing."

Ironically, Aidan's words about brotherly devotion never proved true in his own family. Perhaps, it was the number of years separating his and Andrew's births. He and his older brother never knew a close familiarity, but Aidan would give anything to have his brother's life returned.

Immediately, Aidan assumed a vow to some day be so afflicted: to know love. What Aidan witnessed in Berwick's eyes now rested in Gabriel Crowden's.

"Please God," he murmured as his gaze searched the barren trees on the horizon. "Allow me to one day look in the mirror and observe in my own eyes what I view in my friends' steady gazes."

Reluctantly, Aidan turned his steps toward the morning room. Toward the woman he kissed in a Lincolnshire hunting lodge. A kiss that was the only true memory Aidan held of the past two years. All the others he borrowed from his most intimate acquaintances. A kiss from a magnificently incomparable woman. A kiss and a hope for the future.

Chapter 2

"CERTAINLY NOT WHAT I THOUGHT my life would bring," Mercy told herself in cynical bemusement, but it was honest work and not beyond her abilities. She managed to convince the owners of a small inn in Derbyshire to hire her to replace their regular maid for the week the girl would be tending to a death in her family.

The Pawleys provided their servants two meals each day, along with bread and tea to break their fasts. It was so long since Mercy ate more than an overripe apple or a handful of berries for a meal that it was a real struggle not to wolf down the simple stew Mrs. Pawley placed before her. Mercy's hand trembled as the spoon approached her mouth. She closed her eyes and savored each potato and pea and stringy chunk of lamb as if the finest French chef prepared it. Not that Mercy ever consumed such delicious offerings. *Better than escargot,* she thought with wry amusement. The idea of eating snails turned her stomach on its head. Yet, she heard of the practice, and she knew the dish was reportedly a delicacy most cherished.

"Ye've been doin' without?" Mrs. Pawley said perceptively. Mercy dropped her eyes and nodded. Thankfully, the inn mistress said no more.

The work was backbreaking, but certainly no more tiring than walking from sun up to sun down. At least, it held a familiarity. At Foresthill Hall, Mercy often assisted the few maids her brother employed with the household duties. True, she never washed the laundry, but Mercy assisted her brother's servants with changing the bed linens and airing the rugs. In return, the Foresthill maids agreed to sleep in her room. It was how she and the girls avoided Geoffrey's gaming friends when the men were deep in their cups.

"Another penny," she exclaimed in delight as she swept the floor under the bed of the recently vacated room. It was the third one in as many days. As Mercy fished it from between the slats of wood, she thanked her lucky stars for delivering her to the Pawleys' doorstep. She would not become rich, but when she set out on the road again, Mercy would do so with renewed determination.

"I shall reach London," she told her image in the cut class mirror setting on the small table. When Mercy arrived in Derbyshire, she reached her lowest point: Nearly of the persuasion of lying down in the road and permitting God to decide her fate.

"Odd how a meal and a warm, dry bed can change a person's stars."

For three days Aidan stood attendance upon the Linworth household. He escorted the ladies into the village several times, and he dutifully spent time with Kerrington's son Daniel. Soon the boy would be leaving for school, and the child was full of questions on what to expect and how best to survive. Aidan enjoyed his time with the youth, but the experience emphasized all the things missing in his life.

With Susan's death, Aidan permitted her parents to raise the child. Legally, he could keep the boy, but he made a previous commitment to Shepherd and the Realm; and, in truth, he could not love the child as his son. Every time, Aidan looked upon the lad, especially after Susan's death and the demise of his hopes for contentment in his marriage, he saw his brother's betrayal in the child's face. The boy favored Andrew rather than the Rhodes family.

"Perhaps…" he whispered to the empty room. Perhaps, if he and Susan put their disaccord aside, he might feel different about the child. Perhaps he would call the babe "Son." But any warmth he and Susan once shared dissipated while Aidan served upon the Continent.

Mr. Haley reported Susan's "episodes" to him upon Aidan's return. His once vivacious friend and youthful lover walked the halls of Lexington Arms in a depressed state. Her grief was so great Aidan thought not to marry her, but it was his father's dying wish to know the future heir to the title would remain under Aidan's protection. And the child was Lexington Arms' future. Aaron Kimbolt was Aidan's heir unless Aidan married and produced an heir of his own. He was ashamed to say he wished to hear the word "father" rather than "uncle" when he thought of his title's future.

On Wednesday, Worthing and Godown unexpectedly returned. They came across a bit of luck in their search for a special license. Instead of riding to London and Doctors' Commons, they learned the Archbishop remained at Durham longer than expected, and his friends returned after only three days. Meanwhile, Godown's three aunts and the Realm leader, Aristotle Pennington, arrived on Linton Park's doorstep.

With the extra company, after supper, the ladies retired to the drawing room, and the men enjoyed their cigars and French brandy. Despite their close acquaintance, Aidan felt disconnected from his friends. Each of the other three had an air of completeness, which Aidan had yet to discover. His stomach clutched tightly from loneliness.

"I was not aware of your long standing relationship with Godown's aunts," Aidan ventured when the marquis slipped from the room to have a word with his valet.

The man they all knew as "Shepherd" until only recently scowled. Aristotle Pennington traced his finger up and down the glass's stem.

"I am from the same neighborhood as the former Crowden sisters. Our relationship has seen the test of time."

Evidently, Worthing's curiosity also piqued with Pennington's sudden appearance as escort to Godown's aunts.

"I often wondered how Crowden came to us, especially as the marquis possessed no experience in service to the King prior to joining the Realm."

Pennington remained staunchly stone faced.

"It was a break in regulations," the Realm's leader confessed. "Yet, the boy served well, as I assured you he would."

Worthing nodded his agreement.

"Crowden's skills with languages, the sword, and cunning proved most valuable, and I meant no disparagement, Pennington."

"Perhaps, the truth," Aidan encouraged. "None of us would speak unkindly of whatever you disclose. On the contrary, we would celebrate your happiness. You never led us astray, and we wish you well."

Pennington shot Worthing a knowing look, which appeared to contradict Aidan's words, but the man smiled wryly.

"I held no title, and a man with no title cannot aspire to marry a marquis's daughter. Yet, as I reflect upon those dark days, they drove me to earn my position in the British government." Pennington chuckled ironically. "In many ways, I wield more power than any duke of the Realm."

"Have you renewed your plea to the Dowager Duchess?" Worthing asked curiously.

Aidan looked on as the Realm leader squirmed in his seat. He never witnessed Shepherd so nervous. It seemed even a man of advanced years found love. *Everyone but me*, he thought with regret. Bitterness rushed in to fill Aidan's chest.

"The duchess wishes things settled with Godown before we consider joining, but be known I search for an estate appropriate for the widow of a duke. Bel will relinquish her identity with an exchange of our vows. I wish her role as Mrs. Pennington to give her peace."

Worthing ventured, "I imagine the Duchess holds no worries in that manner."

"And what of your position?" Aidan asked.

He could not imagine the Realm without Aristotle Pennington as its head. The man was a walking history of British military and covert intelligence.

"Who has the knowledge to replace you? You cannot be both a country gentleman and the Realm's leader."

Pennington smiled that secret smile, which always drove Aidan crazy. The Realm's leader shot a enigmatic glance to Worthing.

"I chose my successor. That is all I will say on the subject at this time."

Mercy's newfound optimism floundered when the cold rain began. She set her sights upon London once again. The Pawleys' regular maid returned yesterday, and Mercy regretfully gathered her meager belongings. Mary Purefoy, the maid, graciously permitted Mercy to share her small room for one last evening; otherwise Mercy would be on the road some twelve hours earlier.

Mrs. Pawley fed Mercy a hearty breakfast and gave her a small loaf of dark bread to see Mercy on her way.

"If'n ye are ever in the neighborhood agin'," the woman offered. "Ye must come to us. Mr. Pawley and me be thankful to welcome you."

Mercy was sorry to leave the woman, not only because of the nourishing food and the dry bed, but because the Pawleys showed her a great consideration. It was so long since Mercy knew true human kindness that she thought she would miss the couple's empathy more so than she would miss the Pawley's warm kitchen.

"Congratulations, Your Lordship," Aidan waited for Lucifer to speak his peace to the marquis.

Aidan asked Godown to join him and Lucifer in a private drawing room. It was a bit unusual, but Lucifer Hill served beside the members of the Realm as their eighth man. Hill saved each of their lives at one time or another, and they rushed to save his more often than Aidan could recall. Men who shared such moments held a bond beyond class or station.

"It pleases me you found a worthy mate, my lord."

The marquis smiled that silly grin, which had not departed Gabriel Crowden's countenance since Grace Nelson's appearance in the Linton Park chapel.

"Lady Godown will bring a sense of order to Gossling Hill. I thank you for your well wishes." Godown accepted Lucifer's hand in parting. "Now, if you will excuse me, I must return to the wedding breakfast before the Three Roses think me displeased with my choice of brides."

"A man must only look upon your countenance, my lord, to view your true regard for the lady," Hill asserted.

Surprisingly, the marquis did not contradict the statement. *So Hill sees what I do*, Aidan thought. It was a moment of triumph and regret.

"Be safe, Hill," Godown said graciously. "And keep the viscount from harm."

"I will do my best, Sir." Hill bowed as the marquis exited.

Aidan watched Godown's retreat before he spoke.

"I will remain at Linton Park until Godown's aunts follow the marquis to Staffordshire. Pennington asked for my escort as far as Cheshire."

Hill nodded his understanding.

"Your delay will provide me time to make certain everything at Lexington Arms is set aright before your arrival."

Aidan smiled easily.

"Do not go berating everyone again. I possess no desire to listen to a litany of complaints upon my return."

"You know I hold no patience for those who waste my time," Hill defended himself.

Aidan grasped the man's shoulder.

"And I am a better man for your allegiance, my friend. You will hold to the marquis's warning to take care." He shook Hill's hand. "Did you say your farewells to Hannah?"

"Aye, Sir." Hill nervously reached into his pocket. "Before you leave Linton Park, would you ask Lady Worthing to present this small gift to Hannah on Christmas? It is a token of my devotion."

His friend's voice took on an emotional tone, like sand rubbing against a stone, and Aidan felt the same twinge of jealousy, which plagued him often of late.

Aidan accepted the brown paper wrapped package. It grieved him he would not know the pleasure of giving a simple gift to a beloved one.

"Why did you not give it to Hannah yourself?"

"The woman shed enough tears with my leaving," Hill confessed. "Moreover, I wish Hannah to realize she is in my thoughts when we are separated. It is important for a woman to have something upon which to hang her hopes. Viscount Worthing was saying just the same the other day."

Aidan thought of poor Susan. Had his young wife not had something upon which to pen her dreams? Had such a thought been the source of Susan's bedlam? Had there been a means by which he could have saved her? Had Susan wished to be saved?

"I will see to it personally."

The rain came down in miserable sheets of icy stiffness; yet, Henry Hill barely noticed the elements. His mind remained on the heart-shaped face of Hannah Tolliver. Despite his protests to the contrary, he was sore to leave Lady Worthing's maid behind.

"Nothing to be done but to serve His Lordship," Hill grumbled as he adjusted the reins to keep the open wagon safely in the muddy grooves of the country road. Hill recognized better than most how much the viscount suffered of late, but that particular fact did little to lessen the heartbreak of leaving Hannah behind.

"Ah, my girl," he said to the open countryside. "Think of me often, my Hannah, for I will be thinking of you."

As each water-filled rut in the road wore a sore along his backside, Hill reflected on the past couple of months. In the midst of a misguided kidnapping, Lachlan Charters delivered a mighty blow to the back of Viscount Lexford's head. Not only did His Lordship lose the woman he courted during the chaos, which followed, but also Lord Lexford suffered a worse fate than the loss of a potential love.

"The viscount's memory plagues him, but, in truth, Lexford lost his heart and his dreams long before Charters's attack."

Hill sighed heavily. The weight of so many troubles rested upon his shoulders for he meant to see Lord Lexford happy before Lucifer claimed Hannah as his wife.

"Damn fool," Hill grumbled. "His Lordship should never pursue Miss Aldridge. The girl was not of a nature to appreciate Lord Lexford's gentleman's code. The lady will fare better with Wellston. The earl possesses a wild streak not found in Lord Lexford. And as for the other one: Miss Satiné."

Hill spat the Aldridge girl's name as if it were poison.

"She lacks a spine. Too much like the former Viscountess Lexford. Run away at the first sign of strife."

From an interested distance, Lucifer observed the viscount's pursuit of one female after another, but none could absolve Lord Lexford from his guilt. Lucifer served the viscount since their time together on the Continent, and he suspected he knew more of Aidan Kimbolt than did the viscount's late father.

Lord Lexford saved Henry Hill from a torturous end. Hill and a dozen other British soldiers found themselves prisoners behind enemy lines. He always thought he could escape upon his own, but Lucifer could not leave his fellow Englishmen behind. When the day of their deaths arrived, he made his peace with God and with his decision to stay. But much to his relief, Lord Lexford came charging into the camp, followed by James Kerrington and

Marcus Wellston. Three Englishmen who could fight like twenty good men, and despite Hill's complete exhaustion, Lucifer took up the cause. Within minutes, the four of them stood triumphant. It was a proud moment: One to be savored by a man, who did not know such exquisite glory before then.

The incident provided Lucifer a 'hunger' to be a better person. To return to his letters and to learn from these newfound heroes. At the time, he pledged his allegiance to Viscount Lexford. He gave his word he would serve Lord Lexford for a period of ten years. He did so from gratitude, but his were not all altruistic reasons. Lucifer wished to associate with men of the caliber of those who served as his rescuers. To hitch his stars with such greatness. That choice was made some seven years prior, and although Hill knew Aidan Kimbolt would release him from his vow, as easily as did the British government, Lucifer refused to break his promise. However, the thought of the happiness he could know if he could make Hannah his wife certainly tempted him to beg for his independence.

"Cannot leave His Lordship's service until I see the man well settled. Especially now that his missus's memory haunts him," Lucifer reasoned aloud. "The problem lies in the means by which His Lordship seeks a replacement for the former viscountess. In his misplaced guilt, the viscount looks only upon women, who favor the late Lady Lexford. In my opinion, His Lordship requires a miss who is Lady Lexford's opposite. Lord Lexford should not wallow in his memories. He should place Lady Lexford firmly in the past. The lady was never a true wife to the man."

The rain soaked through her cloak and all the layers of her clothing, but Mercy continued her slow steady walk to freedom. She must find a place to spend the night. December weather in Derbyshire could be quite harsh, and open fields would be no place for a girl alone.

Hill flicked the reins across the horses' backs. The rain greatly delayed his return to Lexington Arms, and irritation hunched his shoulders in the manner, which only Hannah's soft touch could cure.

"It will be a long time before I will see my sweet gel again," he warned his wayward heart.

As they did for the last few hours, Hill's musings might continue along the same lines, but a bizarre sight caught his attention.

"What in Heavens' name?" he exclaimed as he pulled up on the reins.

Sitting on a stile was a gargoyle-like figure. Some four feet in height, whatever it was, it did not move. Having experienced more than one ambush during his years with Lord Lexford and the Realm, Hill proceeded slowly. He reached for his gun before crawling down carefully from the bench seat. Cautiously, he edged closer to the figure for a better look.

"Easy, Boy," he cooed as his hand caressed the horse's rump. Stepping heavily into the thick mud, he steadied his stance by tugging on the harness. Finally, Hill stood before the gray-clad apparition. Despite the icy rain now dripping from his hat and down his back, he smiled.

"Are you not an intriguing sight?" he said with fascination. "I thought you were a witch or a medieval bear come to life."

"Neither," the girl said through chattering teeth.

"I can see you are a wood sprite instead," he said with a chuckle.

The girl pulled her wet cloak closer.

"I require no pretty words from the likes of you," she boldly declared.

She stepped from the stile to stand in a mud-filled puddle. Lucifer noted the wear of her boots. They had many miles on them.

"If you will excuse me…"

The girl picked up a small bag and took several steps in the opposite direction of his.

"Where are you traveling, gel?" Hill called to her retreating form.

"It is none of your concerns, Sir," she said smartly.

Lucifer enjoyed her sass.

"I thought perhaps you might require a ride."

He waited until the count of three to determine if she would accept. The viscount was always telling him not to rush a woman's decision. *The fairer sex prefers to weigh all their options before deciding what is best. We men are the impulsive ones*, Lord Lexford said on more than one occasion.

She paused, but did not turn around.

"What is your destination?"

Hill remained where she left him.

"I mean to finish my journey to Lexington Arms in Cheshire. I am to prepare the manor for the master's return."

⁓⧽⧼⁓

Mercy caught her breath. She knew of Lexington Arms. It was the seat of Viscount Lexford. Upon Grace's return to Foresthill Hall, Mercy and Grace spent a delightful afternoon discussing her sister's brief encounter with the viscount, his associates, and even the Prince Regent. Afterwards, Mercy searched *Debrett's* for each of the men Grace mentioned.

"The Prince Regent actually came to the table and spoke to everyone?"

Mercy's mouth stood agape in amazement. At first, she could not believe her sister's tale.

Grace chuckled in that self-deprecating manner her sister wielded to defend off the least bit of praise.

"Needless to say, our monarch held no interest in me," Grace asserted. "There were several very beautiful women at the table and more nobility than should be permitted in one place. Ignoring the Dowager Duchess of Norfield, who is a beauty even in her advanced years, and Viscountess Averette, Prince George's eye fell heavy on Miss Aldridge. The lady resembles her younger sister, Miss Cashémere, who outshone many with higher titles. They are both very dark of color and strikingly elegant. And there was Lady Eleanor Kerrington, who won the praise of the Queen during the lady's Presentation. She and Lord Worthing only recently married. Lady Worthing is the Duke of Thornhill's sister. She is tall and majestic. I can assure you I faded into the tapestry; yet, it was a moment only few may claim."

Mercy sat spellbound. Living at Foresthill, she held no hopes of having the acquaintance of any of the aristocracy other than her brother's wastrel associates.

"And what of the men?" she asked in curious delight. "Were they exceedingly handsome?"

Her sister's eyes glazed over in quiet contemplation. At length, Grace continued.

"The men in our party, other than Viscount Averette, who grew a good-sized paunch since last you saw him, included several from the aristocracy, who served together during the war and beyond."

Her sister took great satisfaction in ticking off the names upon her fingers.

"Lord Worthing, who is the heir to the Linworth title, led the group when they served abroad. He is magnificently tall and lean. He possesses the most mesmerizing steel gray eyes I ever encountered and a strong jaw, which speaks of his ancestral lines. The Duke of Thornhill is shorter than Lord Worthing, but he is equally muscular in build. He possesses light brown hair, which he wears a bit too long to be fashionable and dark brown eyes. It is my understanding from my time with the Averettes that the Duke recently married his cousin Miss Aldridge, the elder one of which I spoke previously. The bachelors included Sir Carter Lowery, a newly minted baronet and a very affable young man; Lord Yardley, an earl from Northumberland, who is stoical and serious minded, but who I suspect holds very deep emotions; the Marquis of Godown, who is sinfully handsome, and Viscount Lexford from

Cheshire, who is sandy blond of head and boyishly handsome."

Mercy smiled knowingly. If she traveled to Lexington Arms with this stranger, she would have the acquaintance of the viscount, and, perhaps, several of his associates. It could be a means to honor her sister's memory. Grace was a governess, but she dined with the Prince. Could not Mercy assume a position under the viscount's roof and come to know those of the peerage? She turned slowly to best judge the man who offered her an adventure.

Lucifer remained perfectly still so as not to frighten the girl: To allow the truth of his words to take root.

"His Lordship and I served together during the war. Now, I am his man of all means."

The girl nodded her understanding. Hill's instincts told him she was a runaway. She was miserably cold, but she refused to acknowledge her desolation. Lucifer could not resist admiring the woman's defiance: It spoke well of her character.

"If you require employment, I imagine there is a place on His Lordship's staff. That is if you are willing to put in a fair day's work. I am not offering you charity."

Lucifer noted the pleased smile, which graced the girl's lips. Her hood slipped from her head, and with the icy crystals mixing with the red gold of her hair, the woman reminded him of a snow princess he once saw in a painting in a Viennese art museum.

"Why would you offer a complete stranger a position in your master's household?"

Her cultured tongue told Lucifer the girl was no country miss. The woman before him was a genteel lady. That particular fact only solidified Hill's resolve to escort her to Cheshire. He would not leave any woman to suffer as he suspected this one had. He would do the correct thing, the *only* thing.

"Years prior, the viscount saved me from Death's claws. He is a good man, and he would expect me to extend his benevolence to you." Lucifer smiled easily. "If you pardon my saying so, Miss, you appear to come upon hard times."

"Be there children at His Lordship's home?" she asked tentatively. "My sister was a governess. I thought to find a similar position."

Lucifer gave a slight shake of his head. He thought of the child Mr. and Mrs. Rhodes whisked away from a distraught Lord Lexford. Lucifer always thought if His Lordship poured his love onto the babe that the viscount would know peace by now. He took a half step in the girl's direction.

"I fear not, but we can find you some other form of employment. At least, come with me to Cheshire. Spend several days with us. Recover your strength. Fortify your will to travel on."

The girl swayed in place, but Lucifer did not reach for her. She might think he meant her harm.

"I worked at an inn recently," she protested weakly.

"For how long?" he coaxed.

Her eyes closed as if she was silently counting.

"Five days." She paused awkwardly. "The Pawleys fed me and gave me a warm place to sleep."

Lucifer wondered if he might need to resort to kidnapping the girl. She possessed no skills to survive a winter on the road, and Lucifer meant to see her well.

"Five days of charity proves the Pawleys worth knowing, but five days after how many weeks?"

The girl snarled her nose in remembrance.

"Perhaps six."

Lucifer edged closer in anticipation of seizing the girl.

"Would you not wish for more days of warmth and nourishment? I can promise you Mrs. Osborne makes the finest lemon tarts in all England."

The girl looked over her shoulder to the road behind her.

"But Cheshire is the way I came. I cannot retrace my steps."

Lucifer dug into his pocket to retrieve his purse. Fishing several coins from the leather pouch, he extended them toward the girl.

"Come to work at Lexington Arms. Stay, at least, through Twelfth Night, and if you do not care for the place, use these coins to purchase your passage to London or wherever else you wish to go."

"Why?" she asked skeptically. "Why do you insist on offering your assistance?" She looked off across the empty fields. "The last people I trusted stole all my money, as well as my mother's locket. I have nothing of value remaining."

"I want nothing from you, gel. I have me a beautiful angel, who claims to love the likes of me. And I possess a comfortable home and a generous employer. For a man who has not always walked on Heaven's path, I hold many blessings. I think it is time I become the Good Samaritan." He extended his hand to her. "Come, Girl," he encouraged. "You require what I offer."

Although the rain lessened, moisture dripped across her cheeks from her eyes' corners.

"Are you certain the viscount will not object?"

Lucifer breathed easier: He would win this battle. He chuckled ironically.

"His Lordship will likely not realize you were not always part of his staff."

Thoughts of the injury, which robbed Lord Lexford of his memory, were never far from Hill's mind. He meant to see the viscount well again.

He caught the girl's elbow and directed her toward the flat bed wagon he drove. Lucifer knew better than to give the woman time to change her mind. She required a bit of encouragement and a good dose of coercion.

"It might be best if you sit in the back," he suggested. "You may place the blankets about you. It won't be much drier, but perhaps a bit warmer. I will set your bag under the seat."

He pressed the coins into her gloved hand as he lifted the girl to the wagon.

"Sit back," he ordered as he gathered the damp blankets

he stashed in a wooden crate beneath the bench and tucked them about her. "We still have a piece to go so stay as dry as possible."

The girl nodded her gratitude.

"May I...may I know the name of my benefactor?"

She openly shivered from the cold.

"Name is Mr. Hill. Henry Hill, but most people call me *Lucifer.*"

She smiled at him, a smile that uncurled from her heart, and Hill thought she might be one of the prettiest girls of his acquaintance. The smile changed her face completely.

"Lucifer? As in the Devil?"

"My mother once remarked I be devilishly large for my age," he said with a shrug. "The description stuck. I have been Lucifer ever since."

Through lips trembling from the cold, she said, "I am Mer...I am Mary," she stammered. Lucifer heard untruths in her tone. "Mary...Mary Purefoy."

Needless to say, she wanted no one to know her true identity, a fact that confirmed Lucifer's assumption of her being a runaway.

"You should rest, Miss. We will be in Cheshire soon. When we reach Lexington Arms, we will test your skills in making a proper bed for yourself."

Leaving her to snuggle deeper into the blankets, Lucifer climbed onto the bench seat. With a cluck of his tongue and a flick of his wrist, he set the team in motion.

Purposely, he did turn his head again to look at her. He suspected the girl would watch him warily until she recognized he meant her no harm. Instead, Lucifer concentrated on maneuvering the wagon along the rough road, while considering the problem of what to do with the girl he rescued. After some twenty minutes of pure silence, he secreted a glance in the girl's direction. Finding her curled in a tight ball and fast asleep, he chuckled. The woman's countenance spoke of her exhaustion. He knew what it meant to be hungry. Knew also of the hopelessness of those who traversed

English roads in the wake of what some were calling the "year without summer." As an innocent, less scrupulous travelers robbed the girl of her few belongings, but she did not high foot it from where she came. The girl possessed spirit. Her actions spoke of both her desperation and her determination. Those qualities increased Hill's respect for his passenger.

Yet, he worried for her safety. Despite her earlier encounter with disaster, Miss Purefoy accepted his tale after only minor encouragement. Her bravado aside, the girl had not learned her lesson; and his leaving her to her own devices would be a mistake. She trusted him not to defile her. Although not born to the role, Lucifer considered himself a gentleman, but most traveling English roads these days would not come close to that description. Before the woman reached London, some man would have the girl's virginity by seduction or by force. Even now, she slept soundly in a steady rain in a rocking wagon. If not for his honor, he could claim the girl before she could put up a fight.

"The aristocracy," Lucifer murmured in amusement. "The so-called ruling class."

Until he met the members of the Realm, Hill always disparaged the ignorance he found among those of rank, but he quickly discovered Lord Lexford's acquaintances were the exceptions to the rule. He turned his head to study the girl more closely. She was nothing like the women His Lordship usually chose; yet, even on such a short acquaintance, Lucifer hatched a plan of sorts.

"Lord Lexford always preferred his women dark of hair and soft of nature. Exactly like Miss Satiné and Lady Susan," he thought aloud. "However, I think Lord Lexford requires a snow princess. A fiery blonde wood sprite instead of a dark fairy. One full of innocence and a bit of sauciness." Lucifer smiled with the possibilities. "If Lord Lexford could discover happiness, then I would possess no worries for my honor, and mayhap the viscount would hold no objections to my claiming my own contentment."

Lucifer reached under the seat to retrieve the girl's small

bag.

"Let me view what you think to be important in your life, Miss Purefoy."

He glanced again to where the girl's head rested on a half-full seed sack. Removing his glove to lift the bag's latch, Lucifer dug his right hand into the bag's contents. His fingers traced their way through layers of silk and wool. At length, he touched upon a stack of papers, and he closed his fist about the pages. Using his coat to shield the paper from the peppering rain, Lucifer lifted them high enough to where he might read them without removing his eyes from the road.

"Letters," he said under his breath. "With the directions to Mercy Nelson of Foresthill Hall in Lancashire."

Before the girl could discover his deviousness, Lucifer returned the pages to her bag and replaced the satchel under the seat.

"Mercy Nelson," he whispered, rolling the name about his tongue. "Mercy. A much better name for a genteel lady than Mary Purefoy." He chuckled with his next thoughts. "And exactly what His Lordship requires," Hill said with assurance. "A touch of mercy."

Chapter 3

THE RAIN AGAINST THE PANE woke Aidan from a troubled sleep. He rolled to his side to stare at the droplets streaming along the glass.

"How many nights?" he wondered aloud. How many nights did he lay awake with images of Susan's sweet countenance playing across his mind? "On the battlefields," he whispered. "At the safe house in Bombay." Why could he not shake the feeling that if he could simply remember one fact…one particular fact… his world would right itself, and he could place all his foolish dreams of a woman who never loved him behind?

He remained perfectly still for Aidan learned over the past few months that if he did not so much as blink an eye small bits of memory returned. It was in a moment such as this one that he recalled his first sight of Cashémere Aldridge in this very house. He arrived for the prenuptial celebration of James Kerrington and Eleanor Fowler. Aidan played a key role in rescuing Lady Eleanor from Sir Louis Levering. He required no one to remind him of the events at Gavin Bradley's hunting lodge. Aidan observed the situation in his dreams. Recognized how vulnerable Lady Eleanor was, but he also observed the lady's strengths. Levering made an attempt to embarrass and to abuse her. To place Lady Eleanor

Fowler in an untenable situation, while wreaking havoc on the Duke of Thornhill's life. The lady's vulnerability drove Aidan's actions; he risked exposing the Realm's plan to destroy Levering in order to bargain for the woman his Captain wished to make his wife.

Aidan drugged the others involved in Levering's perfidy. Then he claimed Lady Eleanor as his partner. He rested with her in his arms. Felt her warmth along his length. Heard her sobs of relief when she discovered who he was. Tasted her lips and felt the stir in his body's loins. It was the day everything changed for him. The day he experienced humanity after years of deprivation.

When he managed his escape from the hunting lodge, Aidan made a promise to live his life without regret, and he arrived at Linton Park to discover Miss Cashémere Aldridge in residence with her family. The girl was Lady Eleanor's cousin, and to him, Miss Cashé appeared perfect in every way. Lucifer claimed after the fact that Aidan's attraction to the girl was the lady's darker coloring.

"Perhaps, Hill speaks the truth," he whispered. "Perhaps, I seek a replacement for Susan so when I close my eyes I will no longer be haunted by the mistake I made in making the woman my wife."

Concentrating all his thoughts on a dark mark along a table's edge, Aidan stared into his past. She was there–his wife, but not his wife. He could see it plainly. It was after the boy's birth, and he encountered a pale-faced Susan in one of the upper passageways. Seeing her so weak and decimated, Aidan instinctively took her into his arms, a move he long ago abandoned.

"We will see this through," he assured her.

Susan clung to him. Her tears returning and soaking his shirt, but still he held her.

"I am sorry, my lord," she sobbed over and over again. "You deserve better than I."

Unable to withstand the compassion he held for her, Aidan lifted her chin with his fingers, where he might look upon her countenance. Hers was the face, which haunted his days and his nights.

"I pledge we will find a means to make a life together." He brushed his lips across her forehead: It was the first and only gesture of tenderness Susan accepted from him since his return from the East, and Aidan's hopes rose quickly.

"I cannot live at Lexington Arms," she whispered. Her warm breath caressed Aidan's neck. "Permit me to go elsewhere," she pleaded softly.

Aidan stiffened. He held responsibilities to the estate and could not simply leave it behind, and he certainly could not entertain the idea of losing Susan again. Theirs was not an ideal situation, but she was his wife, and Aidan meant to protect her.

"You wish to return to Rhodes End?" he asked cautiously.

"No!" she said adamantly. Susan shoved against his chest for release. "Never there! Promise you shall never return me to my father's home!"

The memory slipped away as quickly as it came.

"Why was my wife so opposed to seeking comfort from her parents?" he reasoned aloud. "How did she come to dislike her own mother and father?"

Aidan closed his eyes in hopes he might recall how the conversation ended, but he could not will the memory's return.

At length, he released the grip he had on the wool blanket covering him. He rolled to his back. The room felt familiar. Although he held no personal knowledge of the fact, Lord Worthing assured Aidan it was the room Aidan preferred when he tarried at Linton Park. It was odd how so many minor details escaped him.

"Minor details and two and twenty months of my life," he grumbled.

Tossing the blanket from his form, Aidan swung his legs over the bed's edge. He donned a robe before stoking the fire and adding more coal. Restless, he made his way to the heavily draped windows. He wondered if Lucifer arrived safely in Cheshire. The cold rain started some three hours after his man departed Linton

Park.

"Hill should have been close to the border when the rain began here," Aidan reasoned aloud. "That is assuming Mr. Hill did not ride into the storm."

Aidan watched the rain a bit longer before forcing himself to return to the bed.

"Home," he said as he squeezed his eyes shut. "Home with all its devils and ghosts."

His plans to return to Lexington Arms to recapture his memory and his life suddenly appeared quite daunting.

"Will I even recognize my staff? Surely those who served the estate for years will be familiar. And what of my quarters? Perhaps this room holds more familiarity than my own chambers."

The possibility caused the knot, which held his stomach hostage since the day he awakened in a strange bedchamber at Chesterfield Manor, to tighten.

"God! Please permit this madness to end?"

"Mr. Hill!" the Lexington Arms cook called when Lucifer entered the warm kitchen. "You returned at last!"

Lucifer smiled easily at the woman.

"Aye, Mrs. Osborne. His Lordship will arrive by mid-week. I came ahead to prepare the house."

Mrs. Osborne looked up with instant tears in her eyes.

"Master Aidan had the worst of it. I pray his return will bring him peace."

Lucifer nodded a similar sentiment.

"We each pray for Lord Lexford's full recovery."

He stepped aside to permit Mercy to slip into the kitchen's warm glow.

"I brought someone with me," he said by way of introduction.

Mrs. Osborne's eyes lit with happiness.

"Would this be your Hannah, Mr. Hill?"

Lucifer flushed with embarrassment. He raised his hand to

ward off the woman's next comment.

"This is Mary…Mary Purefoy. She will be joining us."

The cook looked off anxiously toward the service entrance.

"Does Mrs. Babcock know of Mary's arrival?"

Lucifer understood immediately. The Lexington Arms housekeeper served the estate for some thirty years, and the lady did so with a fist of stone. He would be doing Mercy no favors by placing the girl under Mrs. Babcock's supervision; yet, he saw no other means to keep the girl safe and in a position where he might maneuver Mercy Nelson into Lord Lexford's path.

"Mary's mother was a favorite of the former viscount."

It was a bald lie, and he refused to look at the shocked countenance of the girl.

"The late Lord Lexford promised Mary a position in his household when she came of age. I was to retrieve the girl in October, but with the current master's injury, those plans were placed aside. The Master recently recalled his father's promise and sent me for the girl."

Mrs. Osborne's countenance lightened with hope.

"Then the young Master recovered his memory?"

Lucifer shook his head in the negative.

"Only bits and pieces, I fear, but Lord Lexford recovered his physical vigor. His memory will be returning soon enough."

He noted the look of confusion, which crossed Mercy's countenance.

"I will explain later," he said softly for her ears only.

To the cook, he said, "If you could dish up something warm, I am certain both Mary and I would appreciate it."

He hanged his hat on a peg by the door and motioned Mary to remove her rain soaked cloak.

"If you would keep an eye on Mary, Ma'am, I will call on Mrs. Babcock to inquire on quarters for our newest arrival."

"Come over by the fire, Girl." Mrs. Osborne motioned Mary forward. "You will catch your death with them wet clothes."

Lucifer smiled encouragingly. Mrs. Osborne was one

of the better servants under Lord Lexford's roof. With a sigh of resignation, he squared his shoulders before seeking the estate's housekeeper. He must remain firm with Mrs. Babcock. The lady would not appreciate his interference with "her" household.

"And this was Lord Lexford's wish?" Mrs. Babcock asked suspiciously. "I did not think the Young Master would hold an allegiance to the late viscount's 'external' affairs."

The venom in the woman's tone was worrisome.

"How do we know what this girl's mother says is true? The story plays quite odd. By all who speak of it, the late viscount loved Lady Lexford."

Again, Hill heard the woman's incredulity. He never cared for Lexford's housekeeper, whose gross ignorance, meanness of opinions, and very distressing vulgarity of manner always rubbed Lucifer raw. He could not imagine the woman ever being anything more than a common fishwife.

"It is not of our realm to judge our betters," he cautioned.

When he concocted a tale, which implied that Mercy Nelson could be the former viscount's by blow, he did not anticipate Mrs. Babcock's reaction. It was more disapproval than genuine regard for the current Lord Lexford's supposed benevolence. With all emotion removed from his countenance, Lucifer set his jaw for a confrontation.

"Beware, Ma'am. The girl was raised as a genteel lady. Miss Purefoy desires nothing better than a post of honorable representation. She was promised a position as governess to Lord Andrew's child. As the Rhodeses assumed custody of Master Aaron, I knew not what position to assign the girl."

Hill realized the housekeeper would not disparage any guest of the current viscount's by assigning Miss Nelson household duties.

"If Lord Lexford would choose to take another wife..." he suggested.

"A lady's maid or companion might serve the purpose,"

Mrs. Babcock finished Lucifer's sentence. "However, until that time, I cannot have the late Lord Lexford's issue scrubbing floors. The girl will simply play the role of guest until Lord Lexford decides otherwise."

Lucifer thought his ruse a wise one. He supposed his close association with the Realm taught him the art of deceit. He would need all his previously dormant skills to manage His Lordship's disapprobation. Despite his recent injuries, Viscount Lexford would not be an easy one to fool.

"You are correct, Ma'am. I knew you would see the right of it. The girl will be avowedly useful."

Mrs. Babcock scowled.

"The difficulty will be to keep Miss Purefoy's true familial relationship a secret. Perhaps a *cousin* would be a more appropriate designation than a *sister*."

Hill could not confide to the woman that he considered forming Miss Purefoy into Lord Lexford's cousin, but he thought a "sister" would provide the viscount with time to discover what mattered most in life. He allowed himself great latitude in such points. Society frowned upon an attraction to one's sister, but not so much so with a cousin.

"Yours is a sensible solution," Lucifer said as he made to leave. "And a consideration of kindness."

"Place the girl in the west wing. I cannot have her staying in the private wing. It would not be appropriate."

Mrs. Babcock's "willingness" to accept his story pleased Lucifer. However, Miss Nelson's good opinion was less forthcoming.

"You portrayed me as being born on the wrong side of the blanket," the lady said incredulously. "Surely Lord Lexford will know the truth."

Lucifer escorted the girl into Lexford's private study. He helped himself to a glass of Lord Lexford's finest brandy and poured a sherry for Miss Nelson.

"Now, that is where you erred," he said calmly.

Despite her worn clothing and disheveled appearance, Miss Nelson instinctively assumed a dainty pose on the edge of a cushion. The lady's bearing only went to prove his earlier estimation of the woman he rescued from the road.

"I have a confession of sorts," he began after taking a seat near the hearth. "I am aware you are a genteel bred lady. Your speech and even how you sit in a chair betrays you."

The girl blushed thoroughly, but she squared her shoulders before responding.

"I never portrayed myself as part of the servant class. If you recall, I sought a position as a governess."

Lucifer's admiration for the woman increased. She would not permit Lexford his way in all matters. It would be a refreshing twist for the viscount had no faults but what a serious attachment would remove.

"Yet, you recently held employment as a common maid," Hill argued.

Miss Nelson bit her bottom lip in hesitation.

"My situation will not permit my return to my former home, and I am willing to serve in this household as you prescribe."

Again, there was a lift of her chin, which pleased Lucifer. Yes, the girl would do well for Lord Lexford.

He leaned forward as if sharing a secret.

"I am not your enemy, Miss Purefoy; yet, as it is I who brought you to Lexington Arms, it is I who would suffer at Lord Lexford's hand if His Lordship discovered the truth of your lineage. Especially if I placed you on your knees scrubbing His Lordship's floors." He took a sip of the brandy before continuing. "I must tell Lord Lexford something he will believe. It is not likely His Lordship could not detect your cultured tongue."

He watched as the girl closed her eyes as if seeking another means of escape from her situation.

"Then I shall use the coins you provided me for the stage to London. When I discover appropriate employment, I shall repay you."

Lucifer considered how easily such an innocent would succumb to the less savory ways of London's Society. Within weeks of her arrival in England's capital, Miss Nelson would be either plying her wares behind Covent Garden or be found dead in the stews. Lucifer would not permit either to happen, even if he must imprison the girl in the viscount's west wing until Lexford arrived to deal with the stubborn chit.

"Although we have yet to decide upon the terms of your presence, you found sanctuary under Lord Lexford's roof. Would you prefer to disclose the truth of your journey to the viscount? Would that choice make you feel less deceitful?"

A gamut of emotions crossed the girl's countenance before she shook her head in the negative.

"You do not wish to return to the road, and, truthfully, I believe you are exactly what this household requires," Lucifer said tentatively. "Lord Lexford suffered several losses over the past few years: his brother, his father, and his wife. The house knows Death too as an intimate."

"And what role do you suggest I play in Lord Lexford's recovery?" Miss Nelson asked suspiciously. "I shall not become the viscount's mistress if that is what you are suggesting."

Lucifer choked on the brandy he sipped. The girl was plain spoken, which was refreshing. It was a characteristic His Lordship admired in the eldest Aldridge twin.

"I assure you I would never place you in a compromising situation nor would Lord Lexford act without honor." He sat his glass on a side table. "Do you not see, Miss Purefoy, my tale is the perfect ruse. First, it protects you from what may be perceived as an easy seduction. Lord Lexford would never attempt to know his sister intimately. Secondly, no one would think to search for a woman who poses as an aristocrat's by blow. Moreover, such a distinction would provide you a certain amount of protection. As a Kimbolt, even an illegitimate one, you would no longer know hardship."

"But Lord Lexford shall immediately know of the deception," she protested. "How can you offer assurances His Lordship will extend his benevolence to a wayward soul?"

Lucifer smiled easily; the lady would be swayed.

"I spoke of His Lordship's personal losses, but I omitted one important fact. Lord Lexford suffered an equally great loss in October. An interloper struck the viscount from behind with a large tree limb. The injury cost Lexford much of his memory from the last two years. The only memories of those months are those he borrowed from his most trusted acquaintances."

"Men such as yourself?" she accused.

Lucifer nodded in affirmation.

"I spoke the truth of my allegiance to the viscount, and I do not practice this dishonesty without a heavy heart. My vow to see Lord Lexford well overrides all other forms of friendship. I would move the Heavens if I thought it would give the man peace. I owe him my life."

Miss Nelson's eyes widened in astonishment.

"You have yet to explain what role I will portray in this deception."

"Assist His Lordship's feet to find a new path. Brighten this house of Death with your smile. Save Lord Lexford from the misery that cloaks his shoulders. Do even one-tenth of these tasks, and I will be in your debt forever," Lucifer said earnestly.

Miss Nelson scowled.

"You expect a miracle?"

Lucifer shook his head in the negative.

"Simply do your best by the man. Perhaps, in doing so, you will find a bit of yourself as well."

Lucifer escorted her to a room in the manor's west wing.

"To where does that door lead?" Mercy asked as the candlelight invaded the dark passageway. It was evident that no one else held quarters in this wing.

"No where." Mr. Hill said without emotion, and Mercy's

curiosity piqued from his indifference. "There was a fire some three years prior. Stay away from that part of the house. It is not safe."

"Nearly three years?" she said inquisitively. "Why has the viscount not seen to the repairs? Is Lord Lexford short of funds?"

Mercy knew enough of aristocrats who spent beyond their means. Her brother Geoffrey ran the barony into ruin. Her poor father must be looking down in distress from Heaven upon what became of the estate Thomas Nelson so dearly loved. Her late father took such great pride in his duties to the title.

"No, Miss," Mr. Hill said seriously. The man stared off in distraction. "I believe the viscount chose to leave the ruins as a silent punishment. Lord Lexford blames himself for not saving Lady Lexford. Susan Kimbolt perished in the fire."

A pain of regret stabbed Mercy's heart. The viscount truly knew more than his share of woe. Mr. Hill set about lighting candles and a fire in the hearth.

"There is nothing amiss with these rooms," he assured. "Her Ladyship..." he hesitated.

"Yes?" Mercy pressed.

Mr. Hill paused before answering.

"I should not speak poorly of the dead, but if you are to stay at Lexington Arms, then you should know what occurred to the last Lady Lexford."

Mercy nodded her encouragement.

"Her Ladyship set the fire which took her life. Lord Lexford could not reach her, but the truth is Lady Lexford held no desire to be saved. She chose the fire to end her misery and to punish Lexford for loving her."

"I do not understand," Mercy admitted.

Mr. Hill shrugged.

"I possess no knowledge of the event beyond the words I speak in secret. If one would ask Lord Lexford of the right of what happened that day, His Lordship's opinion would be in sharp contrast to mine. And, in truth, only the viscount knows what occurred. He discovered the fire and his wife long before others arrived to assist with the flames."

Mercy quickly made the connection.

"And since Lord Lexford lost his memory, the truth might never be known."

Hill nodded his head in affirmation.

"The viscount's associates repeat what Lord Lexford told them of that day."

"Yet, as you say, Mr. Hill, no one knows if what Lord Lexford's friends shared is the absolute truth or the viscount's abbreviated version of the events."

"Only His Lordship's conscience can speak of Lady Lexford's motives, and at this time, the man's memories remain sadly silent on the subject."

Although most of the household staff showed her respect in a "distant" sort of manner, Mrs. Babcock's attitude spoke of open disdain with a good dose of hasty indignation. The housekeeper's slights were most determined. Mercy expected some censure, and she attempted to ignore the woman's terse tones, applying the lady's reproach to the housekeeper's long-standing position in the Kimbolt's employ.

Mr. Hill's tale of her illegitimacy would cause many to turn from her, but as much as she did not wish to admit it, the excuse for her unexpected appearance at Lexington Arms held credence. It also provided her the privacy she craved. Mercy spent three days exploring the manor, and she discovered how much she enjoyed the view from the parkland. Except for the section destroyed by the fire, the house was quite spectacular. Despite the less than inviting decor, Mercy loved the spacious rooms.

Mr. Hill spent a good portion of each of those three days assisting her in creating a "story" for the viscount.

"I was thinking," he said as he showed her the stables, "you might make over some of Lady Lexford's gowns to fit. That is if you are handy with a needle."

"Would not Lord Lexford object?" she said in concern.

"First, as I pointed out previously, His Lordship holds no memories of his wife, and besides, men, even those who do not suffer such a devastating injury, possess no mind for frills and lace. Make changes to highlight your fair coloring, and Lord Lexford will never make the connection."

"I think not," Mercy protested. "Mrs. Babcock would not approve of my affront to Susan Kimbolt's memory."

"It is none of the housekeeper's concern," Mr. Hill said adamantly.

"But Mrs. Babcock warned..." She broke off before disclosing the housekeeper's latest reprimand.

"What say the woman?" Mr. Hill asked in suspicion.

Mercy waved away his objections.

"It is nothing. Truly I should have thought the better. I took it upon myself to move a flower vase to a sunnier location, and my doing so upset the housekeeper. I had no right to consider myself the expert on the vase's placement."

Mr. Hill's frown lines met.

"Please do not speak to the woman on my behalf. It would only complicate my situation in this house."

Mr. Hill scowled.

"I will not have you abused by the viscount's servants."

Mercy meant to dissuade him.

"The servants will follow the viscount's lead. I am certain Mrs. Babcock means well. I should be very sorry to be an inconvenience."

"I am not so certain," Mr. Hill argued, "but I will bend to your wishes."

Mercy quickly changed the subjects.

"I also considered my situation under Lord Lexford's roof."

"Go on," Hill said cautiously.

"I took no notice of His Lordship having a secretary. You serve as his man of all means, but who organizes Lord Lexford's day, tends his correspondence, and addresses his needs?"

Mr. Hill said honestly.

"I never knew an aristocrat to employ a female secretary if that is what you are implying."

"I must have some means of repaying your kindness, Mr. Hill," Mercy argued. "Because of me, you placed yourself in a tenuous situation in Lord Lexford's household. If you can be His Lordship's *man* of all means, why may not Lord Lexford refer to his *sister* as his *woman* of all means?"

Mr. Hill barked out a hearty laugh.

"You are quite remarkable, Miss Purefoy. Once Lord Lexford considers his duty to his *sister*, I am certain you will brighten the man's days."

Aidan rode beside the Dowager Duchess's carriage. He never was more thankful to place his feet in Valí's stirrups. He would escort Godown's three aunts and Pennington as far as Cheshire. The crisp December day invigorated him. The only thing, which would make it better, was if he could ride break neck across the surrounding hills, but he promised both Fowler's personal physician and James Kerrington that he would demonstrate restraint. *Restraint.* His mind revolted at the concept. Sometimes, Aidan felt he spent a lifetime practicing restraint.

"You will ride safely," Pennington cautioned as they prepared to depart.

"Not you as well," Aidan said good-naturedly. He tapped his heart. "I swear to practice vigilance."

Pennington smiled easily, and Aidan thought how different a smile made the Realm's leader appear. Pennington long loved Godown's Aunt Bel, and finally, the man found his happiness. Aidan felt guilty for the twinge of jealousy slipping into his chest.

"You were always the first into a fray," Pennington explained. "Never impetuous like Fowler, but the first to place yourself in danger. It was as if you held a desire to die. I think it is time you uncover a reason to live."

Aidan looked off toward the road leading to his home.

"God, I wish it were that easy."

Pennington chuckled.

"I never said it would be easy. Nothing in life worth possessing ever is. Yet, look at me. I found love with a woman I thought never to know."

Aidan swallowed the bile choking his throat.

"Around me, everyone claims a piece of happiness. I wonder if I will be permitted to claim my own wedge or whether by the time I reach for it, Happiness will jerk his hand away and announce he holds no more room for the likes of me." Aidan shook off his maudlin. "Forgive me," he said honestly. "Such is what happens to my composure when I return to Lexington Arms. I know little contentment behind its doors."

Pennington nodded to the duchess. It was time for their departure.

"Perhaps this time will be different. Perhaps Lexington Arms offers adventures, which you never considered. Open your eyes to new possibilities, Lexford."

"Open your eyes to new possibilities," he grumbled as he rode past the gatehouse and Mr. Brown. The estate's long-time servant raised his hat in acknowledgement as Aidan set Valí to an easy gallop. *At least, Mr. Brown is one servant I recognize,* he thought. One of his many unvoiced fears was he would discover several among his employ and in the neighborhood for whom he possessed no name or history. With Sir Carter's assistance, Aidan vaguely recalled, at his wife's request, he released a handful of servants upon his return to the estate.

"Open your eyes," his brain chanted in time to his horse's progress. "Open your eyes," his conscious mind encouraged.

As he came closer, Aidan caught glimpses of the manor house through the bare trees. There were few manor houses he could name which exuded a sense of the aristocracy as well as did Lexington Arms. Of course, there were those houses which were more majestic and those more ornate, but none which spoke so well of the English country gentleman. His revelry was sadly broken, however, when he rounded a curve in the parkland, and the burned out shell of a half dozen rooms of the estate's west wing assumed prominence.

"Open your eyes to devastation," he murmured.

Aidan dragged his gaze from the rotting wood. Dark regret blocked his ability to swallow. Finally, the tree line masked the hollowed out ruins, and he recovered his breath.

"One of my first duties to a new beginning," he swore quietly as he reined in his horse before the main entrance, "is to remove the smear of deceit from my estate."

"Good afternoon, Lord Lexford," a groom with sun-kissed skin and a shock of red hair said as Aidan tossed the man the straps. "Welcome home, Sir."

Aidan scowled as he searched for a memory, but his tongue knew the right words without his thinking on them.

"Thank you, Toby."

The man smiled in response so Aidan supposed he spoke correctly. *Thank God bits of myself remain,* he thought as he slowly climbed the manor's main steps. Before he could release the knocker, the door swung wide to reveal his father's butler. *His butler,* Aidan reminded himself. He was the viscount for some two and a half years, but Aidan could not say he ever felt comfortable in the role. As a second son, he was not groomed for the title. It was a commonality Aidan shared with Marcus Wellston. Only one of the many traits he shared with the Earl of Berwick: A younger son assuming the title; an attraction to the Aldridge twins; and an inability to save someone he loved. He and Berwick were quite the pair until his friend found "his" happiness with Cashémere Aldridge. Aidan gave himself a good mental shake. He had no time for distant memories. His *present* awaited him.

"We are pleased for your return to Lexington Arms, Sir."

The butler accepted Aidan's hat, gloves, and riding crop.

"Thank you, Mr. Payne," he said with confidence. The butler's was a name he readily knew from long before the confrontation with Charters. "I assume Mr. Hill returned safely."

"Yes, Sir. I believe Mr. Hill awaits you along with the other staff in the main foyer."

Aidan grimaced internally. His heart gave his chest a queer jerk of alarm. A formal "welcome" was the last thing he wished. He would prefer to treat this day as any other day in his life. Marking it as an auspicious occasion would only add to Aidan's rapidly growing trepidation. He nodded his understanding before sucking in a steadying breath. Stepping into the main passage, his heart sank. Some five and twenty servants stood stiffly awaiting his recognition. What if he could not recall their names? Would they lose respect for him? Or worse, would they pity him?

Hill met him as Aidan turned the corner. Lucifer's expression said Hill attempted to sway the staff to do otherwise, but someone overruled the man. Hill offered a bow of respect, something with which they long since dispensed, and the simple act sent Aidan's senses on alert.

"Did you see the marquis's family on their way, Sir?" Hill asked as a means to distract him, but his friend's efforts did not fool Aidan. On balance, Hill learned much of his deception from Aidan. As such, Aidan could not shake the idea Hill held an agenda of which Aidan was unaware, and that fact bothered him. Henry Hill was the one constant in his life over the past seven years.

"The Dowager Duchess's coach is safely in route." Aidan's eyes scanned the double row of servants. "I suppose I should make my official entrance."

Hill stepped to the side.

"As you wish, my Lord."

Before Aidan could stop his errant tongue, he said, "Very little in my life is as I wish." With a sigh of irritation, he viewed *his troops*.

"Good afternoon, Lord Lexford," Mrs. Babcock said sweetly.

Aidan never liked the woman, but she served his father and Andrew faithfully, and she performed her duties diligently. Mrs.

Babcock offered Aidan no reason to dismiss her, but he always thought she overstepped her position with her "uppity" ways.

"Mrs. Babcock," he grudgingly acknowledged the woman.

The lady assumed his notice as approval.

"We thought it best to welcome your return. Mr. Payne and I did our best in maintaining Lexington Arms in your absence. I pray you find nothing lacking."

So, this display was Mrs. Babcock's idea. Now, Aidan understood why Hill agreed to this formal review of the staff. When Mrs. Babcock hatched an idea, very few could sway her opinion. And, in truth, the late viscount would take great pleasure in such a display of wealth and position. Aidan's father loved the pomp afforded his position.

"I neither doubt your good intentions nor your abilities, Mrs. Babcock."

To the assembled staff, Aidan raised his voice to say, "Your devotion to this estate and this title are duly noted. I appreciate your generosity."

With the housekeeper's and butler's acknowledgements, as a unit, the servants bowed and dispersed to their duties. With their leavings, Aidan breathed easier.

"If I might speak to you in your study, my lord," Hill said softly from beside him. "I have something of import to share."

Aidan frowned dramatically.

"Could it not wait until I freshen my clothing?"

Hill moved closer to assure privacy.

"My business is of the nature as to require your immediate attention."

Aidan rolled his shoulders to release the tension.

"Very well. If you insist," he said ungenerously.

Mercy impatiently waited for Lord Lexford's appearance. She had an inkling of the viscount's appearance for she observed two renderings of the man in the gallery. In the first, Aidan Kimbolt was no more than five or six years of age. He was the youngest of the three children, and Mercy suspected he gave his nurse a case of the vapors. An impish good nature played in his brownish-black eyes.

"Surely the portrait painter erred in the color," she murmured when she looked upon the rendering, for she never knew another's eyes to possess such richness. The second portrait was one of the viscount, his brother, and their father. She assumed the current Lord Lexford was fifteen or sixteen at the time, while his brother would be in his early twenties. Compared to his brother Andrew, Aidan Kimbolt appeared lanky and boyish, while Lord Andrew sported well-defined shoulders and waist. All three men were exceedingly handsome, even the former viscount, whose age lines only added to his well turned out appearance. Yet, Mercy spent her time searching the countenance of the boy, the one not like the other two in his appearance. The one with the softer lines to his face and the more welcoming slant to his shoulders.

The sound of approaching footsteps warned Mercy of the viscount's arrival, and she rose to greet him. She had second and third thoughts on Mr. Hill's plan to present her as Lord Lexford's relative, but it was too late to change her mind now. Mercy squared her shoulders and prepared to meet the man who would decide her fate. She found herself strangely unnerved by the possibility.

He entered in obvious irritation, and Mercy's heart leapt into her throat. The artist did not err. The viscount's eyes were mesmerizing. All she could say was that they were more blackish brown. The color of the coffee beans she noted on sale in the marketplace. Absurdly long lashes. A wide brow over which a sandy blond curl dropped. Chiseled cheekbones. And a mouth that likely felled countless women. Her sister Grace erred. Viscount Lexford must have been the most handsome man at the Prince Regent's party.

Aidan led the way to the study. He wanted to be done with whatever foolishness Hill concocted. Likely, the man wanted to plea for a return to Linton Park and to Hannah. If Aidan did not feel so vulnerable, he would drive his friend from the estate with a stick. Unfortunately, he held no doubt Henry Hill would remain his salvation. However, after witnessing Mrs. Babcock's display of showiness, Aidan wondered if he made a mistake in returning to Lexington Arms to face his demons.

"Now what is of such great importance?" he began before coming to a stumbling halt barely five feet inside the room.

He gave his head a little shake as if to clear his vision, but the image remained: A fairy goddess in a forest green gown. Red golden locks framed her heart shaped face. A compelling vibrancy surrounded her, and Aidan half expected the image to take flight. His blood heated when he gazed into her eyes: The color of melted chocolate. She was dangerous. This woman was a perfect sin, and Aidan had to remind himself to breathe.

"Pardon...pardon me," he said on a rasp. "I was unaware we had guests."

Without removing his eyes from the girl, he said, "Mr. Hill, would you be so kind as to make the proper introductions?"

Aidan could hear the smile in Hill's tone.

"Lord Lexford, permit me to bring to your acquaintance, Miss Mary Purefoy." His man paused for emphasis, and Aidan wondered what perfidy Hill practice. "Miss Purefoy is your sister, my lord."

Chapter 4

"To HELL, YOU SAY!" Aidan growled.

A heartbeat passed before he digested the situation to discover he was in no mood for whatever game the lady and Hill employed.

"Get her out, Hill!" he snapped. "I have no need of an evening in the lady's arms, nor do I require a mistress. What ails me cannot be cured by a thorough bedding!"

Hill judiciously closed the door before saying, "My Lord, you misspoke."

Aidan opened his mouth to reprimand his associate, but before he could utter a word, the woman's open palm left its print upon his cheek. Aidan's head snapped to the right. '

"You, sir, are no gentleman," she hissed. Next, she turned her anger upon Hill. "You promised me he was a reasonable man, but I should know better. Men who claim social positions are all full of self conceit and misplaced pride."

The woman's gaze fell upon Aidan's countenance, and he thought himself blessed by the passion he found there. Whoever the chit, she was magnificent.

"You are of the same ilk as my brother's associates. Riff raff, all of you."

Aidan rubbed his cheek.

"Are you hoping I will accept another brother, as well as a sister?" he said viciously. "If so, you are sadly mistaken."

The woman blushed thoroughly, but her venom did not lessen. Her eyes darkened in annoyance.

"My brother is Mr. Purefoy's heir. He is fortunate in that regard for he must not contend with the likes of you. In such matters, you and…" She paused awkwardly, and Aidan wondered what she would say if she did not correct herself. "You and Francis are very much alike. You receive the best of what your positions afford. It is only we women who must bend our natures to please a man's whims. Otherwise, we possess nothing of substance."

Aidan watched the breadth of emotions crossing the woman's countenance. One corner of his mouth curved upward in a half grin.

"If this is your way of bending to my will," he taunted, "I am most displeased."

The girl snorted her disapprobation. To Hill she said, "Mr. Hill, if you would make arrangements for my passage, I shall pack my few belongings for the stage. I thank you in advance for such kindness."

Hill's gaze narrowed.

"Perhaps, if we could sit and begin again, things will be more civil."

He gestured to the chairs before the warm fire. Catching the girl's elbow, Hill turned her steps toward the seating.

"Come, my Lord," Hill coaxed.

Aidan shrugged his shoulders in defeat. He knew Hill would not relent until the man had his way; therefore, Aidan chose the most comfortable of the chairs. He purposely slouched in the seat as if he possessed no cares.

"Then be about it," he said aristocratically. "Share with me the lady's tale of woe so I may finally dispense with the road dust ruining my clothing."

He intentionally seated himself before Hill assisted the

woman to her seat. Aidan could not say why he assumed the mantle of a spoiled child. He supposed the problem rested in the nameless wretchedness he had yet to discover at Lexington Arms.

"I possess the power to speed your task, my lord," the lady said with false sweetness.

An enticing pulse leapt to life at the base of her neck, indicating she was well aware of the tension between them.

"Permit me the use of your small carriage to see me to London, and you shall never hear from me again."

"And why should I suffer the inconvenience of losing my small coach for a week when I might place you on the public coach for the flip of a coin?" Aidan said in bitterness.

Hill interrupted their "discussion." With a clearing of his throat, his man claimed their attentions.

"My lord, you are better than this quibbling. I never knew you to act irrational. Please listen to my explanation."

Aidan knew Hill correct, but it felt so good to vent his anger. He held the reputation among his associates as the affable one, but Aidan wished to shed that particular label. He wished to lose the image of a man who always accepted second best. Grudgingly, he attempted nonchalance.

"Have your say, Lucifer."

He would find time to apologize to Hill when they were alone. His man would not place him in a poor light.

"Be quick about it," Aidan added to permit the girl to know his continued irritation.

Hill sat between them. The man took a moment to compose his thoughts.

"I must direct your memory to the time before you traveled to Chesterfield Manor. Do you recall any of the goings on before you called upon Baron Ashton's household?"

Aidan resisted the urge to squirm. Of course, he recalled bits and pieces of the puzzle known as his life, but he was uncertain to what Mr. Hill referred.

"I suspect you must be more specific," he said defiantly.

Hill nodded his understanding.

"Before you made the decision to court Miss Aldridge, you received a letter informing you of Miss Purefoy's existence. You confided in me and asked that I escort the girl to Lexington Arms."

Aidan scowled. Something in Hill's tale went against logic, but he could not pinpoint what expressly spoke of untruth.

"Is the letter still available?" he asked distractedly.

The corners of Hill's lips turned upward, and again Aidan wondered about the man's honesty.

"Not of which I am aware," Lucifer said evenly. "Before I could act upon your mission, Lachlan Charters changed everything. I accompanied Viscount Worthing to Scotland to seek your attacker. During your recovery, I remained with Lord Worthing at Linton Park. It was only with word of your likely return to Cheshire that I recalled Miss Purefoy's fate. I immediately sent word to Staffordshire."

"And Staffordshire is your home, Miss Purefoy?" Aidan asked suspiciously.

The girl shot a quick glance at Hill. Aidan grimaced inwardly. Was he somehow missing an important fact? More than likely, he was missing a hundred or more important facts, but a false one from his past would be a different matter.

"My brother's estate is on the border with Derbyshire."

"I am familiar with the area. May I ask which village?"

"Near Leek," Hill answered for the girl, but the man's response came a bit too quickly.

The lines on Aidan's forehead deepened. There was something odd about this conversation, but before he could define the weaknesses in Hill's story, Aidan made the mistake of looking upon the girl's perfect countenance. Her hair caught the light of the fire, and he could see the flame of life in each silken strand. He wondered what it would be to release the pins, which held her locks tightly in place, and permit the silken strands to run through his fingers. To place a row of kisses along the column of her neck.

"I arrived in the nick of time," Lucifer was saying.

Aidan pulled his gaze from Miss Purefoy's pouty mouth.

"How so?" he said inattentively.

"Miss Purefoy's mother passed, and Francis Purefoy was not of the persuasion to recognize an allegiance to his stepmother's issue. Mr. Purefoy drove his sister from his ancestral home."

Aidan's eyebrow rose in disbelief.

"Destitute, heh?"

Lucifer sat straighter.

"I would not say 'destitute,' my ;ord, but Miss Purefoy's future rests in your hands."

"Such a tenuous position," Aidan said sarcastically.

The girl rolled her eyes, and even Aidan found his attitude amusingly pathetic.

Hill continued his tale.

"Miss Purefoy set out on a solitary journey. Unfortunately, an innocent is fair game to those of unscrupulous purposes. A couple posing as benefactors robbed Miss Purefoy of her few valuables."

Hill's tone changed ever so slightly, and Aidan heard candor in his man's words.

Aidan set forward, his former disdain forgotten.

"Would you recognize the perpetrators?" he said with concern. "Were you injured in any manner?"

He struggled with his unwillingness to accept the overpowering need to determine exactly what occurred.

"Only my pride. My mother's locket…" the girl said softly.

She reached for where the chain should rest about her neck, and Aidan suspected it the second truthful moment he experienced since entering his study.

"The couple claimed their names were Foyle. Mr. and Mrs. Foyle."

"If you will relate what you recall of the pair to Mr. Hill, he will convey the description to the authorities in the area. I am not without influence."

Aidan did not like to think of any woman alone on the

road, and especially a woman who held the countenance of a fairy princess. If evil befell her, Aidan would not possess the pleasure of staring into the woman's mesmerizing features.

Her eyes closed as if recalling the fears she encountered.

"Mr. Hill has been more than kind," she said with admiration.

Aidan's jaw clenched. He did not particularly like the idea of Lucifer being the girl's hero, especially when Aidan chose to play the role of villain.

"Perhaps we should call a truce, Miss Purefoy."

Her eyes rose to meet his, and Aidan noted a flicker of hope.

"Please explain Mr. Hill's claim of our familial relationship."

Again, the girl looked to Hill for support, and Aidan considered the possibility his man of all means made a conquest.

"Before her death, my mother announced the certainty of my parentage."

"And you believe my father is the missing parent?"

He briefly considered the girl's explanation, and Aidan felt the suspicions return. His father was far from angelic. On balance, the late viscount lost his wife some sixteen years prior to his own passing; but Aidan thought himself aware of the women with whom the late viscount associated. He held no knowledge of a genteel woman in Staffordshire. And what made the tale harder for him to swallow was if the girl spoke the truth, Arlen Kimbolt sired Miss Purefoy while Aidan's own mother was still living. He was not naïve enough to know such matters did not occur on a regular basis among men of his social standing, but it pained Aidan to consider the fact while Cassandra Kimbolt still lived, his father betrayed his mother.

"I know only what I shared," she confessed. "Have you no memory of my mother's letter, my lord?"

Aidan wished he could define what part of her story bothered him the most. Unfortunately, as a gentleman, he could not turn her out, especially if the lady possessed no other home. He stood slowly.

"We will act upon discovering the truth of this matter. Until that time, you will remain our guest, Miss Purefoy. I assume Mr. Hill saw to your quarters."

"Mrs. Babcock thought the west wing was best," Lucifer confided.

Aidan shot a sharp glare at the man.

"And you accepted this slight?"

The lady intervened.

"It is of no significance, Lord Lexford. I found nothing wanting in my quarters."

Aidan did not approve. Even if the woman's tale proved untrue, he would never consider the west wing as appropriate housing. Needless to say, Mrs. Babcock's manipulative ways continued. He wondered what the girl did to engender the woman's disapprobation. Likely, the woman thought herself protecting the Kimbolt name. The housekeeper's disdain permeated the manor, and Aidan was of a mind to pension the woman off. The possibility would be something of which he would discuss with his man of business.

"It was my intention upon this return to Lexington Arms to speak to Mr. Hill regarding the necessary repairs for that portion of the house. Hopefully, men can be immediately secured for the work. You may discover your quarters less than desirable under those circumstances."

"If so, I shall report my discomfort." She curtsied. "If there are no other concerns at this time, I shall leave you to discuss estate business with Mr. Hill. Thank you for your kindness, my lord."

Aidan watched her go. He found he enjoyed the gentle sway of the lady's hips.

"Do you speak the truth of the lady's plight?" he asked the one man he trusted with his most innermost thoughts.

Lucifer remained behind him.

"If you ask if Miss Purefoy is in need of protection, I hold no doubt of the lady's distress. I discovered her perched upon a stile during a downpour. After losing her money to the Foyles, she sought shelter on the road in barns and stables. It was only by Fate's good hands I came upon her by accident."

"The condition of the woman's gown fully announces her financial straits, and her speech says she was reared as a lady; but I wish to know whether her claim of blood relation holds merit."

Aidan remained where he stood; he did not remove his eyes from the closed door. It was as if he expected the girl's return.

Hill cleared his throat.

"I hold no knowledge of Mrs. Purefoy's purpose in writing to you of her daughter. You said at the time that you wondered whether Mrs. Purefoy was aware of your father's passing. If the woman held ulterior motives in writing to you when no proof could be found."

Aidan turned to his friend.

"Quite remarkable," he said with a scowl. He hesitated before suggesting, "Needless to say, I must send someone to investigate the lady's story."

"You do not wish me to do so, my lord?" Hill said with a bit of surprise in his tone.

Aidan shook his head in the negative.

"I will require your assistance in negotiating my return to the viscountcy. I will write to Pennington and ask him to set someone to the task."

Mercy's knees were so weak, climbing the main stairs proved difficult, but she kept her chin high and her breathing even. The servants watched her every move, and she was certain several heard His Lordship's earlier disparagements, but Mercy would not permit the possibility of gossip below stairs to worry her. She survived her first encounter with Viscount Lexford, and what an encounter it was: From insult to concern.

In reality, she fallen face first into a most unusual quandary. Normally, Mercy considered herself to be logical and practical and even a bit tedious. Such traits proved useful in her dealings with her brother Geoffrey and with her supposed suitor Sir Lesley Trent.

On balance, Mercy found a means to rise above the debauchery her brother delivered to Foresthill's threshold, and she kept Sir Lesley's attentions at bay while executing her escape. Quite an accomplishment for a girl not yet nineteen years.

However, she feared any measures to which she could claim success would fail miserably short with Lord Lexford. Despite his recent injury, the viscount's suspicious tone spoke of his sharp mind. She and Mr. Hill must practice greater care in what they confided to His Lordship. Moreover, Mercy possessed no skills in dealing with a man who one minute irritated her beyond imagination and who the next stole her heart with his genuine alarm for her welfare. Despite the sting of having her reputation called into question, she discovered she quite enjoyed the small shivers that raced down her spine whenever she thought of the viscount's piercing gaze.

"Miss Purefoy," Aidan said as he stood to acknowledge the woman's entrance. "I am pleased you agreed to join me."

He extended his hand to the lady, which proved a mistake. Aidan thought the earlier tension he experienced when he looked upon the girl an aberration; now a physical zing shot up his arm when Aidan's fingers touched hers. He spent an inordinate amount of time with his ablutions, not because he possessed foppish tendencies, but because the quiet time provided him the opportunity to divine what bothered him about the girl's appearance in his house. Earlier, Aidan replayed the conversation from his initial encounter with the woman to ascertain where the holes in her story rested. Now, if he could keep his mind on the problem at hand rather than upon the lady's pleasing features, all would be well.

"I did not see where I possessed a choice, my lord. Your servant was most insistent regarding my attendance," she said testily.

A wary expression crossed her pale countenance.

Aidan brought the back of her gloved hand to his lips.

"And you did not desire my company?"

Miss Purefoy blushed, and Aidan thought the color made her more beautiful. Decidedly piqued, she spoke in soft tones for his ears only.

"I assumed from your earlier remarks, Sir, you wished to have the truth of my parentage before you weighed judgment upon my role in this household."

He examined the lady's defensive tone for the space of three heartbeats before his exasperation faded.

Aidan led her to a chair and seated the lady before continuing. Motioning a footman to fill their wine glasses, he assumed the seat at the table's head.

"Whether your story proves true," he said in a tone his servants would not distinguish, "you are my guest and will be treated with the utmost respect."

The last part of his speech was for the benefit of those in attendance. Aidan meant what he said. Despite his initial skepticism regarding the story placed before him, he welcomed the idea of the lady's company. It seemed so long since he entertained another in his home. Only once in the months he and Susan shared Lexington Arms did they host a house party. It was at his insistence and a disaster. After the first evening, Susan locked herself in her quarters, claiming the child she carried made her uncomfortable. After three days of strained silence, all the guests made their excuses, never to return. The memory still haunted Aidan. He wondered if he asked too much of his grieving wife: If his insensitivity contributed to his wife's suicide.

Miss Purefoy sipped her wine.

"I am most appreciative, my lord."

Aidan motioned for the first course to be served.

"Then, it is settled."

He placed the serviette upon his lap.

"I thought we might spend our time learning more of each other."

He noted how the lady's spine stiffened, but Aidan made

no comment. Instead, he regaled Miss Purefoy with a tale of falling from the grand oak at the curve of the main drive.

"I broke my arm in two places," he concluded.

"And your mother?" the lady questioned.

"Was quite upset. She thought I might have a crooked arm."

He stretched out both hands before him.

"As you may observe, my dearest mother erred in her estimation of the surgeon father summoned to attend me."

Miss Purefoy smiled genuinely, and Aidan's heart did a small flip in his chest. It was quite remarkable the effect the lady had on him. In London, he accompanied the Marquis of Godown to a house of ill refute, but an attack upon the marquis interrupted Aidan's evening. Godown apologized multiple times for curtailing Aidan's first attempt at enjoying a woman's "charms" after his injury, but, in truth, Aidan thanked Providence for delivering him from the courtesan's lure. He feared he might make a cake of himself otherwise. It was good to feel the tingle of awareness again. He was healing, after all.

"And what tale might you share, my dear?" he said as casually as he could.

With the Realm, Aidan held the reputation of being the one who could easily ingratiate himself into the company of others. *If they only knew how false all my amiable ways truly were,* he thought.

As if she sought a tale he might believe and one in which she would not incriminate herself, the lady looked away. During his ablutions, Aidan made the decision to take Pennington's advice and to treat this situation with Miss Purefoy as an adventure. He would use his finely honed skills to pick apart the lady's story. Meanwhile, he hoped for congenial company as he returned to country society. It was the best of both worlds for him.

"I had few experiences as daring as your tree climbing escapade," she admitted. "Young ladies are not permitted such freedoms. I suppose my most hoydenish ways come from my determination to ride as well as my brother and better than my sister."

"Your brother Francis," Aidan prompted. If he remained silent, the lady misspeak and prove his qualms correct, but Aidan found he enjoyed listening to the girl speak. There was a bit of a Scottish roll of the tongue on certain words, and her eyes glistened when she forgot to protect her story.

She blushed prettily.

"Yes, Francis and my sister Louisa. They were older and knew how to ride long before I could sit upon a saddle."

"And have you become a fair horsewoman?" he teased.

Her chin rose in defiance.

"Quite the expert," she challenged.

Aidan caught a glimpse of a charming dimple, one he would wish to explore in a more intimate setting. He rubbed his hands together in anticipation.

"Excellent. I possess a rather extraordinary stable of fine horses. We will ride together."

"I fear I own no riding habit, my lord," she said in protest.

Aidan feigned a frown.

"A terrible shortcoming, Miss Purefoy. Whatever shall we do to eliminate such a failing?"

His smile widened.

"It is fortunate you possess a relative who can afford the cost of a few baubles and frills."

"Oh, I could not accept such expensive items, my lord," Miss Purefoy said in what sounded of genuine denial.

Her reaction was not of the norm: Aidan half expected the girl to jump at the opportunity to purchase new clothes on his purse, and perhaps even launch herself into his arms, a scenario in which he would gladly participate.

"I did not agree to come to Cheshire simply to place my burdens at your feet."

"Yet, I insist you join me: I desire your opinion on my newest line of cattle."

Aidan frowned for real this time.

"We must concoct a solution."

The girl bit her lower lip in obvious indecision.

"I thought..." She hesitated. "I asked Mr. Hill about the possibility of serving within the household. I hoped for children where I might become a governess."

Aidan's nose snarled: Mary Purefoy was too attractive to be a lowly governess. She would easily become the target of a disreputable master. The lady flinched when she noted his distaste.

"However..." She paused again. "As no children are about, mayhap I may be of service as your secretary. My pen is very well, and I could address correspondence and social invitations. I assume a gentleman of your consequence is often sought by the local gentry as an honored guest."

"You jest," Aidan said a bit more tersely than he intended.

"I assure you, my kord, I did not."

Miss Purefoy's hurt sounded in her tone, and he knew immediate regret."

Aidan sipped his wine to provide him time to consider her suggestion.

"I never knew a female secretary to a gentleman," he said evenly. "But I am not opposed to the idea. Permit me to sleep upon it. I will provide you an answer on the morrow."

Overall, Aidan enjoyed his evening with the lady. Despite their contentious beginnings, they finished their meal in polite silence, but he found no discomfort in the act. He instinctively thought of his wife's reticence and prayed he was not lulled into a false security by a pair of sparkling eyes.

"It was certainly not of the nature of those tedious hours I spent in forced silence with Susan," he reminded himself before immediately experiencing the guilt of betraying his wife's memory. Having someone with whom he could share a meal was a rare treat at Lexington Arms. On the road, Aidan held few objections to dining with Hill or any other man of his acquaintance, despite the gent's social status, but at his home, he was expected to perform as the master of the estate. From the earliest days of his return from the Continent to act upon his duty to his brother's wife, Aidan dined alone. His father took ill; the previous viscount suffered a debilitating stroke before Aidan's arrival from the East. Naturally, Susan was in mourning for Andrew, and she was some six months enceinte at the time. So his wife chose every opportunity to avoid him.

They broke with propriety by marrying so soon, but Aidan's father insisted they secure the heir Susan carried. It was not as if the babe would not hold his place in the line of succession; yet, Arlen Kimbolt was adamant about the necessity of keeping both Susan and the child at Lexington Arms. The late viscount would not see Susan Kimbolt displaced by Aidan claiming another as his wife. He thought at the time that Susan would make the effort to become his wife, but she punished Aidan for Andrew's snub.

"It was a farce," he growled.

Aidan's steps carried him to the window. It seemed of late, he spent many hours staring out on English countrysides. At least this evening, he held a memory separate from the tragedy of this house upon which to reflect.

After the meal, he and Miss Purefoy played a highly contested game of chess over which they discussed some of their favorite books.

"Surely you read the story of Caleb Williams," she insisted.

"I fear at the time of the book's popularity, I was but a lad at school. I am certain my tutors would not think it proper for a viscount's son to read a book which disparages the aristocracy," he teased.

"We must remedy this failing immediately," Miss Purefoy mimicked his earlier tone.

Abandoning the chessboard, the girl caught Aidan's hand and tugged him along behind her until they reached the library. When she finally released him, Aidan felt bereft of the girl's warmth. She selected a paper roll to light several candles.

"I saw that very book," she said as she raised the candle to search the titles. Over her shoulder she chastised, "I was unable to discover rhyme or reason in the organization of this library, my lord."

"I do not recall using the library for more than to meet with my friends," he admitted. "I mean, I read extensively from the selections, but customarily Mr. Hill or Mr. Poley chooses for me."

She smiled then, and Aidan thought the shadows faded.

"Mayhap organizing these titles might prove a worthy task for a poor relation. What say you, my lord?"

The anticipation in her voice brought Aidan unexpected joy. He would take pleasure in making the girl happy.

And, in truth, Aidan approved of the idea immensely. It was a face-saving task for the girl and for him.

"Surely there must be similar duties, which would prove the lady's usefulness, while providing me the pleasure of seeing her more appropriately dressed," he said with the memory of the conversation.

Miss Purefoy quickly found the book in question and presented it to him with a teasing curtsy. Their fingers intertwined for a few brief seconds. The feeling remained long after their release.

"We should retire," she said breathily, and Aidan's own breath caught in his throat.

Disappointment lodged in his chest, but Aidan escorted the lady to her door. Overall, the evening was most satisfying. So satisfying he wished it were light so he might ride out across his estate to wear off the exhilaration skittering through his veins.

He rested his head against the cool pane and imagined the lady's countenance.

"I certainly pray Mr. Hill's story proves a falsehood," he murmured.

A smile turned up his lips' corners.

"It certainly would not do to experience an attraction to my sister."

Slowly, Aidan opened his eyes to look upon his world. For the first time in what seemed forever he felt the glimmer of hope.

Thinking he might actually read some of the book Miss Purefoy chose for him, Aidan turned to where the leather bound volume rested on his bedside table, but before he could take a step to retrieve it, a flash of color along the tree line caught his attention.

He quickly dimmed the lantern and stepped behind the drape for a closer examination. For a few seconds, he thought the break in the gray and green landscape was an invention of his imagination, but then Aidan saw it again: A bit of yellow against a wintry backdrop. Slender and perfect. A woman. Her back to him, but hair he would recognize anywhere. Long and sleek and of the darkest chestnut.

Immediately, Aidan was on the move. Out the door and racing through the passageways. Leaping across stairs and skidding to a halt in the main foyer, he ordered, "The door, Payne." The startled butler scrambled to open the door only a second before Aidan burst through it.

He rushed across the groomed lawn to search for something that no longer existed. His breath came shallow with fear.

"What is amiss, my lord?" Lucifer stood close behind him, and Aidan was once more thankful for the man's loyalty.

He stopped, took a breath, and blew it out again.

"Did you see her?" Aidan growled.

Hill asked in a tone that said he knew the answer before uttering the question.

"See who, my lord?"

"Who else?"

In frustration, Aidan jammed his fingers into his hair.

"Susan."

Chapter 5

"SUSAN? LADY SUSAN?" Hill asked in caution.

Aidan's heart jumped, but he quickly brought his breathing under some form of control. He threw his hands in the air in exasperation.

"I know."

He stormed away from his man. Hill looked on in concern.

"I know," he said to emphasize the point. "I understand my wife is dead. I saw the sexton place her body into the Kimbolt crypt. I mourned her."

Even to him, Aidan's voice held traces of desperation.

"Could you have fallen asleep? Have dreamt of the late Lady Lexford?" Hill suggested.

Aidan turned angrily on the man. He gritted his teeth before giving himself a good mental shake.

"I was awake, I tell you. I watched the evening gather outside my window. I turned to retrieve the book Miss Purefoy suggested. It was then I saw Susan, standing with her back to me."

Hill directed their steps farther from the house after excusing the footmen awaiting Aidan's orders.

"Could your evening with Miss Purefoy prompt the memory of Lady Lexford?"

Hill stood close as if to shield Aidan from the outside world.

Through tight lips Aidan growled his response.

"I had no hallucination, Lucifer."

Aidan hoped his voice did not reflect the panic coursing through his veins.

"And yes, I am aware of the effects of prolonged use of laudanum, but a week after my return to consciousness, I refused all use of the drug. It has been more than six weeks since my recovery, and other than this damnable memory loss, I experience no difficulties. Why, pray tell, would an evening with Miss Purefoy bring on a manifestation of my late wife?"

Hill scrubbed his face with his palms.

"Perhaps you felt guilt over enjoying Miss Purefoy's company."

Lucifer looked about in disbelief.

"I truly have no idea, my lord. However, you taught me to consider all the possibilities."

Aidan's frustration lessened.

"As such, could we examine the area for proof of or a refutation of my tale?"

Hill nodded his agreement.

"I will take the left side and meet you at the opening of the grove."

They searched for more than an hour, but to no avail. There was no sign of his mystery woman. Hill promised to search again with the morning's light; however, Aidan held little hope of vindication. He returned to the window in his quarters to resume his vigil. Subconsciously, Aidan knew *Susan* would not return, but he watched for her nevertheless. From somewhere below, the grandfather clock chimed the midnight hour, and he shot a glance to the ormolu clock on the mantel to confirm the time.

"Nothing to see," he murmured to the darkness surrounding him.

How many nights had he stood watch throughout the

slowly moving hours? More times than Aidan cared to recall. Watching for the Realm's many enemies, but not *his* enemy. His enemy dwelled in this house, among his family. His brother. Such a deep betrayal. His family knew how deeply Aidan affected Susan Rhodes. He spoke of little else for years.

"Had no one been listening?" he growled. "Was I so insignificant as not to have my feelings recognized? Was I only the proverbial 'spare,' after all?"

Aidan rested his forehead against the cool glass.

"No one," he whispered simply to hear his own voice. "No one cared," he reluctantly admitted. "Not since Mother's passing."

The words ripped at his heart, but Aidan knew them to be true.

He turned from the glass and walked toward his waiting bed. He despised sleep. When he slept, all the ills of his world visited him. Aidan collapsed diagonally across the mattress. Grabbing handfuls of the blanket, he draped the woolen linens across him. He should undress: His valet would have a fit in the morning, but for the moment, Aidan did not care. He found the day exhausting, and for once, he hoped it would be enough to permit his mind to know peace.

◈

"Miss Purefoy," Aidan said cheerfully as he entered the morning room. "I am pleased you are an early riser."

He actually slept until four of the clock before the nightmares returned. He reached for a plate to claim a few of his favorites from the breakfast items.

"I am, Lord Lexford."

The lady's melodic tones eased the tension between Aidan's shoulders. Perhaps the woman was what she claimed. Would it not be doubly ironic if his father's death did not only thrust Aidan into the role the late Arlen Kimbolt designed for Andrew, but also provided Aidan with family, at last? With his father's passing, it became common knowledge in the neighborhood that the late viscount's manipulations robbed Aidan of a brother, a wife, and a child.

"I thought I might find something useful to fill my day."

He sat at the table's head.

"I told you previously; there is no need for you to earn your keep," Aidan said softly to maintain privacy.

Miss Purefoy shot a quick glance to where a footman awaited their orders.

"But I insist, my lord," she said in hushed tones.

Her blunt manner of speech did not offend him. Instead, he found her stubborn boldness starkly refreshing.

Aidan also enjoyed the way the December sun, reflecting through the high windows, kissed the golden threads of her hair. A shaft of light caused her locks to glow from within.

"You may repay me by keeping me company."

"I shall do both," she declared.

Aidan spread jam upon his toast.

"We should also see to assigning you a maid," he observed.

"May we wait, my lord? I have no need of a maid to attend to only my needs, and I would not wish to impose upon your staff."

Aidan smiled easily.

"I suppose you mean to insist again."

Chocolate eyes shimmered with amusement, and Miss Purefoy's dimple reappeared. It drew Aidan's eye to its indentation, and he smiled inwardly.

"See how you are learning my ways."

"And people think me the lesser son."

He answered in a jest, but truth rested within the words.

The lady grimaced.

"Never would I speak disparagingly of you, my lord. Even on our short acquaintance, I find you quite unmatched."

Her words caught Aidan unawares. Few, other than Hill and his Realm friends, would come to his defense. It was not as if those with whom he did business would malign him. It was worse: They pitied him. He was the fool who served his family most dutifully and had nothing to show for his efforts.

"It was misplaced banter, my dear."

Silence filled the empty spaces between them. Aidan turned his efforts to the food upon his plate. He lifted the last of the ham to his mouth, but before he could finish it off, the lady stopped him cold with her question.

"When will we gather the greenery for Christmastide, Lord Lexford?"

"Christmastide?"

Dumbfounded, he stared at her in disbelief.

"Yes, Christmastide." Miss Purefoy said with satisfied amusement tugging at her mouth's corners. "As in a fortnight forward."

Aidan placed his fork heavily upon his plate. His expression scrunched up in a rueful manner.

"I did not consider celebrating the Festive Days. I doubt this household acknowledged Christmas or Twelfth Night since before my mother's death some eighteen years prior. Certainly not in the past eight years. For the past four, we were in mourning," he admitted by way of apology.

"But you are no longer in mourning," she asserted.

Aidan hesitated. If he wished to place the past behind him forever, celebrating the upcoming festivities would be a small step in that direction. He responded with a shake of his head at the clarity with which she presented him the truth.

"No. No, we are not. In fact, we experienced enough of Death's hand. I cast my vow for Life."

Miss Purefoy giggled, and Aidan thought it was the sound of Christmas bells. It was certainly the sound he wished to fill his house.

"Then may we choose greenery for the mantels and the staircase?"

"Absolutely," he said with a smile. "Go fetch your cloak and mittens. I will make arrangements for the cutters."

Miss Purefoy rose, and Aidan followed her to his feet.

"And several old blankets, my lord. Do not forget the blankets." She hurried away in excitement.

A few seconds later, Hill appeared framed by the open door.

"You made the lady happy, my lord," he said with amusement.

Aidan returned to his meal.

"We decided to celebrate Christmastide, Hill," he announced.

Without looking at his friend, he waited for the man's protest; however, it did not come.

"It is time," Hill said solemnly.

Aidan excused the footman before he motioned Hill to a chair.

"Do you truly think so? I considered the possibility my memory might not return as I wish it to do, but that does not mean I must give up on life. I should like to know a bit of what Kerrington and the others found. Should not the time be right?"

Hesitation lingered in his tone.

Hill spoke in earnest.

"You suffered enough. If inviting Christmas into this house brings you one full minute of happiness, I think it an act of genius."

Aidan leaned forward to speak in private.

"I have no idea how to go about it. I know nothing of celebrating Christmas. Other than to be a guest at various house parties over the years, I hold few memories of the Festive Days. Where do we begin?"

Hill's smile widened.

"Trust the lady, my lord. One thing I learned from my Hannah is that ladies possess natural inclination on how to make a house livable. They know what makes a man feel comfortable in his skin."

"Will you assist me in organizing this venture?" Aidan asked in hesitation.

Hill stood slowly.

"You bring the lady about, and I will have the men prepared to do your biding." Hill turned toward the door. He said cockily, "And thank you, my lord."

"For what do I receive your gratitude?" Aidan puzzled.

"I am most anxious to observe Mrs. Babcock's countenance when I tell her she has work to do. The old bitty is too assured in her position. I think it about time she earns her keep."

Aidan frowned deeply.

"Tell Mrs. Babcock this is my wish. Do not place the blame on Miss Purefoy's shoulders," he cautioned.

Hill grinned widely.

"Perhaps I will tell her it is my wish, my lord." Over his shoulder, his man said in a mild taunt, "Enjoy the day, Lord Lexford, and be certain to wear your leather gloves. You will require them for the holly."

Aidan never cut evergreens. When he was a child, he and his brother and sister raced about to find the best branches, but the former Lady Lexford refused to permit her children to risk injury. With a deep sigh of both frustration and excitement, he watched as the men gathered supplies for the cut.

"Follow the lady's lead," Hill whispered close to Aidan's ear. He whipped around to see his man walking casually toward the tree line.

With a chuckle, Aidan turned his attentions to the woman by his side. Executing an exaggerated bow, he said, "I am your humble servant, Miss Purefoy."

The lady swatted at his arm. She giggled again, and the sound mystified Aidan. Why had he never acknowledged the magic of a woman's smile prior to today?

"You are dressed too well for a servant, my lord." She gestured to the overspreading branches. "I think it best if we ask some of your men to do the cutting."

Aidan caught at his heart as if she wounded him.

"You think so poorly of my physical prowess, my dear?"

This time Miss Purefoy laughed, and Aidan found that particular sound even more addicting than her giggle.

"I would not wish you to break your arm again, or, Heaven forbid, have you soil your breeches with tree sap."

"You place a trial before me, my lady. Women are infamous for enflaming a man's desire to prove himself worthy, but I will gladly succumb to your challenge."

Throughout his speech, Aidan strutted about like a conceited peacock. He hoped to elicit another laugh from Miss Purefoy's full lips.

She good-naturedly rolled her eyes at his antics, but despite the lady's best efforts, her smile exploded to sparkling effects. Aidan's heart clenched in satisfaction.

"Then Lay on, Macduff, and damned be him who first cries 'Hold! Enough!'"

Another girlish giggle followed Miss Purefoy flourish. She caught up her skirt tail and drifted off toward several hearty evergreens. One of his men trailed after her, and Aidan thought the young gardener the smartest one of those gathered about.

He watched her go before turning to his head gardener.

"You must mold me into the lady's hero."

He caught the man's shoulder.

"Tell me where to begin, Mr. Ryan."

When the man smiled, his wrinkles met.

"You were always the gallant one, my lord."

This time being called "gallant" did not stung. Instead, it was comforting revelation.

Aidan said with new affability, "Please say you hold knowledge on how to please the lady in this matter?"

"I do, Lord Lexford. Come with me."

Aidan followed the man, who served the Kimbolt family for more years than Aidan was alive, into the woodland surrounding the main house.

"We must choose the best holly branches, one loaded with lots of berries to set against the green silk of the leaves."

"Like those?"

Aidan rushed to the stand of holly trees.

"Exactly, my lord."

Mr. Ryan chose a branch.

"Make your cut at the notch so the branch left behind will sprout another for next year."

Aidan listened closely. He never considered how much knowledge Mr. Ryan and his staff possessed in order to keep the Lexington Arms' grounds immaculately beautiful. It made him wonder how many other things about his house of which he never took note.

"Excellent advice, Mr. Ryan," he said with true admiration. "How many should I cut?"

Mr. Ryan laughed agreeably.

"Enough to decorate each mantle within the main rooms, as well as other flat surfaces."

Aidan frowned.

"That many? We will strip the trees bare."

Ryan chuckled at Aidan's naiveté.

"Such is the idea, my lord, but no worry. There are many trees upon the grounds for the birds and squirrels to call home."

The man motioned to a copse of ash and transplanted rowan trees.

"I promised Mrs. Osborne I'd bring back several kissing balls. Would ye be requiring some above stairs, my lord?"

The gardener winked conspiratorially.

The man's suggestion caught Aidan by surprise. "

Whom would I kiss, Mr. Ryan?" he asked earnestly.

The gardener's eyes drifted to where Miss Purefoy chose limbs for the young servant to cut. Aidan's eyes followed. The idea of kissing Mary Purefoy was not as repulsive as it should be.

"Perhaps not, Sir," Ryan said dutifully.

Aidan considered his response. In her innocence, the woman was beautiful, but she was his sister by blood. Even if Aidan feigned an altruistic kiss on the cheek before "accidentally" finding her lips, the lady would recognize his motives for what they were. No, it was better to keep their relationship playful: To treat each other with respect and friendship.

"Hurry on with you, Mr. Ryan." Aidan purposely ignored the man's suggestion. "I will require your assistance to meet the house's need for holly."

An hour later, Aidan escorted Miss Purefoy toward the house. He insisted she return to the drawing room so they both could enjoy some chocolate.

"It will warm you. Your fingers are too cold."

Aidan seated her before the fire.

"And Mr. Ryan fully understands how important the greenery is to the house's celebration."

"What of the ribbon?" she asked distractedly.

Aidan smiled at the lady's singularity.

"I cannot say for certain, but we will seek Mrs. Babcock's counsel."

In calling for the housekeeper's presence, Aidan meant to emphasize to the woman that it was his idea to reestablish Christmastide traditions.

"I am certain the lady will be well aware of what else we might require."

Miss Purefoy flinched, and Aidan wondered of the source of her discontent.

"Is something amiss, my dear?"

The girl quickly shook her head in the negative, but he did not believe her.

"Tell me," he said as he knelt before her to capture Miss Purefoy's hands. "If we are to make anything good of this situation, we must speak the truth. We were thrust together by no fault on our parts; yet, I hope we can carve out a mutual friendship."

She stared at him long and hard. At length, the girl nodded her agreement.

"Mrs. Babcock is not pleased to have me in the household,"

she confessed.

"Has the woman offered you an offense?" Aidan asked in incredulity.

"No. No," Miss Purefoy assured. "But I feel Mrs. Babcock's disdain, nonetheless. She watches me as if the lady suspects I might carry off the best silver."

Aidan chose his words carefully.

"Servants likely carried my initial disparagement with your appearance to their quarters. I apologize if my conceit brought censure to your door. We must set a new tone. Please understand the change will be slow."

"It is of no consequence, my lord. I will find a means to win over Mrs. Babcock. She is a loyal servant and wants only what is best for your household."

Aidan was not so certain, but he permitted Miss Purefoy her delusion.

⁓

They enjoyed the chocolate and the heat of the hearth before Aidan summoned the housekeeper to the room.

"Mrs. Babcock," he said amiably, "Miss Purefoy and I thought to add ribbon and glass balls to the greenery Mr. Ryan will gather to decorate the house. Are there items previously in storage which might be used?"

The housekeeper shot a disapproving glare at Miss Purefoy.

"*I thought*," he emphasized the words, "some of my mother's things might be available. I must surround myself with pleasant memories to nurture the missing ones."

He watched with satisfaction as Mrs. Babcock's expression changed from one of disapproval to one of empathy.

"I am certain any ribbon remaining in storage rotted by now, but there are some lovely glass balls in a trunk in the drying room. I believe some of them were your great-grandmother's. There are others which likely belonged to Lady Cassandra."

"Could they be brought down in time to decorate?" he coaxed.

Aidan's excitement grew with the housekeeper's disclosure.

The lady's prune face returned, but her tone held her professionalism.

"I shall see personally to the decorations, Lord Lexford. It would please the late viscount to know his son reclaimed several of the family traditions."

Aidan could not recall a time when Arlen Kimbolt placed family traditions to the forefront. Only in securing the line did Aidan's father show any passion. Even so, he graciously accepted the housekeeper's words before excusing her to her duties. With the woman's exit, he turned to his sister.

"We should take the coach into the village."

She meant to protest, but Aidan stifled Miss Purefoy's words with his logic,

"I possess no sensibilities when it comes to ribbons. You must save me from making a cake of myself." He assisted the woman to her feet. "Now hurry. I am rarely a patient man."

"Despite your exaggerations to the contrary," Miss Purefoy said after a long assessing look, "I think you a man of great insight."

Then she was gone. Gone before Aidan could ascertain her meaning. In the lady's opinion, was being a man of insight a good thing?

Thirty minutes later, Mr. Hill claimed the reins of the carriage.

"Mrs. Osborne has a long list of supplies in order to create a Christmas feast," his man explained.

"Then you do not mean to chaperone?" Aidan teased.

Hill's eyebrow rose in curiosity.

"Do you require a chaperone, my lord?"

Aidan chuckled in relaxed ease.

"I think not."

He turned to assist the approaching Miss Purefoy into his small coach.

"It is but a short ride into the village," he explained to his companion as Hill climbed into the seat. "Once there, if you think of anything else we might require for the celebration, do not hesitate to purchase it. As I explained earlier, nearly two decades passed since anyone thought to mark the Festive Days at Lexington Arms. My memory of those days is as vague as that of the past two years."

Although he said the words as an apology for his shortcomings, Aidan was not certain he spoke the truth. Since accepting Miss Purefoy's suggestion to decorate his house for the Festive Days, in snatches of colorful images, he enjoyed the vivid memories of those early years of his life.

Miss Purefoy kept her eyes on the scenery outside the coach. Since entering the carriage, she did not look upon him. He knew that observation to be the truth for Aidan watched her exclusively.

"This is very kind of you, my lord. Kind of you to honor a poor relative's whim."

In hesitation, she bit her bottom lip.

"Like you, it has been many years since Christmastide knew a home under my brother's roof."

"Did not your mother insist on bringing the Festive Days into her son's home?" Aidan asked.

The girl blushed thoroughly.

"My...my brother is not easily swayed," she stammered.

Aidan was not certain Miss Purefoy spoke with complete honesty. He possessed the strong suspicion she forgot the ruse she practiced, but he also could not shake the idea he viewed the "real" girl within.

"Then we will form our own family tradition," he said patiently.

Mercy swallowed hard. She cane close to betraying her true devastation to Lord Lexford. The man was so not what she expected. When her sister Grace spoke of claiming the acquaintance of the viscount in London, Grace also confided that the gentleman developed an affection for Cashémere Aldridge. Mercy met the girl but once in the five years Grace served as a governess in Samuel

Aldridge's household. At the time, Mercy found the girl highly opinionated, and not in a good way. Cashémere Aldridge spouted religion as if she were an Evangelical preacher. Mercy could not imagine any man would desire a shrewish woman for a wife, and especially a man of Lord Lexford's ilk.

The viscount was perfect in every way. Handsome beyond reason. By far the most handsome man Mercy ever encountered. Yet, beyond his fine features, His Lordship possessed a cold intelligence, which defined him, and even deeper, there was a sadness, which could destroy him. Destroy her, too, she feared, for she was already very attached to the man.

"We arrived," Lord Lexford announced as the carriage rolled to a halt before a colorful mercantile. "Did you consider other purchases we should make?"

Mercy raised her eyes to meet his.

"We should see to some form of gratitude for your cottagers, my lord."

"You are correct again," His Lordship conceded. "This was a difficult year for those on the land."

"More so than last?" she inquired. "I understood last year beyond the pale."

"True," he acknowledged, but he did not act as if he held a remembrance of what she spoke.

Instead, he spoke from instinct. Mercy wondered how she might assist the viscount in discovering the missing pieces of his life. It would be her hope that in doing so, the man would finally know peace.

"I will ask Mr. Hill to anticipate our needs in this matter. Thank you for reminding me of my duty to the estate. Your empathy is duly noted."

He slid across the seat to reach for the door handle.

Her hand stayed his arm.

"Before the people who depend upon your estate for their livelihood, may I not be your cousin?"

Mercy asked softly. She dreaded facing strangers who

heard rumors of her supposed parentage.

The viscount smiled easily.

"I should have considered the possibility previously. I struggle with how to reconcile what I know of my father's history with our relationship and without causing you pain. From this day forward, you are Miss Mary Purefoy, my cousin from..."

"York," she supplied.

"My cousin from York."

The viscount kissed the back of Mercy's gloved hand before debarking. He first gave Mr. Hill instructions and then reached for her.

"Come along, my dear."

Despite her plain clothing, Mercy never felt so special. Viscount Lexford made her feel as elegantly dressed as a princess in a gossamer gown. When His Lordship was near, Mercy found herself continually a kilter.

"What first?" he whispered close to her ear.

"Ribbons first, my lord," she said with a full smile.

Aidan was uncertain why the woman brought him a sense of purpose, but she did. Contrary to his normally sensible nature, he accepted a complete stranger into a place of honor within his home, and worse, he strove to make the woman happy. In less than four and twenty hours, Miss Purefoy solidly wormed her way into his life, and Aidan would have it no other way. However, he could not dismiss her choice of "York" as her home shire. He wondered if the lady forgot her earlier tale of Staffordshire or whether she meant to mislead others into thinking her more rightly distanced from Cheshire. It was a fact Aidan would include in his letter to Pennington.

He escorted her into the small mercantile. Instantly, Mr. Chadwick, the proprietor was before him.

"My lord, may I be of assistance?"

"My cousin, Miss Purefoy, convinced me it is time for Lexington Arms to shed its mourning ribbons. We will begin with a small family Christmastide celebration. As such, Miss Purefoy says we must have red ribbon and plenty of it."

"Absolutely, my lord." The man bowed again for good measure. "Is there anything else you desire?"

Aidan shot a glance to where Miss Purefoy thumbed fine muslins.

"Please ask one of your daughters to assist my cousin with the purchase of whatever cloth the lady might desire. I wish to speak to Mr. Hill regarding proper supplies for my cottagers; then I mean to choose several personal items."

The shopkeeper rubbed his hands together in anticipation.

"As you wish, my lord."

Although Aidan did not remove his eyes from Miss Purefoy, for a quarter hour he and Hill decided upon what would be appropriate for the estate's tenants. Lucifer thought it a good idea to open Lexington Arms to the cottagers on the day following Christmas.

"It will provide the staff time to organize a basket of staples for each family."

"I agree," Aidan said.

Hill's eyes followed Aidan's gaze.

"Ask the lady's opinion of what we chose and what else should be included."

Aidan scowled.

"You readily bow to Miss Purefoy's opinions. Do you have an ulterior motive, my friend?"

Hill chuckled.

"Only that I like the man I see when you think no one watches you watching the lady."

It was very frustrating to be so transparent.

"You must be daft," Aidan objected, but he strolled toward where Miss Purefoy shoved away the hands of what must be Mr. Chadwick's daughter.

"Give it here," he demanded as he caught the dark blue cloth. He held the material close to Miss Purefoy's cheek. "An excellent choice," he declared. "Now the dark green."

"My lord…" Miss Purefoy pleaded.

"None of your protests, my dear," he replied. "I mean to see my cousin dressed for her station." He turned toward the girl. "Miss Chadwick, I presume."

"Yes…yes, my lord. Serena, Sir," the girl stammered. A quick curtsy followed.

"Miss Chadwick, my cousin requires five new dresses."

"Three," Miss Purefoy corrected.

"Five." Aidan swiftly dismissed her protest. He winked at Miss Chadwick. "And a riding habit."

He looked again upon the pale countenance of Miss Purefoy. He said in sympathy, "Yet, I will not embarrass my cousin by asking her to submit to a fitting today. Instead, we will place the choice of fabrics in your expert hands."

The young girl blushed thoroughly.

"Perhaps you might also recommend a competent dressmaker who would call upon the manor to complete the work."

The girl glanced to where her father assisted a matronly villager.

"I could come, my lord," she said hesitantly. "That is if you hold no objections."

Aidan's eyebrow rose in curiosity.

"You possess knowledge of patterns and fittings?"

The girl eagerly nodded.

"I make clothes for my family, even my father."

Aidan searched Miss Purefoy's countenance for her permission. A brief nod indicated the woman's agreement.

"Then you should come to Lexington Arms tomorrow for the measurements. Bring the cloth and whatever notions you require. Tell Mr. Chadwick I request your services for my family."

The girl smiled brightly.

"Thank you, Sir. It is an honor, my lord."

Aidan caught Miss Purefoy's elbow.

"I have a few items I wish to choose for my brother's family."

He could not call the child by name: The word often choked him. He would send Lucifer to Rhodes's estate with the gifts.

"Mr. Hill made choices for the tenants' baskets. He thought you might examine the items and provide us with a woman's opinion of their appropriateness."

She said softly, "Certainly, my lord."

Aidan watched her cross to where Lucifer conversed with one of the clerks. She was obviously displeased with his high handedness, but Miss Purefoy would change her mind when Miss Chadwick finished the first of the gowns. Oddly, Aidan wondered if it would be so easy to make a woman in which he held a true interest happy.

⁓

Mercy waited for Mr. Hill to finish with his order before she motioned him to the side.

"I wish to purchase a piece of linen to make His Lordship several handkerchiefs. Do you suppose you could conduct the purchase without Lord Lexford knowing? She pressed one of the pennies she found during her stint as a maid into his palm.

Mr. Hill's brow furrowed.

"There is no need for you to pay me."

"I insist." Her back stiffened in defiance. "A linen is far from a fine gift for a gentleman, but whatever I present Lord Lexford will be from my purse. The man will not pay for his own gift."

⁓

Aidan chose three wooden toys for a child he encountered but a half dozen times over the past few years. During his convalescence in Kent, Thornhill apprised Aidan of what the duke knew of Aidan's interactions with the Rhodes family. Evidently, their relationship deteriorated after Susan's death. Aidan possessed no personal memory of this supposed animosity, but the Thornhill assured Aidan it was so. With a glance to where Miss Purefoy spoke privately with Mr. Hill, Aidan made another choice: an impetuous one, but one which pleased him. A small music box. One with a crystal dove upon its silver top.

"Wrap it carefully," he said softly, and Mr. Chadwick nodded his understanding.

Deep in the pleasure of choosing a gift for a beautiful woman, Aidan did not hear the scuff of feet behind him until a throat cleared.

"My lord." Aidan turned to come face-to-face with Susan's father, Jonathan Rhodes. *Speak of the Devil*, he thought. A tight smile spoke of the man's contempt.

"Father Rhodes," Aidan said as a purposeful manipulation of the situation. Strong emotions flooded his chest with an unsavory assault.

Rhodes's expression hardened.

"I was unaware you returned to Lexington Arms, Aidan."

Aidan worked hard to unlock his scrunched fists. He guarded his words: Something about Jonathan Rhodes always made Aidan uneasy. Unconsciously, his jaw clenched in wariness.

"I arrived late yesterday. I meant to send word of my return, but we were quite busy this morning. Was there something of import of which you wished to speak to me?"

Susan's father glanced to where Miss Purefoy selected ribbon for the house's decorations.

"I heard guests arrived during your absence."

"My cousin," Aidan said in explanation, but he knew the servant gossip line likely spoke of Miss Purefoy's true relationship to the Kimbolt name.

Rhodes's expression settled in those aristocratic lines, which Susan perfected in mimicry.

"We hold business, my lord," the man said curtly. "I would call upon you the day after Christmas. I assume you plan to remain in Cheshire as part of your recovery."

Aidan did not appreciate the man's tone, nor did he approve of Rhodes's presumptive maneuver.

"If it is of your concern to know my business, I do," he said autocratically.

Rhodes took a step backward as if Aidan's attitude surprised the man.

"I meant no disrespect, my lord," Susan's father said without true emotion. "Your health is of great importance to the Rhodes's family. I simply meant your staying at Lexington Arms is for the best," he announced with a bit more feeling. "I will call on the twenty-sixth, and I will bring the child with me. It is time the boy came to know his Uncle Aidan or is Aaron to call you 'Father'?"

Chapter 6

THE DAY WOULD BE PERFECT if not for the specter of Jonathan Rhodes's visit hanging over Aidan's head like the sword of Damocles. Over the past fortnight, both he and his staff took on lighter hearts with the addition of the greenery and the lovely ribbon, which Miss Purefoy chose. Each anticipated the Christmas pudding and the goose Mrs. Osborne promised to one and all. Life crept into Lexington Arms on a pair of well-worn boots: Miss Purefoy seemed to fill the air with her enthusiasm.

Earlier in the day, he and his sister wrote notes of gratitude to his household and grounds staff. Tomorrow, Aidan would present each of his servants a gold coin along with the personalized note.

"You do have an excellent hand," he complimented Miss Purefoy as she toiled over one of the last of the messages. Aidan watched with amusement as the lady went about her ritual: a sharpening of her pen, setting of the paper at a precise angle so as not to smudge the ink with the knuckle of the smallest finger of her right hand, the tapping of the pen three times against the lip of the well to remove the excess ink, and the gentle biting of her bottom lip in concentration. Aidan found Miss Purefoy's mannerisms adorably addictive.

She finished the line before looking up. Her smile widened. "I told you I would be of use, my lord."

"I never doubted it, my dear."

Aidan popped another apple tart into his mouth. Between the two of them, they devoured more than they should. As well as the next man, Aidan enjoyed a sweet cake with his tea, but it was not the sweets he found unusual. The odd thing was for the past two weeks, he did not consume more than a single glass of wine at supper. Instead, he enjoyed tea with Miss Purefoy. *Enjoyed* was the key word. He enjoyed the tea, the cakes, and the lady, more so than the finest wines he knew in royal palaces and in the best homes on the European continent.

For the Christmas Eve services, Miss Purefoy joined him in the family pew, which was followed by a sharing of a hearty brew by the villagers and several solemn carols by the children.

"An excellent evening," he murmured to the night's stillness. It was, at least, two of the clock, and Aidan remained from his bed. *The nightmares*, he thought. Although Aidan admitted not all of the dreams of late held frightening events, even those of pleasant times possessed a sense of foreboding. As if they held a certainty Aidan preferred not to recognize. And that was where the true horror waited.

Mercy tossed and turned in bed late into the night. The debacle she left behind in Lancashire weighed heavy upon her mind. It was not as if Mercy regretted leaving Geoffrey's household. Far from it. Despite all the hardships she encountered on the road, Mercy enjoyed her newfound freedom, and she admired the tenacity she displayed. She thought it spoke well of the woman she became: She was a survivor. Mr. Hill's kindness arrived as a balm for her battered soul, but Mercy realized even if she did not make Lucifer Hill's acquaintance, she would know success. On the road, Mercy discovered independence. At Lexington Arms, she found security and acceptance. It was a giddy realization for a girl who knew a vile, sequestered existence.

Her only true regret in the matter rested in her foisting on the viscount the lie of a familial connection. It was so difficult earlier that day when they shared his study to write notes of appreciation. Not difficult to look upon the man's countenance. Never that. Mercy could feast upon his fine features all day and never tire of them. Yet, it was not the man's most excellent appearance she most admired. With the viscount, Mercy felt complete. Felt as if she belonged. Not necessarily in a romantic sense, although she would never reject any overtures of affection Lord Lexford wished to bestow upon her. Being with His Lordship was different from anything she ever knew: The man spoke to her with respect. He sought her opinions. His presence changed everything for Mercy. She knew she would never accept anything less from another man, which likely meant she would spend her life as a spinster.

"Aidan," she whispered to the darkness. Until this very night, Mercy refused the intimacy of his name. "Better I keep it at *my lord*," she warned her foolish heart. "I wish we were truly family so I might see to Lord Lexford's household, and he could manage my safety. That would be lovely. It would be enough to possess a real family."

Restless, Mercy rolled to the bed's side to rise. Catching her sensible robe, she slid it around her shoulders and tied it closed with a ribbon. Retrieving her slippers, Mercy looked about for the book she finished earlier in the day. She would return it to the library and choose another. Perhaps, reading would assist her to sleep.

"I must set my mind to rearranging the disorder found in the library," she reminded herself. "With too much happiness, I enjoyed the prospects of decorating the house and preparing His Lordship's home for Christmastide. Now, I must see to the practical aspects of serving the viscount."

With a cupped flame upon the candle and the book tucked tightly against her body under her arm, Mercy slipped quietly down the stairs. She recalled how, as children, she and Grace would sneak through the manor to discover what their parents placed before the hearth for Christmas Day and on birthdays. Mercy loved the excitement of their sisterly adventures as much as she loved the simple, but heartfelt, presents. Thomas and Louisa Nelson took great pride in treating their modest staff and their children with generosity.

Mercy paused as a draft from below caught the flame to send it dancing with the house's shadows.

"If only," she whispered to the darkened house. *If only* her parents did not die. *If only* Geoffrey did not succumb to the temptations of youth. *If only* Grace did not flee alone into the night. *If only* her relationship with Viscount Lexford held truth.

With a shrug of her slender shoulders, Mercy continued her descent. Her only option was to play the cards she and Mr. Hill dealt. By proving herself worthy of his kindness, she would see that the viscount never knew regret for extending his benevolence to her.

Reaching the library, she eased open the tall door and slipped inside. With her small candle, she lit a brace sitting on a nearby table before snuffing out the light she brought with her. A sigh of approval escaped as Mercy looked upon the shelves lined with books of all sorts.

"If only I could live in such a room," she said softly.

"Could you really remain within these walls?"

Mercy spun around to find the viscount slouched in an overstuffed chair before the hearth.

"My lord!" she gasped. "You gave me quite a fright."

Immediately, Mercy thought of the inappropriateness of their meeting so late and thusly dressed.

"I...I should go," she murmured. Her hands fumbled with the single candle.

When the door opened, Aidan expected Mr. Hill. For the past few years, other than when Aidan tarried with the Fowlers, Lucifer made it his mission to ensure that Aidan found his bed. His man of all means was one of the few who knew how Aidan suffered with the forced marriage and the tragedy, which beset Lexington Arms. Instead of Hill, his lovely "sister" slid into the room.

On this evening, Aidan brought his misery to this particular room because the library always was his mother's pride and joy. As he nestled in one of the chairs before the fire, he chastised himself for not putting more effort into bringing the room to order, if for no other reason than to honor his mother's memory.

He wondered if he made a mistake by returning home. Despite the pleasant hours spent with Miss Purefoy, he could not shake the feeling his house sucked the life from his lungs. He supposed he could remain in his London townhouse, where the ghosts were not so prevalent. His memory loss was like a demon he could not face down. He gasped for air as if he could not breathe– as if he said a prayer for God to release him from the voices in his head, and suddenly the door opened to his Christmas angel.

In silence, Aidan watched the girl. Part of him wished to push her away. To drive Miss Purefoy from his life. His senses said she was not what she appeared to be. But a more basic need simply wished to enjoy her company while he may. On balance, if Mary Purefoy meant to play him, she made no move to demand outrageous sums of money. His purse knew only the cost of a few notions and cloth.

"My lord! You gave me quite a fright!" she gasped when she became aware of his presence. Aidan enjoyed looking upon Miss Purefoy's slender form. The drab gowns she wore during the day did an excellent job of disguising the woman's femininity. In sharp contrast, the thin nightrail and robe displayed curves the woman hid until this moment. Especially with the light behind her, which outlined strong legs and luscious hips.

"I...I should go," she said with a flush of color. The girl turned to leave, but Aidan made short business of the distance between them.

"Do not depart on my behalf." He caught Miss Purefoy's hand, and a tingle of excitement shot up his arm. Aidan shoved away the awareness. "Permit me to assist you in finding a book."

The girl's eyebrow arched sharply.

"I likely know the shelves better than you, my lord. I studied them daily for the past few weeks."

Aidan sighed as if in relief.

"No doubt, my dear, but indulge me a moment. I am in sad need of company."

He meant to take shameless advantage of the lady's good nature to satisfy his self-possessed mood.

A look of concern crossed Miss Purefoy's countenance.

"How so, my lord?"

Aidan silently debated on whether to confide in the woman. On balance, he knew so little of Miss Purefoy, but in the deep recesses of his mind, Aidan could hear his mother's voice telling his late Aunt Janelle that one simply had to listen at a ball or a social to learn all the latest gossip.

"People will tell complete strangers their most intimate details. Every ache. Every sordid mistake they made. Perhaps it is the anonymity. Perhaps it is cathartic simply to say the words aloud," his mother said when she shared a picnic lunch on the lawn with her children. It was so like the former Lady Lexford to pull her children from the nursery to permit them time to be boisterous and childlike.

"We could simply converse, my lord," Miss Purefoy suggested.

"I would think we were quite out of words," he said lamely, but Aidan escorted the lady to a nearby settee. He politely placed a lap rug across her legs to minimize any temptation. He settled across from her. "Should I ring for some tea?"

The lady protested.

"Oh, my, no. Please leave the servants to their sleep. They worked steadily to set the house aright for the Festive Days."

Aidan appreciated Miss Purefoy consideration for his employees.

"Then may I interest you in a glass of sherry?"

"That would be delightful," she said with a bright smile.

Aidan filled a glass for them both. Returning to his seat, he stretched out his long legs before him.

"We managed to extend our informal silence to some five minutes," he said with a chuckle. "Would you care to suggest a subject for our discourse, my dear?"

Miss Purefoy's lips twisted in a tight frown as she searched for a topic.

"I know," she said with bright revelation. "Tell me what you thought of Mr. Roberts's Christmas sermon."

Aidan expected her to bring up the latest London fashions, but he was slow to learn Miss Purefoy was not like other young women. He got caught up in her eyes and did not immediately respond. At length, he admitted, "I am not certain I understood the man's emphasis on what the three kings found in Bethlehem."

She sat forward in excitement.

"Did you not? I thought the whole idea that God might stop time while the world decided what course to take very enlightening. I mean, I often stare into the Heavens and wonder if I would possess the tenacity to follow a star in search of a king."

Aidan held no doubt she would not only follow God's star, the lady would hitch her coach to it to permit the celestial being to tug her along behind it. In truth, he thought her the most remarkable woman of his acquaintance. Her assumption reminded him of one he and Kerrington and Wellston had on one of those less than chilly December nights in Persia. They assumed the role of guardians along a dangerous pass through the mountains.

"Do you miss December snow?" Kerrington asked as he eyed the narrow opening for movement.

Wellston chuckled before answering.

"Cold has its benefits. In northern Northumberland, snow begins as early as October and lasts well into April."

Aidan always was wistfully tied to home, but this particular incident occurred long before Aidan received the news of Andrew's proposal to Susan.

"Do you suppose those in England are gazing upon the same stars as are we?" he asked the silence, which rested heavy between him and his friends. "And what if we followed the stars? Would we find our way home?"

Kerrington's frown lines met.

"I possess no reason to follow any trail, which will return my feet to England."

"Nor I," Wellston concurred.

Their adamant declarations brought on Aidan's scowl. At the time, he thought he possessed a reason to return: A woman for whom he held a tender regard. Perhaps if he arrived in Cheshire earlier than he did, things would be different. Mayhap the condition of his heart would not be one ripped to shreds.

"Decisions," he said to the lady. "Decisions are only clear in hindsight."

Miss Purefoy's lips set in a tight line.

"It amazes me that so many people are titular about the very event which changes everything in their lives. The same way people do not accept God when He gives them the opportunity to make the decision to serve him. Do you not agree that the most contemptible of sinners requires His grace as much as the most loyal of saints?"

Aidan watched the woman carefully; every nerve in his body said she spoke from the heart, but could he trust someone again?

"I often wonder how I might trust a man who possesses only a vague allegiance to God." *Or to family*, he thought bitterly. His heart squeezed, and Aidan tamped down the desolation rarely far from his mind.

"I always thought a man who fluctuated in his dealings with his fellow man or in his relationship with his wife could not truly love God," the lady declared baldly.

If Miss Purefoy thought every man who did not respect his wife ungodly, then England would be filled with infidels. And what would her opinion of him say of his own worth?

"We all feel guilty and ashamed for not being everything to everyone," Aidan murmured.

Miss Purefoy's eyes widened. Her far too wise gaze settled upon his countenance.

"Is that statement the crux of what keeps you from your bed, my lord?"

Despite her evaluation's accuracy, Aidan shook off her words.

"You possess no experience to understand my loss," he said more tersely than he intended.

Instantly, she was on her feet. Aidan expected her to storm from the room, but instead, Miss Purefoy crossed to where he sat and dropped to her knees before him. She leaned against his leg, and Aidan felt her warmth shoot up his body to land squarely in his chest. The lady caught up his hand.

"I would truly not have you know pain."

Miss Purefoy's slender fingers stroked the back of Aidan's hand, and he could not remove his eyes from her steady gaze. Her innocent vulnerability stirred feelings Aidan thought long buried.

"There are events which happen that mark our lives forever. They change everything before and after their occurrence."

"Amen to that," Aidan said sarcastically.

He thought of all the decisions that sent his house into years of mourning.

Miss Purefoy clasped his hand tighter.

"Do you not understand, my lord? God sees your past and defines your future?"

She raised the back of Aidan's hand to her lips and left a tender kiss upon his knuckles. He never felt such complete peace in his heart.

"God knows where you have been," she continued. "He knows your successes and your failures. He knows the peace you desire. The devastation you see. He knows your heart. The disappointments you face and the challenges which lie ahead."

"If He is a benevolent God," Aidan said bitterly, "Why does

He take everyone from me?"

"I am here," she said softly. "And so is Mr. Hill, and the friends with whom you served, and now the families of those friends. You are not alone, Lord Lexford. There are many who care deeply for you. Perhaps God brought you to this time and this place so you could cross over from death to life. From despair to hopefulness. It is fair to grieve, my lord, but not to feel guilty for things beyond your control."

Aidan's breath caught in his chest. The sincerity in the lady's voice pummeled his sensibility. Could any woman be so filled with goodness? His hackles said not, but his foolish heart desperately wanted to believe the promises she purported.

"How can you think so? Your brother drove you from your home. You have no one."

"You err, my lord. I have Mr. Hill and Mrs. Osborne. I have Miss Chadwick as a new acquaintance, and God replaced the most horrid brother with one who looks upon me with kindness."

Damn, he thought. *Hers was the perfect response.*

"Then you enjoy your stay at Lexington Arms?" he asked cautiously.

"How could I not?" she protested. "You gave me a beautiful room and plenty to eat. I know respect and worth. Your estate is pure perfection."

Aidan's eyebrow rose in disbelief.

"I would certainly not refer to Lexington Arms as perfection. There is one wing badly in need of repair, and many of the rooms require new accessories. Several chambers still reflect my mother's time as viscountess."

"Then why not make the manor over in your taste?" the lady suggested. "Make your reign as Lord Lexford memorable. Leave your stamp on the legacy earned. Like the wise men, follow your star to discover what no one in your family ever bothered to know: a man greater than all those who came before him."

"Dare I?" Aidan asked in awe.

The lady's frown lines deepened.

"Why ever not? I would think a man who faced Napoleon's forces and the worst manipulations of mankind would dare anything," Miss Purefoy said adamantly. "Why should you continue to live with the shadows, which haunted you for years? Do you mean to punish yourself for a situation not of your making? If you are not willing to reconsider the possible, who will do so on your behalf?"

Aidan smiled genuinely.

"It would seem I found an advocate in a lost sister."

Miss Purefoy blushed thoroughly. She said obediently, "I spoke beyond my station, my lord. Please forgive me."

Aidan felt perversely pleased by her response. While the girl battled a feeling of discomposure and stole a moment to collect herself, he said kindly, "I made light of your serious consideration, my dear. It is I who should ask for forgiveness." He felt his heart swell with quiet joy. "Despite my ill attempts at levity, perhaps I might request your excellent opinions in making choices for the house."

"Me?" she gasped. "You would trust me?"

She tugged at her long braid, twisting the ends in her fingers in a nervous gesture.

"I would be pleased to be of service, my lord, but should not the next Lady Lexford be the one who will make such decisions?"

Disappointment welled up in him. Just the reminder of his marital prospects caused Aidan's jaw to clinch. His lack of memory and his feelings of loneliness mixed with the anxiety that plagued his days and nights of late.

"It is not my intention to wed? At least, not for many years," he declared.

Cocking her head, Miss Purefoy asked, "Do you not require an heir, my lord?"

Aidan could not stifle the sigh of resignation. He shook his head in the negative.

"My brother left behind a son," he said dryly. "So, an heir is not necessary."

Miss Purefoy shifted uncomfortably.

"Yet, do you not wish to leave the estate and the title to one of your own issue?"

Hell, yes! Aidan wished to scream. He desired a wife and a house full of children, but he accepted the fact he might never recover his memory; and Aidan held the private belief that if he did not learn the contents of the missing piece, he would never accept another into his life. He would know no intimate relationship.

"There is no need for me to pursue a wife in order to secure the Kimbolt line."

His response sounded colder than he anticipated. The sheen of tears in her eyes caught him unawares.

Miss Purefoy took a deep breath before forcing a bright smile.

"Then I shall be pleased to assist you, my lord."

She briefly stroked his cheek with her fingertips. An unfamiliar twinge of expectancy zigzagged its way through his chest. The lady was pretty. No, beautiful. Too beautiful.

"I shall foresee having young Master Kimbolt's acquaintance," she added.

"Then when his grandfather brings the boy for a visit on the day after Christmas, I will send for you."

The sense of dread returned with the remembrance of Rhodes's upcoming visit.

"I could not," Miss Purefoy protested. "I noted Mr. Rhodes's disapproval when the gentleman spoke to you at the mercantile."

Scowling, Aidan spoke through tight lips.

"Mr. Rhodes does not speak to whom is welcome under my roof. The late Lady Lexford's father often acts above his station."

Aidan thought of how the Rhodeses never considered Aidan a proper suitor for Susan. His late wife's parents tolerated Aidan's friendship with their daughter, but only until they realized Aidan's romantic intentions. At that point, Susan's mother limited Aidan finding private time to woo Susan.

Miss Purefoy's lips compressed.

"We shall speak on it again when we are both not so exhausted. It is late."

"Do not leave," Aidan said before she could rise to depart. He stared into her eyes and with reluctance caressed her cheek. "Just a few more minutes," he pleaded.

Her gaze searched his before she nodded her agreement. She sank to the floor to sit at his feet. Miss Purefoy rested her head upon his knee, and Aidan knew instant contentment. He aimlessly stroked her hair while she wrapped her arms about his legs. It was quite the domestic scene. Nothing moved but his hand against the silken strands. Only the occasional snap of the flames broke the silence. Aidan did not wish to talk or to think or to tantalize. He simply wanted this moment of comfort with Mary Purefoy.

Mercy slowly expelled the breath she held. She experienced a brief peek into the life of the man, who fascinated her from the moment of their first acquaintance. And, unfortunately, the fascination did not lessen, especially after learning something of His Lordship's family and his lack of hope for the future. His words of desolation spoke to her heart. She knew such despair while living under Geoffrey's roof. Even though she knew it dangerous to grow closer to the man than her foolish heart already claimed, Mercy wished to know more of Aidan Kimbolt.

Being from a less than stable family, Mercy understood Lord Lexford's reasons for wishing to forget his family's shortcomings. When she escaped Geoffrey's notice, Mercy swore never to accept a man's kindness as anything more than a brief respite from the world's cruelty. The male species brought her nothing but sickening trepidation: Her brother's rakish ways led the barony to poverty's door. Geoffrey's associates threatened to defile her. And Sir Lesley offered her an uncertain future as the mother of his five children. Her head knew she should simply accept the viscount's benevolence for as long as the man extended it, and then she should make her escape when Viscount Lexford's generosity dwindled. Yet, her mind and her heart followed different paths.

Instead of doing the sensible thing, Mercy wanted to touch him. Of late, she dreamed of kissing Lord Lexford. What she would not give to have her first kiss to come from Lord Lexford. Unfortunately, the viscount saw her as someone he must protect, not someone he could love, as a man and woman would know love. *His Lordship thinks you his sister,* her sagacious side asserted. *A gentleman would never kiss his sister, legitimate or not. And it is best the viscount does not act without propriety,* Mercy silently chastised. *You did not accept Mr. Hill's charity to act the seductress.*

Miss Purefoy fell asleep as she rested against his leg. Without realizing she did so, as she drifted off to sleep, the lady gently stroked the back of Aidan's calf just below where his knee bent. Her tenderness touched his heart and stirred his manhood. Aidan never was one to keep a mistress, especially after what happened to Andrew. Now, he suspected he might need to call upon one of the ladies in Liverpool soon. As much as a man can when he feels no connection to the woman beneath him, he thought to enjoy himself with Monique when he and Godown visited Lady Minerva's Parlor Room, but the attack on the marquis brought the evening to an abrupt end.

Aidan leaned forward to support Miss Purefoy's form to the floor. She rested upon her back, her arms and legs bent at odd angles, but he thought her charmingly attractive. She was so innocent. So vulnerable and so damn tempting. The lady spoke her heart without an inner censure to prevent her doing so, and Aidan found her openness delightfully refreshing. With resignation's sigh, Aidan bent to lift her to him.

"You are fortunate, my dear, that my back did not suffer the damage my head endured. Otherwise, you would know no bed this night," he murmured as he buried his nose into the crook of her neck. He inhaled her essence.

Through the thin cloth of her nightrail and robe, Aidan could feel the warmth of her curves as he easily supported her weight. Her slender legs draped across his forearm, and the palm of his large hand cupped the cheek of her hip. An image of the lady naked beneath him drove Aidan's steps forward. He could feel his manhood come to life. *Bloody hell, she is your sister,* his brain told his body, but his body refused such rational thoughts.

Making his way through the darkened halls, Aidan turned toward the stairs. Miss Purefoy snuggled closer, and he drank in the scent of lilacs. He lifted her higher so her breath might warm the skin beneath the opening of his shirt. It was exquisite torture, but one Aidan was willing to bear. Her closeness washed away some of the shame he felt as a Kimbolt.

Reaching her quarters Aidan shouldered her door open. Miss Purefoy left a lantern burning, and Aidan easily made his way to her bed.

"It is time for us to say our farewells," he whispered as he placed her gently upon the pillows. Lifting the heavy braid, he draped it across the lady's shoulder. In doing so, his fingers brushed the fullness of her breast.

His manhood hardened.

"You are so beautiful," he murmured.

He lifted the braid and placed it down again. This time his fingers lingered against the weight of her breast. Aidan would love to caress the globe. To taste the bud. To drink of Miss Purefoy's essence.

With a stifled groan, he shook his head to drive away his errant thoughts. Adjusting himself in his tight breeches, Aidan knew thanks the woman did not awake while he stared down upon her, with his hand cupping his most private parts. The lady would think him quite the deviant. Settling the counterpane across her, Aidan's turned to catch up the lantern. He raised it where the light might shine down upon Miss Purefoy's countenance.

"Sleep well, my Christmas angel," he whispered.

Slipping from the lady's room, Aidan meant to leave the lantern on a small table outside, but a strange click of a door had him turning toward the sound. No one else held chambers in this particular wing.

The door leading to the burned out section of the house stood ajar.

"What the bloody hell!" he growled as he strode toward the partially opened door.

The cold December air seeped through the opening. *As cold as a grave*, he thought as he shoved the door wide and lifted the lantern to cut the darkness. A shiver having nothing to do with the chilly breeze invading his house slid down his spine for the light kissed a solitary figure. His wife stood on the burned out ledge from which she dove into the growing flames. Aidan's shoulders became rigid; his left fist white.

"Susan." His mouth formed the word, but no sound escaped.

Yet, she must have heard him for she glanced his way before darting toward an opening leading to the remnants of the stairs to the ground floor.

Aidan was immediately on the move.

"Susan!" he called. "Please, Susan! Do not run away from me!"

But his entreaties fell on deaf ears. Before he could reach the ledge upon which he last saw her, she was gone. A bitter taste of defeat filled his throat.

Aidan gave chase, but for a man of his size, the burned out skeleton held additional dangers. By the time he squeezed through the opening to descend what remained of the narrow stairs, there was no sign of her.

Did he imagine a woman he was certain he failed? Did his less than chaste thoughts regarding Miss Purefoy manifested themselves as an image of his wife? Looking back on the blackened timbers, Aidan knew it was past time to repair his house and his life. After Christmas, he would impose on Miss Purefoy's good graces to redecorate the sleeping quarters and the rooms for entertaining. He would replace the rooms, which the fire claimed. He would take Miss Purefoy's advice. Aidan would drive the ghosts from his reign as Viscount Lexford.

"Farewell, Susan," he said to the night's stillness, but Aidan's confidence faded when his wife's voice carried across the empty space.

"Never, my lord."

Chapter 7

"AND YOU HEARD Lady Lexford's response?" Lucifer eyed him suspiciously.

Aidan waited until after he excused the staff to their own Christmas celebrations before he asked to speak to Hill privately. He knew his man would find Aidan's tale dubious.

"As clearly as I hear you now," he said more calmly than he felt.

Hill sighed heavily.

"And this occurred after you carried Miss Purefoy to her chambers?"

Aidan omitted the part where he touched the woman. The thought of her soft curves still sent his heart racing, but Aidan abandoned the idea of Susan's image being a twinge of guilt from his actions. He could not recall a time when he hungered for a woman more.

"I know what you are thinking," Aidan said in exasperation.

Hill smiled easily.

"Then why do you not speak for me, my lord?"

Realizing he thumbed his embroidered name on the handkerchiefs Miss Purefoy presented him as a gift, Aidan slammed the open desk drawer harder than he meant to. The lady skillfully placed his initials on a half dozen cloths she gave him as a Christmas gift, but on two, she placed his Christian name on a complementary corner.

"So your cloths are different from those of the late viscount," she explained. "A token of a new beginning."

How Miss Purefoy knew his full name, Aidan was uncertain. Likely from the copy of *Debrett's* in the library. Truthfully, the fact the lady somehow learned he, his father, and Andrew shared the same monogram was beyond his caring. With her gift, Miss Purefoy recognized him as beyond the former heirs to the title, a fact which infinitely pleased him.

Occasionally, Aidan wondered how he and his father would get on if Arlen Kimbolt did not succumbed to his illness. Would his father show patience in teaching his second son the responsibilities of being a viscount? Aidan would never know. It was James Kerrington who came to Aidan's rescue when the title landed squarely on Aidan's shoulders.

"You think I felt shame for enjoying Miss Purefoy's company," Aidan accused. "You think I still blame myself for Susan's death." Aidan could not look Hill squarely in the eye. Perhaps a twinge of guilt did remain.

Hill sat forward in what appeared to be empathy.

"Are those my words or yours, my lord?" he said with concern.

Aidan scraped one hand across his face.

"Damn it, Hill. I require your insights, not your sarcasm," he said testily. Memories of Susan always brought forth Aidan's ire.

Hill's countenance hardened.

"I do not mean to make light, my lord." His man hesitated before saying. "It is odd, Sir, that you never encountered any visions prior to your injury and your return to Lexington Arms."

Aidan's heart lurched.

"Are the images associated with Charters' attack? A delayed symptom of my injury?"

Hill responded in a matter-of-fact tone.

"It would seem prudent to examine the possibility. Is there a man of medicine in the area we might trust in the matter?"

Aidan shook his head in the negative.

"None that would not speak openly of the current Lord Lexford's bedlam, but perhaps a discreetly worded message to Fowler's physician might serve the purpose. The man's professional manner and his knowledge impressed me." Aidan paused before asking, "If we think there is a connection between my return to the estate and these strange sightings, should we be wary of anyone who was not part of my life previously?"

Hill asked cautiously,

"Meaning Miss Purefoy?"

Aidan considered how much the lady's goodness was in sharp contrast to every other memory he held of his estate. Despite his best efforts, he frowned.

"How much do we know of my sister?"

His feelings of doubt increased Aidan's frustration.

His man had an unerring ability to assess a person's true nature, and Aidan often sought Lucifer Hill's opinion on a new acquaintance, whether in London or in the field of battle. On more than one occasion, Hill's intuitive nature saved his Realm group from danger; yet, an odd expression crossed Hill's countenance, and Aidan again wondered if Lucifer hid the truth regarding Miss Purefoy.

"The lady has an irrefutable mystique, but I do not perceive the girl to have a touch of guile in her bones."

Aidan voiced his earlier thoughts, the ones he reasoned while dressing for supper.

"Do you not think it peculiar that you happened upon the very person you sought when you departed Linton Park?"

Hill hesitated, which presented Aidan with another stab of concern.

"You look for deceit, my lord. Can you not take pleasure in the simply joys Miss Purefoy brings to your life?"

"Is the lady honest?" Aidan demanded.

With Miss Purefoy, he was so far off his normal amiability, and he did not know how to rein in his emotions.

In an unconscious gesture, Hill tapped his finger against the chair's arm.

"In all the essentials, you may place your faith in Miss Purefoy."

"But you think my sister keeps secrets?" Aidan pressed.

He wondered if his anger was wrapped up in wanting a forbidden woman, and that fact did not set well with him.

Hill spoke in earnest.

"Do we not all keep our confidences? I cannot imagine you shared your deepest secrets with the woman."

Despite Hill's assurances, Aidan awoke from another fretful night feeling no more satisfied than he had when he crawled into his too large bed the night before. He waved off his valet's efforts to shave him, compleing the task himself. In the field, Aidan learned to tend to his own ablutions.

"Some days we possessed no clean clothes," Aidan had explained to Mr. Poley when the valet complained of Aidan going to breakfast with a smudge of dirt upon his breeches.

"Yet, my lord, that was long before you were Viscount Lexford," Poley protested.

And, most certainly, the man was correct, but the valet's opinion held no weight. If Aidan were to discover the truth among Lexington Arms' ruins, he would begin with the simplest of tasks.

"One point of reference at a time."

"Miss Chadwick," Mercy greeted the girl with a welcoming smile. "You possess impeccable timing. I just thought to have tea. Might you join me?"

Earlier, Mercy asked Mr. Payne to show the girl to Mercy's sitting room. Miss Chadwick was to deliver the first of her creations on this day, and Mercy anticipated the pleasure of wearing something new for Lord Lexford. She abandoned her earlier protests and simply permitted the viscount his generosity.

Miss Chadwick blushed, but she accepted the cup Mercy extended in her direction.

"His Lordship's home is magnificent," the girl said in awe.

Mercy thought it amusing that Miss Chadwick said something similar the other two times the girl called upon the estate to take Mercy's measurements and to do an early fitting of the garments.

Mercy smiled graciously.

"It is a fine estate. Even with the damage to the end of this wing, I think the house possesses an undeniable character."

Miss Chadwick giggled nervously.

"I did not know what to expect. There were terrible rumors that the whole house succumbed to the fire."

The girl's words instantly piqued Mercy's attentions. In the short time Mercy dwelled at Lexington Arms, she noticed how the house's servants, under strict orders from Mrs. Babcock, made a point of not discussing the incident, which cost Lord Lexford his wife. If asked directly, the person would provide a quick, succinct response before rushing away to perform his duties. Even Mr. Hill avoided speaking freely of the event. Perhaps, Mercy might learn something of what most troubled Lord Lexford from a person outside the house. That is, if she dared.

With a steadying breath, Mercy smiled largely at the girl.

"As you observed, only six rooms suffered from the event. The remainder of the house is quite untouched."

The girl's eyes scanned Mercy's quarters.

"Your chambers suffered no damage?"

Mercy spoke in coy tones.

"I could show you the burned out rooms, if you care to see them."

Miss Chadwick fanned her face with her hand.

"Oh my, no," she said upon a throaty rasp. "I could not look upon a place where a woman lost her life so tragically."

Mercy's heart fluttered in anticipation.

"What do the villagers say of the late Lady Lexford?"

She caught the girl's hand in a display of solidarity.

Miss Chadwick glanced about the room as if suspecting an eavesdropper to be hiding in the shadows. She leaned toward Mercy and lowered her voice in secretive tones.

"Although we are not Catholics, the vicar's wife says Lady Lexford should never be buried among good Christians because Her Ladyship took her own life. You were aware Lady Lexford started the fire in which she died, were you not?"

Mercy experienced a twinge of regret for beginning the conversation, but she felt compelled to know more of what happened to drive a woman to seek a fiery release from her pain. She assumed a conspiratorial tone.

"What makes the vicar's wife believe the late Lady Lexford wished to leave all her family behind? Master Aaron was but a babe."

Mercy could not imagine a woman who would wish to leave His Lordship. From what little Mercy discovered of the Kimbolts' relationship, Lady Lexford was Aidan Kimbolt's long time love.

"I heard the fire started in a clogged fireplace," Mercy said baldly.

"Oh, no, Miss." Miss Chadwick's eyes widened with excitement. "The late viscount summoned the current Lord Lexford home to marry his brother's widow, but His Lordship's sacrifice meant nothing to Lady Lexford. Her Ladyship pined for a man who lost his life over another woman. Lord Andrew died in a duel over his mistress. My papa says it was quite scandalous, and Lady Lexford was too weak to endure the shame. The former Susan Rhodes gathered her beautiful gowns together and set fire to them as if she built a celebratory bonfire. Then she stood back and watched the flames spread. By the time, Lord Lexford sought her out, the fire consumed part of the floor. The upstairs collapsed in on the lower level. Although the gossips say he tried valiantly, His Lordship could not reach his wife. When the fire was at its height, Lady Lexford dove in. Deland Simpkins told my father that Lord Lexford reported his wife did not utter a word–not even a scream from the pain when the fire caught her dress."

Again, Mercy could not imagine a woman who would prefer Andrew Kimbolt to His Lordship. She viewed Andrew's portrait in the gallery, and the man resembled his father. The late viscount's portrait showed a square-chinned aristocrat with a broad forehead. Deep ancient eyes filled with determination and autocratic rule, which looked out upon those staring up at him. Mercy imagined Arlen Kimbolt quite implacable. Nothing like the amiable Aidan Kimbolt.

Miss Chadwick continued, "In truth, few in the neighborhood have a care for the Rhodes family. They put on airs others find offensive. No one thought Miss Rhodes worthy to be the viscountess."

Mercy was in unchartered territory. She possessed no right, other than her utter devotion to the viscount, to take an unparalleled interest in the man.

"I suspect we should speak no more of His Lordship's past," Mercy said gently. Giving the girl's hand a squeeze, Mercy was quick to add, "We have but a short time, and I am most anxious to view your creations. My cousin swears your father runs the finest mercantile in the area."

Mercy would add a prayer of forgiveness for yet another lie, but she held no qualms over changing the subject. She had much to consider about what Miss Chadwick innocently shared. As she sipped her tea, Mercy was sorry for how Lord Lexford's family duped him, and she deeply regretted setting her course of deception. She sighed heavily before swallowing the lump chocking her throat. Aidan Kimbolt endured pain from those he held most dear, and the viscount deserved better than Mercy's duplicity.

"It is impossible!" Aidan asserted. It was all he could do to remain in his seat.

As expected, Susan's father arrived promptly at eleven, with the child in tow.

"I have no other choice, my lord. Mrs. Rhodes is not well, and Sophia can no longer oversee the care of the boy."

Aidan scowled his disapproval. What Rhodes suggested would destroy any peace Aidan achieved over the past two years.

"I will gladly support the services of an additional nurse to tend the child."

Rhodes shook his head in denial.

"It is not simply Mrs. Rhodes's frail constitution," the man protested. "It is the boy himself. My wife cannot look upon the child without recalling the tragedy of Susan's death."

"And you think I can?" Aidan said incredulously. "Am I to be punished for loving your daughter?"

Rhodes's mouth thinned into a tight line.

"The boy is your legal responsibility, my lord."

Bloody hell! Aidan long ago tired of being reminded of his responsibility. He did the responsible thing when he joined the British Army in hopes of a career, which would permit him to marry Susan Rhodes. When his lady chose his brother instead, Aidan acted responsibly when he stepped aside to permit his brother's happiness over his own, and he was the responsible one when he returned to Cheshire to claim a loveless marriage.

"There must be some other means."

Even to his ears, Aidan could hear the desperation in his voice.

"I can think of no other solution," Rhodes admitted lamely. "The child is too young to be housed at a school, and as the heir presumptive, the Lexford title holds…"

"Responsibility for the boy's care," Aidan finished Rhodes's thoughts.

He closed his eyes in supplication. How could God test him again? Aidan always considered himself a kind person: One who served his fellow man. Was it so terrible to ask for a bit of happiness? *Evidently,* he growled under his breath. *What am I to do?* He could bury the child in another wing. Open up the nursery. Hire a nurse who would keep the boy from his sight. Continue to pretend the idea of Susan bearing another man's child did not rip Aidan's heart to shreds. Close his eyes to the boy's existence.

"When do you expect me to take possession of the child?" Aidan said grudgingly.

"Aaron awaits his uncle in the yellow drawing room," Rhodes confessed. "I could send over his belongings a bit later today."

"That quickly?" Aidan asked caustically. "With no notice so I might prepare proper quarters for the boy?"

Before Rhodes could respond a light tap at the door brought their disagreement to a stumbling halt. The door opened to frame Miss Purefoy clutching a dark-haired child in her arms. The boy buried his face in the crook of her neck.

"Pardon me, my lord, but Master Aaron had the most dreadful case of the fits. The maid assisting in his care knew not what might cure the young master's woes. The child asks for his Uncle Aidan.

Mercy knew she made a mistake when she approached His Lordship's study and heard the noisy row within, but the lad had the household at sixes and sevens with his screams and tears. Dutifully, Mercy escorted Miss Chadwick to the door after her fittings only to find Lord Lexford's butler and Mrs. Babcock debating on how to settle the child. The housekeeper caught the lad by his arm to give the child a lecture on behaving property.

Without considering how her interference might be perceived among His Lordship's seasoned staff, Mercy rushed to comfort the boy. Scooping the young master into her arms, she carried the child to a quiet corner and rocked him until the boy ceased his caterwauling.

"Shush, my Little One," Mercy cooed into the child's ear.

"Wunkle Waden," the boy sobbed over and over.

Mercy set the child from her where she might look upon

the puffy-eyed countenance. With her linen, she dabbed away the child's tears. The boy held the look of his father. He would never be called handsome, but those with titles and ancestral names held no concern for fine looks.

"You wish to visit with your uncle?" Mercy asked encouragingly.

"Gwanpapa said Wunkle Waden give me cakes," the child confessed.

Mercy smiled easily. The boy knew what was important.

"Then come along with me. We must find your 'Wunkle Waden.'"

Lifting the boy to her, she carried him through the gathered throng of servants outside the drawing room door. To Miss Chadwick, she said, "If you could tarry but a few moments longer, I mean to have His Lordship's approval before you continue your work."

The girl nodded her agreement.

To Mrs. Babcock Mercy said, "Please bring tea and cakes to Lord Lexford's study."

"But Miss…" the housekeeper began in protest. "Perhaps it is best if you do not inter…"

"*Now*, Mrs. Babcock." Mercy emphasized the word before turning toward the stairs.

The housekeeper's continued disrespect settled Mercy's resolve.

Needless to say, Mercy's bravado drained the moment she opened the door to His Lordship's private room. The heated discussion she overheard outside the door left the room filled with stark tension. She faced not only Lord Lexford, but also the man Mr. Hill earlier identified as being Lady Lexford's father, Mr. Rhodes. The expression on Lord Lexford's countenance said it all. His Lordship felt trapped. The viscount was miserably uncomfortable. *But why?* Mercy knew not the answer, but she meant to protect him somehow.

Mr. Rhodes's countenance spoke of disapproval. She saw a

similar look in the man's eyes when he watched her at the mercantile. If possible, Rhodes's vehemence increased. Unconsciously, Mercy shuddered. She supposed Mr. Rhodes viewed her as a threat to his daughter's position in Lord Lexford's household. Little did the man know His Lordship considered Mercy his half sister. However, to protect her, Lord Lexford introduced her to the villagers as his cousin. In the eyes of Society, a marriage between cousins might be acceptable, but never one between brother and sister. A relationship between Lord Lexford and her would never materialize.

Aidan rose to his feet upon Miss Purefoy's entrance. His first thought was of how beautiful the lady appeared. The boy clung to her neck, and the two of them looked so natural together. It was everything Aidan wanted in this house: A wife and a family. But it was not his family. Neither the child nor the woman belonged to him.

"Come in, my dear," he said as he extended his hand in the girl's direction. Aidan supposed he should stop thinking of Miss Purefoy as a girl. She was most definitely a woman.

He noted her hesitation, but Miss Purefoy took perhaps a half dozen steps in his direction. Her fingers caressed the back of the child's head, and she turned to graze a kiss upon the boy's temple. Her tenderness touched Aidan's heart. Then he spotted the scowl on Rhodes's countenance. The man's lips snarled in contempt. Immediately, Aidan's protective nature made an appearance. He did not appreciate the way Rhodes looked upon Miss Purefoy.

"What have you there?" Aidan asked gently.

The lady's eyes met his, and he knew Miss Purefory understood the strange social conundrum in which Aidan found himself.

"This big boy is Master Aaron," Miss Purefoy said playfully.

She encouraged the boy to turn toward where Aidan waited.

His brother's eyes stared out from the child's countenance, and Aidan swallowed the bile of betrayal, which clogged his throat. He managed to respond by keeping his eyes on the lady's countenance. In her face, he found peace.

"You must be mistaken, my dear," he said teasingly. "My nephew is but a babe in a crib." He tickled the boy's side with his finger. "This child is nearly a man."

The child cocked his head as if searching for something familiar in Aidan's countenance and voice. Aidan wondered if the boy held any memory of the long hours Aidan held Susan's child. The hours he resigned himself to loving a babe not of his issue, and if the boy knew how miserably Aidan failed.

"Wunkle Waden?" The child's voice quickly rose in inflection.

Unable to resist, Aidan reached for the child, and with a bit of encouragement from Miss Purefoy, the boy came into Aidan's arms. He pulled the child protectively into his embrace before turning toward Susan's father. The child smelled of baby smells: sleepy tears, and that sweet scent of soft skin and hair. Aidan inhaled deeply.

Rhodes's frown lines deepened.

"Is this not what you wished, Father Rhodes?" Aidan taunted.

Rhodes shot a glance toward Miss Purefoy. The man spoke his disdain through tight lips.

"Mrs. Rhodes would not approve of just anyone tending to the boy."

Aidan took a menacing step toward the man.

"First, you bring my brother's son to my home and demand I resume guardianship of the child. Then you presume to dictate which members of my household may interact with my nephew. You cannot have it both ways, Father Rhodes. If the boy is to call Lexington Arms home, I will determine his future."

Miss Purefoy took a tentative step toward the door and made to leave, but Aidan stayed her retreat.

"Do you hold business elsewhere, my dear?"

The thought of being alone with a child he was uncertain he even liked frightened Aidan more than any enemy he ever faced on the battlefield. What would he do if the child cried? And Heaven forbid the child required someone to change his baby cloths! Aidan looked upon the pink countenance and scowled. Did the boy still wear the cloths?

"Miss Chadwick waits below, my lord. I thought to seek your approval on the girl's designs, but..." Miss Purefoy shot an anxious glance toward Susan's father. "But you hold more pressing matters, and I would not detain the lady longer."

A sharp knock announced the arrival of a teacart and cakes. Aidan's frown lines deepened. How was he to manage a child, a tea service, and a disapproving Jonathan Rhodes all at the same time?

"Ask Miss Chadwick to join us," Aidan instructed the servant, "and tell Mrs. Osborne we will require an additional pot. My cousin will serve the tea."

The maid nodded her understanding before disappearing into the early afternoon passages. Aidan watched Miss Purefoy's countenance carefully.

"If you hold no objections, I would plead for your assistance with the tea service."

"Wakes," the child said as he clapped his little hands together.

Tentatively, Miss Purefoy reached for the boy.

"Come, Little One," she said softly. "Permit your uncle and grandfather to finish their business."

"Wunkle Waden," the child called over her shoulder as Miss Purefoy carried him toward a small settee close to the hearth. "I wike wakes."

Aidan smiled at the boy's enthusiasm.

"Then I charge your cousin to give you two cakes," he said to the retreating forms.

Before he turned to Susan's father, Aidan watched how

naturally Miss Purefoy settled the boy upon the settee with several pillows to support him. Then she poured a generous portion of milk in a cup with just a splash of tea. She offered several spoonfuls of the mixture to the child as she cooed sweet words of nothing throughout. It was a deliciously domestic picture, and Aidan enjoyed every second of it. When she picked up the knife to cut the cake into bite-sized pieces, Aidan returned to the conversation with Rhodes.

"Is this how you mean for the boy's transfer to occur? Sharply and without a proper farewell?"

Aidan spoke softly so as not to relay the tension, which rested between him and Susan's father. The lady already endured Rhodes's disapproving stares on two separate occasions, and Aidan meant to protect her from future aspersions.

"You would replace my daughter with that woman!" Rhodes hissed.

Aidan never liked Jonathan Rhodes. Never took to either of Susan's parents, and he certainly had his fill of people telling him his duties. He still held doubts regarding Miss Purefoy's claim to a familial relationship, but one certainty remained: The lady never asked anything of him beyond his friendship.

"In her sweet gestures, the lady shows more maternal care for the child than did your daughter." Aidan hissed caustically. He continued through clenched teeth, "Miss Purefoy is my cousin. If Andrew's son remains with me, the lady will have a say in the child's upbringing. I value her opinions."

Rhodes shot a deathly glare in the lady's direction.

"Mrs. Rhodes will speak more on this subject when she is well," he rasped.

Aidan's jaw tightened.

"If you leave the boy in my care today, there will be no returning him to Rhodes End. I will not have the child uprooted over and over again. Aaron is a Kimbolt. He will be raised as I say from this day forward."

Rhodes snorted his displeasure.

"I wish to God I never agreed to Susan's marriage to Andrew Kimbolt. The arrangement brought nothing but misery to my door."

Aidan felt his ire rise, and for a change he said the words he always swallowed previously.

"You thought to have your daughter become the future viscountess. You never considered me worthy. After all, I was but a second son. Andrew should be my father's heir, but all your manipulations failed. Susan became a viscountess, but by the time I assumed the title, any tenderness Susan and I once shared was replaced by ambition and perfidy..."

"My lord?" Miss Purefoy's melodic voice penetrated the red-hot hatred, which stole Aidan's tongue. He looked up to see the lady's worried countenance.

He took a deep steadying breath.

"I apologize, my dear." He noted how Rhodes stiffened at hearing Aidan's continued endearments. "My business with Mr. Rhodes knows its end. Perhaps you might pour me a cup of tea while I see Father Rhodes to the door."

The girl eyed Aidan cautiously, but she nodded her agreement.

Aidan kept his expression emotionally blank.

"I will open the nursery. When Mrs. Rhodes recovers, you may make arrangements to visit with the child, but not too soon," Aidan cautioned. "I would have Aaron accept Lexington Arms as his home."

"You are all kindness, my lord," Rhodes said sarcastically.

Aidan smiled at the man's peevishness.

"I learned my lessons at your hand, Father Rhodes."

Rhodes reached for his gloves, but Aidan caught the man's arm. He whispered his threats.

"If you and Mrs. Rhodes persist in your objection to Miss Purefoy, I will use all the power I possess as Viscount Lexford to separate you forever from your only grandchild."

Rhodes jerked his arm from Aidan's grasp before he stormed

from the room. Aidan watched him go, and he wondered if Susan's father would heed the warning. Somehow, Aidan doubted it. Tomorrow, he would contact a man of the law regarding the legal rights of the boy's grandparents."

"Gwanpapa!" Aaron whined.

Miss Purefoy scooped the child into her arms.

"Have no fear, Little One, you are about to go on a grand adventure. A game of sorts."

Aidan joined her in the setting.

"Do you like games?"

"Wirates?" the boy asked with a smile. Aidan did not think the child's smile was one he could associate with Andrew. As selfish as it may seem, that fact pleased him. Aaron's smile came from Susan. It was the one from long before Aidan departed for the Continent: that special smile from a vivacious woman, and he would recognize it anywhere.

"Pirates?" he asked kindly. "I am certain someone in this great house knows how to play pirates." He nodded encouragingly to the boy. "Your grandfather agreed to permit you to spend a few days with your cousin and me."

Aidan rubbed the child's chubby leg with the back of his hand. The boy was built very much like Andrew and the late viscount. Aidan was the youngest of the three Kimbolt children, but he had the makings of his maternal grandfather, who towered over Arlen Kimbolt by nearly four inches. Aidan outstripped both his father and older brother by the time of his eighteenth birthday.

"I realize you do not understand what is happening, but know both your cousin and I will protect you."

The child buried his face in Miss Purefoy's chest.

"Mama?" he sobbed.

It ripped at Aidan's heart to think young Aaron held no memories of Susan. Although the child was but a little over two and a half years of age, Aidan made a vow to relate every recollection he held of Susan Rhodes to the boy. He would repeat the stories over and over until Aaron knew something of his mother. It was what he always wanted the late viscount to do for him. Aidan felt robbed of memories of his mother. It was the first time memories of family eluded him. Lachlan Charters performed the task well the second time. Aidan's father grieved for a woman by never speaking of his wife again.

"Miss Purefoy is not your mother, Boy," he said as he stroked the child's head, "but you will find many at Lexington Arms who love you."

A light tap at the door announced Miss Chadwick's arrival.

"You sent for me, my lord?"

Aidan stood in greeting.

"Yes, Miss Chadwick. Please join us."

He directed the timid girl to a nearby chair.

"I must apologize," he said evenly. "It has been a more difficult day than I anticipated. Yet, I pray you will share some of your ideas for my cousin's attire with me."

The girl's hands were trembling, but she reached for several samples to exhibit upon a small hard polished board.

"Miss Purefoy chose this one for the riding habit and this for a morning dress."

Aidan frowned his disapproval.

"But that is but two garments. I thought we agreed upon five."

Miss Purefoy set the boy upon his feet before joining the conversation.

"My lord, I must protest."

The child tottered toward where Miss Chadwick displayed the other samples.

"Wirates," he squealed and reached for one of the cut squares of material.

Miss Chadwick smiled graciously.

"You are very much like my brothers."

She deftly retrieved the cloth from the child's grasp and replaced it with a small white handkerchief from the hem of her sleeve.

"You must have a proper cap for your head."

Miss Chadwick quickly tied a knot in the cloth and placed it upon the boy's head.

"You look quite dangerous," she teased easily.

Aidan shot Miss Purefoy a knowing glance, and his cousin responded with a sigh of relief. A secret smile blossomed in his heart.

"Miss Chadwick," he began slowly to gather his thoughts. "I have a proposition." Aidan improvised. "Mr. Rhodes chose to leave Master Aaron at Lexington Arms for an extended stay, and neither my cousin nor I hold any experience with children. What say you to assuming the role of Master Aaron's nurse?"

The girl's countenance fell immediately.

"I...I...I possess similar duties in my father's house, my lord."

Miss Purefoy handed the child another bite of cake, which the boy instantly jammed into his mouth before waddling away to explore the room. His cousin sat forward.

"What His Lordship means is not a nurse's role," Miss Purefoy assured. "What Lord Lexford offers is more of a...of a..."

"A lady's companion," Aidan added quickly. "My cousin should have a lady's companion while she resides at Lexington Arms. I occasionally possess duties which take me from the estate, and I cannot have Miss Purefoy going about the neighborhood without a proper chaperone."

The girl's lips thinned in a tight line.

"I am not a lady, my lord. My father is in trade."

"But you are skilled in so many areas," Miss Purefoy protested. "And I do not mind a bit of unconventionality. I believe we would suit well, Miss Chadwick."

"My cousin means to assist me with several improvements about the manor," Adian added. "I am certain she could utilize your keen eye for color in her efforts to redecorate many of the rooms."

"I could also use your assistance in making Master Aaron's

transition a smoother one," Miss Purefoy suggested. "That is until a proper nurse may be secured for the boy."

The child carried over a book to place in Aidan's open palms. With what sounded like a puppy's growl, Aaron scrambled away to find what Aidan assumed was more pirate booty. He wondered who were the boy's playmates at Rhodes End. Likely one of the servants. Aidan did not think to ask Susan's father if the Rhodeses hired a nurse for the child.

"How would this position benefit me?" the girl asked cautiously. "I possess ambitions beyond being a nurse."

"Other than the generous wage His Lordship will provide you," Miss Purefoy said encouragingly, "I shall teach you the way of being a lady. If your dreams lie with a suitable marriage, your time in this household shall pave the way to marrying above your station."

Aidan took up the offer.

"Even if you choose to claim your place among those who earn their livings in London's mercantile district, what you learn from my cousin will serve you well in building your clientele. I will provide you a glowing recommendation. My associates are among England's most influential families. You would possess a ready-made list of clients."

"A duchess. Several countesses. A marquise," Miss Purefoy ticked off the aristocratic ladies on her fingers. It amazed Aidan how well Miss Purefoy understood the ploy.

To each declaration, Aidan indicated his agreement.

"You will be given a room of your own close to the one Miss Purefoy occupies."

"One as fine as the lady's?" the girl asked wistfully.

Aidan and Miss Purefoy nodded eagerly. He suspected Miss Chadwick shared her quarters in town with her siblings.

"A substantial wage. An elegant room. Instruction in ladylike skills and a list of the finest families' connections, which will serve whatever choices you make for the future in exchange for keeping my cousin company in public, assisting Miss Purefoy with her duties at Lexington Arms, and providing expertise in how best to tend a small child. What say you, Miss Chadwick?"

The girl paused in indecision, but she held his gaze.

"It is only one child," Miss Chadwick reasoned aloud. "Much improved to the four I tend now." She watched Aaron carefully carry a china figure to Miss Purefoy. "When would I begin my position?" she said at last.

"I hoped you would consider today as your first at Lexington Arms."

Chapter 8

THEY SPOKE NO MORE of the ruse until after Aidan sent the boy off for a nap with a young maid in charge and after he summoned Mr. Hill to escort Miss Chadwick to the village and to make arrangements to secure the girl's services. At length, they were alone, and Aidan immediately turned to apologize.

"I must beg your forgiveness for my quick tongue. I should never assume your willingness to assist me with my brother's family and to procure Miss Chadwick's services. I should have spoken to you first. If you wish to withdraw from the occupation, I would not think poorly of you."

The lady's lips twitched.

"How could I protest, my lord? Needless to say, I held similar thoughts."

It was the most miraculous moment. He and Miss Purefoy finished each other's sentences, as if they were of one mind.

"I thought you meant not to embarrass me," Aidan confessed.

He could say nothing of how exhilarating he found this new companionship with Miss Purefoy. Was it possible he found someone with whom to share his successes, and perhaps his fears? A very private man, Aidan rarely revealed his most secret thoughts, even with his friends. Only with Wellston, Crowden, and Hill did he speak openly of his qualms on returning home. These were perilous waters in which he waded with Miss Purefoy.

She squirmed with her own excitement, and Aidan discovered another facet of the woman to admire.

"Do not present me with borrowed feathers, my lord," she said teasingly.

Momentarily forgetting to keep his distance, Aidan changed his seat to sit beside her. He caught her hand and brought the back of it to his lips. Belatedly, he realized touching the girl was not the best of ideas. He could maintain his indifference when he interacted with Miss Purefoy, even in a playful manner, but when he touched her, his errant thoughts took a twist toward debauchery.

"Then we will both share the blame or the glory. How should we proceed?"

Unconsciously, Miss Purefoy leaned against Aidan's shoulder, and he turned his head to sniff the lilac scent of her hair. Aidan could not understand why he tortured himself so, but he fell prey to enjoying such pleasures.

"We should see to the nursery. I do not imagine it can be used until repairs and a thorough cleaning are conducted."

Despite how it began, she was so confident, Aidan thought it possible this craziness would turn out well. Without realizing he did so, Aidan's thumb caressed the back of the girl's hand.

"You should likely begin your decoration of Lexington Arms' many rooms with Master Aaron's quarters. I was the last to leave the nursery."

He chuckled. Sitting with Miss Purefoy felt so natural. Her leaning into his body. The weight of her breast against his shoulder. Absolute perfection.

"What do you suggest we do with the boy tonight?" he asked into the comfortable stillness.

A frown line crossed the lady's forehead, and Aidan wanted to smooth it away with his fingertips.

"I would not wish to leave the child alone with only a maid this evening. I am certain the lad will be missing his grandparents. Initially, Master Aaron should stay in one of our rooms."

The fog that clogged Aidan's brain since planting himself beside the lady instantly evaporated.

"Sleep…sleep in one of…one of our rooms," he stammered. "Surely you jest."

When he postured his way through his disagreement with Susan's father, Aidan did not consider the reality of having his brother's son parading about the house. Despite Aidan's best efforts, he stiffened.

Miss Purefoy's frown lines became a positive scowl.

"I would not jest about a child's well being," she said testily.

Aidan released her hand before jamming his fingers into his hair.

"You do not understand," he tersely replied, but a twinge of guilt welled up immediately.

Miss Purefoy cupped his jaw line with both hands, forcing Aidan to stare deeply into her eyes. She studied him for a moment. The girl held no concept of permitting a person his distance. She spoke freely from the heart, and the lady acted upon her impulses. Needless to say, she never knew "Society," especially the social norms regulating actions. If Aidan were not so distressed with the reality of what he did, he would enjoy staring into pools of chocolate.

"I do know," she declared. "I know of your affection for Lady Lexford, and of the lady's turning to your brother, but I also know none of what came before is Master Aaron's doing. You cannot place the father's indulgences upon the babe's shoulders." Miss Purefoy stroked Aidan's temple and brushed the curl from his forehead before saying, "It is important, my lord, for the child to know family, to practice traditions, and to call one place 'home.' We each require a home, my lord."

God! Miss Purefoy had the most mesmerizing voice. Why could he not find a woman with even half of his sister's charms?

"Needless to say, we must do what is best for the child," Aidan said dutifully.

"Master Aaron may remain with me until you secure a proper nurse. Perhaps our Miss Chadwick can speak to someone local."

Somehow, it all came together. Full of excitement, Miss Chadwick returned. His staff managed to find a low trundle bed to place in Miss Purefoy's room for the child. The lady gave orders for the staff to begin cleaning and repairing the nursery on the morrow. Mrs. Osborne led a contingent of staff, which praised Aidan for his generosity. However, he noted Mrs. Babcock and Mr. Poley were of a different mind. Aidan was not certain whether his housekeeper and valet objected to Aaron joining the household or whether their disdain rested in Miss Purefoy's playing a major role in the child's transition. Somehow, he thought it the latter. In truth, despite his staff's enthusiasm, Aidan felt anything but benevolent toward his nephew; instead, he felt trapped. Trapped by his duty to his title.

In the late evening, instead of joining him for a hand of cards, Miss Purefoy insisted upon bringing the boy to the drawing room after supper. The lady sprawled on the floor beside the child to build tower after tower with the wooden blocks Rhodes sent over as part of Aaron's belongings. Each time the tower rose from the floor, the boy took great delight in knocking it over. Yet, slowly, Miss Purefoy coaxed Aaron to stack a few of the blocks before the boy toppled them once more. Apparently, no one ever showered the child with so much attention. It was as if Aidan could see the boy's mind questioning Miss Purefoy's goodness, much as Aidan did.

A pang of guilt tightened Aidan's chest. Sending his brother's son to live with Rhodes proved the best for Aidan's broken heart, but as he watched the child's face light up with each gesture of praise Miss Purefoy offered, Aidan wondered if he sent the child to a home marked with love's deprivation. Aidan could not recall one time Susan spoke kindly of her parents or shared an intimate moment between mother and daughter or praised a father for his affection. Did Aidan make a great error in placing Andrew's son in such a position?

With miserable concentration, Aidan attempted to ignore the laughter coming from a cleared area before the hearth by burying his nose in a book, but he could not recall one word from the page he never turned. Instead, Aidan closed his eyes and listened to Miss Purefoy's and the child's excited whispers. What if Susan waited for his return from the Continent? What if his wife agreed to share his bed? What if she bore his children, rather than Andrew's?

"Mama."

Aidan opened his eyes to see the boy pointing toward the patio door and the worried look upon his sister's countenance.

"My lord," Miss Purefoy whispered.

His gaze followed hers.

"What is amiss?" Aidan said evenly so as not to frighten the child.

Miss Purefoy dropped her gaze to the scattered blocks, but she said softly, "A flash of color at the window."

Aidan was on his feet immediately.

"Keep Aaron close," he instructed over his shoulder as he pulled a pocket pistol from his jacket.

Stepping into the chilly darkness, Aidan surveyed the open lawn.

"Nothing," he grumbled under his breath. Turning to the right he covered the area between the partially opened doors to where the east side of the manor met the front. He scanned each bush and tree for a colorful intruder. Finding none, he retraced his steps to examine the tree line on his left.

"A damn ghost," he growled. "And I am tired of fighting this house's ghosts. I mean to be free of them."

Unsuccessful, Aidan reluctantly returned to the drawing room. With a shake of his head, he warned away Miss Purefoy's curiosity. He was not prepared to speak on the mystery plaguing his house. At least, someone else viewed the apparition, even if the other person was a three-year-old child.

Although disappointed by his refusal to speak on what occurred; the lady gathered the boy onto her lap and began to rock him. She hummed a Scottish lullaby, and Aidan found the sound as comforting as did the child. When Aaron succumbed to the warmth of Miss Purefoy's arms, Aidan lifted the boy to his shoulder.

"I will see him to your quarters," he whispered.

"When?" she asked softly.

Never, he thought, but he said, "Tomorrow. We will speak on it tomorrow."

When Mercy arrived on Lexington Arms' threshold, she held no idea what to expect. Her feelings stung from her brother's betrayal–of Geoffrey's immaturity in performing his duties to her and the estate. Of her brother meaning to "sell" her to Sir Lesley Trent and even to permit Lord Spectre his way with Grace. Geoffrey would look elsewhere while his cohorts practiced the worst forms of debauchery under Foresthill's roof.

Leaving Lancashire behind, Mercy came into Lord Lexford's small world, and, yes, despite His Lordship's extensive travels, Aidan Kimbolt's world was small. He had family–many generations of family looking down upon him and placing the weight of their names upon his shoulders. Mercy wondered why the viscount did not buckle under such responsibilities.

Although it was not perfect, her time at Lexington Arms went much better than Mercy expected. She avoided those, such as Mrs. Babcock, who disapproved of her from the beginning, and instead sought the endorsement of Mrs. Osborne and Mr. Hill. She supposed her easy transition came because she refused to allow disappointment to invade her heart. She found purpose under His Lordship's roof. After their initial contest of wills, Lord Lexford treated her with admiration. Nearly as an equal. A thrill of anticipation woke her each morning. Lord Lexford's kindness was a gift Mercy would forever cherish. And so, with reluctance, she accepted his need for privacy–the viscount's desire to keep his own counsel. Although she did not approve, Mercy could understand.

He entered her room and placed the child upon the small bed.

"I will anticipate seeing you in the morning,"

His Lordship announced as he prepared to leave.

"Thank you for presenting Aaron your attentions."

"He is a loving child," Mercy cautioned.

She watched the emotions crossing Lord Lexford's countenance.

"I understand what you are asking of me and please know I will attempt to open my heart to the boy."

And so it began. In the very practical way of women, over the next week, Miss Purefoy and Miss Chadwick structured their days, and, inadvertently, Aidan's days also. His sister recruited two of the younger maids to assist with Aaron's care. She commandeered the small dressing room attached to her chambers to act as a temporary nursery for his nephew while his staff brought the child's quarters up to snuff. She contacted Mr. Roberts, the local curate, for recommendations for a competent nurse and set times upon Aidan's personal calendar for him to conduct interviews with three candidates.

Miss Purefoy organized his staff for painting and papering the nursery walls, along with new draperies for the sparkling clean windows. A small bed and wardrobe appeared in what would be the nurse's room. A miracle of activity brought Aidan's home to life.

Meanwhile, both his sister and Miss Chadwick spent at least two hours each day with Aaron. They played games with the boy and also spent time teaching the child new words and skills. It was as if his house transformed into a home, and Aidan feared tipping the balance–feared it might all be snatched away.

Hill stood beside Aidan as they watched Miss Purefoy chase Aaron about the smaller of the two ballrooms. The laughter made Aidan hunger to join them, but he remained steadfastly by the door.

"What keeps you separate, my lord?" Hill said softly.

Aidan frowned his uncertainty.

"It is not in a man's domain to tend to a child," he protested weakly.

Hill leaned closer.

"Who is to say what is proper? It would seem to me there is no purpose in being the Master if one bends to the whims of those who hold no knowledge of what is best for a man."

"And how would spending time with my sister and my nephew prove best for me?" Aidan asked sarcastically.

Mr. Hill set a shoulder against the opposite doorframe.

"You returned to Lexington Arms to reclaim your memory, to face your demons, and to begin a new life."

"Reach the point, Hill," Aidan warned.

Hill's tone spoke of the familiarity they shared over the years.

"You must characterize your reign as Viscount Lexford by claiming what is important to you." His man paused, and Aidan wondered if that was all, but Hill continued, "You always desired a family, my lord." Lucifer gestured to the woman and the child. "The only thing missing from the picture is the sweetness of intimacy. Within this room, you will find a woman and a child who are willing to open their hearts to you. You would be a fool, my lord, to ignore what could change you forever."

Aidan felt the shimmer of hope.

"Is it that simple?"

His countenance softened.

Hill chuckled in irony.

"I never claimed it would be simple, my lord, but I possess a theory as to why your previous efforts failed."

Aidan's eyes rested on his friend's countenance.

"I am curious, Mr. Hill. Please enlighten me."

"Your whole life duty to this estate defined you. Lord Andrew was the heir, but it was your internal connection to this land, which made you the true Viscount Lexford. Even so, I believe it is time you complete your duty to Aidan Kimbolt, the man. Do not permit your title to stand between you and happiness. You must look upon your future from a different perspective, one not engraved with your family's name. What will you do if your memory never returns? Will you spend the remainder of your life pining for something elusive?"

Hill stepped closer to keep his advice private.

"I mean no disrespect, my lord, but the late viscount presented you with an impossible challenge. Blinded by your youthful love for Lady Susan, you returned to Lexington Arms with hopes of a future, and since that time, you have been deeply entrenched in this house's misery. You expected your father, your brother, and your wife to demonstrate the same type of devotion to the title, as did you.

"Unfortunately, those to whom you offered your allegiance did not return your loyalty. They dwelled in their selfish desires with no concern for your feelings."

As much as Aidan hated to admit it, Hill spoke the truth.

Hill's hand rested upon Aidan's shoulder.

"You made a grievous error when you did not realize the depth of Lady Susan's despair until it all ended so abruptly. Yet, you were not to blame, my lord. Your life is not empty: You possess friends and family."

Again, Hill gestured to the pair who sprawled on the floor, playing with a pair of wooden horses.

"Family, my lord, who offer you genuine affection, not deceit. Cease thinking of your life in terms of things lost. Rather concentrate on things found. Only then will you know God's blessings. Only then will you discover a reason to celebrate."

Aidan glanced at the man, who acted as father, brother, and

friend for the past seven years.

"And when did you become so wise?"

"The day you rescued Lady Worthing and her maid from Bradley's hunting box, I found happiness. I left behind my foolish ways. Before I met Hannah Tolliver, I built a deep well of self-loathing and only with the lady's love did I find my way back."

"Miss Purefoy is my sister," Aidan protested. "I can never claim her as my love."

Hill cleared his throat as he eyed the girl.

"There are all types of love, my lord, and each has its means to heal a badly bruised heart. Enjoy what the lady offers and rediscover the man you wish the world to see."

"The boy is Andrew's betrayal," Aidan said as a final protest.

"Why not think of the lad as the best part of Lady Susan?"

With that last remark, Hill disappeared into the bowels of Lexington Arms. Aidan listened to his friend's fading footsteps. Then with a deep steadying breath, he stepped into his future.

"What goes on here?" he asked as he strode toward the pair.

Miss Purefoy propped herself up on her elbows, and Aidan's eyes fell on the swell of her breasts, which were readily exposed by the cut of her gown. *Zounds! He required a woman's tender touch soon!* This was not how he hoped to begin this new phase in his life.

"We are describing our favorite horses, my lord."

She shoved a carved animal in his direction.

"Master Aaron likes this one because it can stand on two legs like a monkey."

Aidan's frown lines met.

"A monkey? And what does my nephew know of monkeys?"

"There are illustrations in a book of animals, which Miss Chadwick chose for Master Aaron from the library. My assistant seems to believe our Aaron quite intelligent," the lady declared.

"Perhaps this evening you might share the book with the young master."

Aidan swallowed his trepidation. *Think of the lad as the best part of Lady Susan.* He knelt beside the boy to inger the wooden model.

"Perhaps."

He ruffled the boy's hair. *So like his father's.* The idea was an involuntary response, and Aidan worked hard to drive it from his mind.

He sat on the floor beside Miss Purefoy.

"Miss Chadwick tells me you no longer possess an excuse not to ride out with me. Your riding habit is complete. Together, we could show the boy the horses. I could take Aaron up with me."

"Do you not possess the first of the interviews for a nurse later today?"

Miss Purefoy bit her bottom lip in hesitation.

"Not for several hours. We shan't be gone long." He turned to the child. "Would you like to see my horses?"

"Weal wons?" the child squealed in excitement.

"Yes, real horses," Aidan assured. "So, what say you, Mary?" It was the first time Aidan used her Christian name, and he enjoyed the intimacy of the moment.

His sister glanced to where the child ran excited circles about them.

"How could I disappoint Aaron? Look at him. I prefer his smile to the tears that often wake him."

"Has the boy kept you from your sleep, my dear?" Aidan asked in concern.

Miss Purefoy shrugged away his objections.

"Master Aaron cries out for his mother," she disclosed.

Aidan's eyebrow rose in disbelief.

"I do not understand how that is so. The child's mother passed when Aaron was but two months of age. He can possess no fresh memory of Lady Lexford. Did the boy develop a strong affection for the nurse Rhodes employed to care for the child?"

Miss Purefoy lowered her voice.

"With my encouragement, Mr. Hill sought information from the servant gossip line. From what your man discovered, Mr. Rhodes employed no nurse for Aaron. Mr. Rhodes's servants assumed the boy's care."

Again, Aidan knew guilt. His nephew did not know the care Aidan supposed the Rhodeses would provide their only grandchild. And he wondered what Rhodes did with the generous allowance Aidan provided Susan's parents to see to the child's well being. He would ask Hill to make another discreet investigation into what became of the money.

"I cannot speak my gratitude deeply enough for what you brought to Lexington Arms. You showed Aaron tenderness."

He intertwined his fingers with Mary's.

For several minutes they remained in quiet companionship. At length, the lady slipped her hand in the folds of her dress.

"I must change if I am to take advantage of your offer to ride."

She stood and caught the boy as he skittered past her.

"Come, Little One." Miss Purefoy settled the child in her grasp. "We must dress for the weather if we are to ride with your Uncle Aidan." She offered Aidan a quick curtsy. "The young master and I shall return in a half hour."

"I will send word to the stable for two gentle mounts. I do not suppose Valí will wish to carry a squirming child."

He caught her free hand and brought the back of it to his lips.

"Thank you. I am in your debt."

"As I am in yours, my lord."

"Deland will assist you with adjusting the saddle," Aidan announced when his sister and the child arrived at the stables. "You must know care. The saddle was made for the late Lady Lexford. With your permission, I will order one cut for you."

"That will not be necessary, my lord." She handed the child off to one of the lesser grooms. "However, before we ride again if you would ask your tatter or your saddler to shorten the leather skirt, I would appreciate it."

Aidan watched as his sister spent time in becoming acquainted with the horse. She fed the animal an apple core from the kitchen.

"I shall treat you kindly, my Pretty One," she cooed, and Aidan was a bit jealous of the animal for it knew the woman's tender attentions.

"Are you prepared, my dear?" Aidan asked as he caught her hand.

Suddenly, it struck him how often he sought the opportunity to touch this woman. Even through his gloves, he could feel her comforting warmth.

She came easily to his arms, and Aidan placed his hands upon her waist for the first time. His grip nearly spanned her small waistline. He effortlessly lifted her to the saddle.

"No heroics today," he said as he slid her booted foot into the slipper stirrup.

He meant to permit Deland the privilege of completing these tasks, but Aidan would not deny himself more of the woman's closeness.

"I will be unable to assist you because of carrying the boy before me," he warned.

"I understand, my lord," she said sweetly.

"Humor me," Aidan said softly. "It is my nature to fret."

Leaving her to adjust her weight, Aidan swung up into the saddle of the gelding Deland chose for him.

"Hand me the boy," It was but the third time Aidan held his brother's child since Rhodes unceremoniously left the lad behind a week prior.

Accepting the boy from the groom, he placed the child upon his lap. With a tight hand about his nephew's middle, Aidan issued his warning.

"You must sit still and permit the horse to do the work. Just look how high you are from the ground. Neither of us wishes to fall."

Miss Purefoy edged her mare closer.

"Be my big boy, Darling," she said in   encouragement, and the child nodded his head in agreement.

How quickly the lady formed a relationship with the boy was a comfort to Aidan's guilty heart.

They set out in a slow walk toward the open pasture.

"Your land is beautiful, my lord," she said as she instinctively shifted her weight to the right to maintain her seat. Despite her earlier protest, he would order a saddle made to fit her. Susan was taller and less curvy than was Miss Purefoy.

"Needless to say, I know prejudice, but I think it the finest estate in Cheshire."

Miss Purefoy laughed at his posturing, and Aidan revisited the sound of tinkling bells.

"I do not doubt it, my lord," she said with a wonderfully addictive smile.

For the next hour, they circled several of the surrounding fields at a slow pace, which permitted them to maintain a conversation. They spoke of the weather, of which fields he would fallow in the spring, and of several of the natural geographic features. The child was surprisingly well behaved; the boy pointed to rocks and trees and streams, and Aidan indulged the boy with the names of each. He did not know what to expect. The only young child with whom he ever spent time was Fowler's daughter Sonali. He and his Realm associates took turns over the years to attend the girl. It was a shame he knew more of his friend's daughter than he did his own nephew. Both children called him "Uncle Aidan," but until the past week, Aidan held an allegiance to only one.

The boy slumped against him in a deep sleep, and Aidan examined the child's angelic countenance. He searched for Susan's classic beauty, but the boy's looks spoke loudly of the Kimbolt blood flowing through his veins.

"The young master is quite precious," Miss Purefoy said wistfully.

Aidan spoke honestly, "I had no idea how it would feel to know this child."

Miss Purefoy adjusted her seat as the mare danced a prissy step. "Young Aaron has a quick mind."

Aidan watched her carefully. The horse began this outing very docilely. Now, it pranced and bucked as if it wished to run briskly across the open field.

"Yes," Aidan said distractedly. "The lad has many questions."

He shifted the boy in his grasp so he might catch Miss Purefoy's reins if the mare broke form.

"Perhaps we should turn back."

Miss Purefoy executed another countermove to bring her horse in line again. She was truly an excellent horsewoman, one far superior to any female of his acquaintance.

"I agree," she said with obvious concern. "I never knew a horse so skittish."

"If you wish to run her," he suggested, "just do so where I might keep you in sight."

He knew enough of the animal to know the mare loved to run. Aidan regretted bringing the boy. He could not ask Miss Purefoy to carry the child on such an unreliable horse. Nor could he leave Aaron in order to tend the lady.

"Would you mind, my lord?" she asked as the mare turned in a tight circle.

Aidan did mind; yet, no other alternative presented itself.

"Take care, my dear."

When Miss Purefoy tapped the mare's right side with the riding cane Deland provided her, the mare bolted forward in a frantic bid to unseat its rider.

Instantly, Aidan's heart lurched. Despite recognizing the lady's expertise with horses, he knew riding sidesaddle held dangers beyond an ill-bred horse. He fastened his jacket about the boy to hold Aaron more securely before he kicked his horse's flanks to give chase.

At first, Mercy enjoyed the crisp wind, which stung her eyes and throat, but it was not long before she realized she was in trouble. The mare did not simply race toward what appeared to be a deep riverbed, but the animal did its best to dislodge her. She adjusted her seat again, but Mercy could not release her foot from the slipper stirrup. Her boot caught on the metal. If she attempted to jump from the animal's back, she would be dragged along beside the animal; even so, knowing the danger and avoiding it were two different scenarios. Seconds later, when the mare kicked out from under her, Mercy prayed aloud, "Dear God…"

Aidan watched in horror as Miss Purefoy bounced in the seat. He held the boy to him with one hand and his horse's reins with the other. Why did he not think to bring a groom with him? *Because you enjoy the lady's company and did not wish to share Miss Purefoy's attentions with others.* The realization of what such thoughts could mean nearly brought Aidan up short, but he had no time to analyze his motives. Miss Purefoy was in trouble.

"Hold tight, Boy," he said over the thunder of the gelding's hoofs.

Aaron whimpered when jarred by the animal's gait, but the child did not put up a fuss, and for that, Aidan knew gratitude.

Ahead of him, the unthinkable happened. The mare skidded to a halt to kick up its back legs. Miss Purefoy's hold loosened on the reins, and the lady went flying over the mare's head. At the last second, her foot pulled free of the stirrups, and she landed heavily in a clump of dried vegetation.

Aidan reined in the gelding. Clutching the boy to him, Aidan was on the ground and running to where she laid curled in a ball. As he reached Miss Purefoy, he unbuttoned his coat to release the child.

"It is well," he said as calmly as he could. Frightening the child would serve no purpose. "Permit me to see to the lady," he said as he kissed the boy's forehead.

Thankfully, Aaron obediently stood near while Aidan rolled Miss Purefoy to her back.

Although a bit labored, the woman's breath caused her shoulders to rise and fall.

"Easy," Aidan cautioned, as he said a quick pray.

He slid his hands up and down her legs and arms to check for broken bones. Aidan wished he had time to enjoy the sensation of touching Miss Purefoy so intimately. He brushed the dirt from her cheek. *God! She was so beautiful!* Why should such a perfect woman be his sister?

"Do not move," Aidan warned as her eyes fluttered open and closed.

"My…my lord?"

The lady's lips formed the words, but no sound escaped.

"I have you." Aidan removed her bonnet and touched her hair's silken strands. It was heaven. She groaned her discomfort, and he placed his desires aside.

"I must see you safely to the house."

"The boy?" she whispered.

Aidan looked up to view his nephew playing with a small stick in the dirt. He frowned. He could not expect Miss Purefoy to hold Aaron while he carried them both to the manor. More than anyone, Aidan understood the ramifications of a severe injury.

"Aaron is safe," he said. "But I cannot say the same for you."

He glanced to where the gelding waited. The mare skittered away, likely returning to the stables.

"I cannot leave Aaron behind." Aidan did not take well to abandoning her, but, by nature, he was a practical man. "The cold ground may not be comfortable, but I do not want you to move," he told her. "I will not be more than a half hour." Unable to resist, he caught her hand. "Do you trust me?" he asked softly.

"With my life," she said honestly, and Aidan's heart

clutched tightly in his chest. When he asked, she affirmed what he already knew. Implicitly, he was aware of their unspoken bond. How long was it since anyone gave over so completely to Aidan's protection. *Never,* he thought. The lady's devotion was a heady experience.

"I will never fail you," Aidan promised. Without thinking, he brushed his lips across hers and then lingered just a brief moment to feel the warmth spread through him.

"Rest," he said upon a rasp.

Pulling away from her was one of the most difficult things Aidan ever did. He stood to look for his nephew.

"Come, Boy," he called. "We must play the lady's heroes."

Immediately, Aaron scampered to where Aidan stood. Whoever tended the child taught Aaron to respond quickly. Aidan paced away to catch up the gelding's reins.

"You will ride with me again," he told his nephew.

"Kiss," the child said plainly.

"We have no time for kisses," Aidan said as the child moved from his reach. "Come along, Aaron."

He motioned the child to him. Chasing the boy in a game was unacceptable, and Aidan could not leave Aaron with the lady while Aidan sought assistance.

The child looked up in bewilderment, but he remained stubborn.

"Kiss."

Then Aaron bent over Miss Purefoy to plant a wet kiss on the lady's cheek. Aidan never observed anything like it.

"Thank you, Darling," Miss Purefoy said lovingly.

Aidan recognized how the lady wished desperately to sit up and take the child in her embrace, but she resisted doing so because Aidan looked on. She caressed the boy's hand.

"Now assist your Uncle Aidan by bringing me another horse. Later, we shall have lemon tarts."

"Yes, Ma'am."

And just like that, the child returned to Aidan's arms.

As he lifted the boy to him, Aidan declared, "I mean for you to rest, Miss Purefoy. No cheating."

Chapter 9

HE KISSED HER. Well, not really a kiss. A brush of his lips against hers, but Aidan wanted more. He wanted a long, heated sampling of her lips. Wanted to view her mouth swollen from his kisses. To taste her lips fully. To kiss Miss Purefoy until she clung to him and begged for more. *Your misplaced desires had you lingering longer than appropriate,* his rattled senses warned. Aidan wanted to drape himself across her. To stretch out beside the woman and drive the madness away. To know the lady naked beneath him.

"Find a medium," he growled as he turned the gelding toward the stables.

Aidan prayed he did not frighten the lady away. Prayed she would not consider leaving simply because his masculine impulses ruled his brain.

"Kiss," his nephew said with a smacking sound. "Kiss." Smack. "Kiss."

"Do not remind me, Boy," Aidan groaned. "I was a fool."

He could not imagine what the girl thought of him. If her story held true, Miss Purefoy was his sister. Much to Aidan's chagrin, his lust held no sense of propriety. Yet, what if the lady proved to be false? How could he treat her with kindness if she showed her deception? In such a scheme, Aidan would be forced to drive her from his home and his life. He would lose either way. The truth was the woman had him in knots.

"Pool," Aaron chanted his new word. "Pool."

Despite chastising himself for his actions, Aidan could not stifle his chuckle.

"No sense announcing my shortcomings to the world," he said as he clutched the boy to him

Before Miss Purefoy, Aidan would never accept Rhodes's returning Aaron to Lexington Arms. Instead, he would utilize every legal trickery his purse could employ.

Aidan brought the horse to a halt inside the circle before the stable. Several grooms ran to do his bidding. He handed Aaron to the youngest.

"Carry Master Aaron to Miss Chadwick. Bid the lady to tend the child, and tell Mr. Payne to send for the physician. Miss Purefoy's horse threw her."

"Aye, Sir."

The boy of fourteen rushed away toward the manor's servant entrance. Over the young groom's shoulder, Aaron waved farewell with both hands, and despite the chaos, Aidan raised his hand to the child.

"Is the lady badly injured?" Deland asked.

Aidan's fear for the lady caused him to speak more forcibly than usual.

"When I return, I want to know what the bloody hell happened."

Waving off the groom's explanation before the man began, Aidan turned the gelding in a close circle.

"I have no time for excuses. I must see to Miss Purefoy's safety."

Mercy waited until she heard his horse's retreat before she touched her fingers to her lips. The warmth remained. Lord Lexford kissed her.

"Not an actual passionate kiss," her mind warned her

unwise heart. But His Lordship meant to kiss her. It was not as if he thought to skim a kiss upon her cheek, and she turned her head at the last second.

"No, his mouth pressed against yours," she said in awe. "Deliberately and for several seconds."

Her first kiss: It was a moment that would stay with Mercy always.

"I am glad it was he," she said aloud.

Mercy wondered what it would be to know such a man intimately. When Geoffrey meant to hand her off to Sir Lesley Trent, Mercy attempted to reconcile herself to permitting the baronet his marital liberties, but she quickly came to the conclusion she could not tolerate Sir Lesley's touch. The baronet was old enough to be her father.

"It would be too reprehensible," she declared when Grace broached the subject several nights before her sister's disappearance. It was then Mercy resolved to flee if no other alternative became available.

Slowly pushing herself to her elbows, Mercy took a long lazy look at her surroundings. Her head throbbed, and every muscle in her body ached, but she survived what might kill another.

"Thank Goodness, I fell from a horse previously."

She glanced at her legs to find her garments about her knees. Even without the gentleman present, Mercy blushed. Lord Lexford looked upon her as such. The idea of such intimacies brought another rush of color to Mercy's cheeks and an unusual warming to her most secret place.

She sat forward to spread her habit over her exposed legs.

"My boot?" Mercy said with a frown. She prayed she did not lose the footwear. She possessed no other boots, and she would not wish to impose further on His Lordship's kindness.

"I thought to stand," she admitted as she brushed twigs and dirt from her clothing. "Poor Miss Chadwick," Mercy groaned. "Serena's work was for naught."

Aidan should change horses, but he refused to waste precious time. He held no true idea of the extent of Mary Purefoy's injuries, and Aidan meant to ferry the woman to Lexington Arms where he might oversee the woman's care. In the near month of their relationship, Aidan knew contentment for the first time in many years, and he was sore to part with her presence in his life. He received an initial report from Pennington regarding the lack of information regarding Miss Purefoy's claim of a familial connection; however, Aidan ceased to care. Needless to say, he remained exceedingly curious, but he was satisfied to permit the lady's possible deception to continue if it meant his heart no longer ached with loneliness. He decided that even if Miss Pruefoy were not his sister, he would offer the woman a place in his home. At least, the thought of such an offer was his decision when he watched the lady playing with Aaron in the ballroom. He might have other thoughts when he discovered the whole truth.

"Accept what is right in your life for now," he told his all-too-practical mind.

Aidan broke through the wooded area, which separated the parkland from the fields. It did not surprise him to observe Miss Purefoy staggering to her feet: the lady was a stubborn one. He slowed the gelding from its mad gallop and enjoyed the view. Miss Purefoy in a dark green riding habit stood framed against the greens and browns of the riverbed. With her loose red-gold locks, the lady resembled a wood sprite come to life. It was a magnificent portrait, one of which Aidan wished to commission in the future.

He came within the length of the open field when, to his dismay, a shot rang out, and the lady spun to the left before dropping to the ground. Aidan kicked the gelding's flanks hard, and the horse responded accordingly. As he raced to where the lady crouched, his eyes searched the tree line on the other bank. The river was shallow as it were several weeks since a substantial rain fell, and it was easy to see beyond the path leading to the other side. He kept his concentration on the only area, which would afford the shooter coverage. At length, he saw it: a flash of red.

Aidan slowed the horse to slide to the ground. Running crouched over, he was at Miss Purefoy's side, placing himself between her and the shooter.

"Are you badly injured?" he asked without looking at her.

The single shot volley he carried would be of no use at this distance.

The lady's sob ripped at Aidan's heart.

"It burns," she rasped.

Again, without looking at her, Aidan fished his linen from his pocket. He shoved the cloth into her hand.

"Here," he said as gently as he could.

They were in an exposed position. No cover was available, and Aidan felt very vulnerable. *Who shot at Mary?* His mind repeated the question. It was intentional. Aidan held no doubts of the shot's purpose. A hunter would not mistake the lady for a deer or other animal. Her hair would tell whoever fired the shot that his target was human in form. *Then who? Had the lady's enemies followed her to Cheshire?* It was important for Aidan to discover more of her story before it was too late to protect her. Whether a familial connection proved true or not, Aidan remained confident Miss Purefoy fled her demons.

The sound of horse's hoofs had Aidan spinning to the rear. He looked up to see Mr. Hill's approach.

"What happened?" Hill said as he slowed the animal to a halt.

Aidan finally looked at Miss Purefoy. She was crumpled against him. His jaw was tight, and his tone laced with disbelief.

"Someone shot at Mary."

"Where?" Hill's eyes scanned the tree line.

Aidan gathered the woman to him.

"Other side of the river. A flash of red. Like a man's waistcoat."

"I have it," Hill said as he removed a long rifle from a strap along his saddle. Hill won the gun from an American in a card game in Belgium, and it was one of his friend's most treasured possessions.

"See Miss Purefoy to the house."

Aidan nodded his agreement. He did not think Mr. Hill would discover anything, but it was best to investigate. Only the one shot meant the attack was likely one of intimidation. In his years with the Realm, Aidan learned intimidation meant the victim had something the perpetrator wanted. As he pulled Miss Purefoy closer, Aidan wondered what secret the lady held that would set someone against her.

"Find me when you return to the manor."

Aidan watched as Hill edged his horse down the slope, across the narrow stream, and up the incline on the other side before disappearing into the late afternoon shadows.

"Come, my dear. You had a difficult day."

He lifted Miss Purefoy into his arms for the second time in their short acquaintance and was again surprised by how light she was.

"Allow me to place you on my horse, and then I will see to your injury."

Aidan enjoyed how the woman clung to him–how she gave over to his care. It was important to him that others viewed him as competent. Aidan rode in Andrew's shadow for too many years not to question his abilities.

Carrying her to his horse, Aidan lifted her to the saddle. She caught the horn for balance, and he noted her grimace, but Miss Purefoy did not so much as whimper. She was as brave as she was beautiful.

Carefully, Aidan swung up behind her and settled the lady against him. Like a soothing fire on a chilly night, Miss Purefoy's warmth crept into his body.

"Permit me to look at where the bullet struck you."

Aidan wrapped his hands about her, and Miss Purefoy

turned her cheek into his arm.

"I fear I am a terrible coward," she said weakly.

Aidan eased her fingers from where she still held his linen against her skin. Fortunately, the bullet did not penetrate her skin. *Her creamy white skin*, his lust announced.

"It does not appear to be serious," he said encouragingly.

"Shall it leave a scar?" she asked against his bicep.

Aidan chuckled.

"It will not blemish your beauty, my dear."

He gathered the reins into his right hand, but before Aidan could set the animal in motion, Miss Purefoy looked up into his countenance. Aidan's breath caught in his throat. They were mere inches apart. Close enough to kiss her again. Kiss her properly.

Innocently, she asked, "You think I am beautiful?"

Aidan's smile turned up his lips' corners.

"You have no need to fish for compliments, my dear."

Miss Purefoy blushed, but her gaze held.

"No one..." she paused. "No one ever spoke such a compliment in my presence," the lady confessed.

"Then the men of your village must be blind or exceptional idiots," Aidan declared. "For you are one of the most beautiful women of my acquaintance."

The lady frowned, and he wanted to smooth away the lines in her forehead.

"One among how many?" she asked boldly.

Aidan laughed lightly. Before kicking the horse's flanks, he kissed her forehead where the lines remained. He gathered her closer to him.

Miss Purefoy snuggled into his body, but she said, "You avoid my question, my lord."

Aidan smiled easily. Yes, she was a stubborn one; the lady would not permit him a distraction.

"I mean, being one in a hundred is not so prestigious as being one in a dozen," she reasoned.

He nuzzled her shoulder and enjoyed the scent of lilacs.

The flower's fragrance became his favorite over the past month.

"Let me see," he began in a playful tone. "Unfortunately, the most beautiful women of my acquaintance are married to my closest friends."

"Is that fact why you find them so attractive, my lord? Must a woman be unattainable before you take notice of her beauty?" she challenged.

Aidan's muscles tightened about her. Miss Purefoy's question was one he never considered. Did he purposely place barriers in his life to prevent his finding happiness? Did he take some sort of perverted pleasure in punishing himself?

$$\sim\!\!\sim\!\!\sim$$

Mercy inhaled deeply. She would fill her lungs with the scent of Lord Lexford. *He called her beautiful,* and Mercy's heart melted immediately. Surely, Sir Lesley declared her *comely,* but never beautiful. Only Lord Lexford chose that particular word to describe her. It was a giddy sensation.

Teasingly, she asked, "Is that fact why you find them so attractive, my lord? Must a woman be unattainable before you take notice of her beauty?"

Mercy assumed His Lordship thought of her as "unattainable," especially as his sister, but when he stiffened, she tightened her arms about him.

"I apologize, my lord. I meant no aspersion."

Lord Lexford casually kissed the top of her head before responding.

"None taken, my dear." He hesitated. "I long thought myself immune to the manipulations of Society mamas. Perhaps I only permitted myself to see a woman's finer qualities after someone else laid claim to the lady's affections."

"If it would not distress you, would you speak to me of your friends and their ladies? I know their names and titles, but I never experienced London Society. I am in awe of it."

"Some day I would enjoy showing you about the Capital," His Lordship declared.

Mercy sighed deeply. It was a delightful dream: She would walk arm-in-arm with Viscount Lexford along Bond Street, and heads would turn to see such a handsome couple.

He slowed the horse to a walk and adjusted his hold to bring her more securely into his embrace. Mercy enjoyed the feel of His Lordship's body along hers. It was a thoroughly naughty thought, but she could not remove the smile from her lips. From deep in his chest, Lord Lexford sighed in what she assumed was resignation.

"At one time, I thought to court Cashémere Aldridge for my own, but the lady preferred the Earl of Berwick."

Mercy held the acquaintance of Miss Cashémere once when they were both young girls in the schoolroom. Cashémere Aldridge possessed gorgeous black hair and emerald green eyes. Mercy considered her sister's connection to the Aldridge family and forcibly swallowed the desire to comment on her knowledge of Miss Cashémere.

"Although I am certain it was awkward at first, you demonstrated true friendship in stepping aside," she reasoned.

"Berwick is the one with whom I share the most experiences, and I could never separate him from the woman he so plainly loves."

The viscount maneuvered the gelding across a footbridge.

"I thought I wooed Miss Cashémere, but, in reality, I knew Miss Satiné. They are twins and are two of a kind."

Mercy thought glumly, *Another woman of dark hair.*

"Miss Satiné went abroad with her guardian Baron Ashton. I doubt she will return to England any time soon. Their older sister married the Duke of Thornhill. The Duchess resembles her sisters in color and height. The lady's name is Velvet, and she is as fine to look upon as the fabric of her namesake."

Mercy's misery increased. She observed renderings of the late Lady Lexford. Susan Kimbolt was dark of hair and slender in her stature.

"The Marquis of Godown married his love the week before

I returned to Lexington Arms. I cannot say I would think the new marquise would make a fine showing, but Godown had the right of it. The marquis's bride showed her fair countenance at their wedding."

"And the lady's looks?" Mercy asked softly.

"Hair of brown with golden tints." He turned in at the gatehouse. "And then there is Viscountess Worthing. It was with the Worthings I shared my time before returning to Lexington Arms. It is the viscountess I admire above the others."

"Is Lady Worthing of the same nature as the others?" Mercy asked morosely.

How could Lord Lexford truly find Mercy beautiful if every woman His Lordship admired was dark of head?

"Oh, no," Lord Lexford said wistfully. "Lady Worthing is tall and lithe of figure. Well, not so lithe at the moment as the viscountess is enceinte. The former Lady Eleanor Fowler possesses reddish golden hair and pale blue eyes."

Mercy raised her head to study his countenance.

"And of all these women, it is Lady Worthing you hold in deepest affection?"

The viscount laughed ironically.

"I cursed myself on more than one occasion for not traveling to London for last Season. Perhaps if I had, it would be I who would be welcoming a child in a few short days."

Mercy felt the pang of regret. If only Lord Lexford looked upon her with the same admiration as he did Lady Eleanor Kerrington, perhaps Mercy could convince Lord Lexford her lie was nothing but a ploy to save face, and the gentleman would forgive her. As it was, His Lordship loved Lady Susan Kimbolt and deeply admired Lady Worthing. Mercy possessed nothing to offer him. Both women never kept secrets, which could ruin them. *At least, Lady Worthing is fair of head,* Mercy acknowledged with a bit of jealousy.

"And you discovered nothing beyond this piece of shrapnel?" Aidan asked Hill as they shared a brandy in manor house's private study.

"Boot prints where the dampness remains beneath the trees, but the path leads to the main road to the village. Any number of people crossed that particular stretch of land," Hill shared.

"It was not an accident," Aidan declared.

Hill nodded his head in agreement.

"But why would someone make Miss Purefoy a target? And how would our shooter know the lady was alone?"

"Could it be a warning shot?" Aidan hissed. "A means to inform the woman that she did not escaped her enemies?"

His gaze demanded Hill maintained eye contact.

"Speak to me of the truth. Do you possess knowledge of Miss Purefoy's past, which you did not previously disclosed?"

His man shook his head in denial.

"Nothing, my lord."

Aidan studied Hill carefully. He could not abandon the idea Hill hid an important fact, but pressing his friend would prove futile. When Hill chose to confide in him, Aidan would know the secret and not before.

"We should place some of the men as guards about the estate."

"I will see to it." Hill paused. "How fares Miss Purefoy?"

"Mr. Jamison says the lady will heal quickly. Miss Purefoy claims only her pride to be bruised."

"I am glad of it," Hill said earnestly. "By the way, the mare returned to the stall." Hill's expression became one of concern. "Deland is most distraught, my lord. The groom cannot understand what occurred. Deland swears he added extra padding to fit the mare's back, but when he removed Miss Purefoy's saddle, the horse's back sported saddle galls."

"Do you believe him or do you think Deland makes excuses

for ill work?"

Hill sat forward to press his point.

"Of all the grooms, I find Deland the most diligent. He genuinely grieves for Miss Purefoy's injury. If the lady simply knew difficulty with her horse, I might rest the blame on Deland's oversight; however, when one combines the saddle being under padded with the attack upon the lady, I tend to believe the groom. Perhaps, Miss Purerfoy's attacker called at the stables before making his presence known in the open."

Silence filled the space between him and Hill for several seconds.

"Your conclusion is a sound one." Aidan's heart slammed against his ribcage. Adamantly, he said, "I will not have Miss Purefoy know of your suspicions. Neither will I permit another to harm her."

Aidan appeared at Miss Purefoy's chamber door early the next morning. He missed her at breakfast and wanted to assure himself of her progress.

"My lord," she said on a gasp when the maid admitted him into her quarters. "You honor me."

She appeared a bit rumpled, and Aidan thought her deliciously attractive.

"I required the assurance of your recovery, my dear." He remained close to the door. "I thought perhaps you might wish to spend time in the library. I know I am not the best of patients, and I assumed you of the same nature."

Miss Purefoy shoved herself to a seated position. Although she kept the blankets close, Aidan noticed the prominent bandage at the edge of her gown's neckline. The bullet grazed the lady's shoulder blade.

"Might we set the servants to the task of reorganizing the library? It would do me well to be of service during my convalescence. Moreover, later today you have another interview for Master Aaron's nurse, and I would not wish to take you away from your duties."

Aidan smiled at how her mind worked. The woman was always planning and organizing.

"I will speak to Mrs. Babcock immediately and return for you in half an hour. I will not have you attempt the stairs alone."

"It is not..."

"Necessary," Aidan finished her protest. "You forget, my dear, I am the master of this house," he said teasingly. "And I choose what is necessary."

He presented Miss Purefoy a quick bow before reaching for the door latch.

"By the way, your boot survived your mishap."

He placed the footwear on a nearby table.

"Deland returned it to Mr. Hill." Smiling at her, Aidan said, "Be about it, my dear. I mean to see you well quickly. I find I do not care to dine alone."

Aidan carried Miss Purefoy through Lexington Arms' passageways to rest upon a chaise in the library, not because one of the footmen could not do the job equally as well, but because Aidan enjoyed having the lady close.

"We are all at your beck and call," he announced to the room. Mrs. Babcock objected to Aidan's interruption of what the woman termed the staff's "routine duties," but he reminded the estate's long time housekeeper that "his" wishes would prevail. It was essentially what he said to Miss Purefoy, but not with the same tone or intent.

Miss Purefoy's smile widened, and Aidan could swear sunlight flooded the room. He was very much attached to this woman's charms.

"I think it best if we remove every book and thoroughly clean each shelf. We should dust the books, as well, and examine them for loose bindings. Those found in need of repair should be set aside until those repairs are completed. Books are too precious not to be treated without respect."

Her excitement grew and so did Aidan's.

"What say you, my lord? Shall we organize the books by titles or authors?"

"Authors," Aidan announced.

He enjoyed the way Miss Purefoy always deferred to his position.

"Then authors it is," the lady agreed.

Aidan took over from there.

"From what I observed this job is not as daunting as it first appears. The majority of the books are already arranged alphabetically by author. We will each take a section and first remove the books, which do not belong. Then we will place those 'lost' books on the shelf where they should be alphabetically. Afterwards, we will clean and organize each shelf."

"We?" Mrs. Babcock said skeptically.

"We," Aidan asserted.

He removed his jacket and handed it to Miss Purefoy.

"I was never been to object to a bit of dust upon my hands." To Miss Purefoy, he said, "You, my dear, are to design other improvements we might make in this room."

He retrieved paper and artist pencils so his sister could make sketches and notes, an activity Aidan observed her doing when the household carried out her instructions for the nursery. She was obviously a "list" person.

Mrs. Babcock's countenance spoke of the woman's disdain.

"This room has been a showcase for the past half century. The late viscount would be most displeased."

Aidan said incredulously, "You forget yourself, Madam. Arlen Kimbolt is no longer the master of this household. I am Viscount Lexford."

The housekeeper dropped her eyes in a subservient manner, but her actions did not fool Aidan.

"I apologize, my lord."

"As this was my mother's favorite room, it will be restored to its former glory and as my cousin sees fit." Aidan suggested judiciously, "Perhaps you should see to rearranging the duties of the others while we begin our work in here."

With a poorly disguised glare in Miss Purefoy's direction, Mrs. Babcock made her curtsies.

"Odd," Aidan said under his breath.

Miss Purefoy paused to collect her composure before leaning forward to speak privately.

"Perhaps not so odd. Likely, you did not take notice previously."

Aidan left the women to their cleaning, but Miss Purefoy's words clung to him like a winter cloak. Did his distress upon being forced to return to Lexington Arms blind him to the real goings on under his roof? Did he refuse to take notice of what became of his family's title? Grudgingly, he waited for Mr. Payne to show in the scheduled candidate for a nurse for Aaron. Aidan would prefer to remain in the library with Miss Purefoy. The woman made a game of finding various volumes, and the maids scrambled to do Mary's bidding. It was intoxicatingly lively wherever she was, and Aidan ached for what the lady brought to his household. Now, if he could simply resolve his growing desire for her, Aidan would find some peace at last.

At a rap on the door, he looked up as Payne escorted a freckled faced girl of possibly twenty years into the room.

"My lord, this is Miss Hanson. She is Mrs. Osborne's niece, Sir."

Miss Purefoy convinced Aidan to permit the girl an interview. Reportedly, his cook pleaded with Mary to intervene in Miss Hanson's behalf, and, as usual, Aidan agreed with Miss Purefoy's suggestion. He chuckled at his own domestication.

"Thank you, Mr. Payne. Would you ask Miss Chadwick to bring in Master Aaron?"

"Immediately, Sir."

Aidan rose and gestured to a nearby chair.

"Please, Miss Hanson."

He waited for the girl to seat herself on the edge of the cushion before he continued.

"I am to understand you are Mrs. Osborne's niece."

"Yes, Sir. The late Mr. Osborne and my mother were brother and sister."

The girl's lips trembled, but her voice was strong. At least, he did not intimidated Miss Hanson completely.

"And what of your qualifications, Miss Hanson? How might I judge you as competent to tend my nephew?"

Aidan sat across from her.

The girl shot a quick glance about the room and sighed in admiration.

"I...I possess four younger brothers and sisters, and last year I served Mr. Shankler after his wife passed in childbirth. The gentleman kept Mrs. Titus as the wet nurse when he decided to return to Edinburgh, but I held no desire to leave Cheshire, Sir."

A light tap announced the arrival of Miss Chadwick and the child.

"Wunkle Waden," the boy squealed as he scampered to meet Aidan's open embrace. It still amazed Aidan how quickly the child wormed his way into Aidan's heart. He caught the boy's shoulders and turned him to where Miss Hanson looked on.

"This is Miss Hanson."

Aidan balanced Aaron upon his knee. The boy's eyes widened, but he did not shy away.

"Miss Hanson asked permission to escort you on a walk about the grounds."

"Wout side?" Aaron asked in anticipation.

"Yes, the lady will escort you outside to play. You must mind her most loyally though."

"Yes, Sir."

Without further ado, Aidan handed off the child to the girl.

"Miss Chadwick will show you the boy's quarters. Be certain Master Aaron dresses for the elements."

His order surprised the girl, but she caught Aaron's hand,

made her curtsy, and turned to follow Miss Chadwick. He liked the fact Miss Hanson understood his intentions: Aidan would judge Miss Hanson's competency by observing her interactions with the child.

He looked up to see Miss Purefoy framed by the open door.

"I thought you were to send word when you finished for the day," he said a bit testily.

Aidan once again fought the warmth her appearance brought to his heart.

As he did previously, Miss Purefoy ignored the others in the room.

"A woman may only remain a lady of leisure so long before she requires more challenging endeavors, my lord."

Despite everyone looking on, Aidan smiled. He adored the familiar teasing tone Miss Purefoy adopted with him.

He extended his hand to her.

"Then come join me, my dear. Miss Hanson is escorting Aaron outside so they may learn more of each other."

Miss Purefoy bent to kiss the top of Aaron's head.

"Hello, my darling," she whispered. "You must be a good boy for Miss Hanson," she instructed.

"Yes, Ma'am."

"Then hurry along."

She watched the two women and the child depart before saying, "You, Sir, are quite ingenious."

Aidan chuckled. "You came to recognize my manipulations."

He caught her hand and gently led her to a nearby chair. Aidan noted each gingerly step Miss Purefoy took; the lady was likely severely bruised. He would not mind kissing well each of those bruises.

"You mean to know if Miss Hanson can truly contain Master Aaron's enthusiasm for the outdoors."

Aidan seated himself across from Miss Purefoy. One thing they quickly learned about the child was Aaron possessed an enormous reservoir of energy, which required thoughtful planning to control.

"How Miss Hanson fares will prove her true credentials."

"Devious, thy name is Lord Lexford," Mary teased.

Aidan chuckled again.

"I am pleased you approve. Now tell me how I may serve you. What *more challenging endeavors* did you set for yourself?"

Miss Purefoy retrieved a book from where she placed it on a side table.

"Miss Chadwick compiled this sample book over the past few years. In it, she placed bits of cloth of many shades. The pages are bound only by ribbon," she explained as she opened the handmade book upon her lap. "By doing so, a person may remove and compare the pages for complementary colors. See these two pages hold shades of red. These three hold blue, and so forth."

Aidan moved to where he might better view the samples. There were squares of cloth and paper and ribbon and even of wood and leaves.

"Interesting," he said as he turned yet another page.

Miss Purefoy bit her bottom lip in hesitation. Aidan knew she still did not feel comfortable speaking for his household, but he relied upon her opinions.

"I thought we might seek cloth of this shade to replace the two worn chairs in the library."

She pointed to a sample of golden hues.

"I do not think you would need more than those changes to bring life to the room. We might rearrange some of the pieces, but the furniture is sturdy and speaks of a masculine quality. The drapes and rugs are due a thorough cleaning, but those could wait until spring. With the beeswax shine, the room will sparkle."

Aidan took the book from her and turned several more pages, flipping back and forth between two samples.

"I agree," he said distractedly. "This one is beautiful, but it is too dark. It would act in opposition to the drapes. You possess a good eye for color, my dear."

He returned the book to her lap.

"Tell me what you would choose for my imprint upon Lexington Arms."

Miss Purefoy blushed.

"I possess no occasion to view your chambers, my lord," she said softly.

Occasionally, Aidan reminded himself they were together for but a month. Miss Purefoy filled the empty spaces he knew forever.

"Needless to say, I will show you my quarters at a later time, but perhaps for the time being, I might give you a hint by choosing from Miss Chadwick's samples."

He turned the pages carefully so as not to dislodge the samples from the wax, which held them.

"Here." Aidan pointed to a deep purple swatch of cloth.

Miss Purefoy did a poor job of hiding her disapproval.

"Oh, no, my lord. That will never do. You are an earth color," she declared.

"An earth color?" Aidan's lips turned up in amusement.

"You must wear and use the rich shades of the land," she asserted. "Blacks and browns and greens."

It was odd: Those were the colors he associated with her. The earth and the blues and grays of the sky.

"Why would anyone assume you would choose the color of royalty? You possess no false airs, and if ever there was a man who saw the goodness in all, it would be you, my lord," she said earnestly.

The woman never hid her feelings. No artifice existed in her speech, except, of course, the possibility of their familial connection. The lady's praise was a balm to Aidan's bruised soul.

"The purple tones were my father's choice," Aidan admitted. "I never thought to change them."

Miss Purefoy caught his hand.

"It is not kind of me to speak poorly of a man I never met, but you are not of the same ilk as the late viscount. In fact, I doubt there is another quite like you."

Chapter 10

"BLOODY HELL! The woman knows exactly how to enflame my dreams," Aidan growled as he undressed for bed.

Hours passed since Miss Purefoy's innocent pronouncement, but the lady's words still haunted him. He glanced about his chambers. As was customary, Aidan moved into his father's suite of rooms after Arlen Kimbolt's death. At the time, he saw the move as symbolic of his transition into the title. As the younger son, Aidan thought it important for appearances to assume his father's position, but now he wondered if he erred. He looked upon the drapes of plum and the bed linens of a similar shade and regretted the decision.

"Certainly not of my taste," he said as he tossed his shirt upon the back of a chair.

"What is not to your taste, my lord?" his valet asked from the dressing room door.

Aidan often forgot about Mr. Poley's presence. When he departed for the war, Aidan left behind Mr. Stewart, the elderly valet, who served him throughout his youth and university years. The late viscount pensioned off the man. After Aidan and the others rescued Mr. Hill, Lucifer often served the role of valet, but it was as much a part of the ruse the group practiced, as it was a subservient position for Hill. In reality, Aidan looked on Hill as one of his most trusted friends.

When he returned to secure the Kimbolt line by marrying his brother's widow, Aidan never considered the idea he would one day inherit his father's title, the late viscount's chambers, and Viscount Lexford's valet. Aidan simply accepted all three as part of his responsibility to the estate.

"I was considering of late redecorating these quarters. I asked Miss Purefoy for suggestions."

Mr. Poley looked up from where he folded Aidan's freshly laundered clothes and frowned.

"Do you think that decision a prudent one, my lord?"

Aidan's eyebrow rose in curiosity: Mr. Poley rarely expressed an opinion; that is until of late. Yet, with Aidan's sister's arrival both his valet and his housekeeper became more vocal.

"Do you disapprove of my changing the décor of *my* private quarters or is it Miss Purefoy to which you direct your dissatisfaction?"

Mr. Poley froze, and a multitude of emotions crossed the valet's countenance.

"I...I apologize, my lord. It is...it is none of my...of my concern how you conduct your viscountcy."

Aidan bit back his curse. He realized several of his father's servants, especially Mrs. Babcock, disapproved of Aidan's treating Miss Purefoy as family. Others disagreed with his placing Mr. Hill in a position of oversight; yet, none of the others understood him the way Lucifer and the lady did. His growing dependence on Miss Purefoy's opinions and his continued reliance on Hill's should worry him, but Aidan felt secure in the knowledge that both spoke honestly of his past and his future.

"Then I will keep my counsel," he said aristocratically. "You may be excused for the evening."

"As you wish, my lord."

Mr. Poley gathered Aidan's soiled clothing, bowed, and turned toward the dressing room, but Aidan's ire continued to simmer. He stopped the man's exit.

"Mr. Poley, I will be most displeased if I discover my decision to shed my father's feathers becomes part of the servants' gossip line. I hope I make myself clear in this matter."

"Perfectly, clear, my lord."

⟨⟨⟩⟩

"Mama!"

The child's voice rose in alarm. Mercy pulled the blanket tighter about her. She certainly did not want to relinquish the bed's warmth to stumble through the darkness to comfort the boy. She did so every night since Mr. Rhodes deposited the child in Lord Lexford's care. Mercy adored Master Aaron, but it would be wonderful if the boy would discover a means of calming himself. Just this one evening, she would love to return to her dreams of the viscount's endearing smile.

"No, Mama!"

The child's alarm brought Mercy fully awake. Tossing the linens to the side, she bolted from the bed. Scanning the room for where the sound of shuffling feet came, Mercy's eyes noted a brief flash of light as the dressing room door closed quickly.

"Aaron! Aaron, where are you?"

"Mar!" the boy called.

It was the child's attempt to say "Mary." Aaron had only done so for the past few days, and the boy's familiarity with her warmed Mercy's heart.

Mercy's head snapped to the right.

"Stop!" she ordered, but whoever it was who had the boy was running. "Stop! Stop! Stop this instant!"

Without considering the consequences, Mercy was running too. She flung open the exterior door in time to see the culprit hurrying toward the burned out rooms. She could not understand why the wall sconces were out, but the passage remained draped in darkness.

"Stop!" she screamed to the retreating form.

Immediately, she was on the move. Aaron was crying

loudly, but the figure paid the boy no attention. In his retreat, the interloper overturned small tables to block Mercy's way. The noise of the breaking glass and wood only added to the chaos. Deftly jumping over the scattered debris, Mercy ignored the ploy; yet, despite her daring, she was too late. The figure disappeared into the open darkness, and the door to the ruined section slammed shut just as she reached it. As she caught the latch to follow, a bolt on the other side slid into place.

"No!" she pleaded as she pounded her small fists against the wood. "No!"

The constant tapping ripped Aidan from a sound sleep.

"My lord!" a servant called. "Please, my lord!"

Aidan stumbled from his bed to yank the door open.

"What is amiss?" he growled.

A young footman in a wrinkled shirt looked about anxiously.

"Mr. Payne reports screams coming from the west wing, Sir."

"What?" Aidan shoved the man to the side and was running through the shadowed passageways

"Break it down!" he heard Hill order as he turned the corner.

"What happened?" Aidan caught Mary's arm and dragged her from Mr. Hill's way.

Her lip trembled, and she looked uneasily toward the half broken door. "Someone…someone took Aaron. I could not reach the boy in time."

"Stay here," he ordered. "Hill, the servants' stairs." Aidan did not wait for Lucifer to respond. Instead, he entered the empty room adjoining the burned ruins and flung the window wide. Aidan climbed through the opening and precariously perched upon a narrow ledge and a protruding hunky punk. Thankfully, he had no time to don his boots. They would not serve him well in such precarious matters. His toes dug into the soft mortar between the bricks. From behind him, he could hear his men hit the door again. By the sound of it, someone found an ax.

Aidan took a deep breath to steady his next move. Surprisingly, it took only three long loping straddles to edge through the shell of the charcoaled rotting timbers. Edging about the corner, he scanned the area, but saw nothing unusual. Then a movement to his right announced he was not alone. He swung wildly to cuff his attacker on the chin just as a solid chunk of wood hit him firmly in his chest; thankfully, the blow did not dislodge him. Aidan swung through the crumbled window and chased his attacker, who nimbly outdistanced him. He attempted to ignore the many nails and splinters upon which he stepped, but they slowed his progress.

A light suddenly cut the darkness as his men breached the door.

"Aaron!" he heard Mary call as she followed the men through the opening. "Aaron, answer me!"

"Mar!"

Aidan looked up to see the child perched upon a charred crossbeam.

"My God!"

He halted his chase. Aidan jumped from the burned platform, which was once part of the flooring of the second level. He landed in a pile of broken boards and debris, but he scrambled to find his footing.

"We need more light," he demanded. "Easy, Boy," he said softly. His nephew's eyes announced the boy's terror. "Do not move."

"Kared," the child whined.

Aidan swallowed hard. How could he reach the child? He looked around frantically for something upon which to climb. Above him, he heard Mary's soothing voice.

"Do not move, my Darling," she cooed. "I am coming for you."

"No!" Aidan hissed.

Miss Purefoy hung precariously over the edge of a scorched section.

"There is no other means, my lord."

Aidan stared up at her perfect countenance.

"I am not certain the wood will hold your weight," he said as he examined where the boy clung tightly to his perch. "I will catch Aaron if he falls."

"But how do we convince the boy to jump to the safety of your arms, my lord?" Mary argued. "Master Aaron is but a babe." Tears misted her eyes. "And his gait is too unsteady to cross the wood on his own."

She hastily shoved away the tear crawling down her cheek.

"The wood held long enough for our intruder to place the child in such a perilous situation. Surely, it will hold for a mere woman to rescue the boy."

Aidan hated not possessing options. He did not want Miss Purefoy in danger.

"Move slowly," he said, at length.

With a nod of agreement, Mary edged toward a connecting crossbeam. Despite the close proximity of his men, she caught the hem of her gown and gave it a good tug, which rent the material. She took the ends and wrapped them about her legs creating a pair of short Cossack style pantaloons. His men blushed, but like Aidan, they looked on in admiration.

"Magnificent," he murmured.

"Do not move, Darling," she encouraged as she worked on her creation. "I am coming after you."

"Kared," Aaron continued to sob.

"I know, my pet, but I mean to assist you. Just remain still for a few more minutes."

She knelt to crawl along the beam on all fours. The wood was likely six inches in width, and Aidan prayed it would hold her weight.

His men held their lanterns and candles high to light her way. Hill appeared beside Aidan.

"What is Miss Purefoy doing?" he whispered.

"Rescuing the boy," Aidan said on a soft exhale. "We must catch them if they fall."

Hill nodded and sidestepped the clutter scattered about the floor. "I have the girl," he said softly. "You take Master Aaron."

It made sense. Hill was heavier and taller than he, but Aidan wished to be the lady's hero.

"Your reflexes are faster than mine, and the boy is unpredictable," Hill said as if his man thought to soothe Aidan's pride.

"Look at me, Darling. Do not look down." Miss Purefoy edged closer to the child. "I am almost there. Be my brave little man."

"Want my room," Aaron bawled.

"I know, Darling," she said softly. "Soon. You must know I shall permit nothing bad to happen to you."

The boy nodded, but the tears streamed down Aaron's cheeks. Aidan heard the board groan as she neared the middle.

"Slower," he cautioned as he centered his weight and extended his arms above his head in case the child shifted before the lady could reach him. He watched anxiously as Miss Purefoy sucked in a quick breath before starting forward again.

"Just a few more inches," she told the boy.

Aidan admired how she never looked away from the child.

As she neared, Mary said, "When I reach you, you must not move, my pet. Not until I tell you. We must practice care."

As Aidan watched nervously, Mary lowered her weight upon the beam so her legs hung over either side of the wood.

Aidan breathed a bit easier, but the ordeal was far from over. Mary slowly extended her right arm.

"I shall touch you, Darling. Do not be frightened. Permit me to see to your safety."

Keeping her balance, Miss Purefoy carefully scooted forward on the beam as if she were on a tittering board.

"Mary loves you, Darling," she coaxed. "I shall permit

nothing to harm you."

The child's eyes grew even larger, but thankfully, Aaron listened carefully to what the woman's said. The boy remained perfectly stationary. At length, she was close enough to capture Aaron into her embrace.

"Oh, my pet," she comforted the child as she lifted the boy to her. Mary kissed the side of Aaron's head. "You were so brave," she repeated. "I am so proud of you."

"Kared," the boy said on a sharp squeal.

"I know, Darling," Mary said encouragingly. "Now, I must assist you down from here."

The idea did not occur to the child before that instant. Aaron turned his head to look about him in fear.

"No!" he demanded and tried to squirm away, but Miss Purefoy caught him tightly to her.

Aidan's breath hitched when he thought they would both tumble over backwards, but she smartly countered the child's move with a shift of her weight, just as she did when riding sidesaddle.

"Yes!" she demanded with a slight shake of the child's shoulders. "Your Uncle Aidan is below us, and he means to see us both down safely."

As she spoke, Mary's gaze lingered on the far corner, but Aidan assumed she settled her own fears. He had no time to take a proper analysis of what caught the lady's attention. Aidan was too busy judging the child's descent for he held no delusions Miss Purefoy did not intend to drop the boy into Aidan's arms.

As predicted, before the child could send up another alarm, the lady lifted Aaron by his arms and swung the child over the edge of the beam. The boy shrieked in fright, but Miss Purefoy ignored Aaron's protestations. "My lord?" she called over the boy's loud cries.

"I am here," Aidan declared. "Release him on three. One. Two. Three."

As if in slow motion, the child dropped from the height.

Aidan looked on in amazement as only a screech of surprise broke the night's silence, but in a split second the boy's weight hit him hard enough to knock the air from Aidan's lungs. Nevertheless, he wrapped his arms about the child and held on for all his might.

"I have you," he repeated several times before the child went silent. "I have you," Aidan said again for good measure.

From above a round of cheers broke the night.

From the shadows, Mr. Payne appeared by his side.

"Give me the young master, Sir," his butler said. "You and Mr. Hill must assist the lady."

Aidan kissed the boy's head. "We must see to Mary," he said as calmly as possible. "Permit Mr. Payne to hold you for a few minutes."

He wiped the child's tears away before handing his nephew to the elderly butler.

With a deep sigh of relief, Aidan returned to where Miss Purefoy remained perched on the beam above him.

"I do not suppose you could crawl back along the wood the way you came," he said in concern.

The lady held perfectly still, and her expression turned to one of dread.

"I doubt such a scheme is possible, my lord," she said without looking in his direction. "The wood is split in the far corner."

An unbecoming hint of dismay laced her tone.

Aidan's eyes followed hers. He briefly considered the peril.

"Bloody hell!" he growled. "Mr. Hill!" he said urgently.

Aidan cursed himself for permitting the ruins to stand as a silent tribute to his late wife. His former foolishness never ceased to amaze him.

"I am here, my lord," Hill said softly from behind him. "You catch the lady, and I will brace you."

Aidan chuckled, "You were always the stable one."

He did not remove his eyes from the precarious position in which Miss Purefoy found herself.

Hill said with an easy taunt of familiarity,

"One of us must wear the cloak of immovability."

"My lord," Mary called. "Did it hurt when you broke your arm falling from the oak?"

Aidan smiled easily. She was incomparable.

"Absolutely!" he said firmly. "But I promise you will know no pain, my dear. I will guard you with my life."

"I trust you, my lord," Mary declared for all those who looked on. "On three, Sir. One. Two. Three."

With the count, Miss Purefoy swung her left leg over the beam just as it cracked under her weight. Aidan positioned himself beneath her. Unlike the boy, Mary dropped quickly, a muslin-clad bullet. When she hit him, he fell backwards, but Hill's bulk took the impact. A loud grunt announced Hill's sturdiness as the three of them collapsed in a pile of legs and arms.

A swish of cool night air deposited his sister in Aidan's arms; but despite the exquisite feel of Miss Purefoy's bare legs brushing against his, Aidan could not enjoy the moment. Foremost, his staff peered over the edge of the burned sections of the flooring as Aidan's hands searched Mary's body for any broken limbs, and secondly, Lucifer Hill was not a comfortable mattress upon which to bed a lady.

From everywhere at once, people surrounded them. Mrs. Osborne and Miss Chadwick lifted Miss Purefoy to a standing position and wrapped a blanket about her.

"You poor dear," Mrs. Osborne said as she caught Mary about the waist to lead her away.

The warmth disappeared with the lady's retreat, and Aidan rolled to his side to check on Hill. He made it to his knees before he said, "Are you injured?"

Hill groaned and stretched his arm above his head.

"Next time I catch the girl and you become the one on the bottom."

Aidan's lips turned up in a smile. It was this man with whom he shared countless adventures and schemes. He pushed himself to a crouched position and extended his hand to Lucifer.

"Come, my friend. I owe you a drink."

"Make it two."

Hill's fingers closed around Aidan's hand.

"Anything you want. I am forever in your debt," Aidan said heavily.

Hill permitted Aidan to pull him to his feet. Always in the past, Lucifer would remind Aidan of his own debt, the one where Hill promised to serve Aidan for ten years. The man meant as an actual servant, but it was not in Aidan's nature to place such a fierce fighter in a menial role, so Aidan made Lucifer Hill his companion, his friend, and his confidant. Hill became the "eighth" member of a seven-man team, and when Aidan returned home to his personal demons, Hill traveled with him. Henry Hill put his life in limbo to be Aidan's most trusted associate. Now, Aidan regretted his dependence upon the man. It was selfish of Aidan to keep Hill from knowing Hannah Tolliver as his wife; therefore, Aidan silently vowed to set his life to right as quickly as possible and then say farewell to Lucifer Hill.

"We should see to Miss Purefoy and the boy." Hill shoved the hair from his face.

Aidan laced his arm about Lucifer's shoulder in companionship.

"It was a good night," he said with a laugh.

"Being a hero is hard on a man of my advanced years," Hill declared good-naturedly.

"I am not certain the lady requires a hero," Aidan confided. "Did you see her? As calm as the smoothest sea. I never knew anyone like her."

"Miss Purefoy suits you, my lord. In the past month, I heard you laugh and observed your contentment." Hill halted their steps. "Grab happiness, my lord. Grab it with both hands and hold on for all you are worth."

Aidan's heart lurched with anticipation.

"According to your own tongue, the lady is my sister."

Hill's eyes spoke of mirth.

"The woman is more family than you ever knew, Lord Lexford."

Before Aidan could reply, his men surrounded them.

"The dang'us thing I ever seen," Deland declared. "I thought all three of you be dead."

"Wunkle Waden," the boy reached for Aidan, and Aidan accepted the child's embrace. Each time he did so, he wondered why he denied himself such moments. Aaron was not his child, but it did not mean Aidan could not love the boy.

"You were very brave." He ruffled Aaron's hair.

"Have cakes?" The child patted Aidan's cheeks.

Aidan smiled as the boy's singular thoughts.

"As soon as I set some men to search for our intruder."

"We have it, my lord." Deland lifted his gun in response.

"Did you see which way the person ran?" Aidan asked Hill.

"Toward where the stream narrows behind the copse."

Aidan noted how Hill rubbed his shoulder. He would have Mr. Jamison attend Hill in the morning.

Aidan hefted Aaron higher. To his men, he said, "I must see to Miss Purefoy and Master Aaron."

To his friend, Aidan said, "Hill, you should come with me. We must inform the magistrate of this break in."

Hill nodded his gratitude as he fell into step beside Aidan.

"My lord," he said privately. "Did you notice who rushed to our aid?"

Aidan caressed the back of Aaron's head. The child rested his head on Aidan's shoulder.

"The footmen...the kitchen staff...the maids...the grooms..."

"And who was not among those responding to the alarm?" Hill prompted.

Aidan stumbled on the graveled path, but he listened carefully to what Hill did not say. His mind raced to understand the predicament, which hanged over his house.

"The only one I do not recall seeing was Mrs. Babcock."

"True," Hill confirmed. "And Mr. Poley. It seems to me if a man's master was called out by an intruder under his roof, a valet would respond to assure himself said master required no assistance."

Aidan paused briefly before they entered the house. A sharp flare of dread stabbed his heart.

"I so rarely think on Poley's service unless I require a fancily-tied cravat," he admitted. He looked about to assure privacy. "I reprimanded Poley earlier for his impertinence."

"I will discover where Poley kept his own company," Hill said softly. "Do not mention our suspicions to the others."

Despite his request for his favorite cakes, the boy was asleep by the time Aidan entered the drawing room where Miss Chadwick flitted about an obviously shaken Miss Purefoy. Someone retrieved the lady's robe and slippers, but Mary hovered close to the hearth as if she could not know enough of the fire's heat. Aidan wished to catch her up in his embrace and warm the woman with his body. Instead, he placed the boy on a nearby chaise and covered Aaron with one of Susan's shawls. The item was reverently left where it laid since before his wife's death.

"Master Aaron appears none the worst for wear," Miss Purefoy said shakily.

Aidan glanced at his nephew's innocence.

"I imagine, on the morrow, he will be full of tales of his adventure. I fear Miss Hanson will find her first day as Aaron's nurse a challenging one."

Miss Purefoy shivered again.

"Do you think it best to move the young master so far from where the rest of the household rests, my lord?"

Aidan understood her fear for the child. He was not happy with how easily someone breached the lady's private quarters, but that particular situation would change with the morning light. Aidan would send word to London for Pennington to assign several of the Realm recruits to Lexington Arms until this matter knew a settlement.

"Mr. Hill will see to extra men to secure the entrances into the house," he assured her.

Realizing belatedly this discussion would best be held without Miss Chadwick, Aidan asked the girl to see to Aaron. He instructed a footman to carry the boy to Miss Chadwick's room and to stand guard outside the door.

When the shopkeeper's daughter disappeared into the night, Aidan placed three chairs close together before the fire. He poured Miss Purefoy a sherry, and he and Hill a brandy.

"We have much to discuss," he said as he joined them.

Miss Purefoy looked about in puzzlement.

"I do not understand, my lord."

"We are family," he said simply. "I cannot have you fearing to sleep under my roof. In order to alleviate your anxiety, you must speak of what will bring you peace. If you think my idea of securing the house's entrances is not adequate, I wish you to voice your concerns. In this matter, I am your servant."

Miss Purefoy blushed thoroughly.

"My lord, it cannot be so," she protested. "I cannot presume to speak of your responsibility."

"Oh, but you must, my dear." Aidan smiled easily at her. "Mr. Hill and I find you quite remarkable, and I will not have you relinquish that exemplary quality simply because you do not experience safety at Lexington Arms."

"It is true, Miss Purefoy. His Lordship and I often admire your ingenuity and your steadfastness," Hill declared.

The lady's face scrunched up in disapproval.

"I do not appreciate your levity at my expense, Sirs."

"What levity?" Aidan said honestly. "I mean what I say. I know few men who would risk what you did to save a small child. The fact you completed an unselfish act speaks highly of the person I know."

He watched as the lady's shoulders shifted, and she sat

more erect. Aidan smiled secretly: Miss Purefoy would recover from her fright.

"Then we know agreement regarding increasing the number of guards set about the estate?" Hill asked tentatively.

Again, the lady frowned, but this time in deliberation.

"Should we not first determine why someone would choose to kidnap the young master?"

Aidan's mouth twitched in amazement. Miss Purefoy narrowed the problem to its core truth. The lady had the makings of a reliable Realm agent: daring and intelligence.

"What do you suppose the person's motives?"

"Ransom," she and Hill said together.

"I have not had the opportunity to search your quarters, my dear, but I would venture to say no demand for money exists within." Aidan already considered the possibility of ransom.

Miss Purefoy bit her bottom lip in concentration.

"Perhaps whoever took Master Aaron from his bed meant to have the ransom note delivered after the boy was secured."

Aidan refilled her sherry glass and Hill's brandy.

"Perhaps."

He liked how the color returned to Miss Purefoy's cheeks. The sherry and the lady's constant need to be of use warmed her and restored Mary's normal curiosity. Aidan made a mental note not to permit Miss Chadwick to tend Miss Purefoy too closely. The shopkeeper's daughter had a tendency to smother her charges with her maternal instincts. Aidan preferred his "sister" with a bit of fire in her stomach.

"What can you tell us about the man who took the boy?" Hill asked.

Miss Purefoy said enigmatically,

"Who said it was a man?"

"Most assuredly the perpetrator was a man," Aidan declared. "Although I did not have a clear look at the person who threw the wood block at me, my attacker dressed as a man."

"And the shadow I chased through the woods was a male.

A woman would not move so," Hill added.

Miss Purefoy's nose rose in indignation.

"First, Mr. Hill, although I would agree most women would not take to running about dressed in men's clothing, you must agree the possibility exists."

"Certainly, my dear," Aidan said as he sat forward to listen more carefully to the point Miss Purefoy made. "But could you enlighten us as to why you believe the kidnapper could be a woman?"

"The boy, my lord," she said confidently. "Master Aaron called out for his mother. He said 'Mama' over and over again. It is a word we heard the child use previously, but never in reference to a man."

Chapter 11

AIDAN AND LUCIFER sat up long after Aidan insisted Miss Purefoy find her bed. He instructed Mr. Payne to permit everyone extra sleep in the morning after such a trying night. Deland reported no signs of the intruder. The lack of any tangible details frustrated Aidan, but he kept his concerns private. Was there a connection between his three sightings of "Susan" and the taking of his nephew?

"The question is whether these sightings are related to my return to Lexington Arms?"

Aidan could not seem to shake the idea his memory loss played into the strange happenings.

"Do you ever sleep?" Hill said groggily as he entered the morning room.

Aidan could not recall when he last slept a full night, and the lack of memory had nothing to do with his head injury.

"A few hours." He gestured Hill to join him at the table. "I am wondering if Realm recruits are enough reinforcements for the house," he said privately.

"I will ride into the village and find a few willing souls to guard the grounds at night." Hill paused before asking, "Will you inform Rhodes of what occurred?"

Aidan scowled.

"I think not. Rhodes always considered me less than my father and my brother. My inability to protect my nephew would only prove the man correct."

"I never held any respect for an idiot," Hill said loyally. "And Jonathan Rhodes is the epitome of an idiot."

Aidan nodded his gratitude before excusing the waiting footman.

"Any word on Mr. Poley?"

"According to Mrs. Osborne, late in the evening, Poley complained of a toothache and took himself off to see Mr. Charles in the village. As far as the cook knows, your valet did not return last evening. The woman commented on the unusual circumstances, as your valet rarely leaves the estate."

"So do we know whether Poley actually saw Mr. Charles?" Aidan ventured.

The pitch of Hill's voice remained low.

"I mean to know the truth of the tale."

"And Mrs. Babcock?" Aidan did not discount Miss Purefoy's idea that the intruder could possibly be a woman.

Hill glanced about to assure himself of their privacy.

"The housekeeper contends she partook of laudanum to ease the pain of a stiff shoulder. Mrs. Osborne concurs such is Mrs. Babcock's habit."

"No wonder the woman is so lethargic at times," Aidan said caustically.

"There is very little of the housekeeper to admire," Hill declared.

Aidan placed his serviette on the table.

"See me later today." He stood to leave. "I must post a letter to the Home Office before Miss Purefoy awakes. I plan to spend my day with the lady and my nephew. I fear both suffered from their ordeal."

"And these are my quarters," he announced as he led Miss Purefoy and Miss Chadwick into his private chambers. Even though Aidan recognized Miss Purefoy's opinion before she spoke the words, he waited impatiently for the lady's assessment of his quarters' décor. After three days of carefully watching her well-crafted reactions to everyday household business, Aidan decided to distract Miss Purefoy with a new project. By his sister's words the woman loved to be of service; he would use that particular fact to assist her in conquering her fear of his house. What better way to overcome her hesitation than to make the lady familiar with each room?

"I am thankful you warned me of the color," Miss Purefoy said honestly. "Otherwise, I might make a terrible guffaw upon observing the inappropriateness of these furnishings for you."

Aidan squeezed her fingertips.

"I would never wish you a social indiscretion, my dear," he said teasingly.

"This will not do, my lord," she continued. "I cannot imagine you comfortable in such surroundings."

The lady's words rang true. Aidan never claimed this room as his own. Instead, he forced his father's cloak about his shoulders and pretended to be something he was not. He "was" the viscount, but he was "not" Arlen Kimbolt. His temperament, his tastes, and his opinions differed greatly from his father's. Aidan saw the world at its worst and its best, while the late viscount knew only the title and the estate.

Aidan graciously accepted the truth. With an easy smile, he said, "I will leave the choices in your most capable hands."

Miss Purefoy turned to her companion.

"We should sketch the furnishings."

Miss Chadwick nodded and removed a sheet of paper from the artist pouch she carried at her side. As the girl seated herself at a nearby table to make basic renderings of the room, Miss Purefoy strolled about Aidan's quarters to examine items more closely.

It was odd. He never permitted a woman entrance into his private quarters. When Aidan and Susan first married, he asked his wife to lie with him in this room, but his viscountess adamantly refused. That fact in itself added to the oddness, but what truly brought forth Aidan's awareness was how natural Miss Purefoy appeared. As if the room came alive when his sister entered. She gently caressed several items on the desk. Aidan swallowed hard. It was very intimate to permit her touch of his personal belongings.

"When you make your choices, I will ask Mr. Poley to move my things to another room while the workmen complete their tasks."

The words sounded breathy even to Aidan's ears, and Miss Purefoy glanced up suddenly, as if realizing the inappropriateness of her actions.

Without thinking of the consequences, Aidan gestured to his left. He simply knew he must maneuver Mary away from Miss Chadwick so they might be alone for a few minutes. Of late, Aidan only felt complete in the lady's presence, and the idea of leaving his father's legacy behind appealed to him.

"Would you care to see the dressing room?"

Miss Purefoy took a tentative step in the direction he indicated.

"I...I suppose I should be...should be aware of its arrangement."

The lady blushed, and Aidan realized she thought of his small clothes.

Taking her hand, he brought her to his side. Whispering in her ear, he said, "Mr. Poley is most efficient in his duties."

Miss Purefoy's color deepened, but she accepted his hand on the small of her back as they moved across the room. When he opened the door to the narrow dressing area, his finding Mr. Poley hard at work surprised Aidan. The valet appeared equally unawares, but the man managed a proper bow.

"Did you require my services, my lord?"

The valet avoided making eye contact with Miss Purefoy, a fact that irritated Aidan.

"No, Poley," Aidan said with a bit of suspicion.

Why would Poley be found at work at the precise moment Aidan chose to show his quarters to the lady? Did the man spy upon him?

"Miss Purefoy and I examine my chambers in anticipation of setting workmen to executing the changes I ordered."

The valet shot a glance in Miss Purefoy's direction before saying, "Of course, Sir."

"I pray your tooth pain eased, Mr. Poley." Aidan said perversely. The muscles of Aidan's jaw tightened.

The valet's expression showed confusion before the man schooled his emotions.

"Much better, my lord. Thank you for your consideration."

The man hid something, and Aidan did not like it.

"I feared you fared poorly as you did not return to the estate until the wee hours of the morning on the evening we experience the attempted kidnapping of my nephew," Aidan said cautiously. "I thought to send someone to search for you, but no one appeared to possess knowledge of your whereabouts. Later, I discovered your suffering forced you to seek Mr. Charles's assistance."

Aidan turned a sharp gaze upon the valet.

Mr. Poley shifted his weight uncomfortably.

"I did not intend to remain so long in the village, my lord, but Mr. Charles's special painkiller was more than I could tolerate I am ashamed to say, I was not fit to ride afterwards. I apologize, Sir, for my shortcomings. I did not realize you would require my services, Lord Lexford."

Aidan could not find the falsehoods in his man's story, but he meant to examine it more closely. He would send Hill into the village to speak to Mr. Charles. He pushed past the man.

"Although I must admit to tending to my own needs when I lived abroad," he prefaced his statement so the valet would know his standing in the Kimbolt household remained on shaky ground. "Your services were missed, Mr. Poley."

He caught Miss Purefoy's elbow.

"Come along, my dear."

Aidan gestured the lady through the adjoining door before he realized what he did. The drapes remained closed, but Aidan required no light to see the room. Even if the sunlight streamed through the dusty windows, he would still fill the cold dread, which lodged in his stomach.

"My mother's room," he whispered to the emptiness.

He entered the room only twice in the past eighteen years: once as a ten-year-old child grieving for his mother and a second time when he attempted to convince Susan to agree to change her residence from the west wing to the suite meant for the viscountess. They had a noisy row, which set the servants gossiping for several days. Six months later, Aidan buried any hopes of knowing Susan as his wife.

Miss Purefoy's soft hand slid into his.

"It is not necessary to change anything within, my lord," she said gently.

Aidan did not move. For a dozen elongated seconds, he did not breathe. Crippling anxiety held him immobile.

"I wish to see it in the light," he rasped.

"Certainly, my lord," the lady said with a comforting stroke of his arm.

Aidan remained in place as Miss Purefoy moved swiftly across the room to drag the drapes to the side and to admit the light. His gaze searched each corner for the ghosts he suspected lingered in the shadows.

"The former Lady Lexford...my mother...always welcomed her children in this room. If we were not in the nursery or the schoolroom, Aylene and I were in her presence, playing with toy soldiers or drawing pictures or sharing cakes and tea."

"Not Andrew?"

Aidan gave a slight shake of his head.

"No, Andrew was several years older than Aylene and I.

He was at university when my mother passed. While my sister and I played our childhood games, Andrew was learning of his responsibilities to the estate, practicing to be the viscount."

Miss Purefoy stated the obvious.

"Your brother would better join his siblings."

Aidan took a step closer to the bed.

"Spending time with my mother remains one of my most cherished childhood memories. I hoped to marry a woman who would agree such moments were important to a child's development. I even foolishly thought as their father I could show my children love also."

From quietly beside him, Miss Purefoy said, "It is a magical picture you create, my lord."

Aidan grimaced in a rueful manner. He was not certain when she returned to his side, but he brought her into a loose embrace.

"It was a foolish dream," he said bitterly, ashamed of his moment of vulnerability.

Miss Purefoy gave him a hard shake. Her gaze never wavered from his.

"I shall tolerate no disparagements, Lord Lexford. I speak for my sex when I say your dream is one any woman would embrace."

Despite his growing despair, the lady's loyalty brought a smile to Aidan's lips.

"Not every woman," he contended. "My wife shunned the possibility. In the few short months Susan lived after Aaron's birth, I recall but a half dozen times she showed tenderness toward my brother's child. Toward her child."

He heard the snit of disapproval Miss Purefoy attempted to hide, and Aidan found he desired the lady's endorsement.

"I cannot speak to Lady Susan's mental state for I know no one who experienced such incapacitating grief, but I would imagine the previous Lady Lexford's circumstances did not permit her a clear head."

Despite his heartache, Aidan agreed. With a determined smile, he turned Miss Purefoy where she might view the room.

"What should be changed in this one?" he said with feigned joviality.

A long pause followed. So long Aidan did not think she would answer.

"Actually, the colors are not as severe in this room as in yours," she said kindly. "I would keep the lilac, but add a leafy green and the purest white to brighten the room. Several of the pieces are too heavy and too dark for most contemporary tastes. Nevertheless, I think them quite interesting in their design. I would move them to one of the guest rooms. That wardrobe, for example, has a distinctive cut, and in a room with rose tones, the color would take on a mahogany shade."

Aidan studied the piece in question.

"I believe you correct, my dear. The chest belonged to my maternal grandmother. I suppose my mother held onto it in remembrance. It would please me to see it showed to its best advantage."

Miss Purefoy leaned against him, her back plastered along his front. Aidan rested his chin on her head and his hands on her upper arms.

"Thank you," he whispered, "for permitting my dream to live. For permitting me to hope again."

The work began in earnest before the week was out. Miss Chadwick's sketches and Miss Purefoy's detailed lists had men scurrying to meet both ladies' wishes. Aidan enjoyed the activity. It made his house appear alive. Between Mr. Hill, who volunteered to oversee the workers, and Mr. Chadwick, who meant to see his daughter's vision successful, additional men were hired to complete the work with record speed. Aidan moved into a room across from his quarters so he might keep his eye on the progress.

"A new beginning," he told himself repeatedly.

"What have we here?" he asked as he casually strolled into

his bedchamber. It was the second week of the transformation, and he looked upon the busy workers with anticipation.

Hill glanced up from where he studied Miss Chadwick's drawings.

"These women possess great vision," Lucifer said jovially.

"Too great?" Aidan asked in curiosity.

He observed his friend with suspicion.

Hill laughed easily.

"Certainly not, my lord. This mausoleum required a change since long before the former viscount passed." He gestured to the sketches. "Look at how the ladies incorporated the morning light to keep the room warm in the winter. I swear sometimes I think God created women to see the truth of a man's soul."

Aidan examined the drawings.

"Miss Chadwick certainly holds a talent for such work," he mused aloud.

Aidan would be pleased to recommend the lady to others.

"What is this?" he pointed to a side view of the room.

"Miss Purefoy suggested a natural wood frame along this wall." Lucifer gestured to the wall opposite the hearth. "The men will remove the faded paper before painting this section a milk swirled green. Then a panel made from this hardwood will be added."

Hill handed Aidan a sample sliver of the wood.

"The panel will be cut to interlock tightly, but it will only cover the lower third of the wall. A thinner molding will lock the sections in place."

Aidan studied the cut of the wood. His expression lightened.

"I like the concept. Too much of this wood would overpower the room, but against a paler tone it would accent the color."

Aidan admitted he would never think such a combination attractive, but the idea certainly appealed to him when he saw the wood and the paint streak on a scrap of paper together.

"The maids finished the drapes. By this time next week, you will have new quarters, my lord."

Aidan's smile widened.

"Who would think a woman could change my life so completely?"

※

Mercy could hear the distinct timbre of His Lordship's voice, but she did not seek out the man. Instead, she accepted the task of separating his mother's clothing into items to be donated to the poor and those to be placed in storage. She layered cotton paper to wrap the pieces to be kept in a chest in the drying room.

"Do you suppose Lord Lexford would object to my claiming several pieces? I would use them as style examples from the past."

Miss Chadwick folded the items to be sent to the church for the poor.

"I am certain His Lordship would consider a donation an honor, Serena," Mercy said graciously.

Their relationship progressed nicely, and although Mercy did not hold much in common with Miss Chadwick, she appreciated the girl's loyalty and the way the shopkeeper's daughter took on each challenge with equal enthusiasm. Miss Chadwick would prove a worthy competitor for future business opponents.

"I shall take these below so Mrs. Babcock may see to their preparation for Mrs. Roberts's committee."

"I have but one more drawer to empty. I shall meet you in my quarters after you dress for supper."

Mercy folded a silken undergarment. Her fingers traced the delicate lines and soft detailing. Neither she nor Grace could afford such luxury. Even when their father was alive, they did not know expensive pieces of clothing. Baron Thomas Nelson was a very practical man. Mercy may favor her mother in appearance, but she was definitely her father's daughter in personality. With resignation, she continued her task.

Arms full of day dresses and outerwear, Miss Chadwick paused at the door.

"Might we spend time with the harp before the evening meal?"

Mercy showed Miss Chadwick the basics of the instrument, and the girl mastered the delicate, but commanding, touch required in record pace. Mercy thought it all part of Miss Chadwick's disposition. Serena possessed the heart and soul of an artist.

Mercy nodded her agreement.

"I shall speed my task."

When Miss Chadwick departed, Mercy took a private moment to examine the room. It possessed an alcove with a window seat, which overlooked the rose garden. During the summer, the scent of roses would fill the room. A deep sigh escaped her lips.

"Not for you," she said sadly before turning to the remaining drawer.

When Mercy finished a few minutes later, she made one last turn about the room. It was important to remove all the items. She would not have any of the former Lady Lexford's beautiful pieces soiled by the workmen. It would destroy His Lordship to observe his mother's belongings being treated with anything but the up most reverence. Moreover, she felt a special allegiance to this room. It was where Aidan Kimbolt knew happiness. From the items to be kept, she would ask Lord Lexford to choose one or two, which held special memories. Mercy would find a means to display them as part of the room's décor.

"Nothing remaining in the drawers," she said to the empty room as she closed the last one in the chest.

Her eyes scanned the room.

"Such a lovely suite. What could keep Lady Susan from this room? Even empty, it is the most welcoming place in the manor."

Taking note of the desk, which Serena emptied, Mercy made to take a final look before returning to her quarters to dress for supper.

Crossing to the small escritoire, Mercy opened and closed each compartment. When she closed the bottom drawer, a thud had her searching again. Nothing appeared within, but she knelt before the opening.

"And what have we here?" she asked as she extracted a

leather bound volume from the space. A wooden sleeve attached to the bottom of the drawer above hid the book. Taking it to the window seat, Mercy thumbed through the pages.

"Lady Cassandra's journal," she murmured in serious contemplation. "Should I share this with Lord Lexford?"

Mercy read a short passage, which spoke of a disagreement Lady Cassandra had with the late viscount.

"Perhaps I should peruse the passages before I share them. If there is anything within which would negatively color His Lordship's memories of his mother, then it is best if this volume stays hidden. The man experienced enough pain, and only the fond memories of his mother remain as part of his dream of a future."

Mercy tucked the journal between several sheets of paper before slipping from the room. In the hall, she glanced toward where His Lordship's voice could be heard in conversation with Mr. Hill. To the passage's stillness, Mercy vowed, "I mean to protect you, Aidan."

Unable to avoid the temptation Lady Cassandra's journal offered, Mercy excused herself early to return to her quarters. When His Lordship announced his intentions to accept Squire Holton's invitation to play cards, Mercy seized the opportunity to feign a headache.

Excusing the maid, Lord Lexford insisted Mercy permit, she quickly undressed and crawled into bed. Mercy carefully opened the book to the first page.

"Lady Cassandra's sixteenth birthday," Mercy said wistfully.

Geoffrey's drunken friends marred Mercy's sixteenth birthday. They pounded upon her chamber door, offering vile suggestions. The next morning, the staff informed her that the first of the silver plates from her grandmother's service went missing. Geoffrey's response to the discovery was to discharge the housekeeper.

Mercy read the entry with interest. Lady Cassandra Morrison was the daughter of the Earl of Hartwood, and her sixteenth birthday was the first night of the girl's acquaintance with Lord Arlen Kimbolt. Seven years her senior, the former Viscount Lexford had just come into his title shortly before he presented himself to Lady Cassandra as a potential suitor. Needless to say, the viscount's attentions thrilled Lady Cassandra.

Imagining the exuberance of a young girl straight from the schoolroom, Mercy fingers gently traced the words on the page. If Andrew greatly favored his father, Mercy knew something of the young viscount who set his sights on the daughter of an earl. Mercy saw renderings of Lady Cassandra in her late twenties, but the emptiness found in the lady's eyes in the drawings did not match either His Lordship's memories or the words of happiness found on the journal's page. Mercy wondered what happened to bring about the change.

Encouraged by Lady Cassandra's spirit, Mercy continued reading of the early days of Kimbolt's courtship. Evidently, Lady Cassandra reserved this particular journal to record her interactions with Viscount Lexford, and Mercy imagined how the earl's daughter hid it away from family and servants. It was full of young girl thoughts of marriage and duty to husband.

Apparently, Arlen Kimbolt was singular in his pursuit. He presented Lady Cassandra with flowers and small trinkets, which the girl faithfully kept as proof of the viscount's affection. When she had her Come Out, Kimbolt followed the girl to London to make his intentions known before all of the *haut ton*.

Mercy thought the viscount's actions a bit peculiar. Most men waited until the age of thirty to marry, but the previous Lord Lexford made his choice in his early twenties. Perhaps it was because he came into his title so early on, only two years after reaching his majority.

There were months during their long engagement in which Lady Cassandra did not see Viscount Lexford, but from her words, she appeared quite content with the idea of marrying

Arlen Kimbolt.

At the end of her second Season, the lady wrote, "Arlen officially spoke to Papa, and I expect him to make his addresses to me tomorrow. Papa wished for me to be more than a viscountess, but I am content. I hold the viscount with tender regard, and I expect to find happiness in Cheshire. Mama says a late summer wedding would provide the family time to arrive in Yorkshire."

Despite Mercy's best efforts, she sighed with contentment. Lady Cassandra's words spoke of the dream of every woman of finding fulfillment in marriage. Mercy could not help but wonder if she would ever know a husband and a family. As often as she told herself she would not wish for more than what she found at Lexington Arms, Mercy could never quite abandon her own schoolgirl dreams, ones very much like those of Lady Cassandra Morrison.

Mercy turned the page in anticipation of reading more of the woman's bliss. Instead, these words greeted her: "I am a fool. I thought Arlen affected me, but I quickly came to discover my husband knows nothing of respect and regard. He only thinks of himself.

"He brought me to this house, a place greatly in need of repair and of the generosity of my dowry, and he left me to manage a reluctant staff while he tends to his mistress. After our wedding night, Arlen spoke harshly to me of how poorly prepared I was to please a man of his tastes. What did he expect? An earl's daughter is not a common tart. What shall I do? I cannot return to York. As my husband has so kindly informed me, I am his property, and he can do with me as he chooses. I must learn to call Lexington Arms my home, but I shall never love one thing within its walls."

Tears streamed down Mercy's cheeks. "Perhaps the simple life I have under the current Lord Lexford's roof is for the best."

Yet, she knew it could not always be the way it was now. Some day Lord Lexford would choose a wife, and another woman would not tolerate the position Mercy currently garnered in Aidan Kimbolt's life.

"I must leave soon," she decided. "When the weather turns toward spring, I must return to the road. I am already too attached to the viscount."

After reading several more of Viscountess Lexford's passages, Mercy thought to burn Lady Cassandra's testimony to a life of despair. She certainly could never permit Lord Lexford to read of his mother's misery. It was painfully plain Aidan Kimbolt adored Lady Cassandra's role in his life. It would tear at the man's heart to realize how poorly his father treated the viscountess.

Sadly, even as her heart told her no good would come of reading more of Lady Cassandra's wretchedness, a part of Mercy felt compelled to learn details of the viscountess's story. Needless to say, the lady found a means to survive in a loveless marriage, and from Lord Lexford's accounts, his mother discovered love beneath Lexington Arms' roof: Lady Cassandra born the late viscount three healthy children.

"Surely, they resolved their differences."

Mercy cried herself to sleep long after she closed the pages of Lady Cassandra's diary. She cried for a woman she never met, but one she admired over the hours after midnight. She also cried for a weak man who destroyed what could be a most satisfying love. And, finally, Mercy cried for Aidan Kimbolt for she knew what the diary held would crush His Lordship's hopes for a happy marriage.

A light tap on the door drew her attention from the dresser where she sat, ineptly placing her hair in a loose twist.

"Come," she called lacklusterly.

The door opened to reveal the man over whom she spent her sleepless hours.

"Miss Chadwick informs me you are still out of sorts this morning," Lord Lexford said with true concern. "Should I send for Mr. Jamison?"

Mercy shot a quick glance to where she hid Lady Cassandra's diary.

"Thank you, my lord. I suspect a full night's sleep will cure what ails me."

A profound sadness crept into her heart.

He stepped farther into the room.

"I will not have you work yourself into a sick bed. I insist you leave the oversight of my mother's quarters to Miss Chadwick and Mr. Hill."

He came to stand behind her, and Mercy watched him through the mirror's reflection. Aidan Kimbolt was an exceptionally kind man, and the woman who eventually won his heart would be fortunate indeed. The thought made Mercy all more aware of her responsibility in assisting the viscount to keep his heart in tact. Learning his mother's secrets would wound him forever.

Resting his hands upon her shoulders, the viscount said, "While Miss Chadwick and Hill see to their duties, I plan to assume charge of your care. I will have your maid bring you a light breakfast, and I will ask Mrs. Osborne to prepare a draught to assist you to rest properly."

His Lordship lifted her to her feet, and Mercy readily accepted the comfort of the viscount's embrace.

"I must put aside my selfish need to have you at my table," he whispered close to Mercy's ear. "To permit you time to heal properly."

Lord Lexford caressed her cheek, and Mercy fought the tears pricking her eyes.

The viscount studied her countenance carefully, and Mercy realized her expression spoke the words she purposely stifled.

"Is there something other than a headache, which troubles you? I never witnessed you so distraught. Did someone treat you unkindly?"

Despite her best efforts, the tears escaped. "Everyone at Lexington Arms treats me well, my lord. I found family here," she said through trembling lips.

"You are family." He brushed loose curls from Mercy's cheeks. "This house knows life because of you."

Sorrow tugged at Mercy's heart. She must never speak the truth of what she discovered to this man.

"You are the best Lexford this estate ever knew." *Far superior to your father,* Mercy thought. "Promise me you shall mark my praise as your personal motto, my lord."

She peered deep into His Lordship's expressive eyes.

Confusion crossed the viscount's countenance.

"I would promise you anything, Mary Purefoy."

"Then heed my words: You must not permit anyone to prevent your happiness. You are the finest man I ever encountered, and I would see you fulfilled."

Their eyes met and held. His Lordship leaned forward slowly as if to kiss her. Mercy's breath shallowed, but she stepped from his embrace. She could not permit herself to become more attached to this man. She pretended to return to her ablutions.

The viscount cleared his throat.

"I am to meet with a gentleman regarding Master Aaron's future, but I will not be long from the estate. If you require anything beyond your maid's duties, please send for Mr. Hill."

Mercy returned to her dressing table.

"I shall rest, my lord. Thank you for your concern."

He bent to kiss the top of Mercy's head, and she wished desperately to lift her chin and accept the viscount's tenderness.

"As you wish, my dear."

With that, he left her alone, and Mercy grieved for what might be.

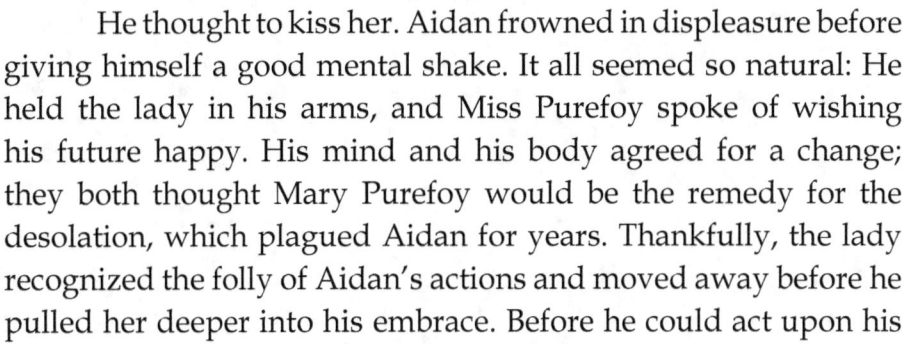

He thought to kiss her. Aidan frowned in displeasure before giving himself a good mental shake. It all seemed so natural: He held the lady in his arms, and Miss Purefoy spoke of wishing his future happy. His mind and his body agreed for a change; they both thought Mary Purefoy would be the remedy for the desolation, which plagued Aidan for years. Thankfully, the lady recognized the folly of Aidan's actions and moved away before he pulled her deeper into his embrace. Before he could act upon his complete desire for the woman.

"An absolute fool," he chastised as he reined in the horse before the solicitor's home. "You lost your previous good sense."

Mr. Taylor agreed to locate a man of the law who could protect Aidan's rights with his nephew. Aidan also wished more information on what illness consumed Susan's mother. From the servants' gossip line, Aidan discovered several examples of peculiar behavior since Susan's passing. Earlier he confided in Hill, "If necessary, I will use Sophia Rhodes's illness to keep Susan's parents at arm's length. I will not permit my wife's parents to ruin their grandson's life in the manner in which they destroyed the child's mother. Despite my initial qualms, Aaron is a Kimbolt."

Chapter 12

"YOU WISHED TO SPEAK TO ME?" Mr. Hill asked.

He arrived within moments of Mercy's sending for him. She suspected he anticipated her message. After Lord Lexford's departure, Mercy took her tea in her sitting room before sending for the viscount's man.

"Please come in, Mr. Hill. I have something of import of which I require your discretion."

A raised eyebrow and a twitch of his lips said she piqued his interest.

"Should I close the door?" He tilted his head to one side, studying her.

"By all means."

It was her turn to study him. Mercy gestured to a nearby chair. When he settled, she took a deep steadying breath before beginning. In the hours following her reading of the diary, Mercy decided to seek Mr. Hill's advice on how best to be rid of the former viscountess's words.

"In our renovations of the Lady Cassandra's suite, I stumbled upon the viscountess's personal diary."

Hill sat forward. He eyed her squarely.

"I assume you did not share Lady Cassandra's writings

with Lord Lexford?"

A completely outlandish flush of color rested upon Mercy's cheeks.

"I made the decision to read the viscountess's diary before I turned it over to His Lordship. Viscount Lexford suffered from his memory loss, and I feared something within might affect Lord Lexford's recovery."

Hill rested his forearms on his thighs.

"And why would you think anything within his mother's diary would damage Lord Lexford's state of mind?"

Wondering how much to disclose, Mercy bit her bottom lip in hesitation.

"His Lordship shared several idyllic scenes from his childhood. Lord Lexford's memories are so fragile I feared exposing the viscount to shadows from his past. No marriage is perfect, and I was certain after perusing a few of the passages that some of the information within could cloud the viscount's understanding of what happened behind closed doors."

"Did Lord Lexford say anything to lead you to believe things were not what he purports them to be?" Hill asked in concern.

Mercy shook her head in the negative. She wondered why she ever agreed to betray such a handsomely disturbing gentleman. Lord Lexford placed Mercy's already chaotic world in more turmoil; yet, she would never regret her time with the man.

"Call it female intuition. The current Lord Lexford does not hide his emotions well. If His Lordship was aware of what I discovered, the news would torment him."

Mr. Hill kept his expression purposely bland.

"For a man trained in complicated charades by the best in the British government, when it comes to his own affairs, Lord Lexford wears his thoughts upon his sleeve."

Mercy wondered if Mr. Hill could see what was happening between her and the viscount, or rather what she hoped deep in her heart was happening.

"I meant only to read a few of the entries–to determine

whether to share the book with His Lordship," she explained.

Mr. Hill stated the obvious, "But you read more than a few."

Mercy closed her eyes and heaved a heavy sigh.

"The whole book," she confessed.

Hill scowled.

"Is what you discovered within the pages so dire as to have you pretend a sickness you do not possess? Lord Lexford sincerely worries on your behalf."

Tears formed in Mercy's eyes. She despised herself for yet another deception directed toward the viscount.

"The entries are truly dreadful," she said vehemently.

Mercy retrieved the book from where she hid it among the pillows.

"You must read some of the entries for yourself to determine if I speak the truth."

She placed the book in Mr. Hill's outstretched hands.

"I marked the most important ones. The early entries speak of the late viscount's lengthy courtship of the former Lady Cassandra Morrison."

Mercy moved to stand over him. Mr. Hill opened the book to the entry, which initially set her tears flowing.

"Read this one first."

She pointed to a passage and stepped away.

When he finished, Hill said, "It is not uncommon among the aristocracy for a man's mistress to know more of the gentleman than does his wife. The current Lord Lexford would not approve of his father's actions, but this information would not be devastating. Moreover, His Lordship believes your birth resulted from such a relationship."

Mercy paced the small space from the door to the settee.

"Keep reading, Mr. Hill," she insisted.

Hill flipped to the next page Mercy marked with strips of foolscap torn into small squares. As he read, Mercy's pace increased. She wrung her hands in anxiety. At length, she sat awkwardly on the edge of the settee and examined Mr. Hill's countenance as the man skimmed one entry after another. His expression spoke of the horror Mercy knew the previous evening.

"That bastard," Mr. Hill growled, and Mercy made no effort to chastise Hill's remark. His words spoke to the indignation she experienced on the viscount's behalf. "Of all the twisted schemes," he said incredulously.

"Do you now understand why we must never share these passages with Lord Lexford?" Mercy asked anxiously.

Mr. Hill frowned deeply.

"Lord Lexford has a right to know what occurred."

Mercy pressed, "How shall such knowledge alter the viscount's life for the good? There is nothing but more pain within these pages."

Mr. Hill flipped through the book.

"Where do the entries end?"

"Shortly after Lady Aylene became ill. Lady Cassandra does not write daily. It is as if the viscountess saved this book to record her greatest happiness and her deepest despair."

Mercy leaned into the cushions.

"I ask your assistance in ridding this house of Lady Cassandra's diary."

Hill's lips thinned into a tight line.

"I am not certain we possess the right to make that decision."

"Yet, we must," Mercy insisted. "I shall not permit Lord Lexford to know additional pain."

Although Mr. Hill promised he would see to disposing of Lady Cassandra's diary, Mercy still spent countless nights lying awake considering Lord Lexford's reaction if he discovered the truth. She looked upon certain members of the household with dismay. Her knowledge of the perfidy practiced by the late viscount's most trusted members of his staff troubled her. The only peace she knew during those troubling weeks was the look of contentment upon His Lordship's countenance. Lord Lexford took well to the changes she made in his home, and that particular fact gave Mercy some solace.

"The family wing possesses an air of freshness," Lord Lexford said as he seated her for supper. "I am most pleased."

"Are you truly, my lord?"

Mercy considered the changes perfect. Each room knew fresh paint and new fixtures. She kept the maids busy with sewing new draperies and coverings for the chairs. Assuming she was still at Lexington Arms in the spring, she would set the staff to beating the Persian rugs.

The viscount smiled easily at her.

"I am so pleased, I mean to host a small house party to permit my friends to observe my good fortune at possessing a talented sister. Moreover, such a party will provide Miss Chadwick an introduction to Society families who will sing her praises. It is what we promised the lady in payment for her companionship and her expertise with both the boy and with the renovations."

Mercy's heart plummeted.

"When...when would you place the date, my lord?"

She would leave before his friends arrived. It was one thing to foist a deception upon the viscount, but quite another to do so upon Lord Lexford's dearest friends. She would not embarrass the man by appearing at his side and pretending a familial relationship. Mercy would not play him a fool before those he counted as his intimates. Despite her qualms over the role she played in Mr. Hill's ruse, Mercy considered herself as an essential part of His Lordship's recovery. What she accepted from Lord Lexford, Mercy repaid in her devotion to his household.

"How long will it take to finish the guest rooms?" he asked casually.

Mercy swallowed her sorrow. She would name the date of her self-imposed expulsion from Lord Lexford's life.

"I cannot imagine the task could be accomplished...could be accomplished in less than six weeks," she said in true distress.

His Lordship appeared deep in thought and did not notice

her misery.

"Six weeks. Then the first week of April. A pleasant time to travel."

Mercy forced herself to ask, "How many guests would you ask to Lexington Arms?"

She thought, *Please make it a large number. I cannot bear the thought of leaving you.* The more rooms to finish the longer Mercy could delay her departure.

"I originally thought of only sharing the changes in the house with those I served on the Continent, but I hold no objection in your adding names to the guest list."

Mercy's heart raced.

"Oh, no, my lord. I possess no one beyond these walls."

His Lordship's frown lines met.

"We should take in part of the Season. You should develop your own acquaintances."

Lord Lexford's kindness brought tears to her eyes. The viscount meant to treat her as his family.

"When the spring comes, you should enjoy Society, my lord, but as for me, I am content to remain behind with Master Aaron."

Before he could insist she accompany him to London, Mercy redirected the conversation.

"Tell me who to expect."

His Lordship's smile widened.

"Lord and Lady Worthing. Her Ladyship should be free to travel by April. I heard from the viscount, and they welcomed their daughter Amelia to Linton Park."

"The nursery will host another resident. Aaron will be excited," Mercy observed.

"I did not consider the nursery as part of the house's renovation, but it the first room which knew your touch, is it not?" Lord Lexford said with good-natured enthusiasm. "I never hosted a party where children must be accounted for." His Lordship's smile grew. "I believe I like the idea."

He sipped his wine.

"I will be pleased to share the changes more suited for a child with the Kerringtons. They will hold a real appreciation of what you and Miss Chadwick accomplished."

"Who else, my lord?"

Mercy made mental notes of how many rooms and something of each guest. She would see His Lordship's house immaculate. The task would be her personal "farewell" to the man.

"I am uncertain of the Duke and Duchess of Thornhill. The Duchess should be six or seven months with child by then."

He ticked off the others on his fingers.

"The Earl and Countess of Berwick, Baron Swenton, and Sir Carter Lowery. I suppose I should also consider Sir Carter's brother Lord Hellsman and his new bride."

Mercy would love to hold the acquaintance of the people who meant so much to His Lordship, but she was certain the Countess of Berwick would recognize her and spoil Mercy's pretense.

"With the opportunity to view his lady love again, Mr. Hill should be beside himself with anticipation," she said softly. "But what of the marquis?"

Lord Lexford frowned.

"Naturally, I will extend an invitation to Lord Godown, but the last message from Viscount Worthing confirmed what we all expected: The marquis's rushed wedding to a woman he suspected of practicing a deception proved the lady's true colors. Lord Godown banished his bride to one of his minor estates."

"Is there no room for a reconciliation?" Mercy asked in concern.

Men of Lord Lexford's ilk, evidently, were unforgiving. She did not understand how any man could drive his wife from his home. Surely, the marquis did not know the full circumstances. Despite what many believed, artifice was not a ploy most women practice.

Lord Lexford spoke in disdain.

"The marquis knew several attacks of late, and all evidence points to Lady Godown's involvement."

Mercy never heard the viscount speak with such bitterness. Did Lexford's miserable marriage cloud His Lordship's view of how best to embrace the difficulties of marriage? Mercy witnessed her parents' sometimes-loud rows, but she was certain Thomas and Louisa Nelson adored each other.

"Then why did Lord Godown marry the woman if he suspected her of deviousness?"

His Lordship's mouth thinned to a wry smile.

"The marquis thought to hide his heart, but Lord Godown affects his wife. We can never know when love will present itself. Unfortunately, love can often cripple a man."

Mercy's heart clenched tightly in her chest. She held silly schoolgirl dreams of Lord Lexford's forgiving her deception, and even perhaps falling a bit in love with her; but his words of finding love did not match his dreams of family contentment. Which did he truly believe? If given the opportunity, she would remain by His Lordship's side forever.

"I shall add the marquis and Lady Godown to my prayers. Perhaps God shall find a means to their happiness."

It happened when he least expected. Weeks passed since Aidan's last sighting of Susan's "ghost," so long, in fact, he began to believe the apparition was but a fragment of the fear he experienced upon his return to Lexington Arms. If not for the shot, which wounded Miss Purefoy and the attempted kidnapping of his nephew, Aidan would pronounce the ghostly visions a remnant of his recent injury: His mind playing tricks upon his conscious thoughts.

For the second time in a month, he spent a pleasant evening playing cards at Squire Holton's modest home, but he was well aware of the lateness of the hour. Since the war's end, the number of poor who took to the road as amateur highwaymen increased significantly, and Aidan remained on alert.

He was on his property, but still some distance from the main house when he heard a snap of a twig off to his right. Instantly, Aidan's senses intensified. He slowed the horse to a halt and gently patted Vali's neck to keep him calm. Aidan's eyes searched the darkness for any movement.

Then he saw it: A flip of white moving swiftly away. For a brief second, he thought it might be a deer, but the figure caught in hesitation in a shaft of moonlight. It was definitely a female in a dark gown and cloak. The white perhaps a petticoat.

Aidan slid off the horse to give pursuit. The woods were too thick to follow on the stallion, especially in the dark. Retrieving a gun from an inside holster, he trailed the woman further into the woodlands.

Crouching low, he used the filtered moonlight to search for any signs of the way the figure went. At length, he came across a distinct boot print in the soft earth. Whoever he followed turned toward the stream, which fed the River Goyt. It was the same stream by which Miss Purefoy was recently injured, and that particular fact kept Aidan cautious. If his quarry was not a female, he might think poachers plagued his property in his absence. Aidan increased his pace. His years with the Realm taught him to track his enemy in the worst of conditions.

Even so, his training presented him a false sense of superiority. Like many men, Aidan considered females the weaker sex. Therefore, he did not expect the assault when it came.

He followed the few markings to an outcropping. A slight incline rose to a rocky ledge. Cautiously, he climbed the hillside, taking time to place each of his steps so as not to dislodge the stones and signal his approach. If he were fortunate, Aidan would corner the intruder upon the upper point with no means of escape.

Silently, he crept over the rocky edge to stand upon the flat surface. Aidan scanned the area: Nothing. He somehow underestimated his opponent. He made an uncharacteristic error. The footprints led him to this particular spot. Aidan would stake his reputation as one of His Majesty's agents on his ability to trail any unknown intruder. Yet, despite his confidence, he frowned when he stared hard into the empty space.

"Bloody hell," he growled under his breath.

This was not a wise choice, a voice in his head advised.

In frustration, Aidan briskly searched the confined area. He knelt on all fours and leaned over the flat surface to observe the area beneath the outcropping. There was no way down on the other side for the ledge dropped off to the water below. Nothing moved. He stood to walk about the ledge, instinctively looking for any clue to the mystery, which trailed him to Cheshire.

Shadows stretched across the valley, which formed his pastureland, Aidan felt the frustration wan, and his fear rose quickly in his chest. The air teemed with pungent odor of dread. Silence drifted upon a heavy breeze. Aidan jammed his fingers into his disheveled hair. Attempting to settle his breathing, he closed his eyes to calm the tension knotting his shoulders. He turned his head to listen to the sound of the falling water. Somewhere below him, the thin line of dampness worked its way toward the stream. The rain from earlier in the day gave the water more force, creating a small waterfall.

Opening his eyes, he replaced the gun in its hidden pouch, but before Aidan could return to his horse, he found himself struggling to keep his balance. Every pore in his body spoke of awareness, but the warning came too late. His boots could find no purchase on the broken rock face. Someone struck him from behind. Not like before with Lachlan Charters. Not enough to injure him, but hard enough to send him tumbling head first toward the water below.

Aidan kicked out in hopes of finding a deeper point in the water. Luckily, the ascent was not high, but neither was the stream known for its depth. Aidan was facing another serious injury or even death if he did not time his descent perfectly. He barely had time to make the necessary adjustments. Fortunately, his previous injury did not dull Aidan's instincts, nor did it color the childhood memory of jumping from the rock face on a summer day.

The water was a cold knife cutting through his senses, and Aidan's reflexes curled his body into a tight ball before he struck the rocky bottom. Intuitively, he kicked against the rough underbelly to propel himself to the surface. Alas, the tight cut of his jacket and the weight of his boots worked against Aidan's success, but he managed to break the water's surface and gulp in the chilly night air.

He treaded awkwardly as his boots filled with water. Aidan turned his body to the side and attempted a life-saving stroke. Reaching the shore was tantamount. Otherwise, the frigid water would rob him of his life's breath.

In a little over a minute, Aidan crawled upon the shallow bank. With a significant effort, he pulled his weight to drier land. At length, he collapsed upon the grassy bank. Gulping for air, he rolled to his side.

It was cold, and he was soaked through; and Aidan knew he could not rest long, but he made no effort to recover further. He simply turned upon his back to stare up at the stars, the same ones he looked upon in Persia and said his prayers for direction in his life.

"Why did you bring me here?" he asked the stillness. Through trembling lips, he confessed, "I do not understand what it is you expect of me."

Turning his head to the right, Aidan's eyes returned to the outcropping. His wife looked down upon him. Aidan could not see her countenance because her hood cloaked it in shadow, but, nevertheless, he knew it was she.

"If you are alive," he shouted as he shoved himself to his elbows, "I expect you to return to Lexington Arms. To me and to your son."

He sat upright, but Aidan's eyes remained on the stationary figure staring out over the water below.

Susan did not speak, but a shake of her head in the negative denied Aidan's demand. She turned toward the back of the rocky ledge; yet, before she disappeared into the darkness, he heard her say, "Your home offers nothing but misery."

⟊⟊⟊

"You sent for me?" Mr. Hill appeared at the library door.

Whenever the viscount spent time away from the manor, Mercy developed the habit of waiting in the library for Lord Lexford's return. Then she would quickly scurry through the servants' entrance to hide in her quarters as if she did not acknowledge his absence. It was a foolish act, but she could not seem to control her desire to know of the man's safety.

"Yes."

She wrung her hands as she paced the open area before the hearth. Mercy would expose her vulnerability by permitting Mr. Hill to know of her obsession.

"I apologize for drawing you from your quarters, Mr. Hill."

The man smiled wryly.

"How may I be of service, Miss Purefoy?"

Mercy hesitated but an elongated second. What did her silly pride matter if there was a chance Lord Lexford knew harm? Moreover, she long ago abandoned any artifice in her dealings with Mr. Hill.

"His Lordship has not returned from the squire's card game."

She shot a quick glance at the mantel clock.

"It is more than an hour past the time Mrs. Holton would permit the squire his entertainment."

"And what do you wish of me? Lord Lexford holds no need of a nurse maid," Hill said without judgment.

Mercy ceased her pacing.

"I have no idea what should be done nor even if I dare express my alarm. Speak sense to me, Mr. Hill."

Hill entered the room and gestured to two chairs before the fire.

"Perhaps we should converse privately."

Mercy shot a glance toward the darkness beyond the

window. In frustration, she joined Mr. Hill.

"I have no right to worry over Lord Lexford's safety," she confessed.

"But you do so, nevertheless," Hill said evenly.

Mercy bit her bottom lip in indecision before sighing heavily.

"His Lordship is essential to my days."

"And you to his," Hill declared.

The man's words sent Mercy's heart skittering; yet, she was a practical person.

"I can be nothing more to Lord Lexford than a poor relation," Mercy tentatively expressed. "Yet, that knowledge does not keep me from considering the viscount's happiness above all others."

Hill leaned forward to rest his forearms along his thighs.

"Do you wish to be more than Lord Lexford's sister?" he asked earnestly.

Mercy closed her eyes to steady her emotions.

"Lord Lexford will never act the scandalous role of Lord Byron and his sister Augusta," Mercy rasped as tears pooled in her eyes' corners.

"However?" Mr. Hill encouraged.

"However, I would devote my life to His Lordship's comfort," she reluctantly admitted.

Hill smiled easily.

"Then perhaps we should devise a means to prove you a viable choice for the viscount."

"Do not be foolish, Mr. Hill," she chastised. "When Lord Lexford discovers our betrayal, His Lordship will drive me from his home. I shall never see the viscount again, and you shall likely require another position."

Hill chuckled.

"I imagine Lord Worthing could see me through."

He leaned back into the cushions.

"Leave the truth to me."

Mercy groaned; she dreaded the possibility of the viscount

learning of their ruse.

"In the time being, may we consider the lateness of the hour?"

Hill good-naturedly accepted her change of subject.

"Do you wish for me to search for Lord Lexford?"

Mercy jumped on the suggestion.

"Would you? I cannot sleep until I know His Lordship's return to the manor."

Hill grumbled as he donned his heavy jacket. Why he left his warm bed in the first place Lucifer would never know? Now, he was going out into a cold night to search for a man who would gladly remove Lucifer's head from his shoulders if he knew the lie Lucifer practiced.

"At least the girl admits her interest," he said with another deep smile.

Catching the door latch, Hill jerked it open to find the viscount leaning heavily against the frame.

"My lord!"

Lucifer reached for his friend and pulled Lexford into the muted warmth of the kitchen.

"You are soaked to the bone."

Lucifer could not imagine what occurred. He jerked off his coat and wrapped it about the viscount's shoulders. Directing Lexford to a straight-backed chair, he said, "Here. Sit."

The viscount's teeth chattered, and his lips assumed a bluish hue. Hill swung the pot upon the hook over the banked fire before adding several more logs and new kindling.

"We will have you warm in only a moment."

He glanced at the icy cast on the viscount's cheeks.

"What happened?" Hill asked curiously.

Yet before Lexford could respond, Miss Purefoy appeared on the servants' stairs.

"Mr. Hill, I mean to go…"

The lady froze in mid sentence.

"My God!"

Miss Purefoy rushed to Lord Lexford's side. Catching his hands between hers, she began to rub them briskly.

"Oh, my dearest," she said sweetly as Lucifer looked on. "We shall tend you, my lord."

∼❧∼

Aidan could barely recall finding his way to the manor. With the disappearance of the figure who knocked him from the rock shelf, he laid upon the muddy bank for a long time, analyzing each of the half dozen appearances of his "wife's ghost." From the beginning, Aidan assumed his guilt manifested itself into Susan's form, but now he thought otherwise. A ghost could not hit him with such a force as to send him toppling over the rock face.

So, if the "ghost" was not his imagination, then he possessed more troubles than he initially expected. Someone wished to kill him, and on this evening made a marked attempt. Forcing his weight to a seated position, Aidan stared in the direction where he last saw Susan's figure, but for once, it was not his wife's countenance, which materialized. Instead, he saw the lovely image of Mary Purefoy. The lady motioned him to come to her, and Aidan wanted what she offered: a feeling of belonging.

And so he stumbled and crawled along a path to where he left Valí. Mounting the horse, Aidan rode home in a shivering mix of soaked clothes and a needful heart. He kept the image of Miss Purefoy beckoning him before him, and when he finally reached the servants' entrance, after releasing Valí to find his way to his stall, Aidan half expected to discover the lady waiting for him.

When Mr. Hill opened the door, Aidan felt both the relief of surviving his ordeal and the disappointment of his dream. Without much enthusiasm, he permitted Hill to attend him. Oddly, his mind dwelt on the lady, and as if he willed her to him, Miss Purefoy appeared. Despite his misery, Aidan smiled.

"We shall tend you, my lord." The lady turned to Lucifer. "Mr. Hill, fetch His Lordship some brandy. I shall support him to his room."

Aidan wondered at the obvious look of amusement on Hill's countenance.

"Should you not fetch the brandy and permit me to tend the viscount?"

"Can you walk, my lord?" Miss Purefoy ignored Hill's suggestion.

Aidan was not certain his legs would cooperate, but if his effort meant wrapping himself about the woman, he would make the effort. Painfully, he nodded his agreement and reached out his hand to Lucifer for support. As bad luck would have it, his body expressed its objections to the idea, and he swayed in place.

"Easy," Miss Purefoy said as she rushed to brace him with her body. "I was so worried for you, my lord."

She fussed over him, tightening Lucifer's coat about him.

"I summoned Mr. Hill to search for you."

Then the image was not simply a dream: The lady's desire guided Aidan's return. The idea brought a zing of warmth to his heart. He glanced to his man, and Lucifer gestured the truth of the woman's words.

"Th...ank you," Aidan said through trembling lips.

He knew her to be extremely practical so the lady surprised him when she shooed Hill upon his way. As appealing as having the woman clinging to him seemed, Aidan realized he was no match for the stairs leading to his room. Nevertheless, the woman remained confident.

"Come, my lord," she said as she turned him toward the servants' stairs.

Aidan's feet felt as heavy as boulders, but he managed to shuffle his way toward the open door. Yet, when he reached the first step, his body balked at the necessity of climbing the stairs. With a sigh of defeat, he said, "I cannot...mount...the steps."

He leaned heavily against the door. The back of his head rested against the wood, and Aidan held his body in place by grasping the side of the door.

"Oh, my poor Aidan," Miss Purefoy said as she braced him

with her body.

Having the lady so close brought Aidan's senses to alert, and the sound of his name upon the lady's lips brought him a different type of warmth.

"You must know care, my lord. You are too precious to us."

Miss Purefoy caressed his cheek, and Aidan turned his head to rest it in the lady's palm. It was many months since his head knew such confusing thoughts, but this time he did not fear the unknown. When the lady rose on tiptoes to offer him her mouth, the thought of the cold, which held him captive for the last hour, dissipated immediately.

"My Aidan," Miss Purefoy whispered.

Her breath warmed Aidan's cheek before her lips pressed against his.

At that moment, he was *her* Aidan. The heat returned to his lungs, and Aidan reached for her. Mary Purefoy was the most remarkable woman he ever encountered, and his arms held her tightly in his embrace. His once chilled fingers pressed Miss Purefoy closer while his tongue swept the seam of her lips. Although tentative, the lady's kiss was as sweet as honey from the comb. Miss Purefoy's mouth opened enough for Aidan to slide his tongue inside; she gasped, but the lady clung to him, permitting Aidan to taste her completely. He wished for her surrender–finally to acknowledge his desire for her. *God!* He forgotten how sensual a kiss could be! He certainly did not kiss Cashémere Aldridge as such, and if he held Miss Satiné in a tight embrace, Aidan possessed no recollection of the moment. And sadly, Susan never permitted Aidan such liberties.

The lady teetered on the brink, and Aidan's heart rejoiced. He did not push her response. If the woman came to him, it would be Miss Purefoy's choice. He would not take advantage of an innocent. Instinctively, he felt the give of her body.

He thought he could continue kissing the lady forever–to feast on her until his hunger was sated, but the sound of a distant shuffling of feet brought Aidan to his senses. He quickly set Miss

Purefoy from him at the same instant Mrs. Osborne entered the kitchen.

"My lord?" The cook shot him a suspicious look. "Is something amiss?"

Aidan swallowed deeply to push away his desire.

"I had...had a riding...accident. Miss Purefoy and...Mr. Hill...are assisting me to my...to my chambers."

Aidan spoke to the cook, but his gaze remained on Miss Purefoy. Even in the dull light from the fireplace, he could see her lips swollen from his kiss. To his delight, the lady was having as much difficulty as he in recovering.

Mrs. Osborne said doubtfully, "Where be Mr. Hill?"

"Here, Ma'am."

Hill stepped into the room carrying the brandy decanter.

"I thought His Lordship might require something to warm his bones. Lord Lexford's horse spooked and provided His Lordship with an unscheduled dip into the river."

Aidan suspected Lucifer observed Aidan's embrace of Miss Purefoy. At a minimum, Mr. Hill overheard Aidan's explanation of a riding mishap for Hill added details Aidan did not disclose.

The cook's gaze softened.

"You'll catch yer death, my lord," she said as she rushed to set a second kettle upon the fire. "I'll have the tub for a hot bath brought up shortly. Kant be having ye takin' ill."

Aidan could easily read the lady's thoughts. Mrs. Osborne feared consumption might take him also, but she erred. The kiss he shared with Miss Purefoy meant Aidan possessed something for which to live, and live he meant to do.

"Perhaps Miss Purefoy could retrieve clean clothing from my quarters," he suggested.

He must maneuver Miss Purefoy away from the cook's observations. They would speak on what transpired between them, but the conversation would wait until a more convenient time.

"Mr. Hill is capable of assisting me here in the kitchen. God only knows we encountered worst conditions during our war years."

Everyone always gave sway when Aidan spoke of his service, and he would use that particular fact to his advantage.

"I see no reason to have the tub carried above stairs at this hour. That is if you hold no objections to my converting your kitchen into my dressing room."

The lady fussed with the fire.

"This be yer house, my lord. Ye be free to do what ye think best."

Aidan stepped past Miss Purefoy to block her from the cook's view. He slid his hand around hers. Desire shot up his arm, but he made himself gently squeeze her fingers in encouragement.

"I am pleased you agree, Mrs. Osborne," he said evenly. "Claiming Lexington Arms as distinctly my own is exactly what I intend to do."

Chapter 13

SHE KISSED HIM. Unconsciously, Mercy touched her fingers to where the warmth still remained on her lips.

"Like a common tart!" she moaned as Mercy climbed the last of the stairs leading to His Lordship's chambers.

Lord Lexford protected her by sending Mercy for his clothing. If she turned to face Mrs. Osborne, the cook would easily observed the look of bewilderment upon Mercy's countenance and the swelling of her lips from the pressure of the viscount's kiss.

"Why?" she groaned softly as she tapped upon Mr. Poley's door.

Hearing the bolt released, Mercy straightened her shoulders to meet Mr. Poley's usual disdain. She would never permit Lord Lexford to know the condemnation Mercy encountered daily from certain members of His Lordship's staff. She would not dwell long with Aidan Kimbolt, and there was no reason to set him against his servants purely for her to avoid a few moments of discomfort. She was the outsider, not they. Mercy would send the valet to retrieve the viscount's clothing. She certainly could not enter Lord Lexford's quarters without bringing more censure upon her head. Moreover, viewing His Lordship's bed and rifling through his clothing would engender thoughts no lady should possess.

The valet's door cracked but a few inches. The man held a candle aloft.

"Yes, Miss?" he said flatly.

"Your master had a riding accident."

Mercy doubted the pretext the viscount gave was the truth. She personally witnessed the expertise, with which Lord Lexford rode, and she knew his horse's temperament; however, the staff would accept whatever excuse Lord Lexford offered.

"He was thrown into the water and requires dry clothing."

Mr. Poley opened the door wider. He shot a quick glance across the hall toward his master's room.

"Is His Lordship waiting elsewhere? Why were you sent as Lord Lexford's courier? It is well past a lady's bedtime."

Mercy customarily would answer the man's question and be on her way, but the valet's impertinence enflamed the anxiety coursing through her.

"It is not of my station to explain myself to yours," she said aristocratically. "Be about your duties. Lord Lexford awaits your services in the kitchen."

"The kitchen?" the man called after her.

Yet, Mercy's nerves had all the turmoil she could handle for one day. She walked briskly away. She meant to find her bed and bury her head under a stack of pillows.

"Stupid. Stupid girl," she chastised herself as she entered the dark quarters.

Despite how easily Lord Lexford wormed his way into her heart, Mercy realized she did not deserve the viscount. A woman who spoke untruths could never own such happiness. She took a moment to stoke the fire before undressing. Mercy performed her nightly ritual without thinking on it.

"You played the fool," Mercy told her reflection as she set before the mirror to brush her hair.

Her misery only fortified the idea she must leave soon.

"All you did this night was to speed your departure. You

may no longer linger until the date of His Lordship's house party. Lord Lexford is too great a temptation."

⚬⚬⚬

"The person who attacked me was a living, breathing woman," Aidan told Lucifer. The appearance of his valet did not please Aidan, but he accepted the man's assistance with as much grace as he could muster. In truth, Miss Purefoy did the practical thing by sending Mr. Poley rather than to return to the kitchen, but that particular fact did not quench Aidan's desire to hold her again.

Lucifer sipped his brandy.

"Then your *ghost* cannot be Lady Lexford."

"No." Aidan paused. "I am not certain whether the idea pleases me. I am grateful my mind is not conjuring up specters to punish my guilt, but I do not look upon the situation with comfort. Someone attempted to kidnap Aaron, to kill Miss Purefoy, and to drown me. All this chaos started with my return to Lexington Arms."

Hill closed his eyes as if searching for the correct words.

"Did you consider the possibility of the person behind this design as being Jamot? I certainly would not put it past that crazy Baloch to devise some scheme to find Shaheed Mir's infamous emerald. I do not imagine Mir will welcome Jamot home until the Baloch completes his mission."

For an elongated moment, silence greeted the question while Aidan considered Hill's conjecture.

"Last I heard, Jamot was in Liverpool. Likely, with the number of ships coming and going from the port, he can hide more easily there than in other parts of England."

"Liverpool is not so far," Hill reasoned. "While you were in Cheshire someone broke in the manor. Rummaging through drawers and such. I believe the culprit to be Murhad Jamot."

Aidan frowned.

"Why did you not inform me of this development previously?"

Hill shrugged.

"I was not aware of the incident until I returned from Scotland. By then, you were recovering from your attack. Only thought of it again recently, after the attempt to steal the boy. I started asking question of those below stairs. Two of the grooms reported seeing a dark-skinned man running from the house. They gave chase through the woods, but did not catch the intruder."

"You think Jamot meant to trade Aaron for the emerald?"

Hill sat his glass on a side table.

"It would not be the first time the Baloch used kidnapping to learn more of the missing emerald. Miss Sonali. Miss Aldridge. Hell, at first, Lord Worthing considered Miss Satiné's abduction Jamot's doing. That is until Miss Cashémere recognized Charters' family name as to the coach's letting."

Aidan voiced other schemes in which Murhad Jamot was involved.

"The Baloch meant to intimidate Thornhill by wounding Lady Eleanor in Hyde Park, and he arranged that elaborate trap for Miss Cashémere and Miss Satiné in the glass cone."

Aidan's fingers tapped out a staccato upon the chair arm.

"Could Jamot hire a woman to impersonate my wife?"

Hill thought on the possibility.

"Jamot is a cagey opponent, my lord. He showed himself intelligent enough to learn the intimate details of each of the Realm members' lives. To exploit any weaknesses. As masters of grand estates, you and your associates are fodder for the local gossips. Servants and villagers alike speak freely of what they know of your lives. It was the means by which Jamot knew of Miss Aldridge's returning to Lord Averette's Scottish home and how, when he sought a place to hide Miss Sonali, Rahmat Talpur knew of Thornhill's Cornish home. Mir schools his agents well in discovering vulnerable points."

"I require more information on Jamot's most recent appearance in Liverpool," Aidan reasoned.

"Is not Sir Carter still in the port city, seeing to the

dismantling of the Chinese ship?"

Aidan stood.

"I will be away from the house for several days. Reportedly, Pennington rushed to the Dowager Duchess of Granville's side and left Sir Carter in charge. The baronet and Swenton take over the case."

"What of Lord Godown?"

"The marquis searches for his wife. Lady Godown saved the marquis's three aunts, but then disappeared into the night. Lord Godown belatedly discovered his wife's honesty; however, he was too late to salvage his marriage."

"I am sorry to hear it," Hill said earnestly. "The marquis knew enough sorrow. I pray for an early resolution to his troubles."

"I pray for the same for each of us."

Mercy heard the door open and close, but she did not open her eyes. Likely, Lord Lexford sent Mercy's maid Millie to check on her, especially after Mercy did not return to the kitchen last evening. If she kept her eyes closed, the girl would think her asleep and leave. As if Mercy could sleep with thoughts of dashing viscounts dancing through her mind.

Someone leaned over her, and so Mercy concentrated on keeping her breathing even and her eyes tightly closed.

"You are so beautiful," a decidedly masculine voice whispered, and Mercy's heart lurched to a halt.

How could she breath when the man who regularly stole the air from her lungs lingered above her? His warm hand stroked Mercy's shoulder before giving it a gentle shake.

"Mary," he coaxed. "Mary, wake up."

Mercy reluctantly opened her eyes. It was her recurring dream: She would awake to find Lord Lexford only inches from her. The viscount's eyes would relay his desire, and he would kiss her most thoroughly before declaring his love. She often gave her imagination free will, and just for a moment, considered her dream real. Mercy gave herself a mental shake, but the image of the man remained before her, and, yes, desire was evident in his expression.

"Is something amiss, my lord?"

She attempted to make her voice sound groggy from sleep.

Lord Lexford caressed her cheek and slid a lock of hair behind her ear. Mercy resisted the urge to turn her cheek into his large palm.

"No, my dear," he said gently. "I decided to travel to Liverpool at first light, and I did not want you to think I purposely avoided you after..."

Mercy swallowed hard.

"After what happened in the kitchen?" she asked through trembling lips.

The possibility did not occur to her earlier: Perhaps His Lordship would send her away. Her forwardness was a deplorable habit. Mercy always thought she would name the day of her departure, but the viscount could find her impertinent and decide to rid himself of her company.

Lord Lexford's lips twitched in what appeared to be amusement, and Mercy's misery deepened.

"Yes," he said with what sounded of a tease. "Yes, what happened between us below stairs."

"I apologize," Mercy rushed to say.

Above all else, she must save face. Mercy must prove herself indifferent so she might remain with Lord Lexford.

"I worried over your return, and in my joy, I...I acted... acted foolishly."

His Lordship scowled fiercely.

"Then you did not mean to kiss me?"

Mercy shook her head in the negative.

"No more so than you after my riding accident," she declared falsely.

Mercy shoved herself higher in the bed.

"We are great friends, you and I. So you see. I only meant to comfort you. To warm you. To express my gratitude for your kindness."

Lord Lexford straightened.

"I see."

The man presented her a sharp nod, but he did not look too pleased by the news. He jammed his fingers into his hair.

"Then it is I who should apologize. I drew you from your sleep for no reason."

The regret in his voice touched Mercy's heart.

She schooled her expression.

"I would always wish to know of your whereabouts, my lord. I thank you for your consideration. If I went down to breakfast only to find you gone, my earlier anxiety would return."

She took a slow, steadying breath and attempted to smile.

"And what earlier anxiety would that be?" the viscount suspiciously demanded.

Mercy forced her breathing to normal.

"My initial anxiety regarding your late return from Squire Holton's entertainment. Then witnessing your condition, and at length, my self censure for the folly of my actions."

Mercy could not look upon His Lordship's countenance. Since coming to Lexington Arms, she became quite the practiced liar, and Mercy found she did not approve of the change.

The viscount widened the space between them.

"I will be away but a few days," Lord Lexford said stiffly. "A week at most. Mr. Hill will see to your needs in my absence."

"I mean to begin the guest quarters for your house party," she said lamely.

Anguish filled her soul. Mercy felt more than the physical space between them increase. Her words changed Lord Lexford's ease with her. She supposed it the correct thing to do, but somehow the thought of distancing herself from the viscount brought tears to her eyes.

Lord Lexford offered the proper bow.

"That would be delightful," he said without emotion. "I will anticipate your efforts on my behalf. Now, if you will excuse me, I must seek my bed. It is not many hours before I intend to depart."

Mercy wished to throw her arms about his neck to share a moment of intimate splendor, but she said, "Safe journey, my lord. I shall keep you in my prayers."

As expected, Lucifer saw him off.

"You should spend some time in your own pleasures," Hill stated baldly.

Aidan shot a quick glance at the house. Although he could not see the lady's windows, just knowing Miss Purefoy rested within played havoc with Aidan's emotions. He slept very little. At least, his lack of sleep came from the remembrance of the kiss he shared with the woman rather than the nightmare associated with Lexington Arms.

"And you think burying myself in some nameless woman will resolve what ails me?" Aidan said defensively.

Hill's expression did not change.

"There be only one thing, which will offer you salvation, my lord; yet, perhaps a few hours of mindless pleasure will provide you the opportunity to clear your mind of what bothers you."

Aidan could think of only one woman for whom his body called out.

"I will consider your counsel, but of late, such trivial connections lost their glory."

Hill stepped away as Aidan mounted.

"As you wish, my lord."

"Protect the lady and my nephew," Aidan said needlessly.

He knew, like him, Mr. Hill would lay out his life for Miss Purefoy and Aaron.

Many hours later, Aidan dismounted before The Golden Apple. He took his time on the journey, providing Valí ample rest. He could have changed horses at one of the inns, boarding Valí until his return journey, but Aidan preferred the stallion to all others in his stable. Since returning to England, he made several shrewd purchases from Tattersall's: He hoped to build a line of championship horses for racing and breeding. He learned much of thoroughbreds when he was in the East. It was another means in which he differed from his father and brother, who held with the old ways. Strangely, over the years, Aidan came to despise his lack of tradition–even to keep his ideas secreted away so no one could criticize; yet, of late, he was more comfortable talking of his dream. Squire Holton and Mr. Verity both commented on how much they would wish to view his stables in hopes of setting some of their mares to stud.

Aidan stretched his sore muscles and looked about for familiar faces. When in the Liverpool area, Realm members frequented The Golden Apple.

"Lexford? Is that you?"

Aidan turned to see John Swenton striding toward him. He smiled when both he and the baron ignored the customary bow and instead opened their arms for a male embrace of brotherhood.

"What brings you to Liverpool?"

Aidan was truly glad to see his friend. Although he was closer to Marcus Wellston and Gabriel Crowden than he was to the baron, Aidan required the familiarity of those who knew him best.

"I experienced several unusual incidents at Lexington Arms since my return. Lucifer assumes Jamot could be involved. As the Baloch was last seen in Liverpool, I thought it best to begin my investigation in the port city."

Swenton chuckled ironically.

"I doubt Jamot will show his face in Liverpool any time soon. Sir Carter left few stones unturned since the marquis spotted the Baloch on the Chinese ship involved in the kidnapping of Lady Godown and Lord Godown's aunts."

"I only heard bits of the story of that night," Aidan admitted.

Swenton directed Aidan toward the inn.

"It is a complicated tale, but I will be pleased to regal you with the sordid details over the evening meal. The baronet and Lord Yardley will return late, and I will be glad of your company."

Aidan paused outside the main door.

"Why is Yardley in Liverpool? Please say the earl and countess are not experiencing difficulties."

Aidan would not wish for Wellston and Lady Yardley to know unhappiness. Despite his initial interest in Miss Cashémere, Aidan preferred to think Yardley found contentment with the woman. Aidan's tattered hopes hung on each member of the Realm finding love. Godown already lost his wife; Aidan would not wish another to suffer.

"When you observe the silly grin on the earl's face, you will possess no doubt of Yardley's marital felicity. It seems Baron Ashton returned to Chesterfield Manor without Miss Satiné. Ashton is quite distraught, and Lady Yardley came to Manchester to see to her uncle's health. Lord Yardley thought to give his wife and Ashton some private time to reestablish their relationship."

Aidan's lips turned down in a frown.

"And what of the lady? Surely, Ashton would not willingly leave Miss Satiné behind."

Swenton eyed Aidan cautiously.

"Do you plan to renew your addresses to Miss Satiné?"

The baron's reaction was not what Aidan expected. Perhaps, there remained something from the story of Ashton's nieces that slipped Aidan's memory. He shook his head in the negative.

"I hold no interest in Satiné Aldridge. My own memories of the lady are those repeated by others. In fact, until I saw Lady Yardley recently in London, I held no true memory of Miss Cashémere's appearance. If the countess did not stand at Lord Graham's ball beside Thornhill's duchess, I might not recognize her. People often forget my memory possesses large holes in it. Now that I viewed Lady Yardley, I am aware of Miss Satiné's appearance. Because I hold a memory of a kiss, people believe it was one with Miss Satiné."

Swenton's lips thinned into a tight line of disapproval, and

Aidan was quick to add, "Yet, I cannot say for certain the lady and I were thusly involved. I know only of a kiss. It might be one I once shared with Susan or with another beautiful woman. In my recollection, I cannot see the lady's countenance, only can I recall the feel of her lips."

Aidan would not tell Swenton that he knew perfectly well the woman in the image was Lady Eleanor Kerrington. Nor would he admit the kiss he exchanged with the "Captain's" wife changed Aidan's life.

"Miss Cashémere and Miss Satiné were thought to appear as one," Swenton said sadly. "But from what Yardley reports via Ashton, Miss Satiné altered her appearance with powders and creams."

Aidan lowered his voice.

"Then Charters did not leave the lady with child?"

Swenton frowned deeply.

"Apparently, motherhood is no longer a concern, but Miss Satiné took the assault as a means to reconstruct her image. According to Baron Ashton, Miss Satiné chose to ply her beauty and her charms in a most scandalous manner. The baron no longer retains any control over the woman; therefore, he left Miss Satiné with her latest amour."

"Latest?" Aidan said incredulously. "How can there be a latest? Miss Satiné is but four months upon the Continent."

Swenton's tone spoke of personal anguish.

"One never knows how a person will react to the tragedies in his life. Miss Satiné deserves our pity, not our censure."

~~~

"Then there is no sighting of Jamot?" Aidan asked.

With the return of Sir Carter and Lord Yardley, Swenton made his excuses and disappeared for the evening. The baron always was the most stoical of their group. John Swenton often sought his own company. Regrettably, after his disdainful remark regarding Miss Satiné's actions, Aidan recalled the rumors surrounding Swenton's mother. Supposedly, the woman deserted her husband and son for a life on the stage. None of the their group knew for certain the truth of the gossip following Swenton's title, but the baron often called upon a woman outside of Vienna whenever he could do so beyond his service with the Realm.

Sir Carter's expression hardened.

"Not even a rumor of the Baloch. I begin to think Godown made a mistake."

Before the return of Lowery and Wellston, Swenton filled the time and the awkwardness from Aidan's earlier remark with the tale of how Godown unexpectedly called upon Swenton over Christmastide. The marquis's Aunt Bel recognized the fact the marquise was with child. Godown accidentally overheard the conversation and thinking the child another's banished Lady Godown from his home. Aidan was not certain he approved of Godown's actions, but he understood the man's pain of betrayal. Aidan knew a similar feeling in dealing with Susan's turning to Andrew. Then the marquis retreated to Yorkshire. When Pennington sent Swenton to Liverpool to assist Sir Carter with a lead on the opium ring, Godown accompanied the baron.

"Sir Carter took out a small boat to spy on the Chinese ship," Swenton confided. "The baronet retrieved what he thought was a boy from the water, only to discover Lady Godown dressed as a lad. The marquise escaped the ship in hopes of saving Godown's aunts. I thought from the look upon Godown's countenance when he saw his wife's suffering that the marquis would forgive her, but when Her Ladyship explained how Jamot assisted her in her escape, the Godowns had a very bitter-sounding row. Words are often more dangerous weapons than are swords or guns."

Swenton looked off for a moment as if recalling a distasteful incident before continuing.

"Godown assisted with boarding the ship. The infamous Lord Spectre turned out to be Lady Gardenia's lover and cousin. It was all very scandalous. The marquis weathered the worst of it, but I do not envy his having to go through the rumor line again.

"When Godown ferried his aunts to safety, the marquis,

like his wife earlier, claimed to observe Jamot on board the ship. Sir Carter swore otherwise. The baronet spent the last month examining every detail past and present in his investigation."

They both had a good laugh at Lowery's expense for they knew the diligence with which Sir Carter attacked every part of his duty to the Realm.

Now as Aidan surveyed the baronet's face, he noted the lines of stress etched about Sir Carter's eyes and forehead. When Carter revisited the tale upon his return, Aidan sensibly said, "The marquis would never make such an error."

The baronet scrubbed his cheeks and eyes with dry hands, attempting to drive weariness away.

"I know," he said with a deep sigh. "But the lack of information is maddening." Sir Carter stood heavily. "Berwick and I are to search a suspicious warehouse tomorrow. I would be pleased if you would join us."

Aidan nodded his agreement.

"It will be as old times." Yet, he knew "old times" could not be recovered so easily as marching into a warehouse with a gun drawn. "Old times" were more elusive than that.

Sir Carter staggered toward the door.

"Good evening, Gentlemen."

With the baronet's departure, Aidan turned to his closest friend.

"We have not spoken privately since before your wedding."

Wellston called upon Aidan at Chesterfield Manor and offered to withdraw from his marriage to Miss Cashémere Aldridge rather than to damage Aidan's and the earl's relationship. At the time, the Berwick's happiness was bitterer to swallow than the physician's mixture, but it was the correct thing to do. Aidan could not love a woman who preferred another. He attempted to salvage a relationship with Susan and failed miserably. He learned his lesson.

Wellston thumbed his glass.

"I should have called at Thorn Hall," he said guiltily.

Aidan chuckled self-consciously.

"I will not deny the fact I would enjoy a sensible conversation. The duke is so besotted by his duchess, he practices no caution, but it was best if you set your marriage to right. How fares Lady Yardley?"

Wellston's eyes glazed over in delight.

"Cashé is phenomenal. I never knew a woman who could change a household so drastically. A woman who could take a bachelor's house and make it very feminine, but still inviting."

Aidan could think of one such woman.

"It is I who lost his mind. When Lady Yardley is not near, I am searching the manor for her. I placed the countess's desk in my study so Cashémere would be within my view, and I would be less distracted."

Wellston barked out an ironic laugh.

"Even so, when Cashémere is in the room, I find I prefer watching her mannerisms. The way my wife twirls her hair about her finger or bites the tip of her quill…it is all so mesmerizing. I am as besotted as the duke, only my obsession lies in the duchess's younger sister."

The earl shrugged away his confession.

"Can you imagine such a scheme?"

Aidan swallowed the sigh of envy.

"I noted the same expression upon the countenances of both Thornhill and Worthing as I observe on yours. Hell! Even the marquis looks upon his wife as such. I am infinitely jealous."

Wellston sat forward in concern.

"Is there no one in your life, Lexford?"

Aidan's thoughts went immediately to Mary Purefoy, and although it was not customary among men to discuss "romantic" musings, he confessed, "Actually, I inherited a poor relative, who set my house on its ear."

Men of his and the earl's ilk would deny a conversation about love and dreams if confronted by an outsider, but Aidan and Wellston repeatedly survived life and death drama in their years of service. Such duty to country changes a man's perspective of what is acceptable.

"Is the lady pretty?"

Aidan closed his eyes to conjure up Miss Purefoy's countenance.

"So much so I no longer recall Susan's image."

Luckily, the earl did not comment on Aidan's unguarded confession.

After an exaggerated pause, Aidan said, "Unfortunately, mayhem settled under my roof. My nephew returned to Lexington Arms, but someone attempted to steal away the boy. On another occasion, an unknown culprit sabotaged Miss Purefoy's saddle and took a shot at the woman. Two days prior to my coming to Liverpool, someone pushed me from a promontory to the stream below."

Wellston spoke in incredulity.

"All this since your return home at Christmastide? Why did you not send for assistance? We are a brotherhood, Lexford?"

Aidan considered the sincerity in the earl's voice. He spoke through his tight throat.

"It is worse. I have seen what appears to be an apparition. The ghost of my wife showed herself on four occasions. Although my home offers nothing but misery, Susan declared she will never leave Lexington Arms."

Over Aidan's objections, Wellston roused both Sir Carter and Swenton from their beds so Aidan could repeat his tale. He explained each incident in terms of what precipitated the sightings. Aidan spoke of Miss Purefoy's appearance, of the changes the lady made in his household, and of her bravery in saving Aaron's life. Even so, Aidan purposely omitted the fact Miss Purefoy was his father's by blow. He refused to analyze his reasons. He told himself he protected the lady's reputation, but a little voice in his head said Aidan did not want to admit the obstacles between them. He wanted what Wellston found in Lady Yardley, and Aidan strongly suspected his hopes hanged heavily upon Miss Purefoy's shoulders. Moreover, he held no desire to revisit the reasons his marriage failed.

"And you believe Jamot had a hand in these attacks?" Sir Carter asked.

"The Baloch used similar tactics in the past, and Hill reminded me of Jamot's earlier reconnaissance of my estate," Aidan admitted. "It seemed only logical either to confirm or to eliminate the Baloch as a suspect."

Sir Carter shook his head in the negative.

"It is not as if Jamot is not capable of such chaos, but none of these attacks upon your house and estate are original, and if I know nothing more of the Baloch, I know of Jamot's pride. He might taunt you, but he would formulate a plan specifically designed to annoy you. I cannot imagine the Baloch would sink to petty teasing."

An expert at heights, Wellston easily scaled the walls of the warehouse to permit the Realm agents inside. For the first time ever, Aidan did not experience the excitement of the chase. Instead, he felt the folly of rushing into the unknown; after all, although his was not the traditional example of a family, Aidan possessed those who cared for his safety. Miss Purefoy's and Aaron's futures depended upon his remaining the head of the viscountcy. So, despite his prior mode of operation, Aidan was not leading the charge into danger.

"Do not consider resistance!" Sir Carter ordered.

There were a few minor scuffles, but surprisingly the men found within the warehouse surrendered without a confrontation. Aidan breathed a bit easier, but he kept the weapon leveled upon the group. Despite knowing, he participated in more than a hundred such attacks, the experience felt foreign, as if he were a mere recruit again.

He followed Swenton's lead and isolated the group's leaders. On alert, Aidan's eyes scanned each movement of these dealers in opium.

"Escort these men to our cells," Sir Carter ordered the young recruits known as Henderson and Van Dyke.

According to Sir Carter, these two were the most promising of the post war enlistees.

"Aye, Sir." Soon all but three men were secure in one of the Realm's secret holding facilities.

Aidan had yet to release his grip on the gun.

"Are you well?" Wellston asked quietly from beside him.

Aidan nodded his agreement.

"Felt like some new conscript," he confessed. "I suppose I lost some of my previous bravado along with my memory."

Wellston chuckled in easy familiarity.

"I am pleased to hear it," his friend said. "As I climbed the wall outside, I had the sudden thought of what would happen to Cashémere and to Trevor and to my estate if I fell and broke my neck."

"We are growing older, my friend," Aidan spoke with relief. "We should leave the heroics to Sir Carter's new young bucks."

Wellston's smile widened.

"I was thinking something similar."

"Your Lordships!" Swenton called from the open door to a small office. "You must see this."

Aidan and Wellston hustled to join Swenton and Lowery.

"What is amiss?" Wellston asked as he led the way.

Sir Carter was pouring over unfurled maps.

"It appears the opium lines stretch to your neighborhood, Lexford, as well as into Manchester."

Aidan and Wellston leaned over either side of where the baronet studied the maps. Aidan's finger traced the line, which led dangerous close to the village his estate supported.

"Do we know what these symbols mean?" he asked distractedly.

"Never seen them before," Sir Carter said just as abstractedly. "We will question the prisoners, but it may take some time to 'convince' them to cooperate."

"This is ominous, but Lady Yardley and I will not be in Manchester long enough to do more than sound an alarm," Wellston reminded them.

Aidan continued to examine the map, memorizing details and praying his ability to retain such facts would not be interrupted by his memory loss.

"Why not involve Baron Ashton? From what you shared, the baron requires something to serve as a distraction from his trials with Miss Satiné; and he is former Realm."

Wellston caught Aidan's eye as they peered around Sir Carter.

"Yours is an excellent idea. Will you return with me to Chesterfield Manor to convince the baron?"

Aidan nodded toward Sir Carter.

"Should we not earn Lowery's approval before we change the prescribed plan?"

"Since when did either of you listen to orders?" Sir Carter pronounced testily.

Aidan placed his arm around Sir Carter's shoulders.

"Since when did you lose your sense of humor?" he teased, good-naturedly.

Swenton said without looking up from a box of papers he unearthed beneath a loose floorboard.

"Since Carter heard Pennington placed Lowery's name in the hat to replace him once Pennington marries the dowager duchess."

Aidan's smile turned up his lips' corners.

"Really? That would be excellent, Lowery. I can think of no one who deserves the position more."

"Other names are on the list," Lowery said with a shrug of self-consciousness. "More prestigious names. I am only a newly-minted baronet."

Wellston reminded their friend, "Pennington has no title, and he served the Realm for several decades."

"Neither did Pennington possess military experience," Aidan added.

Swenton stood to add his find to the documents on the table.

"The others are correct, Lowery. You have as good of an opportunity as your competition. However, I do wish you would find your amiability again."

"It is as Swenton says; do not sacrifice your principles," Aidan added sagely. "You can be an efficient leader and still show compassion. If you must change to earn the position, is it truly worth having?"

"Pennington never relinquished his ideology," Wellston reasoned.

"Pennington worked his way through the ranks," Lowery groaned. "I keep thinking if I could capture Jamot…"

"Do not overanalyze it," Swenton warned. "Earn the position on your own terms."

Lowery sighed heavily.

"I know you speak the truth. I suspect I caught a bit of my father's fever. I kept the baron away from Lawrence and Arabella during my brother's courtship of the lady. A man with Baron Blakehell's ambitions is difficult to refuse."

They were all well aware of how the baron manipulated Carter's older brother.

"You never wanted to be the baron's favorite son in the past, why would you do so now?" Aidan asked suspiciously.

Lowery looked away in disconcertion.

"Waterloo was not enough for the baron to see me. Neither was the Prince Regent's presentation of the baronetcy."

"Blakehell sees you, Lowery," Wellston advised. "Your father does not know how to express his pride. I felt the same with Trevor and Myles before me, but the earl finally said the words I most wanted to hear. Give the baron time."

Having shared the intimate moments meant only for those who weathered tragedies and tribulations, Lowery nodded sharply, but he did not respond. Understanding stood righteously between them.

"Then we agree: Wellston will recruit Baron Ashton to head the Manchester investigation. Pennington cleared the baron of any wrongdoing in that matter with Viscount Averette."

"Agreed," their trio responded.

Wellston reached for his gloves and the Manchester map.

"I will return this by week's end. Are you coming, Lexford?"

A knot of anxiety tore through Aidan's stomach. He would prefer to return to Cheshire.

"Permit me to retrieve Valí from the stable."

As he followed his best friend from the room, Aidan's heart pounded in his ears. He was returning to the site of where he lost his memory. He wondered if the visit would restore some of the missing details or leave him more confused.

Chapter 14

"To WHERE MIGHT YOU BE OFF, Miss Purefoy?" Mr. Hill asked as she passed him in the upper passageway.

Mercy set her steps beyond the guest chambers to which she directed her efforts in the viscount's absence. Lord Lexford departed four days prior, but to Mercy it felt a lifetime. Mr. Hill took Mercy into his confidence and explained the reason for Lord Lexford's quick withdrawal and the suspicions the viscount held. His Lordship meant to solve the mysteries shadowing his house. Mercy understood the viscount's need to control his world; however, she did not wish to think on Lord Lexford being in danger. The man was too essential to her.

"You are too efficient, Mr. Hill," Mercy said good-naturedly. "You hold no need for my opinions. The room came together nicely. We should set some of the men in preparation for the adjoining suite tomorrow. I located a bed and wardrobe in the west wing, which will complement the rose tones in both rooms. And I would place the chest from Lady Cassandra's room within the suite."

"Just tell Mr. Payne what you desire, and he will instruct the men to move the furniture." Mr. Hill stepped closer for privacy. "You deftly avoided my question, Miss Purefoy. You are dressed for the cold, so I assume you mean to partake of the grounds."

Mercy nodded in the affirmative.

"The house is too silent. Even with the hammering and workers scurrying everywhere, the rooms lost their appeal as a distraction."

Thankfully, Mr. Hill did not comment on Mercy's confession.

"Lord Lexford would not approve of your going out alone. Take Miss Chadwick or Millie with you."

"Serena joined the seamstresses to explain how she wants the drapes to hang," Mercy protested.

Mr. Hill spoke in firm tones.

"Then take your maid. His Lordship charged me with your care, and I will not permit you to wander the estate grounds alone."

Mercy frowned, but she accepted the man's need to secure her safety. After all, she was not as familiar with the area as was he, and in many ways, it was wonderful to know someone would grieve for her if something untoward happened.

"I shall not be long."

Aidan's anxiety rose as he dismounted before Chesterfield Manor. He barely acknowledged the young groom who hustled forward to capture his and Wellston's reins. Aidan stared at the façade he last glimpsed as he and Fowler rode away from Baron Ashton's home the previous October. As he relaxed into the leather squabs of the duke's carriage, Aidan gloomily realized he held no memory of ever entering the baron's home, and today, the same feeling of fear crept through Aidan's veins. There was something ominous about entering the manor after so many months–as if its walls knew a secret they refused to disclose. With a few deep breaths, he made his feet turn toward the open door. People within would recognize him from his weeks of recovery under the baron's roof, but he could not return the acknowledgement by pronouncing a once-familiar name. Unwelcome feelings of pity rushed to his heart, and Aidan worked hard to school his expression.

He supposed even Wellston forgot the fact Baron Ashton remained a stranger to Aidan until his friend whispered, "Follow my lead."

Aidan nodded his gratitude, but Wellston's gesture did little to ease Aidan's anxiety.

"Good day, my lord," the baron's butler greeted Wellston. "I sent a maid to inform both the baron and Lady Yardley of your return."

The man accepted Wellston's gloves and hat.

"Thank you, Mr. Whitcomb." The earl emphasized the man's name, and Aidan gave a quick nod of understanding.

"And Viscount Lexford," Whitcomb continued. "The staff will be pleased to know of your continued good health, my lord."

Aidan accepted the man's greeting with simple words of "thanks." He handed the butler his hat, gloves, and crop before looking up to see a slightly graying man approaching. Although he possessed only a faint memory of Fowler explaining how Richard Breeson accepted the position as Ashton's steward, Breeson's was one face Aidan could easily recall.

"You brought us well-known company," Breeson greeted the earl with the ease of long years of being together. Richard Breeson once served as Wellston's batman and lost an arm in battle saving the earl from a blind attack from an enemy soldier. In payment, Wellston provided Breeson a position on the Tweed Hall estate. When Ashton required a new steward, Wellston nominated his long time servant.

Despite being more than a bit anxious over greeting so many forgotten faces, Aidan kept a welcoming smile upon his lips. His may be a familiar countenance to this household, but beyond Wellston, and now Breeson, Aidan recognized none within. Even the rooms felt unfamiliar because Fowler insisted they leave for Kent on the day the physician pronounced Aidan well enough to leave his bed. That particular realization plagued

Aidan, but something else, something infinitely more personal, scratched at his memory. He supposed it something to do with the reason he came to Chesterfield Manor: He meant to woo Miss Cashémere with the intention of marriage. Yet, even recognition of that distinct fact did not satisfy the "itch," which begged to be discovered. Aidan certainly hoped some day all the searching for answers would end, and his memory would return.

He extended his left hand to catch Breeson's left.

"Good day, Breeson. I forgot you joined the baron's staff."

"Breeson settled down," Wellston explained. "He married Faith Molson, the physician's daughter from our village."

Aidan smiled genuinely for the first time since entering Chesterfield Manor.

"Then I wish you happy. You deserve it, Breeson."

"I cannot speak to deserving Mrs. Breeson, but I am more than content."

Although Aidan truly wished the man well, a pang of envy appeared. Except for his own sorry state, it seemed everyone found someone to return his affections.

A woman he knew to be Lady Yardley appeared upon the stairs, and Wellston met his wife's descent to catch her up in a tight embrace.

"Marcus!" she squealed, but the lady lifted her chin for Wellston's kiss. No one among their class ever showed affections before others, but Aidan's friend ignored propriety. Instead of being repulsed by the earl's actions, Aidan swallowed his jealousy. He set his sights on Miss Cashémere Aldridge long before Wellston recognized the lady's beauty. If he were successful, it could be he making a cake of himself over his wife rather than being an admiring stranger. Wellston's loving gaze rested upon his wife, and that simple gesture made Aidan feel worse. Fate had a way of turning the world on its head.

The lady broke from her husband's embrace to greet Aidan.

Extending her hands to him, Lady Yardley said, "Lord Lexford, you are most welcome, Sir. I was so pleased to hear of your return to health."

He noted her sorrow-filled gaze asking for forgiveness.

"Thank you, Lady Yardley."

Aidan lifted the woman's hand to brush his lips across her knuckles. Immediately, he wondered where the spark of recognition went. Needless to say, the woman was his best friend's wife, but according to what all the other Realm members assured him, Aidan once was very besotted with the lady. Should there not be a zing of desire, something similar to what he felt whenever he touched Miss Purefoy?

"My life took a turn for the better of late."

"And your memory, my lord?" she asked softly.

Aidan searched the lady's countenance for a flicker of familiarity. Whatever existed between them disappeared. They would begin anew as friends.

"I must report no progress on that particular front, my lady."

A pronounced frown formed on Lady Yardley's lips.

"Time has a way of healing all ills, my lord." She glanced to her husband. "Uncle Charles is in his study. He asked we join him there."

"This way." Wellston motioned toward the stairs. Aidan dutifully placed Lady Yardley on his arm, but again he felt nothing more than the uncomfortable nagging of missing details from his life.

Reaching the point where Wellston awaited them, Lady Yardley wrapped her arm through her husband's to walk between them. Aidan swallowed hard. The past was better left to its misery. The situation remained awkward, but he knew he must push through it or lose Wellston's friendship, something Aidan was not prepared to do.

"Uncle!" Lady Yardley called as they entered the room. "We brought you company."

A man rose heavily from where he sat behind a dark wood desk. The room was sparsely furnished, but Aidan approved of the décor. It spoke of a well-organized mind.

"Ah, Lord Lexford," the baron said genially. "I am pleased you returned to Chesterfield Manor. Perhaps you will be a good omen for the estate–will herald the return to normalcy."

Aidan kept his voice even.

"As much as I pray for a resolution of your latest tragedy, I would prefer not to wear the cloak of the Angel of Hope."

He noted Wellston's pronounced frown.

"My life remains in disorder," he added quickly, "and I would not wish it upon another."

"But I thought you spoke earlier of your fortunes turning for the better," Lady Yardley reasoned.

Aidan remained where he stood while Wellston seated his wife. He thought of the red gold-framed countenance of Miss Purefoy's lovely face, and a smile tugged at the corners of Aidan's mouth.

"My life knows the golden glimmers of anticipation. I discovered a familial connection of which I was unaware, and my nephew returned to his father's home. Moreover my house is glowing from a much overdue renovation; nonetheless, my memory from the time of my arrival from the East to the present remains elusive. In truth, I walked into this house with only the earl's and Mr. Breeson's countenances as part of my memory. Forgive me if I do not wish to be the bearer of lost expectations."

"You sound bitter, my lord," Ashton observed as he sat once again. The man appeared exhausted by the exertion.

Aidan's conscience twanged.

"I do not mean to add sullenness to the situation, but, of late, speaking honestly serves me well."

Aidan looked upon three guilty countenances. He should feel regret for placing these three in an discomforted moment, but perhaps it would be better to clear the fog hanging over the room.

"Not a day goes by, my lord, where I do not know remorse for my actions in precipitating your injury," Lady Yardley said softly. "I never meant to hurt you, my lord."

"But you did hurt me, Lady Yardley. You treated my honest regard as a playing chip to discard at your whim."

Aidan found saying the words were not as satisfying as he anticipated, but he still found the moment infinitely more rewarding than pretending nothing occurred, which was exactly what propriety would expect of him.

Wellston stepped between Aidan and Lady Yardley.

"If anyone is to blame, it is I. If you have a grief to air, it should be with me, Lexford. I encouraged Cashémere."

"I have no grief with anyone within these walls," Aidan said earnestly. "I told you honestly to follow your heart; but neither can I pretend we always played fairly between us. It does not mean I hold you in less regard than I did previously. The situation simply requires us to begin anew; you, Lady Yardley, and I must acknowledge our past, *all* of our past. We must accept the fact that Fate pulls the strings, and we are but marionettes."

"Lord Lexford is correct," Ashton said sagely. "We cannot change what occurred yesterday or a week ago or several months long gone. If it were possible to do so, I would turn over the incriminating information I possessed on Viscount Averette. If so, my sweet Satiné would be in Cheshire and preparing for her first Season."

"My sister shall return soon," Lady Yardley assured her uncle.

"I appreciate your kindness, Cashémere, but I must face the possibility that Satiné is even now lost to me forever."

He motioned Wellston and Aidan to chairs.

"Please join us, Lord Lexford. Together we will find a means to a better situation. The future may not hold what we originally planned, but we welcome it nonetheless. Doing so is better than the alternative."

Aidan thought of Mary and Aaron. Neither was part of his plan, but they each enriched his life. He would cherish their time together.

"You may return to the manor, Millie."

Mercy's maid openly shivered from the cold.

"I mean to spend a bit more time outdoors."

For once the young girl did not argue with her. Mercy twice walked the length of the groomed parkland, now dormant from the winter's frost. Although her fingers and toes screamed for a warm fire, she turned her steps toward the outcropping where Lord Lexford took his fall. Although she trusted His Lordship's version of the story, Mercy's practical side said it impossible for either ghost or human to disappear into solid rock. She would inspect the area to discover answers to the questions, which nagged her waking hours.

A quarter hour brisk walk brought her to within the vicinity of the scene Mr. Hill described. No longer did the water pour from the rock face as per His Lordship's rendition of the events. Instead, a steady trickle of water slid down from above. Mercy followed the sound to look upon the area in daylight.

The outcropping was little more than the side of a hill swept away over the years by the cut of the stream flowing into the River Goyt. It stood some fifteen to twenty feet above her head. The sight sent a shiver of dread down Mercy's spine.

"His Lordship is fortunate he survived the drop," she murmured. "How sad we all would be with a different outcome."

With a quick prayer for Lord Lexford's continued health, Mercy explored the base of the hill. She easily found where the viscount made his ascent. Deep heel prints announced where Lord Lexford stood. It would be natural to assume whoever His Lordship chased used the same path. It was the easiest means to the top. But no footprints, other than Lord Lexford's, showed in the damp earth.

Mercy braced her hand against the sharp rocks. She surveyed the path several times.

"If the woman His Lordship chased did not climb the path

to the top before him," Mercy reasoned, "how did the lady reach the top and when did she arrive? Needless to say, Lord Lexford did not push himself into the water."

Mercy walked the outline of the small hill, checking for another means to the top, but only the one path provided a foothold for a weary traveler or a devious culprit.

"Where?" she said over and over. Mercy reasoned that if the woman did not lead the way to the ledge, Lord Lexford's attacker hid away and waited for the opportunity to strike.

"Where?" Mercy continued to think aloud.

Her fingers traced the rough sandstone. When she reached the steady plop, plop, plop of the water moving through the cracks in the rocks, Mercy ducked behind the thin stream. Then she saw it: a rough zigzag opening in the rock's surface. An opening large enough for a person to enter or exit the area if bent over. Mercy considered her alternatives: She could seek out Mr. Hill's assistance or she could explore the area privately. What if the opening held answers to questions His Lordship did not think to ask? There was really only one choice: she must protect Lord Lexford.

Ducking through the small opening, finding a lantern and flint on the ground and protected from the splash back of the water by a large boulder surprised Mercy. Balancing the lantern on a flat surface, she struck the flint three times before a spark caught the piece of a twig she found inside the opening. Using the twig, Mercy quickly lit the candle's wick. She thought it odd the candle was not a cheap rush candle or tallow, but rather one made from wax. That fact meant whoever placed the candle within was a member of the gentry. The poor could not afford such candles.

Lifting the lantern higher, Mercy examined what appeared to be a cave in the hillside.

"Who would think?" she said in awe. "Surely, Lord Lexford is aware of this place, but if so, how is it the viscount did not think of the possibility previously?"

Curious, Mercy explored the open space. It was not large, but not so small as to feel cramped. The lantern's light drifted upward where a gentle slope appeared to go straight to the summit.

"The ghost's path?" she questioned. Mercy would explore the possibility before she exited the cave.

On the left there was a narrow opening through which a person turned sideways could fit. Permitting the lantern to lead the way, Mercy squeezed through the opening to emerge into a long tunnel.

"A person familiar with this passage could easily hide from someone who searched for him," she thought aloud. "Even if that someone recognized the smaller opening to the cave."

Mercy hesitated before venturing farther. She held no idea whether the tunnel might lead deeper into the side of the hill or whether it dipped into the earth.

"Do I venture forth?" she asked the blackness.

"I would not if I were you."

A dark-faced man stepped from behind a large boulder to block her way. At first, her foolish mind thought him the ghost of a copper miner, covered in mine dust. She saw sketches of such apparitions in one of the few books remaining in Geoffrey's library. The man trapped her. She was too far from the narrow opening to run for safety. The shadows hid the man's features, but Mercy did not underestimate him. He was tall and lean, but muscular, like the Black Dog of legend fame.

"Put the lantern down on the rock beside you," he said with a gesture of the gun he held.

The man's tongue rolled with a heat over the hard English vowels. Mercy heard his accent before. This man was one of her brother's associates. Geoffrey found her. She swallowed the groan of defeat filling her lungs.

"What are...what are you doing here?" she asked.

Mercy had to know what Geoffrey meant to do with her.

The man chuckled.

"I thought to call on my old friend Lord Lexford," the man said baldly. "I always use this secret way when I make my social calls."

Did the man mean to make light of the power he held over her? He remained hidden by the semi-darkness as if he wished to keep his identity secret. Mercy wondered if he could see her better than she could him. Thinking thus, she edged away from the light.

"Did the viscount send you to find me?" the man taunted.

Mercy nearly blurted out the fact His Lordship was elsewhere, but she kept her tongue in check.

"Actually, it was Mr. Hill's idea for me to explore the opening. He would not fit easily into the space."

"I never liked the man," the stranger admitted with a touch of disdain.

Mercy searched her memory for the man's name. She saw him but twice in her brother's company. Even so, the stranger was memorable, especially when compared to the other riff-raff with whom Geoffrey associated. His skin tone spoke of a man long from his home. Back in Lancashire, her first impression of her captor was "dangerous." That feeling did not dissipate.

"Is Mr. Hill waiting for you?" the interloper asked curiously.

"By the stream," Mercy lied.

"I am sorry to hear it."

The man's eyes traced lines up and down her body. It took all of Mercy's willpower not to cover herself with her hands.

"I thought we might learn something of each other," he said seductively.

Mercy bit back her fear.

"There is no time for niceties," she said as bravely as she could. "I should be going."

She edged backward toward the narrow opening. If she could maneuver through before the man reacted, Mercy might be able to outrun the stranger.

"Your name, my pretty?" the man demanded.

Mercy slid her left foot closer to the opening.

"Mary," she said evenly.

Mercy watched her captor closely, attempting to anticipate

his movements.

The man's tone said he scowled.

"Mary. Mary is something a man does. It is a perfectly plain English name, but it is not a proper name for such a beautiful woman. You require a name as distinctive as your countenance. You should be Anahita or Zam-Armtay. A name which distinguishes you among women."

"Yet, Mary is my name," she said a bit testily.

The man narrowed the distance between them, and Mercy's fear rose quickly to close her throat. She swallowed hard.

"We have a bit of a problem," her captor's tone changed from teasing to warning. "I do not wish to be the bearer of ill news, but I cannot permit you to return to Lord Lexford's house to raise the alarm."

Mercy's heart slammed to a halt. She spoke to trembling lips.

"You mean to return me to my brother?"

The man's countenance screwed up in confusion. He caught Mercy's arm and dragged her toward the light. Mercy pulled hard in the opposite direction, but the stranger was too strong for her. Her leather boots slid easily over the damp smooth floor.

"Who are you?" he demanded; his hand clamped her wrist tighter as he caught up the lantern in his other hand. He lifted it to look upon her countenance, and Mercy prepared herself for the worse.

When the light flooded her features, she braced herself for the moment of recognition. Mercy erred: The man did not come for her. Instead, he was Lord Lexford's enemy. Her mind searched for the memory of his name.

"Talpur."

The stranger's identity slipped across her tongue.

However, her recognition only deepened the man's scowl.

"Talpur died in the cellar of the Duke of Thornhill's Cornish home. How do you know my countryman's name?"

Mercy set her mouth in a tight line. She would say nothing

more. She stubbornly stiffened and pulled in opposition, but it was in futility. The man was as strong as she anticipated.

He jerked hard to pull her beside him.

"Let me look upon your countenance."

He set the lantern on a flat shelf in the stone face. Then he grabbed Mercy's chin to lift it where he might examine her features.

"I looked upon this countenance before, but from afar."

The man's thumb rubbed roughly over Mercy's lips.

"Your brother believes you dead or employed in a brothel," he declared baldly.

Instantly, tears pricked at Mercy's lashes. It broke her heart to know Geoffrey made no effort to find her. She expected as much, but having the truth of her brother's lack of responsibility to his family hurt more than she could ever speak.

"I wonder what the knowledge of your hiding in Cheshire is worth?"

Mercy wanted to beg the man not to betray her, but she remained silent. She would not provide her captor the pleasure of hearing her pleas.

"I imagine Sir Lesley would be most generous, but then perhaps not so much. I cannot think the baronet would desire Lord Lexford's leavings."

Mercy rose to the viscount's defense.

"His Lordship treated me with nothing but respect."

Despite her earlier vow to keep her counsel, Mercy turned her head to the left.

"What do you plan to do with me?"

The man caught her roughly about the neck and returned Mercy's chin to its former position.

"I could make you my leavings instead," he said sinisterly.

Mercy's fear roared to life again. There would be no one to save her; if she were to survive this encounter, it would be of her own design.

"I was on the road for six weeks. Perhaps I have no honor

to steal."

She infused as much bitterness into her words as she could.

"Unlike your fine English gentlemen, men of my country care not for such trivialities," her captor insisted.

"Fah!" Mercy declared. "There are few men on this earth who would treat a woman thusly. The male pride is too ingrained to allow a woman forgiveness."

The man barked out a laugh.

"You are wise beyond your years."

He frowned deeply.

"Talpur once took such liberties with the woman I hoped to make my wife. I am pleased the one known as James Kerrington took the bastard's life."

It was Mercy's turn to frown.

"Yet, you freely use your countryman's name."

Her capturer smiled deprecatingly.

"As you cannot be Mary, I would never be able to call myself Benjamin or Martin. My countenance would betray my foreign beginnings." He said wryly, "I suppose I could choose Shahryār. Thornhill's duchess likened herself to Scheherazade."

The man's true name arrived on a note of clarity.

"Then you are the one known as Jamot?" she accused.

"And you are Miss Nelson?" he countered.

From outside the enclosure another called her name.

"Miss Purefoy!" Mercy stiffened. It was Mr. Hill.

"You spoke the truth," the man announced. "Mr. Hill awaits you."

Mercy shifted her shoulders to a defiant slant.

"You cannot take me with you for Mr. Hill will follow. Your only opportunity for escape is to permit me to return to His Lordship's home."

"Miss Purefoy!" The sound was closer.

The man glanced anxiously toward the opening.

"I could lie in wait and kill Lord Lexford's man."

"How do you know Mr. Hill is alone? Two grooms

accompanied him earlier," Mercy challenged.

A bond of dread knotted her stomach.

The sound of someone moving overhead reverberated in the enclosure. As Mercy suspected, anyone in the cave would know the movement of a person above. The man tightened his hold about her neck.

"If I release you," he bargained hastily, "will you keep my secret? How will I know you will not betray me the moment you step outside this tunnel?"

"I do not wish to return to Lancashire," Mercy admitted. "I shall keep your secret if you do not tell my brother or Sir Lesley of my whereabouts," she bargained.

"Miss Purefoy!" Mr. Hill's voice called more urgently.

Her captor's expression took on a dark warning.

"If you betray me, I will find you and kill you."

Mercy thought she would rather die than to return to her brother's care.

"You must trust me," Mercy encouraged. "We must each walk away and never look back."

The man smiled as he loosened his hold.

"As if we were once lovers."

Mercy swallowed hard and resisted the urge to rub the burning sensation upon the side of her neck.

"When I am through the opening, douse the lantern."

Boldly, she stepped away from him. Setting her feet in action, she walked briskly away. Without turning her head, Mercy squeezed through the opening to reenter the cave. She peered into the muted daylight. Mr. Hill was nowhere in sight, and so she slipped through the space. Mercy would like to look back, to assure the man did not follow–did not point his gun at her back. Instead, she clung to the wall so Mr. Hill would not see her until she was in the open. Finally moving past the falling water, Mercy stepped into the winter sunlight.

"Mr. Hill. Down here!" She pulled her cloak closer to hide her struggle with the stranger, half afraid of what Mr. Hill would do if he discovered the Baloch on Lexford property.

Hill's expression twisted as he peered over the edge of the rock shelf.

"I looked everywhere for you. You sent your maid back."

Mercy glanced anxiously toward the cave. She thought she could see the man watching her. With a lift of her chin, she called to Mr. Hill.

"Come down, Sir. I could use a strong arm on which to lean. I am in need of your strength, Mr. Hill. I am most anxious to return to the safety of Lexington Arms."

Chapter 15

HE STAYED AT CHESTERFIELD MANOR for three days, but Aidan's heart remained tied to his home in the adjoining shire. He missed the tinkling laughter Miss Purefoy used to pepper her speech, and Aidan longed for a hug from his nephew. He would readily admit to indifference to the boy in the beginning, but now he was quite smitten with both the child and the lady. Wellston and Lady Yardley's love filled the baron's household, and although Aidan held few hopes for the intimacies his friend found with Miss Cashémere, he possessed the resemblance of a family, and Aidan was anxious to return to his estate.

He and Wellston spent exhaustive hours bringing Baron Ashton up to snuff on the activities of those involved in the opium ring. They also assisted the baron in identifying agents to include in his set of contacts. Aidan lost some of the details of his earlier participation in the investigation, but the other Realm members summarized what Aidan reported to Pennington. Like so much of the prior years, he could not lay claim to specifics; therefore, Aidan spent his time with Ashton by bringing the baron up to strength on changes in Realm procedures since the time Ashton served his country.

Now, as Aidan turned Valí into Lexington Arms' main

gate, he looked up in anticipation. It was the end of February. Soon, his tenants would be in the fields, and spring would bring new life to the land. For the first time since his youth, Aidan meant to spend time working beside his people. Perhaps then, he could erase any memory of his father's reign as viscount. Although Arlen Kimbolt served the estate well as a financial steward, Aidan knew his father's obsession with securing the Kimbolt line draped the title in rumors and innuendos. Andrew's duel. Susan's early widowhood. Aidan's speedy courtship of his brother's wife. All were a result of his father's manipulations. It was time for Aidan to rule his estate as he chose, not as Arlen Kimbolt would do it.

"You made judicious changes within the house," he told himself. "For once since waking with a black void in my memory, I think my lack of recall a blessing. I possess fewer restrictions on my conscience."

The thought brought an ironic chuckle to his lips. Reining in Valí before the main entrance, Aidan was barely from the saddle before the door opened to reveal Miss Purefoy with Aaron in her arms. It was a scene of pure bliss, and Aidan could not hide his smile of approval.

"Wunkle Waden!" the boy called and squirmed to be free of the lady's embrace. At length, Miss Purefoy placed the boy on his feet, and the child scrambled to reach him. Aidan scooped the boy up and tossed him gently in the air; delightful squeals followed.

Aidan caught the child close to him and held Aaron tightly.

"Did you mind Miss Hanson in my absence?"

The child nodded readily, and Aidan's smile grew wider.

"I am very proud of you, Lad."

He ruffled the child's hair.

"Welcome home, my lord," Miss Purefoy said sweetly. "You were sorely missed, Lord Lexford," she whispered as she slid her hands about Aidan's proffered arm. Instinctively, Aidan flexed his muscle so the lady might know something of his strength.

"I am pleased to return to Lexington Arms' warmth," he said for the benefit of the staff lingering nearby. When he departed less than a week prior, Aidan was not satisfied with the lady's explanation for the kiss they shared. Now, Miss Purefoy's genuine expression of happiness at seeing him brought him a feeling of giddiness. No one but his mother ever displayed such joy with his appearance. In that moment, Aidan wished his staff to oblivion so he might catch the woman to him and bury himself in Miss Purefoy's sweetness. Somehow, he thought the woman might actually welcome him.

He handed the boy to one of the footmen.

"After your nap, I will show you the new pony," he told Aaron.

"Pomise?" the boy said with excitement.

"Only if you take a proper nap. I will ask Miss Hanson for a report," he warned as sternly as his good humor would allow. "Now, off with you."

For a second time, he fluffed the boy's hair. Only a few short weeks prior, the child's resemblance to Andrew pricked Aidan's pride. But with the boy's return to Lexington Arms, all he saw was Aaron, not his brother's betrayal. Aidan knew those changes were a direct result of Miss Purefoy's presence under his roof.

"I should leave you to your business," the lady said softly from beside him.

Aidan caught her hand.

"I insist you join me for tea," he said to deflect any criticism of her earlier boldness. "I spent my time with Lord and Lady Yardley, the barons Swenton and Ashton, and Sir Carter Lowery. We should add Baron Ashton to the guest list for my house party."

Aidan was certain he never witnessed a more enchanting sight as the flush of color kissing Miss Purefoy's cheeks.

She dropped her eyes before saying, "As you wish, my lord."

Aidan did not like the lady in a subservient pose; he preferred Miss Purefoy with a spark of devilment in her eyes.

"Exactly. And I wish your company."

He tightened his grip upon her hand and tugged the woman

along behind him toward the yellow drawing room. Once inside, Aidan closed the door behind him before turning to her. Lifting Miss Purefoy's chin, he spoke earnestly.

"You must never again act the role of my underling. Not before my staff. Never before my neighbors or friends. Until I choose a wife, you are the mistress of this house." Miss Purefoy's eyes searched his countenance. "Do you understand my wishes?"

The lady nodded weakly. Aidan preferred a more definitive response, but he would not insist too strongly. If she were to claim Lexington Arms as her home, it must be on Miss Purefoy's terms. Aidan's thumb stroked her cheek. He thought to kiss her again–to know her warmth, but he knew the folly of acting upon impulse. A letter from Pennington found him in Manchester. It was a simple message: Realm agents discovered a Mary Purefoy working as a maid in an inn in Derbyshire, a place near where Hill reportedly came across "Miss Purefoy." When Aidan first read the carefully worded note, he felt the instant emptiness of loss. If Pennington's words were accurate, and Aidan held no doubt they were: Miss Purefoy lied to him.

At first, he was angry. Angry at the charade, but he knew this woman, perhaps better than he knew any female in his life. Miss Purefoy lied to become a member of his household. The question to her motives remained unanswered. In the meantime, she offered him honest work to repay his kindness.

On the day of the letter, Aidan vowed to discover the truth of her ruse, as well as what drove Miss Purefoy from her home. In addition, he meant to uncover how the lady persuaded Mr. Hill to join in her deceit. The deciding factor regarding the woman was the realization that if Miss Purefoy was not his sister, then the feelings, which kept his emotions a kilter since the day she walked into his life, were not taboo. That particular knowledge sped Aidan's journey home. He meant to see whether the lady felt the same or whether her few flirtations were part of an act. He would confide his suspicions to no one, not even Lucifer Hill.

He tilted her chin up for a closer inspection. His fingers

trailed a line down her neck.

"As long as we understand each other, Mary, we will write our own rules."

⸙

Mercy did not know what to expect with Lord Lexford's return, and the viscount certainly surprised her. She fretted all evening and most of the night regarding her encounter with a man she knew to be an enemy to Lord Lexford and his associates. That fact ate away at her conscience. To think she protected a man, who provided the opportunity would easily take His Lordship's life, increased her anxiety. How could she live with herself if her silence brought disaster to Lord Lexford's door?

"What am I to do?"

She stared out the window at the rolling lawns, still brown from winter's touch, but with blades of green peppering the groomed areas with the promise of spring. Her finger traced a figure of a man and a woman in the moist mist covering the pane. In her mind, she imagined the happy couple caught in a waltz, like the caricatures she once saw on a flyer for a grand assembly hall she held no hope of attending.

"Set the work to order," Mercy said with a catch in her voice. "Set the work and then leave. Your presence in this house places Lord Lexford in danger."

Tears streamed down her cheeks as the moist droplets ruined the crude picture she created.

"Set the work to right; gather your belongings, and leave behind the only man you will ever love."

⸙

"What say we go into the village later?" His Lordship asked as he seated her at his breakfast table.

She missed this simple act during his time in Manchester.

"I must speak to my solicitor regarding funds for Aaron's education and care. Mr. Taylor contracted with others to draw up the proper papers. I thought you might wish to call in at Mr. Chadwick's to choose more samples. We might have tea at the inn if you have a care."

Yesterday, Mercy had a good cry. Today, she planned to enjoy every moment remaining of her time at Lexington Arms.

"That would be delightful, my lord. Perhaps before we go, I might show you the completed work and discuss what I planned for the other suites. I wish your approval for the renovations."

"I am certain whatever you chose is tastefully done, but I would enjoy a tour of the rooms. Let us have our breakfast and then plan our day."

Aidan could not recall a more pleasant time. Although Miss Purefoy refused his offer of placing a desk for her in his study, he managed to convince the lady to spread her samples upon a table near the large windows in the room. As he assisted her in bringing the samples from her small sitting room to his private study, all Aidan could think upon was Wellston's description of Lady Yardley. He wondered if Miss Purefoy possessed any mannerisms, which would entrance Aidan in the same means as Wellston described.

Now, he followed her into the rose toned guest rooms.

"My Goodness!" he exclaimed. "I cannot envision this space being the same chambers as before."

"Have I displeased you, my lord?" Miss Purefoy asked tentatively.

Aidan caught her hand and brought the back of it to his lips to brush a kiss across the lady's knuckles.

"On the contrary, I find it as exquisite as I do you."

Aidan purposely lingered before releasing her hand, and she rewarded him with a quick intake of air. It was very satisfying to know what he suspected about their connection proved true.

Something deep flashed in her eyes, but her tone spoke of censure.

"You should not speak thusly, my lord."

The color rose to her cheeks.

Aidan lifted her chin with his fingertips.

"I speak the truth."

He traced a line from her chin to the base of Miss Purefoy's neck.

She asked through trembling lips, "What brought on these changes, my lord?"

"No changes," Aidan insisted.

He surveyed her delicate features.

"I simply spent the past several days observing my best friend and the woman I once thought to claim as my own, working at making a life together. I returned to Lexington Arms with a renewal of my resolve to do the same."

Miss Purefoy said uncertainly, "Yet you possess no wife."

Again, the lady blushed, and Aidan understood to where her thoughts traveled. Her words made him bolder. He peered into her wide, chocolate colored eyes.

Aidan smiled easily.

"I have no wife. 'Tis true. But I possess family. You and Aaron. You said so yourself. I can grab a bit of happiness, can I not?" He paused for emphasis. "You mean to remain by my side, do you not? Tell me you hold no plans to leave Lexington Arms."

The fact Miss Purefoy hesitated worked against Aidan's confidence.

"We knew since my arrival, I would one day take my leave of your kindness."

Again, the lady's lips trembled.

"Why?" Aidan asked honestly. "Why must you leave me?"

"Because one day you will choose a wife. You said as much only moments ago. You shall know the tenderness of a wife and the joy of a family." Her gaze met his. "Please promise me when you welcome your own children, you will not neglect Aaron. The young master holds a great capacity for love."

Aidan studied the lady's sincerity. He could not understand the contrasts. From Pennington's message, Aidan held no doubt Miss Purefoy practiced some form of deceit, but when she spoke of his nephew, he knew the lady spoke without artifice.

"Most assuredly Aaron will recognize my affection. Until I produce an heir, my nephew is my second; and even after I have a son, Aaron remains in the line of inheritance. Today, I mean legally to remove all claims the Rhodeses may hold to the boy, as well as to dictate funds for Aaron's care if something would happen to me."

He led her farther into the room.

"Do you not wish to know the joy of family also?"

Miss Purefoy looked off, but tears teased her eyes. Her lips twisted with what appeared to be long-suppressed emotions.

"Every woman wishes for a husband and children. In our society, family defines a woman's worth; yet, I am likely to spin my years in isolation. I hold no hope of knowing a husband."

Her words bothered Aidan more than he would admit. He could not imagine her as a spinster. Aidan desired the woman, but he was not prepared to make her a marriage offer. A twinge of guilt shot through him. Perhaps he should rethink a possible seduction. If the lady could not trust him enough to confide in him, especially after all this time and all they saw together, Aidan would never know peace. Susan led him to believe she would wait for him to earn his fortune; instead, she accepted Andrew's overtures. And the Aldridge twins schemed against him, as well. Aidan would not permit another woman her deceptions. The corundum remained. What should he do with the fictional Mary Purefoy?

"Explain your vision for this room," he said to redirect the conversation.

Several hours later, His Lordship escorted her into the village. Their earlier exchange remained with Mercy. She purposely asked Miss Chadwick to accompany them. The girl appeared happy to visit with her family while Mercy shopped. It was the perfect solution to Mercy's avoiding His Lordship's attentions.

"I will call for you in an hour." Viscount Lexford said as he assisted her and Serena from the carriage. He held the door to the shop for them before disappearing into a building several doors away. At length, Mercy released her breath.

From the moment of the viscount's return, Mercy's emotions rolled in the way of a stormy sea.

"I mean to go upstairs unless you require my assistance," Serena stated.

"Enjoy your brothers and sisters," Mercy assured.

As Serena moved away, Mercy nodded to Mr. Chadwick before drifting off toward the fabric samples. She possessed plans for three more rooms before she would leave Lexington Arms. It was all so bittersweet. Mercy never felt so alive in her life, and yet so dead. With the viscount's encouragement, she discovered new facets of her personality, which Mercy once admired in others. It was a heady feeling to recognize her growing maturity. Yet, she despised the untruth lying between her and Lord Lexford.

Mercy removed her notes from her reticule and set to work making choices. A half hour later, she set aside selections from Mr. Chadwick's limited stock and instructed the shopkeeper on what he should secure from London. With the time remaining, Mercy looked about the store. It would be exquisitely pleasurable to purchase many of the items on display: a finely polished chain that would look lovely with her missing locket, a lace-trimmed handkerchief, and a pair of kid gloves.

"Miss?" A small dirty-faced boy tugged on Mercy cloak. "A man told me to give ye this."

He shoved a folded note into Mercy's hand.

Immediately, she wondered if Lord Lexford would be detained. Looking up to study the street beyond the shop window, she asked, "What man?"

"Fine gentleman, Miss. Gave me two pence to be certain you git his note personally," the child said in self-importance.

"Thank you," Mercy said with a smile for the boy.

Inside, her stomach rolled with dread. With a quick glance to make certain no one observed the exchange, Mercy strolled toward a deserted corner of the shop. Unfolding the paper, she turned her back to the store's interior. Bringing the note to the light, she read, "You thought I would not discover your whereabouts, but you erred."

No signature, but Mercy knew it was either from Geoffrey or Sir Lesley. No one else would have a care for her absence from Foresthill Hall. Oh, why did she tarry so long in Cheshire? *Because you are in love with the viscount*, her foolish heart answered.

Mercy caught at the windowsill. Her legs meant to buckle, but she willed herself to remain erect. Instead, her eyes searched the street for any sign of either her brother or the baronet, but only the usual villagers went about their business.

Mercy read the note again. It said nothing of how the person found her. Likely, the one known as Jamot betrayed her. She was a fool to think he would not. The note also did not indicate when "he" would come for her. How long did she have? A day? A week? A few hours?

If the mystery writer was Geoffrey, her brother would likely demand a payment from Viscount Lexford to keep her identity secret, or worst yet, demand His Lordship marry Mercy. Geoffrey would desire the connections, but as much as Mercy wished to be Lord Lexford's wife, she would not permit his alliance with the likes of Baron Geoffrey Nelson. Her conscience pricked her like the devil.

And if the author of the note were Sir Lesley Trent, the baronet would ruin Lord Lexford's reputation. She possessed no doubt Sir Lesley would find a means to bring gossip to the viscount's door. When she considered the scandal of Andrew Kimbolt's duel and the secrets hidden in Lady Cassandra's diary, Mercy knew she could not permit the chaos to follow him.

A shiver of dread ran down Mercy's spine. Her only choice appeared to be a return to Lancashire. She would never see Lord Lexford again. The viscount would be glad to see her go, and all she did for him would be a reminder of her lies.

"Why are you hiding in this corner?"

A familiar voice asked close to Mercy's ear, and she looked up to see Lord Lexford's beloved countenance.

"My Goodness! You are not well," he said in concern as he caught Mercy's elbow to support her. "You are too pale."

She must really be distraught if Lord Lexford took note.

"Why did you not send word for my speedy return?"

"It is nothing," Mercy said as he braced her stance. "I simply have one of my headaches."

For once, Mercy's headache had a true source. Her whisper of a voice spoke of her distress.

Viscount Lexford whispered in reprimand.

"I will not have you suffer."

He placed Mercy's hand on his arm. Mercy allowed Lord Lexford to direct her steps toward the door. She could not think clearly.

"Chadwick, I mean to see Miss Purefoy home. The lady is not well. I will send the carriage back for Miss Chadwick."

"That is not necessary, my lord," Chadwick assured. "Serena is healthy enough for a good walk."

"Nonsense," Lord Lexford insisted. "Your daughter is part of my household. The carriage will return shortly. Please be so kind as to inform Millie. She awaits her mistress at the inn."

"Aye, Sir."

Mercy knew the note's author likely observed how the viscount cared for her. Lord Lexford was the kindest man of Mercy's acquaintance, and the manner in which His Lordship saw to the comfort of a simple shopkeeper's daughter spoke volumes of the man's character. Despite his training as an agent of the British government, Lord Lexford was a vulnerable target for those with unprincipled manipulations–those such as her brother, who would sell his sister to a distasteful old man, in order to recover part of Geoffrey's debts. Mercy must find a means to protect the viscount from a connection not worthy of him.

In the carriage, Mercy sat with her head pressed against the soft squabs and her eyes closed. She wished to block out the chaos surrounding her. When the viscount lifted her to his lap, she rested her head on his shoulder. It was another exquisite moment to add to her memories of the man.

"Thank you, my lord," she whispered against the rough skin of his neck.

A scruffy stubble showed upon his chin. Mercy found the contrast of dark and light quite mesmerizing. She kept her eyes focused on Lord Lexford's cheek. As the carriage rocked gently, Mercy filled her lungs with the scent of him. She etched upon her memory, the clean smell of soap, mixed with spicy sandalwood. The combination would forever remind her of Aidan Kimbolt.

She had not stirred from her quarters since the viscount escorted her to her room a day and a half prior. Mercy wished to hide under the blankets forever, as if being safely in Lord Lexford's home would drive away her "phantoms." Yesterday, she gathered her few personal belongings and placed them where she might easily retrieve them. She also carefully counted the coins Mr. Hill presented her in anticipation of her leaving. Today, Mercy constructed a letter to His Lordship and another to Mr. Hill. This evening, after everyone took to his beds, she would leave in the night's middle.

"Like a thief," she told her reflection in the windowpane.

The candlelight flickered from a draft behind her; yet, Mercy did not turn her head. She made her decision.

Earlier, Millie assisted Mercy with her nightclothes and unknowingly delivered a message, which sealed Mercy's fate.

"Miss," the girl said tentatively, "when I be waitin' fer ye at the inn like His Lordship be sayin' a young lord approached me."

Mercy's stomach plummeted, but she schooled her expression to one of surprise.

"A young lord?" Mercy worked to keep her voice somber and her gaze steady.

"Yes, Miss. Fine looking with London clothes and all."

The girl spoke with excitement while Mercy's mind raced with possibilities.

"The lord said he be knowin' ye from yer home, and he

acted mighty disappointed when he sees Lord Lexford escorting ye to the viscount's carriage."

A young lord, Mercy thought. So the author of her note was her brother. It made sense. She previously noted the dark-skinned Baloch in company with Geoffrey.

Another headache blossomed within Mercy's head. She rubbed her forehead with her fingertips before quickly dropping her hands to her side. Swallowing heavily, Mercy forced even tones to her response.

"I cannot imagine who the gentleman might be."

"All I knows is he be mighty nice to me," the young maid said wistfully. "Bought me a glass of beer while I waits for His Lordship's carriage to return. Asked me questions 'bout how long you was at Lexington Arms, but I not tell him nothing. I swears it, Miss."

"I hold nothing to hide," Mercy said graciously.

With practiced politeness, she thanked the girl for her service before Mercy retrieved a book from the table to execute the ruse of reading in bed.

"That shall be all I require this evening, Millie. You may be excused."

The girl curtsied before shoving her hand in her apron's pocket.

"The gentleman asked me to give ye this note."

Reluctantly, Mercy accepted the folded paper. She casually placed the note on the table as if it was of no significance; yet, when the maid exited, Mercy snatched the paper from the surface to read:

"I will be waiting for you three days hence beside the stream where Lord Lexford took his plunge."

"Three days hence," Mercy murmured. "This is the second day."

She must be gone before dawn, but Mercy had one more task. At length, the clock downstairs struck eleven, and Mercy blew out the candle before sneaking quietly from her room.

On soundless feet, she crept along the corridor until she came to the door she sought. With sweaty palms, Mercy turned the latch and eased the door from the frame to slip into the muted light of the dying embers of the fireplace. Closing the door behind her, she turned the lock until a soft click announced no admittance. Mercy tentatively stepped into the room. Her knees trembled, but despite her sheltered upbringing, her heart knew she made the correct decision. With a deep breath to steady her nerves, Mercy walked into the semi-circle of light.

Her heart jumped with expectancy as a dark figure rose from a chair turned away from her.

"Mary?"

Concern rose in the viscount's voice.

"Is something amiss? Should I summon a physician?"

Mercy despised the fact he called her "Mary" instead of her given name. She wished desperately for the viscount to know the real Mercy Nelson.

"No, my lord," she said softly.

"Then why are you here?" he asked without censure.

The fire's reflection in the viscount's eyes made Mercy think of the desire she observed in Lord Lexford's eyes whenever he looked upon her, and the thought embolden her.

"I thought we might share a glass of sherry. I have not seen you since we returned to Lexington Arms yesterday afternoon."

The viscount took several steps in her direction, but stopped short.

"I fear I have no sherry in my quarters," he said with an easy smile. "I could offer you brandy."

His gaze met and locked with hers.

Mercy shook off his offer. For a moment, she paused in controlled intensity.

"Brandy is not a drink for a lady's taste."

"Then I will send for the sherry or retrieve it myself."

Lord Lexford started past her, but Mercy stopped him my placing her hand on his chest. Through the fine lawn of his shirt, she could feel the erratic beat of the viscount's heart. It matched hers perfectly. His breathing shallowed as he leaned closer.

"Mary, you play with fire," he said on a rasp. "If you remain, I mean to know you as a man knows a woman."

Mercy's chin rose. She stared lovingly into his eyes. Eyes, she would never forget.

"I am well aware of your desire, my lord," she said baldly.

The steadiness of her voice surprised her. Her erratic pulse slowed. Even if she could not escape Geoffrey, Mercy meant to spend one night in the arms of the man she loved.

"But are you aware of mine, Lord Lexford?"

Chapter 16

AIDAN STOOD TO SEND Mr. Hill upon his way, but a muslin-clad Mary Purefoy brought him up short. The soft glow of the fire kissed the lady's fair skin, and Aidan felt the tug of desire in his groin. As if she fought the urge to cover herself, the lady twisted her hands together before her. Yet, surprisingly, when he inquired as to her reason for coming to him, she said boldly, "I thought we might share a glass of sherry."

Only if I can drink it from the flat of your stomach, his body screamed. Aidan took a step in her direction.

"I fear I have no sherry in my quarters. I could offer you brandy."

His heart pounded out an erratic rhythm. Aidan's eyes remained locked upon the lady's countenance, and she slanted an odd look in his direction.

Miss Purefoy shook off his offer.

"Brandy is not a drink for a lady's taste."

He wanted her to stay. Aidan had no idea what Miss Purefoy planned, but he meant to discover her purpose.

"Then I will send for the sherry or retrieve it myself."

He started for the door, but her hand on his chest halted Aidan's progress. A thrill of elation spread through his veins. He lifted her chin with his fingertips, tilting her head where he might look upon her lovely countenance.

"Mary, you play with fire," he warned. "If you remain, I mean to know you as a man."

Her chin took on that defiant slant Aidan came to love. A smile tugged at the corners of the lady's mouth. Their gazes fastened as he explored the depths of the woman's resolve.

"I am well aware of your desire, my lord," she declared in a clear voice. "But are you aware of mine, Lord Lexford?"

A wash of moonlight caused her hair to gleam like liquid gold. Her figure was perfection: rounded hips, full breasts, and a small waist. Desire rushed in, but Aidan firmly put it in its place. He would require all his faculties; yet, somehow, Aidan thought the battle already lost.

He inhaled her scent. He would never smell lilacs again without thinking of her. At the moment, he wished desperately to know her real name. To whisper it in her ear. He looked deeply in the dark brown eyes that were now so familiar. Aidan could wait no longer to know her heat along his body. He pulled her into his embrace, and the lady came willingly.

"Oh, God, Mary, I dreamed of this moment," Aidan murmured.

He placed a line of kisses from her temple to her chin. At length, his mouth covered hers in a blazing kiss, which declared his need for her.

She came into his life at a most inopportune time, but the woman opened his closeted existence to a new world. Mary Purefoy, or whatever her name might be, presented Aidan a part of him long left behind.

Her arms moved about his neck, and Aidan pulled her closer, lifting her hips where he might grind his erection against her vee. Hungry to taste her again, when her lips parted, he slid his tongue along the seam and plunged in. Desire raced straight to his brain. Never did Aidan feel such unrestrained passion. He loved the feel of the soft tissues of her mouth on the tip of his tongue.

When she ventured to touch her tongue to his lips, Aidan's ardor soared. He made a practice of never kissing the women he paid for sexual pleasure, and Susan never shared such intimacies. He could barely catch his breath.

In a passion-drenched moment, he released her mouth.

"I must have you," he growled.

Aidan prayed she would not refuse. Her body trembled beneath his touch.

"Come with me," he coaxed.

She looked at him in bewilderment, but the lady did not attempt to move away. Instead, she curled herself about him, her arms tightening about Aidan's neck.

He caught her left hand and brought it to his lips. He kissed each of her fingertips, sucking lightly on her index finger before whispering, "Will you lie with me, Mary?"

A faint smile spread across her lips.

"I will, my lord."

Never did Aidan know such joy. He caught her hand to tug Mary along behind him toward his bed. She shivered, but her expression never changed. Miss Purefoy accepted the fact this night would be the one in which they would join in the most basic of dances. Her boldness should have spoken of the lady's loose morals, but Aidan knew in his heart she was an innocent, and this night would change their lives forever.

"Are you frightened?" he asked as he recaptured her in his arms.

Mary bit her bottom lip. Despite what he said earlier, Aidan meant to provide her the opportunity to change her mind.

"Of you, my lord? Never. Of not pleasing you? Infinitely so."

Her voice held the promise of sensuality, and Aidan felt himself grow harder. Her words were a salve to his racing pulse.

"You please me more than you know," Aidan rasped.

He ran his hand through her hair. It was the golden silk he knew it to be. He wound the strands about his palm, drawing her closer. He nibbled upon her ear, running his tongue along the lobe. The lady's body grew warmer, and Aidan lifted her hips so she could feel his heat. After tonight, he would commit himself to this woman. That knowledge brought a twinge of doubt, but Aidan realized if Mary desired him as much as he did her, then he would be helpless to stop what he began. Somehow, they would make a life together. Their connection would prove strong in molding their futures.

The lines of the lady's countenance spoke of her classic beauty. She was all female, and all his. The invisible threads between them tightened. Her arms snaked about his waist, and Aidan lowered his mouth slowly to hers. A fire ignited between them.

His hands trembled as he reached for the ribbon tie of her robe.

"You possess one last opportunity to withdraw," he growled.

"Kiss me, " she whispered.

Aidan's lips touched her tenderly before sliding down her neck to suck on the point where the vein throbbed in anticipation. His tongue circled the pink scar where the bullet grazed her skin. The thought of how he could have lost her before he had the opportunity to know her intimately sent a shiver down his spine. He tightened his embrace. With one hand, Aidan tugged the ribbon lose and guided the cloth from her shoulders. With a swish, the robe slid to the floor. Aidan's hands explored her arms, her back, the rise and fall of her hips. Through the thin muslin, her breasts stood erect. Aidan's mouth went dry, but he remained hungry: Hungry to taste her.

Desire crowded Aidan's chest as his fingers fumbled with the few buttons keeping him from the ecstasy her body promised. At length, the gauzy material slid over her creamy shoulders to reveal Heaven on Earth. He caught her wrists to prevent Mary from covering her breasts.

"You are exquisite," he rasped as his eyes scanned her

curves.

She was everything Aidan never knew he wanted in his life and in his bed.

The lady's hands smoothed the lines of his shoulders, and she whispered his name: "My Aidan."

He lifted her to his bed. Watching the lady as lust rose in his veins, Aidan dragged his shirt over his head. Unbuttoning his breeches, he slid the cloth from his hips taking his small clothes with them. Mary's eyes widened as the stiffness of his erection was exposed.

"I promise I will not hurt you," he said warmly as he crawled across the bed to recapture her mouth.

Skin against skin. Heat wrapped with heat. Aidan recalled the two times they kissed. Each kiss had excited him beyond reason. Excited and confused him. But kissing Mary when no barriers remained between them drove all the confusion away. Nothing ever felt so right. The sensation of his skin against hers sent ripples of need to his erection.

His kiss started tenderly, but it quickly grew to raw need. The intense desire in the lady's expression captivated him. His mouth slanted over hers. Mary's hands skimmed his chest, his waist, and his back. As the passion unfurled deep within him, Aidan lowered his head to place gentle kisses upon her breasts. His erection jerked in expectancy while Aidan laved her nipples before sucking firmly. Mary rewarded him with a groan and a digging of her nails into his back. She arched, driving her breast further into his mouth.

"Aidan," she moaned.

He raised his head to look upon her.

"Yes, my love?" he asked adoringly.

He enjoyed his name upon her lips. Slowly, methodically, Aidan blew upon the dampness to tease the nipple, making it bead harder.

On a self-possessed breath, she confessed, "It is too much."

"When I am with you, it is never enough," he declared

huskily. "I mean to possess you."

His mouth returned to her breast. This time her fingers moved through Aidan's hair. With each lick of his tongue, Aidan's desire intensified.

He balanced his weight on his forearms as his mouth returned to hers. Aidan meant to brand Mary Purefoy as his–to demand her surrender. Her body trembled, and he realized she was close to knowing pleasure for the first time.

Her tongue challenged his, and he took full advantage of the moment to slide his hand along the flat of her stomach to her most private place. His fingers traced the dampness up and down her folds. She writhed beneath his touch, as if she searched for something only he could provide. When he bluntly entered her dampness with first one and then a second finger, Mary's hips rotated against his hand. Aidan's thumb massaged the nub while his fingers entered and withdrew. At length, a cry of pleasure escaped her lips as Mary's legs slammed shut about his fist. Aidan took great pleasure in milking the last shudder from the lady's body.

When she trembled weakly, Aidan leaned forward to kiss her tenderly. He slowly withdrew his fingers, wiping her dampness along the blankets.

"I want you more than I could ever tell you," he whispered as he kissed her temple. He caught her chin in his large palm. "Mary," he said hopelessly.

She caressed his cheek with tremulous fingers. Her gentleness moved Aidan in ways he could not anticipate. His former concerns melted immediately. She lied to him about her name, but everything about the woman said her emotions were real. He tugged her into his arms, and Mary's body molded tightly to his. Aidan rained kisses over her face, her hair, her shoulders, and her neck.

His body yearned for this woman. She was a vibrant, sensual woman. A sensual woman who belonged to him. Only he would ever know her. Raising his head, Aidan devoured her with a searing gaze.

"You are so beautiful," he said huskily.

He kissed her again–a sizzling kiss, which left them both breathless.

"So unbearably beautiful."

He braced his rigid body above hers: His manhood thick and swollen. He straddled her legs, and with a nudge of his knee, Aidan opened her further.

"I will treat you gently," he said through taut lips.

Unable to remove his eyes from her, Aidan's hands searched her body. He would worship the pure ivory of her skin. Pay homage to the thrill of knowing this woman forever. She strained high as he tormented her nipples. She blinked blindly, pleasure flooding her and causing his manhood to jerk in response.

Mary's body arched against him. He caught one pink nipple in his mouth. He laved it with the wet wash of his tongue. He licked and nibbled freely; and she bit her bottom lip to stifle her cry of pleasure. Her ragged breaths plunged him toward an early release, but Aidan swallowed his building desires. He reveled in every soft whimper from her lips.

His swollen head probed her opening. Sweat exploded on his brow as Aidan attempted to control his hunger. His near uncontrollable desire for her humbled him. He meant to drive into her until they were one person. Aidan gritted his teeth as he entered her; Mary's heat swallowed him inch by inch, and his muscles bunched tight across his back. The perfection of the sensations came close to pulling him apart, but Aidan held. His entry finally met the membrane protecting her virginity, and Aidan flinched with regret for their actions; yet, he was beyond stopping. He kissed her again, a long sizzling kiss, which left them both gasping for air.

Awashed in pleasure, Aidan's eyes closed so he might enjoy the mounting frenzy. The sensations thundered through him as he pushed past the wall with one hard thrust.

"Mary," he chanted in slow releases of ecstasy.

The frenzy grew. Her body rubbed against his turgid flesh. His mouth sought hers, only releasing her when rewarded with a heated moan. Aidan gritted his teeth and increased his pace. When Mary joined him in the blending of their bodies, a shudder wracked him as his seed exploded deep inside her. The air filled with the sound of raspy mews. She spasmed against his heat, and Aidan was at peace with a beautiful woman. He collapsed upon her, his breathing erratic, but Aidan had the oddest feeling he finally came home.

Mercy clung to him with every ounce of strength remaining within her bones. She understood the mechanics of what would occur between them, but she held no concept of the intense emotional connection, which would tie her to Lord Lexford forever. His possessiveness thrilled her. Being claimed by Aidan Kimbolt was an honor indeed. Her heart pounded so hard she thought it might explode.

Yet, a small part of her regretted their joining. Mercy sought his room because she loved Lord Lexford more than words could describe, and it was her intention to know him once before she departed Lexington Arms. However, His Lordship would never reciprocate. He did not think upon her as she did him. The viscount freely shared his body–freely whispered words of desire in her ear, but words of affection remained unsaid.

"God!" he groaned while air slowly seeped into her lungs. Awareness returned as he buried his head into the curve of Mercy's neck. At length, the viscount rolled to his side taking her with him. He wrapped her into his embrace and pulled the bed linens over them. She rested her head upon his shoulder. He smoothed one hand across her hair as he slipped into the stupor of sleep. Mercy remained beside him, listening to the return of the steady beat of his heart. If she could remain so always, she would never complain.

His Lordship's breathing indicated his body meant to know sleep. Mercy settled along the length of him. When Lord Lexford accepted the exhaustion, which crept through his bones, she would return to her quarters, gather her belongings, and steal out into the night's darkness. His fingertips sent heat up and down Mercy's arms.

"I know," the viscount said sleepily, "Mary Purefoy is not your real name. Will you not trust me with your identity?"

Mercy feared this moment from the day she crossed Lord Lexford's threshold. The letter she left on her bureau addressed to him would explain everything, so she said, "It is a long complicated story, my lord. We shall speak of it in detail upon the morrow."

He kissed her forehead.

"I will permit you your secrets for a few hours more, but know I mean to have the truth from you."

Mercy waited until His Lordship's breathing indicated the soundness of his sleep before she pried herself from his grasp. Dressing quickly, she exited his suite through Lord Lexford's dressing room. She did not chance releasing the exterior door's lock in fear of waking him. Before going to his room, she arranged her gown and cloak and packed her bag. Mercy took only the gowns she brought with her from Lancashire–none of what the viscount purchased for her, other than the music box. She saved the coins Mr. Hill presented her, and Mercy meant to purchase passage to London.

"Running away?" a familiar male voice said as she slipped into the darkness of the kitchen's garden.

Mercy spun around to find Lucifer Hill sitting upon a small bench.

"My Goodness!" she gasped. "You presented me quite a fright."

Her hand fluttered at her throat.

"You did not answer my question," Mr. Hill said stubbornly. "It is a regrettable habit, Miss Purefoy."

Mercy's shoulders shifted in defiance.

"I am leaving; it is time, Mr. Hill."

The man stood to tower over her, but Mercy held her ground.

"Without a proper farewell to either me or His Lordship? Do we mean so little to you?"

Mercy glanced lovingly at the house behind her.

"You know that is not true. I saw His Lordship, and I left a proper note for both you and him."

"Yet, at this moment, Lord Lexford knows nothing of your flight?"

Mercy dropped her eyes in sorrow.

"It would make little difference; it is better this way. Those from whom I sought release followed me to Cheshire."

Mr. Hill caught her arm.

"Lord Lexford and I would protect you if you require a shield."

Tears rolled down Mercy's cheeks. Apprehension griped her.

"I cannot ask either of you to place yourself in danger in my behalf. Moreover, there are more devious means to exact revenge on Lord Lexford than to stand in defense of my honor. Some of low connections would claim his good name if I remained at Lexington Arms."

"Should you not permit the viscount to decide if he wishes to deny the connections?" Mr. Hill reasoned. "I would not imagine His Lordship would turn from whatever scandal you name. I observe how Viscount Lexford looks upon you. The man cares for you deeply."

Mercy wished she could be assured of the viscount's affections, but she chose to terminate their relationship. She shared his bed because she loved him, not because she wished to trap him in marriage; and Mercy held no doubt His Lordship would extend an offer of marriage. He was an honorable man.

"I am not worthy of Lord Lexford," she said simply. "Now, if you will excuse me. I must hurry to catch the coach at the inn."

Mr. Hill did not release her.

"If you are set on leaving, I will take you as far as Warwickhsire. The wagon is loaded with wool. I mean to set when Deland has the horses to harness."

Mercy's heart leapt with pleasure. It would be comforting not to travel alone. The possibility of unscrupulous men upon the journey frightened Mercy beyond reason.

"Lord Lexford would not approve of your involvement in my departure."

"I am the one who brought you to Lexford's notice. I should be the one to see you upon your way."

Tipping her head to one side, she considered Mr. Hill's offer carefully. Mercy would gladly accept his protection.

"I do not wish for the others to know I departed."

Mr. Hill nodded his understanding.

"Take the lane to just past the gatehouse. I will come for you on the main road."

"Thank you, Mr. Hill. I pray you shall not regret the gesture."

Aidan rolled over to caress her breast. He had four hours of sleep, enough for him to desire her again, but she was gone. Aidan frowned as he glanced about his quarters. Even the lady's clothing disappeared. He rubbed a dry hand across his face in an effort to clear his thinking; yet, nothing wiped away the memory of burying himself deep within her liquid heat.

"So sweet," he murmured to the empty room.

And she was. Sweet sensuality and sweet innocence. Just considering her soft moans brought another erection. Aidan understood why she returned to her room. Miss Purefoy could not be found in his bed; yet, acknowledging the sensibility of the lady's actions did little to relieve Aidan's renewed hunger. He buried his nose into the bed linens. The scent of lilacs lingered, and he inhaled deeply. His eyes closed to summon forth another dream of Mary Purefoy. Tomorrow, Aidan would discover her name, and then he would make his addresses. Soon, she would be in his bed every night. And soon the hollow emptiness would no longer well up with guilt for failing Susan.

The sharp knock at his chamber door brought Aidan from a sound sleep.

"Who knew?" he thought as he staggered toward the door, after wrapping a robe about his naked body. He thought of the pleasure of having Mary Purefoy beneath him and of finally having a full night's sleep.

"A woman and sleep could be complementary."

An ironic smirk touched his lips as he jerked open the door.

"What is amiss?" he growled at his properly clad butler.

Aidan realized it must be later than he anticipated.

Mr. Payne took a reflexive step backward.

"A message, Sir."

The man extended a silver salver.

"From Sir Carter and delivered by a special express."

Aidan swallowed his groan.

"When?" he asked distractedly.

"Only moments ago, Sir."

"Thank you, Mr. Payne. Please tell Mr. Hill I need to speak to him."

Aidan turned toward his quarters.

The butler cleared his throat.

"Mr. Hill departed early for Warwick, Sir."

Aidan scowled his disapproval.

"Of course. I forgot."

He broke the seal and scanned the hastily written note from the baronet. Sir Carter required Aidan's assistance with a possible lead on the opium line.

"Mr. Payne, send Mr. Poley in, and tell Deland I require a horse immediately."

"Yes, Sir."

"Also, please inform Miss Purefoy I will be away from the estate for several days on urgent business."

Aidan poured water to wash his face.

Mr. Payne bowed.

"Yes, Sir. I will make a point of conveying your message when the lady comes down for breakfast.

Aidan shot a quick glance at the clock upon the mantel. It was shortly after nine. He smiled. So the lady slept longer, as well. Normally, they both breakfasted by eight and started their days.

He despised being drawn away without first making his addresses known to the lady, but, hopefully, Miss Purefoy would understand. When he returned, Aidan would arrange a romantic evening to prove his honest regard. He would propose. Although he could not speak of love, Aidan realized he and Miss Purefoy held a deep respect for each other. It was more than many aristocrats possessed in their marriage. It would be enough. He would not risk his heart ever again.

Miss Purefoy's body swayed against his shoulder. She fell asleep an hour into their journey. Hill knew he must discover what the lady planned before he released her to the London coach. By the time he could return to Cheshire to inform Lord Lexford of her direction, Miss Purefoy would possess a four day advance on the viscount. Lexford would never find her if Hill could not convince the woman to confide in him.

A deep rut in the road jarred her awake.

"Where are we?" Miss Purefoy asked as she stretched her neck and shoulders.

"Nearing the border of Staffordshire," Hill explained. "I fear with the wagon laden so heavy with wool that our journey will be slower than if you traveled by coach."

Miss Purefoy smiled easily.

"On the coach, I would possess no shoulder to support me. I am quite content, Mr. Hill, for your company, however much time remains."

Hill studied her countenance.

"Are you certain this is the best choice for you and His

Lordship? If you fear Lord Lexford's retribution for the deception we foisted upon the viscount, I can tell you from experience Viscount Lexford's temper flares quickly, but it pales just as fast. He will forgive us both once he admits his heart is engaged. Say the word, and I will turn the wagon about. We will be home before nightfall. His Lordship will not complain if I set out on a different day with the wool."

Hill watched as indecision crossed her expression, but the lady shook off his suggestion.

"You paint a beautiful picture, Mr. Hill, but my betrayal lies deeper than calling myself Mary Purefoy, half sister to Viscount Lexford," she murmured with definitive regret.

Hill sighed heavily. He nodded his head with forced politeness.

"If that is your wish, I will see you safely upon your journey. Lord Lexford would expect nothing less. I thought we might stop at an inn for a bite of breakfast. That is, if you hold no objections to being seen with the likes of me."

His companion smiled warmly. It was the same smile Hill knew stole the viscount's heart. The lady presented him a knowing look, her sparkling eyes saying more than mere words. Miss Purefoy's thoughts rested on Lord Lexford also. She squeezed Hill's hand.

"You are my guardian angel, Lucifer Hill. I would be foolish to deny your company."

Hill directed the horses through a difficult section of the road before responding.

"Lord Godown keeps a small reiver's hut on the edge of his property. I use it often when I am in the area. The marquis regularly restocks the place with food and clean linens. It will mean a shorter day today and a longer one tomorrow, but it will keep us from taking refuge in an unsavory inn. I would not have you exposed to the likes of The Purple Goose. Yet, please know the marquis's hut is nothing more than one large room with a lean to behind. I could ask at the main house for sanctuary. Lord Godown is to London for his aunt's engagement party; yet, I am certain his staff could find us appropriate lodging."

The lady frowned deeply.

"I would not wish to involve the marquis in my difficulties. Beyond your loyalty, Lord Lexford speaks of the Earl of Berwick and Lord Godown as his closest friends."

Hill smiled at her diplomacy. He was nothing more than a farmer, who learned to operate in the world of aristocrats. He mastered much while serving with Viscount Lexford, but Hill held no delusions of his own worth.

"We are mature enough to share the shelter of the room without making propriety an issue. I am not so high in the instep to look poorly upon your kindness, Mr. Hill."

"If Lord Lexford extends his forgiveness, Miss Purefoy," Hill pleaded. "Please accept the man's promise and make an honest man of the viscount. Your tenacity is exactly what Lexford requires for his happiness."

A tear escaped the corner of the lady's eye.

"Your word picture is the perfect portrait upon which to latch my dreams, Mr. Hill. Perfect, indeed."

Chapter 17

AIDAN SPENT FOUR DAYS in disguise infiltrating a group, which transported the opium into the various shires. It was the role HE regularly played in the Realm. Aidan assumed many faces and accents to secure information. Those involved in the shipments knew both Lowery and Swenton so Sir Carter sent for Aidan. For three days, he dressed in filthy clothes and spoke with a Scottish accent. Sir Carter even arrested Aidan's "character" as part of the group. Later, if he met any of those involved, Aidan's "Kell MacLeary" would claim escaping his gaolers.

Aidan enjoyed stopping the supply line into his home shire, but he held no delusions of the British government driving opiates from its shores. Most people thought men placing themselves under the power of the opium from the beautiful poppy plant were a problem found exclusively in London's slews, but the growing use of the drug was everywhere, among the rich and the poor, and the city dwellers, as well as common villagers. The fight would know no end.

Aidan hoped to arrive home before his household retired for the evening, but it was near eleven of the clock when he used his key to enter the manor. He was exhausted, but his desire to see Miss Purefoy guided his thoughts for the past three hours, and he wanted to look upon her countenance before another minute passed. He would not wake her, but Aidan meant to sneak into her room and satisfy his obsession with the woman.

Avoiding the main stairs, he circled through the servants' quarters, making his way toward the west wing. Aidan would steal a quick peek and then seek his bed for the evening. He would surprise the lady at breakfast tomorrow.

Quietly easing the servants' door open, he stepped into the muted light of the passage. Aidan clung to the shadows. He was Lexington Arms' master, but he would not embarrass Miss Purefoy by permitting others to view him entering the lady's room. If he were to make Miss Purefoy his wife, Aidan would not have her name defamed by his actions.

"Her name," he whispered to the stillness.

The words brought a new recognition. Aidan must maintain the ruse of their relationship. The realization stayed Aidan's progress. His household and the neighborhood thought of her as "Mary Purefoy." Calling the lady by her given name would not be an issue. He could claim "Mary" as the lady's middle name or pet name.

"Yet, how will the banns be called?" he reasoned.

Aidan did not consider the ramifications of his decision to make the woman his wife.

"A special license will be required and in another parish."

He slid down the wall to sit upon the floor. There were so many issues to which he never gave reflection. How had he not thought this through before he became involved with the woman?

"Because your lust controlled your motives."

He chastised his foolish lack of forethought. It was certainly not characteristic of him. True. He often walked about with his heart upon his sleeve, but his logic always prevailed until he met Miss Purefoy.

"The lady has you bamboozled," he said ironically.

Aidan circled his legs with his arms and rested his forehead on his knees. His chest contracted. He wondered how things might play differently. If he made the lady his wife, he would become part of the perfidy, and he was not certain he cared to begin his new life in a bed of lies. In reality, he knew not the depth of the woman's deceit.

"What if Miss Purefoy was another Doña Marina or like Samson's Delilah? The possibility existed. Aidan knew only of her assuming another's name. *What if she came to Lexington Arms to learn his secrets? Did not all of the unusual happenings of late begin after Miss Purefoy's arrival?*

What was he to do? Not an hour passed in which Miss Purefoy was not in his thoughts. If he looked at a new horse to add to his stable, he also examined the mares in hopes of finding a horse with a personality Mary might enjoy. If he recorded items into his expenditure ledger, Aidan would think on the role Miss Purefoy played in turning his once stale existence into something exciting. And he could not shake the image of Mary writhing in pleasure beneath him; yet, it was folly to permit his heart its reins.

His mind might not recall what happened with Susan's depressed state, but it knew the scent of Mary Purefoy as if God ingrained her mark on him. Aidan knew the taste of her lips and the feel of her body clinging to him. Tight and hot. And how perfect it felt to be deeply embedded in her.

Just the thought of Mary Purefoy erased all the evils in Aidan's world. He would never forget her, and he could certainly not ignore the fact he took the woman's virginity. He vowed to keep his distance, but Miss Purefoy overwhelmed his resistance. He made the mistake of allowing her into his heart. God! Did he love her? He never thought to love again.

He should send her away, but Aidan suspected it would not be that easy. The possibility shook him to his core. He lost so much. Lost his dream, the one to which he clung for so long. Now, he wanted the dream again. He wanted a wife and a family; yet, was he willing to risk his heart crushed again to claim a bit of happiness?

Aidan leaned his head against the wall and closed his eyes.

Silence, thick and despairing, cloaked his shoulders.

"What am I doing? I played the role of tinker and gentleman, but my trickery was in behalf of the British government."

Suddenly, an idea so dreadful it rocked his composure exploded in Aidan's head. Could Miss Purefoy repeat lines in a theatre greater than a country assembly? Could she be an agent for the Realm's enemies?

Aidan wished for his memories to return so he would possess a point of reference by which to judge what happened of late. As if something was missing, an aching pain filled his heart. He felt all of the uncertainties were held in the lady's delicate grasp.

He had no idea how long he sat as such. Somewhere below, a clock struck one. Slowly, Aidan forced himself to his feet. He returned to his home with grand plans only to second-guess his choices.

"I cannot go forward until I speak to the lady."

Dejected, Aidan turned his steps toward his quarters.

However, the sound of a door opening behind him had him spinning around to meet what he instantly knew was an intruder. Other than the two at the head of the hallway, no rooms in this part of the house were occupied. Aidan expected to meet, at best, a familiar thief, but he was not prepared to face Murhad Jamot; however, that was who stood before him.

"What the bloody hell!" he exclaimed.

The Baloch smiled warmly as he unsheathed a long knife at his side.

"I was told you were away," he said in heavily accented English.

Aidan edged toward the light. He did not think he could retrieve his gun from his inside pocket without the Baloch noting the movement. He would face the Realm's enemy bare-handed. Aidan could set up an alarm, but he was better trained to fight this intruder than were his most burly footmen.

"Who spoke of my absence?" he demanded.

Jamot took a defensive stance.

"You have those upon your staff not so loyal. I visited your house previously."

"So I heard," Aidan snarled.

His eyes searched the hall for possible weapons.

Several seconds ticked off before he asked, "What brings you to my home for a second look?"

The Baloch stood perfectly still, and Aidan could not help but to admire the man's bravado. Murhad Jamot did not fear dying. Aidan wondered if his enemy could read him as easily. Until of late, he had little for which to live, but with Miss Purefoy in his life, he held a reflection of hope. Despite his earlier misgivings, Aidan doubted he could give her up.

"I search for the emerald," the Baloch said matter-of-factly.

Aidan chuckled ironically.

"After all this time, you still believe one of us involved in Ashmita's escape had something to do with Mir's emerald? And here I gave you credit for more intelligence. I begin to think you have no desire to return to your home. England grows on you." Aidan flexed his fists, waiting for the Baloch's attack.

"As for this God-forsaken damp country, you are welcome to it." The Baloch scowled. "Yet, Mir expects by diligence."

Aidan actually felt empathy for the man. Mir sent his tribesman on an impossible mission, and, unfortunately, Jamot would never be welcomed home unless he succeeded. The man was in permanent exile.

"You will never know fruition."

Jamot smiled dryly.

"We will see."

The smell of smoke interrupted a long pause.

"What have you done?"

Aidan charged forward, and Jamot countered with a move, which placed Aidan on his backside and the Baloch towering over him.

"I did nothing, Lord Lexford," Jamot hissed. "But you

possess many enemies, and several reside under your roof."

Aidan made no countermove. The Baloch held the advantage of a weapon. Aidan desperately wanted to know of whom Jamot spoke. Possibly his memory loss had a source close to home.

"You claim solidarity twice. Name your compatriots," he growled.

Jamot smiled deviously.

"That would be too easy, my lord. Why do we not negotiate? I will name those who opened your doors to the likes of me if you will return Mir's emerald."

Aidan scooted backwards out of the Baloch's reach.

"I will permit you to search my house without fear of incarceration if you provide me the names of those who mean me harm. If you find the emerald, it is yours. I simply want my life to know normalcy."

Aidan stood gingerly to face Jamot again.

The Baloch sighed.

"It is the wish of many men, but I possess only two names to share. Are two names enough to whet your taste, my lord?"

Jamot switched the knife to his less-dominate hand, and Aidan wondered what the man planned.

"As I claim nothing to hide, your terms are most amenable."

"Nothing to hide is it, my lord? Then why did you place young guards about your estate?"

Jamot maintained his threatening stance.

"Perhaps you should study your family tree as closely as have I. I find my strength in knowing my enemy's weaknesses."

Annoyance chewed upon his patience.

Aidan said testily, "What does all your tosh mean? Just speak the truth. My temper knows enough of the world's manipulations."

In frustration, he unconsciously jammed his fingers into his hair. Aidan knew he should not ask, but he could not stop the words.

"Is Miss Purefoy one of my enemies?"

The Baloch smiled knowingly.

"Miss Purefoy?" he said with satisfaction. "Is that the lovely lady's name?"

Aidan's heart sank.

"Do you know Miss Purefoy?"

He was so certain he could have the woman without his heart being involved. Unfortunately, Aidan suspected misery would soon become his companion.

The knife rested again in the Jamot's right hand, and he gestured with it.

"I have not had the acquaintance of Miss Purefoy, but I do know a Miss Nelson."

"N...Nelson?"

Aidan could barely get the word out. His throat closed in dread.

"As in the marquis's wife?"

But before he could ask more, a door opened at the end of the hall, and a young gentleman with whom Aidan held no knowledge stepped into the muted light. With hair as dark as the night sky, the man held a presence of authority.

"Talpur?" The stranger spoke with a Northern accent. "Have you..."

The intruder broke off when he spied Aidan.

Aidan asked suspiciously.

"Talpur?"

The Baloch shrugged.

"It is as it should be," he said softly.

"We must go," the stranger called urgently.

Aidan wished he could see the man clearly, but Jamot stood between him and the Englishman.

Jamot began to back away.

"I fear our negotiations took a divergent path, my lord. You must discover the answers on your own."

Aidan stalked Jamot's retreat.

"You entered my house for the last time. You come again,

and I will kill you."

The Baloch laughed. "And here I thought we came to an understanding, Lord Lexford."

Without removing his eyes from Aidan, Jamot executed a flamboyant bow before turning toward the still open door through which the gentleman disappeared.

Aidan gave pursuit, but he pulled up when the smell of smoke became more pronounced. Instead of giving chase, he followed the scent of burnt timber to open the door leading to the area, which haunted his house and his dreams forever. Flames rose from the shambles of the former west wing of Lexington Arms. His heart stumbled to a halt. He could lose it all.

He turned toward the main stairs. In a panic, Aidan called out the alarm.

"Fire! Fire! Fire!"

A footman appeared.

"What is amiss, my lord?"

"The west wing," he huffed. "Another fire! Rouse everyone!"

Without waiting for the man's response, Aidan returned to the wing. He must warn Miss Purefoy. Skidding to a halt before her door, Aidan pounded with both fists.

"Mary! Mary! Do you hear me? Mary! Please."

"What is the danger, my lord?" He turned his head to find Serena Chadwick clutching a robe to her chest.

"There is a fire, Miss Chadwick. I need you and Miss Purefoy out of the house immediately."

The woman glanced toward the open door and the smoke billowing into the hall.

"Miss Purefoy is gone, Sir. She left while you were absent from the manor. In fact, the night of your leaving from what we can decipher."

Aidan could not comprehend how what Miss Chadwick said could be so. He and Mary finally knew sweet intimacies. He meant to make his addresses to the lady in the morning.

"Gone?"

"Yes, Sir."

The sound of his men rushing to his aid brought Aidan from his stupor.

"Tell Miss Hanson to take Aaron to a point of safety outside. Stay there until I come for you."

"Yes, Sir."

The girl rushed away to do his biding. Aidan glanced to Mary Purefoy's room. She spent the night with him; and then the lady departed.

"Just like all the others," he whispered.

The tumult surrounded him, but not all of the chaos came in the form of the fire. Aidan shoved his heartache aside to bark out orders.

"You two organize the water buckets. You check the nearby rooms to make certain the fire did not spread to the rest of the house. You others, come with me."

Aidan led the way outside. The water line formed, and he stripped off his jacket to join it, but before he could heft the bucket from Deland, one of the grooms caught his arm.

"There be someone in the fire, Sir."

Aidan's eyes followed along the line of the young groom's arm.

"Damn!" he growled.

"Do we know who it is?"

A woman was tied to the center post close to where Miss Purefoy rescued Aaron. Through the flames, Aidan could see the brown and gold of the day dress he commissioned for the woman. She writhed and pulled at the ropes.

"Good Lord!" he groaned.

He rushed to the door leading to the yellow drawing room. It stood open upon the night. It was likely the entry point for Jamot and his accomplice, but Aidan had no time to investigate the scene. A woman's life rested in his hands. He lost Susan in a fire, but the suicidal plunge into the fire's center was his wife's choice. *This was different*, he told his reasonable side.

Climbing the servants' stairs two and three at a time, Aidan emerged into the same hallway where he encountered Jamot earlier. Now, thick smoke filled the air. Dropping to the floor, Aidan crawled along the passage to the open door.

Emerging into the open space, Aidan tottered on one of the braced joints before claiming his balance. From his vantage point, he could see the fire line was a large circle about a makeshift bonfire in the middle of the open space. Flames danced high, but the fire was not as dangerous as he first thought. Aidan bent low to direct his men.

"Place water on the circle first."

He lay out along the beam and gestured to those below.

"Deland, direct part of the men to pull the timbers from the bottom. Spread it out. Not all the pieces hold fire!"

"Aye, Sir."

Aidan began to work his way toward the girl. Secretly, he hoped it was Miss Purefoy. In fact, the possibility of Jamot's accessory teasing Aidan by placing Miss Purefoy in danger would be the script if the Baloch was in charge. Jamot enjoyed pure drama. Instead, the girl was a wide-eyed Millie Joseph, Mary's maid. The reason the girl wore Mary's gown would be addressed once Aidan saved her.

The heat from the flames below streamed upward, but the fire would not reach them. The stacked timbers and broken furniture were not so high. Even so, it was a dangerous situation. The structure was less than stable. To reach her, Aidan must walk across a narrow crossbeam. He wished Wellston near. The earl would easily dance along the distance. Aidan glanced up at the girl.

"I am coming for you, Millie." He edged along the beam. "Do not be frightened."

Wide pleading eyes met his. Either Jamot or the Englishman gagged her with a large handkerchief tied about her head and covering the girl's mouth. She groaned a response he could not identify.

"Just a few more minutes," he said as he tittered on the board, his arms spread wide to counterbalance his steps. He wondered how the man lured the girl to such a dangerous spot.

At length, Aidan reached the braced point where four large beams met to form a double cross. Aidan went to work loosening the knots. First the gag.

"Thank you, my lord," the maid whispered on a throaty cough.

As if the culprit never meant for the girl to suffer, the knots were not too tight. The situation was a message to Aidan: His enemies could wreak havoc with Aidan's household, and he was helpless to stop them. When the last knot gave way, he tossed the rope to the floor below.

His men followed his instructions. They dragged the fiery timbers from the pile and attacked them with buckets of water. White smoke trickled upward, but it was not as thick as previously.

"Come with me, Millie," Aidan said as he caught the maid's hand. "We must cross the beam to safety."

He stepped onto the cross beam and gently tugged the girl's arm so she might follow him.

"Do not be frightened. I will not permit you to fall."

The maid nodded her agreement, but Aidan noted how her breath came with a ragged catch.

"Do not look down. Keep your eyes on my shoulder," he ordered.

She bit her lip, but Millie allowed him to lead her onto the beam. Aidan said a silent prayer that the wood would hold their combined weights. He recalled how another cross beam gave way from under Miss Purefoy, and the lady certainly was feather light. The image of Mary in her muslin-clad pantaloons led to one of her naked body beneath him. He paused to steady his progress.

"Easy." Aidan looked up to see John Swenton reaching his hand out to Aidan. His friend had his other arm wrapped about a support post.

Aidan did not know whether to laugh or to frown. He left

the baron behind in Ellesmere Port some eight hours prior. He certainly did not expect to see Swenton so soon.

"Nice knowing you appear when most needed," Aidan said sarcastically.

The baron smiled easily.

"Always glad to oblige."

Swenton stretched his hand in Aidan's direction.

"Now take my bloody hand and stop with the heroics."

Aidan did as he was instructed. Stepping to safety, he turned to brace Millie's final steps. With Swenton's assistance, he managed to direct the girl to the ledge marking the room's former floor. Swenton caught Millie's other hand and led the way along the narrow framing. At length, the three of them stood in the west wing's hallway. Smoke settled along the floor.

Aidan called to the servants rushing to assist them.

"I want windows and doors left open to air out the rooms. Temporarily move Miss Chadwick and Master Aaron into the newly finished rooms."

He shot a questioning glance to Swenton, who nodded his agreement.

"The baron will also require a room."

"Yes, Sir." Mr. Payne organized the maids and several footmen.

"Millie, you will accompany me and the baron to my study. I possess several questions, which require answers."

The girl trembled, but she nodded her understanding.

Mrs. Osborne wrapped her arms about the girl's shoulders.

"I'll see Millie below, Sir, and then I'll bring in refreshments. This looks to be another long night."

"That it does." Aidan scrubbed his face with dry hands. "Thank you, Mrs. Osborne. Baron Swenton and I will follow momentarily."

With the exit of the cook and Millie, Aidan directed Swenton to a private corner where they might speak.

"It is not that I shun your company, but what sent you after me? We parted only hours prior."

Swenton took a second glance around the area.

"Lowery questioned the prisoners further. One indicated Jamot might be using the name 'Talpur' and was in the vicinity of Lexington Arms. I followed to warn you. I am to meet Sir Carter in London at week's end to attend Pennington's engagement ball."

"In the chaos, I forgot about the celebration for Pennington and the dowager duchess, and as for your warning, you are too late. Jamot was here. I stumbled across him in this very hallway, along with a young Englishman of whom I held no prior knowledge."

"Jamot was in your house?" the baron asked incredulously. "What occurred?"

Unwelcome feelings of pity filled Aidan.

"We tussled. Jamot taunted. He shared some cryptic statements regarding my household. Then his compatriot showed, and I discovered the fire. Jamot and the Englishman escaped while I attempted to save my manor and all in it."

Aidan's frown lines met in a tight knot.

The baron considered what Aidan communicated.

"Likely the reason your local inn was full. I stopped there before seeking lodging at your estate. I planned to speak to you on the morrow. Perhaps I should return to the village. I suspect two rooms suddenly become vacant."

"Although I expect you correct, I am in need of your good sense in discovering what is actually occurring under my roof. Jamot claimed two of my employees admitted him last autumn and again tonight. Moreover, I discovered from Miss Chadwick that Miss Purefoy departed Lexington Arms the night I rushed off to join you and Lowery."

Swenton studied Aidan's features, and Aidan attempted to hide the turmoil churning in his stomach.

"What else?" the baron demanded. "You keep some facts private."

They exchanged a sorrow-filled glance.

Aidan considered keeping his counsel, but he knew the

baron to be trustworthy.

"What I confide in you must be kept secret until I can interpret the truth behind the lies. You must not speak of what I am about to share with the others."

"I promise."

Aidan murmured a self-deprecating curse. He clenched his jaw against another rush of despair.

"I should not believe him. I know Jamot rarely speaks honestly."

He paused to compose his thoughts.

"Jamot claims... Jamot claims my Miss Purefoy is really Miss Nelson."

"A relative of Lady Godown?" Swenton asked skeptically.

Aidan stood perfectly still; he dared not breathe–dared not to put into words his worst fears. Bile scorched his throat.

"I know from Pennington's investigation that the real Mary Purefoy is a maid in an inn in Derbyshire, but even with that knowledge, I never thought the woman meant me harm. Yet, if what Jamot speaks is true, my 'Miss Purefoy' is the sister of the woman the marquis suspects of staging several attempts on his life, as well as being the younger sibling of a man who played a role in bringing opiates to English shores."

Chapter 18

SURPRISINGLY, THEY SPENT a comfortable night in the marquis's hut. Lucifer enjoyed 'Miss Purefoy's' company. They played cards before the hearth and spoke of home.

During the evening, Hill sought answers to his questions. When he first uncovered the lady's name to be Mercy Nelson, Lucifer did not make the connection to Gabriel Crowden's estranged wife. The two women did not favor each other in looks, and "Nelson" was a common surname. He executed a private investigation and uncovered the lady's roots. With the discovery, Lucifer thought to drive Miss Nelson from Lexington Arms, but when Hill observed the difference in Aidan Kimbolt, Lucifer decided he must find a means to bring the viscount and Miss Nelson together, rather than to drive them apart. He suspected he was more than a bit successful in his manipulations. When the lady appeared suddenly in the kitchen garden, the girl held the look of a woman well bedded.

"Do you wish to tell me what is in the note you left for me?" Lucifer said casually as he played a card.

Miss Nelson studied her hand.

"I expressed my deepest gratitude for your kindness."

She blushed deeply.

"Is that the extent of the note?"

The lady placed her cards aside.

"No. There is more…"

She paused as if deciding whether to speak of what she wrote.

"I want you to know I spoke of a discovery I made in the last week. One which could affect His Lordship's happiness, and so I did not include the information in Lord Lexford's farewell. I shall leave it to you to decide if the viscount is to be apprised of my finding."

"I understand the need for discretion," he said earnestly. "You piqued my interest."

Miss Nelson sighed deeply.

"Last Friday, when I went for my walk, I stumbled upon an opening behind the waterfall."

Lucifer screwed up his face in concern.

"What kind of opening? A cave?"

"At first, I thought it a cave," Miss Nelson admitted. "But there was a lantern and flint close to the opening, and a narrow passage between the rocks, wide enough for a person to squeeze through. There is also a steep slope, which appears to lead to the outcropping."

She hesitated, and Hill wondered if she would speak the full truth. At length, she continued.

"I lit the lantern in hopes of exploring what turned out to be a tunnel, but I encountered a man within the depths."

"Did he hurt you?" Lucifer asked in incredulity.

Miss Nelson shook her head in denial.

"Your calling my name frightened the stranger away."

Lucifer watched her expression. The lady meant to disclose only what she thought important to the viscount. Hill belatedly wondered if her brother recruited the girl to spy on the Realm. From what Lucifer knew, Baron Nelson held ties to the infamous Lord Spectre, who kidnapped Godown's aunts and Lady Godown, as well as a close association to Jamot and the opium ring.

"What else can you tell me of the man and the cave? Did you recognize the intruder?"

She hesitated again, which spoke volumes.

"The man said he used the tunnel previously to enter Lord Lexford's house."

Lucifer knew immediately the culprit was Jamot. What he did not know was the connection between Miss Nelson and the Baloch.

"I did not possess the opportunity to explore the tunnel. I hoped you would seek out an answer for I strongly believe many of the 'ghosts' who plague His Lordship's house enter and exit through the opening."

"The woman who appears as Lady Susan?" Lucifer pondered aloud. "No wonder the apparition easily disappears each time we give chase."

Miss Nelson leaned forward as if to share a secret.

"What I could not understand is why Lord Lexford is not familiar with the tunnel."

Lucifer did not consider that particular fact.

"Could it be part of his memory loss?"

She shook her head in the negative.

"The memory loss covers the past two years. Would not the viscount hold knowledge of the tunnel from his youth?"

"I do not know," Lucifer said cautiously, "but I mean to discover the way of it."

After their guarded talk, Lucifer spent a restless night. He wondered what devious forces overtook the viscount's household and how this new information related to Lady Cassandra's journal.

Hill was anxious to return to Lexford's side before more mischief occurred. In Warwick, Miss Nelson remained with him while he sold the wool at a market. It was late in the afternoon when Lucifer purchased a ticket for the mail coach, the only transportation available to Bedford, where she could make connections to London.

"Promise me you will not venture into London's East Side.

Also, promise you will find housing at one of the three places I listed for you last evening, and you will seek employment first from one of the fine houses I included."

Lucifer purposely sent Miss Nelson to homes of relatives of the Realm.

"Use my name as a reference."

He handed her another small piece of paper.

"If you are in need of assistance, you know my direction. Send word, and I will come immediately."

Miss Nelson frowned her disapproval, and he understood immediately.

"In case you do not wish Lord Lexford to know of your whereabouts, I included the directions for my Hannah. She will contact me in confidence."

Lucifer would not tell the girl Hannah knew only a few letters. Lady Worthing agreed to teach Hannah more as time went on. Meanwhile, Her Ladyship read Hill's letters to Hannah and transferred Hannah's response to paper. Lucifer would speak to Lord Worthing and apprise him of the possibility of Miss Nelson contacting Hannah.

"I promise," she said softly.

Lucifer pressed part of the profits from the sale of the wool into her gloved hand.

"Save it for emergencies," he insisted.

"I cannot. It is too much," Miss Nelson protested.

"Lord Lexford would have my head on a platter if I gave you less. You will need it while you search for employment."

The lady threw her arms about his neck and planted a kiss on Lucifer's cheek.

"You are absolutely incredible. God blessed me when our paths crossed."

"You met the gentleman the day you awaited your mistress at the inn?"

Aidan attempted to keep his voice calm, but the maid's

naïveté drove him to distraction. He asked her the same questions several times in hopes Millie would contradict herself. Yet, the maid did not vary from her tale. That fact bothered Aidan more than the girl's involvement with a man who was obviously a fast-talking rake.

Millie admitted to sneaking out to meet the young lord she called "Lord Spectre." The man's name provided no new information. He and Swenton were both well aware the original "Lord Spectre" was Benjamin Talbot, a man who blamed Gabriel Crowden for the lost of his title. Talbot was currently incarcerated in Old Bailey, awaiting execution for attacking members of the aristocracy. Yet, if the man who invaded Aidan's house earlier used the same name, it meant the intruder was involved with Baron Nelson, which proved Mary Purefoy was truly Miss Nelson, the baron's younger sister. The thought was a knife to Aidan's heart.

"As I told ye before, I didn't admit Lord Spectre. I might've been out to meet him on other nights, but I would never let a stranger into yer house, my lord," the maid said anxiously. "Ye must believe me. Lord Spectre was mighty upset when I told him Miss Purefoy left. He gave me a note for the mistress, and then she leaves."

"Do you know the contents of the note?" Swenton inquired.

"No, Sir," she answered quickly. "Lord Spectre sent Miss Purefoy a note when she be in the mercantile, but ye be takin' my mistress home early."

Aidan now understood why Miss Nelson went so pale while she waited for Aidan's return from the solicitor's office.

"And you wear your mistress's dress because…"

He clenched his fingers into a fist rather than to shake the full truth from the girl.

The maid blushed thoroughly.

"Miss Purefoy leave all them fine clothes behind, and I be thinkin' they be wasted away hangin' in her wardrobe. The mistress be so kind, I thought she not mind if'n I wear somethin' nice to meet with Lord Spectre."

The girl's tale made Aidan cringe. The young maid obviously knew intimacies with this unknown lord, and Aidan would possess no choice but to send her away to await news of whether the girl was with child. Later, he would decide if he would permit Millie's return to his household.

"You will remain in the kitchen with Mrs. Osborne or in your quarters. I will decide your fate on the morrow."

Aidan rang for Mr. Payne. He provided the butler instructions for what remained of the night.

After the servants exited, Aidan addressed Swenton, "Do you possess any insights?"

"Likely no more than do you." The baron sipped his brandy. "I would say you must determine whether these are separate incidents or whether they are somehow connected."

Aidan slouched in his chair.

"I have no idea where to begin."

"Perhaps a few hours of sleep will bring clarity."

Aidan murmured, "I doubt I will ever sleep again."

Immediately he thought of the sound sleep he experienced following his intimacies with Miss Purefoy. *Miss Purefoy*, he thought caustically. *I suppose I must begin to think upon her as Miss Nelson.* Aidan stood heavily.

"As I have much to accomplish tomorrow, I will bid you good night."

Swenton followed Aidan to his feet.

"It is a great responsibility, but one you were born to bear."

Aidan shook off his friend's response.

"I am the second son, the one meant for the military. The viscountcy was designed for Andrew."

Swenton placed his hand on Aidan's shoulder.

"I know little of Andrew Kimbolt, but this title–this estate–has your name on it. Andrew would be found wanting."

Aidan made another tour of the house before he retired. He checked every room, every door, and every window. The west wing held the faint smell of smoke, but he would set the staff to cleaning and polishing tomorrow. He climbed the stairs to the nursery to check on Aaron. His nephew slept soundly in his small bed. Aidan bent to stroke the child's cheek. He held hopes of marrying soon and filling the nursery with noisy children, who would be playmates for Aaron.

"It will be just us two," Aidan whispered as he pressed a curl behind the child's ear. "We will run a bachelor household."

Leaving the boy to his slumber, Aidan first checked Miss Chadwick's room before stopping before Miss Nelson's door. He closed his eyes to conjure up her image. What he would not give for the door to open and the lady to greet him with her mesmerizing smile!

Aidan's fingers trailed gently along the wood. Although she betrayed him, he could not shake the empty feeling in his chest. As if something important was missing. Why did he not send her away the first time he laid eyes upon her? The question tore at him. *Because she filled your world with her spirit.* Aidan's throat constricted. His heart squeezed tight. Had the lady been so unhappy with him? Could she not trust him with her secrets? With her heart?

On impulse, Aidan entered the room. Someone cleaned and polished the furniture, but Miss Purefoy's scent still filled the space. Aidan closed his eyes and inhaled her essence. Bile rose in his throat and the bitter taste of acid filled his mouth. It was all he could do not to groan his disappointment at losing her. With the assistance of the hall sconces, he could make out the gowns he purchased for her draped across the back of a straight backed chair and the brush she chose upon a visit to Mr. Chadwick's shop upon her dressing table. Feeling suddenly very empty, Aidan sat upon the lady's bed.

"Why?" he asked the stillness. "Why share yourself with me and then leave?"

Dejected, Aidan leaned backward across the counterpane. He draped his forearm across his eyes. His legs hung down over the bed's edge. Aidan was not certain he wished to sleep in his chambers. The room held too many memories of Miss Purefoy's joy in redecorating his quarters and of her body wrapped about him in ecstasy. Aidan caught the edge of the counterpane and rolled over in the bed to lie diagonally, drawing his knees up under him. His eyes closed to bring her image forward. Within minutes, he dreamed of the woman who once occupied the room.

"Good morning, my lords." Lucifer Hill bowed to Aidan and Swenton. "I understand we experienced another fire last evening."

Aidan glanced up from his breakfast. He awakened early, still wrapped in Miss Purefoy's bed linens. He groggily made his way to his dressing room and purposely avoided looking upon his chambers. He meant to leave his memories of the woman behind. He reasoned he managed to do so with Susan, a woman he loved throughout his youth. Therefore, Mary Purefoy would be easy to obliterate from his reminiscences. After all, the woman was a part of his life for a mere ten weeks.

"Come join us." Aidan gestured to an empty chair. "I excused the staff for services."

Hill filled a plate from the items on the table.

"Did you two not think of Sunday service?" he sat casually.

Swenton explained, "Lexford and I thought while no one was listening to our every word, we would use the time to discuss last evening's events."

"I know some of the details from what the grooms shared, but would one of you care to apprise me of the missing information?"

Aidan spent the next quarter hour summarizing what occurred and what the maid disclosed.

"Do we have an identity for the Englishman?"

Lucifer asked between bites of ham.

Aidan shook his head in the negative.

"I sent a quick report to Pennington. Hopefully, he will set men to the investigation."

"According to the maid, the gentleman sent the absent Miss Nelson two notes, but we can find no trace of the messages. Likely, the lady burned the evidence," Swenton shared.

"So you know Miss Purefoy's true identity?" Hill said cautiously.

Aidan bit back his retort. He regarded his friend with open displeasure.

"Then I did not err in my belief you knew the lady's secret from the beginning."

Despite his best efforts, Aidan's tone spoke of his seething anger.

Hill placed his knife beside his plate. As he always did, his friend looked Aidan in the eyes.

"Aye. I knew her name."

Aidan threw his serviette across his plate and pushed his chair from the table, placing distance between him and a man he thought to trust.

"Why?" he said irritably. "Why would you assist the lady in perpetrating a deception against me? Did she seduce you into doing her bidding?"

The idea of Miss Nelson sharing any type of intimacies with Hill made Aidan see red. He wanted to punch someone, preferably Hill.

Lucifer said quietly, "You know Miss Nelson had no eyes for the likes of me, and as to the lady practicing a deceit, it was my lie, not Miss Nelson's. The woman wanted to beg for a position as a maid or a governess. It was I who elevated her to a familial relation."

Aidan rose to pace the area before the serving tables. He glared at Hill. Physical pain clawed at his heart.

"You still have not explained why you chose to act against me."

"I did not consider the tale to be in your detriment. I acted only to protect the lady. If she remained on the road, sooner, rather than later, some unprincipled man would make a whore of her. She had no other resources."

Aidan cursed under his breath. He knew what Hill proposed was the truth, but he did not appreciate being the target of his friend's deception.

"I would protect the woman from whatever drove her to the road."

"Aye. I hold no doubt of your benevolence, my lord, but you are assuming Miss Nelson would place herself under your protection. I can assure you the lady would adamantly refuse. I spent a good half hour in a steady rain convincing Miss Nelson that you would provide her gainful employment."

"When the marquis came to York before Christmas," Swenton offered, "Godown spoke of the conditions under which his lady and her sister lived. Geoffrey Nelson gambled away his family's fortune. Godown purchased Nelson's markers. He owns the estate and placed the baron on a strict allowance. It is my understanding Nelson struck Lady Godown when she refused to follow his orders. The baron regularly entertained those who would ill use both sisters. They abused the man's household until the majority of the females fled. The only thing which protected the younger sister from the baron's cohorts was Nelson planned to marry her off to a wealthy baronet."

Aidan looked to Hill. He grimaced in a rueful manner.

"Were you aware of these charges?"

"No, Sir. I discovered the lady's name when I read it on several letters she hid in her baggage. I simply saw a woman in trouble. I did not make the connection until I did a bit of snooping on my own."

In resignation, Aidan sat heavily in his chair. He released a heavy sigh.

"If Miss Nelson required protection, why did she run away?"

He wanted to say "from me." Why did she run away from me? But Aidan swallowed the phrase.

"I know the excuses the lady gave," Hill said honestly.

Aidan scowled. A hint of exasperation colored his words.

"Did Miss Pure...Miss Nelson explain her motives to you before she departed? Did you see the lady? Had you prior knowledge of her plan?"

Aidan certainly did not like the idea of Miss Nelson confiding in Hill and ignoring him.

Nervously, Hill cleared his throat.

"I suppose I owe you another confession. I offered Miss Nelson transportation to Warwickshire."

Aidan said disbelievingly, "You assisted Miss Nelson in her escape? How could you act so foolishly?"

Hill flinched at Aidan's angry tone, and an immediate twange of guilt arrived.

Swenton smiled easily. He softened Aidan's words.

"The viscount means he is experiencing difficulty understanding your motives."

Aidan curtly nodded his agreement.

Hill shrugged his shoulders unrevealingly.

"Surely you know, my lord, of Miss Nelson's stubborn nature. The lady was determined to leave. I thought it best if I accompany her."

The baron interrupted Aidan next remark.

"Did you manage to discover the lady's reason for leaving Lexington Arms' safety?"

Hill responded earnestly, "I suspect Miss Nelson feared her brother would learn of her whereabouts and insist upon claiming the Kimbolts as among his close connections. I doubt the woman held knowledge of the restrictions placed on Nelson by Godown. She was from her home for four months–long before the marquis married Grace Nelson."

Aidan thought upon what Hill shared. Hill's was a shrewd guess. Did his man speak the lady's inspiration? Did Miss Nelson left Lexington Arms to protect him?

"What is the lady's given name?" he whispered hoarsely.

"Mercy."

Aidan sucked in a deep breath.

"Mercy. The perfect name."

He did not look upon Hill's countenance. He suspected his friend's mouth turned upward in a knowing smirk.

"What was Miss Nelson's destination?" Swenton asked.

"I placed her upon the coach to Bedford," Hill emphasized. "From there, she planned to travel to London."

Aidan spoke in disbelief.

"London? If Miss Nelson is as naïve as you fear, London is a dangerous place!"

Hill's lips most definitely took an upward turn. Aidan wanted to wipe the superior grin from his friend's countenance.

"I provided Miss Nelson with a list of legitimate boarding houses and another list of households in which to seek employment. All of them with Realm connections."

Aidan absorbed Hill's information with satisfaction, but then he panicked.

"Miss Nelson has no funds!"

"You will discover a shortage in the market payment for the wool," Hill confessed.

Relief raced through his veins.

"Thank you," Aidan said honestly.

"Could the Englishman you observed with Jamot be Geoffrey Nelson?" Swenton wondered aloud.

Aidan thought on the possibility.

"I doubt it. The man's hair was dark as coal. Although Miss Nelson does not favor Lady Godown, the sisters both are fair of head. Miss Nelson is blonde, while the marquise has a lighter reddish-brown hair."

"I have seen Nelson," Swenton admitted. "Lady Godown favors her brother."

Aidan immediately wondered whom Mercy Nelson favored. He asked the question to which he did not wish to give voice.

"Could the man be the baronet of whom you spoke earlier?" He did not like to think of Miss Nelson pledged to another.

Swenton screwed up his mouth in doubt.

"You said the intruder was young, perhaps in his middle to late twenties. I understood the baronet was more than twice the girl's age. Been married twice. Has five legitimate children by two previous wives and another family in a neighboring village."

Aidan's frown lines met. Irony did not escape him: He experienced relief that Hill saw to the lady's safety, but he would feel better if Miss Nelson resided under his roof. He held no wish to make Baron Nelson a familial connection, but having the marquis, as an intermediary, would lessen the scandal associated with the baron's immaturity. Aidan wondered why Godown assumed the salvation of Lady Godown's brother. If Gabriel Crowden knew of Nelson striking Lady Godown, the baron would have a high price to pay. Women thought of Gabriel Crowden as the dashing prince of the Brothers Grimm tales, but, in reality, the marquis was a lethal opponent. No matter the poor connection, Aidan owed Miss Nelson a marriage proposal. A gentleman knew his duty.

"I wish Miss Nelson shared her fears."

"Did not the lady say anything of her concerns in the note she left in your name?" Hill asked.

Aidan asked doubtfully,

"What note? I know of no message from Miss Nelson. Millie spoke of messages sent to her mistress by the unknown lord, but nothing of a farewell letter."

Such a note would do well in soothing Aidan's broken heart.

"Miss Nelson swore she left a note for you and one for me," Hill insisted. "The lady mentioned doing so on several occasions."

Hill stood to take action.

"We should search her quarters."

Aidan motioned Hill to return to his seat.

"Last evening, I examined the lady's rooms before I returned to my quarters. I thought to learn more of Jamot or of her involvement in my house's invasion."

He would not admit to sleeping in her bed rather than to be alone in his.

"There were no notes."

Hill placed his serviette on the table.

"I think it would be prudent to look again. I asked Miss Nelson the contents of my note, and she readily confirmed her parting words. Perhaps you missed something in the chaos."

Swenton followed Hill to his feet.

"I agree with Hill. The notes could be a possible clue to solving this mystery."

Aidan thought such a search an effort in futility, but he followed his friends up the main staircase.

"I cannot believe the maids did not straighten the bed linens," Hill grumbled as he jerked the counterpane across the surface.

Aidan noted Hill's expression when he spotted bootblack smeared on the material. He shot Aidan a quick glance, but his friend judiciously relayed nothing suspicious in his tone or his actions.

"No notes here," Hill said as he lifted the pillows to look under them.

"None here either," Swenton said from the desk.

Aidan pretended to search, but he did not expect to find a message.

"The lady misled you, Hill."

His friend shook his head in denial.

"Other than the lie I foisted upon her, Miss Nelson spoke honestly. If the lady swore to leaving her farewells in a note, the letters should be in this room."

"Then to where did they disappear?" Aidan asked.

Hill's frown deepened.

"Needless to say, the maids would not remove them. Whoever cleared the room would report their existence to Mr. Payne or Mrs. Babcock."

"Perhaps the maid Millie removed them," Swenton suggested. "Did she not take Miss Nelson's gown after the lady's departure? Surely, if she came in to borrow the garment, Millie would possess knowledge of the notes."

Aidan gestured lacklusterly toward the door. He was not certain he wanted to read Mercy Nelson's farewell. Her words would likely squash his heart.

"Lay on, Macduff. And damned be him that first cries, 'Hold, enough!' Millie is confined to her quarters."

Moments later, Swenton led the way into the maid's lodging.

"Millie, we have another question."

The maid scrambled to her feet.

"Yes, Sir."

"When you removed your mistress's gown did you observe a note addressed to Lord Lexford?"

"Aye, Sir," the girl said readily.

Then she scowled.

"That be not completely true, Sir. You see, I kant read. So I asked Mrs. Babcock what the papers were about. Mrs. Babcock didn't seem pleased by the discovery. She be sayin' it weren't proper for a lady to write to a gentleman unless they be engaged. At the time, we didn't know whether Miss Purefoy be returnin'."

Swenton continued the questions.

"What happened to the notes?"

"Mrs. Babcock be sayin' she would give them to Mr. Poley to decide if'n Lord Lexford should be seein' them."

The girl shot Aidan a regretful glance.

"I be sorry, me lord, if'n I did wrong."

Aidan had the suspicion everything changed without his participation.

"It will all come to right, Millie."

He was not certain whether he meant his words for the maid or him.

Hill said from behind him.

"I suspect we should have a closer look at Mr. Poley's quarters."

Aidan sighed deeply in resignation. He led the way toward his valet's rooms, but he paused before turning the latch. He addressed his friends in agitation.

"Do you recall your analysis regarding my valet and the housekeeper after Miss Nelson saved Aaron?"

Hill nodded his understanding.

"I asked which members of this household did not respond to the crisis."

"It just struck me that neither Poley nor Mrs. Babcock made an appearance during the fire last evening," he said softly. Cynicism crept into his tone.

Swenton spoke with determination.

"As both are at services, it seems the appropriate time to search their quarters without interference."

Chapter 19

MERCY SIPPED THE TEA she ordered and waited for the next coach. If not for Mr. Hill, she would possess no such luxury. The man protected her from the onset of their acquaintance. She was fortunate to find such an honorable man.

For the hundredth time, she eyed the table of four gentlemen and clutched her cloak tighter. The oldest of the four made overtures in her direction, but the youngest returned the man's attentions to the cards. From what she overheard the innkeeper say to his wife, the four men spent last evening in a highly contested card game. The innkeeper expected the card players to be residents of the inn for several days.

"You know they be staying as before," the innkeeper said. "So you need to keep a fit stew in the pot. They will play until one be the victor."

Mercy forced her eyes to the window. If the stage was on time, she had less than a half hour before she would be on her way to London.

The sound of chairs scrapping along the wood floor announced a break from the game. Mercy stiffened and dropped her eyes when the older gentleman sauntered clumsily in her direction.

"I know what would bring me luck," he said loudly.

Mercy shot a quick glance about the room. Other than the four gentlemen, the innkeeper and his wife, and her, the inn's common room was empty. From the look upon the innkeeper's countenance, she would receive no assistance from the man. A proprietor would never speak out against a paying customer, and especially one of the aristocracy. If she knew nothing else, Mercy was aware of class differences.

"What say you?" the man leaned down over her, and Mercy could smell the stink of stale cheroots and alcohol on the his breath. "Come bring me luck, Sweetheart, and I will split my winnings with you."

In an attempt to place distance between her and the man, Mercy pushed further into the seat. "No, thank you, Sir," she said meekly. She hoped her subservient response would be enough to defer him, but the man sat heavily in the chair beside her.

"Am I not handsome enough for you?" the man slurred his words. "You are a pretty one." He reached to stroke her cheek, and Mercy recoiled from his touch.

"Leave the girl alone, Monroe," a deep male voice said from beside them. Mercy glanced up to see the same younger gentleman as before. "We have cards to play, and the girl has a coach to catch."

Monroe looked up and scowled.

"There is still time. The girl has at least twenty minutes before the coach. I can be quick when I need to. You will wait the game for me, will you not, Stafford?"

The young gentleman said with more firmness.

"I think not."

He gestured toward the table.

"Return to the game before we are at odds. I would dislike losing you as an acquaintance."

Mercy did not breathe. The one called Stafford meant to protect her, and she prayed his friend would agree. She noticed the signet ring upon the gentleman's finger. It was not Mr. Stafford;

the man was Lord Stafford.

"What is the girl to you, Stafford? Do you want her for yourself?" the one known as Monroe charged.

Lord Stafford took a combative stance.

"I have no desire to deprive you of your enjoyments, Monroe, but I will not stand by and watch you force yourself on the girl." He paused for emphasis. "I will ask you a final time to return to the game before I name my seconds."

Mercy did not blink; she made herself invisible by her inaction. The older man glanced at her before assessing Lord Stafford's unspoken threat. At length, Monroe heaved his weight from the chair. She waited in breathless horror.

"No need to be surly, Stafford," the man said genially. "I meant no harm."

"Of course, not." Lord Stafford gestured his tablemate past him.

Yet, the young lord waited until Monroe pulled out his chair to return to the table before he said softly, "Are you well, Miss?"

"Yes, my lord." Mercy licked her dry lips. "My gratitude, Sir."

Lord Stafford nodded sympathetically.

"Have a safe journey, Miss."

Mercy expelled a ragged breath. She quickly swallowed the last of her tea, gathered her bag, and hurried to the door. She would await the coach on the wooden walkway before the inn. Remaining inside was too dangerous.

The time passed slowly as she ticked off the minutes in her head. The coach was late, and Mercy became more anxious with each passing minute. She glanced toward the door where the inn mistress waited.

"Do you suppose I have time to tend my needs?" she asked politely.

"The coach will change horses. You have mayhap ten minutes," the inn mistress said matter-of-factly. "But Billie be late so he won't be happy to wait for you."

Mercy looked up to see the dust stirred up by the approaching coach.

"I promise to hurry," she said as she scurried about the corner of the building.

The small lean-to allotted for women to use for personal necessities was not much, but it did provide a certain degree of privacy. Mercy sat her bag away from the bucket left in place of a chamber pot. She held her breath as she squatted precariously over the offending item. Evidently, the innkeeper's staff neglected their duties. The area smelled of human waste, but Mercy muscled through because she knew it would be many hours before she would have a similar opportunity.

Finishing quickly, Mercy straightened her clothes, grabbed her bag, and scurried toward the front of the building. She could hear the whinny of the horses and the jangle of the harness. Rushing forward, Mercy skidded about the corner of the inn, and slammed hard into a man's well-toned chest. Strong hands reached out to steady her stance, and Mercy looked up into a familiar face.

"You were correct, Talpur," a sinister voice said to the shadow of a man behind him. "The one known as Lucifer saw our pigeon to Warwick."

Mercy fought the tears pooling in her eyes. She thought to beg for her freedom, but she knew her pleas would fall on deaf ears.

"What do you intend to do with me?" she asked with a slight tremble in her voice.

The man caught her chin and forced her gaze to fall on his countenance. She once considered him handsome and held hopes that Geoffrey would pledge her to this man. Yet, the face that stared back at her lost its appeal. Her captor's eyes bore into hers, and Mercy caught a peek of the evil buried deep within the man before he shuttered it away.

"I plan to return you to my father," he hissed. "The baronet requires something to distract him or he will likely stumble into my business, and I cannot have that. It would be a shame to dispatch pater before his time."

Mercy's blood ran cold. She never suspected Mathias Trent of being anything but an obedient son. She always knew if she married Sir Lesley, Mathias would not provide for her or his younger siblings with Sir Lesley's passing; yet, she never considered him as a leader. He was another Geoffrey Nelson! A pawn in a large, inexplicable game.

"Trent, we must leave," Jamot said softly.

Mathias glanced over his shoulder.

"See if the innkeeper has a horse and saddle for the lady. Our Miss Nelson is an excellent rider."

"I doubt the innkeeper will have a side saddle," Jamot cautioned.

Trent smiled deviously at Mercy. Fierceness spread across his features, and Mercy knew real panic.

"If that be so, my father's intended will be showing her wares to all those who care to look."

Trent continued to grip Mercy's arm so tightly it would show bruises tomorrow.

Mercy's mind raced. She required a means to escape, but few possibilities existed. She doubted she could outride both Mathias and Jamot. She prayed some bit of luck would look kindly upon her; yet, she held few hopes of regaining her freedom. Mercy closed her eyes to bring the image of Lord Lexford's countenance into focus. She left the viscount behind in order to shield him from these people–these twisted individuals. With that realization, Mercy opened her eyes to confront her future.

<hr>

"Nothing!" Aidan grumbled. "Not even a trace of a clue." He, Swenton and Hill examined ever corner of Mr. Poley's room before moving on to Mrs. Babcock's.

"What did you expect? You presented Poley and the housekeeper too much sway within your household because you wished nothing to change," Hill said seriously. "In fact, you spoke often of Poley's disapprobation, as well as Mrs. Babcock's caustic remarks. Perhaps you wished to ignore the abuse because you never thought of yourself as the master of this estate."

Insult arrived on a high note.

Aidan's temper flared.

"What are you suggesting?"

His fist curled at his side.

Swenton stepped between Aidan and Hill.

"Lucifer gives speech to what you know, but never acknowledged. We all joined the Realm in retribution for those parts of our lives over which we held no control. Kerrington required forgiveness for his first wife's death in child birth; Fowler wished to remove the stigma of his father's reputation; Wellston, a desire to save others because he could not save his sister; and Crowden, a necessitate to prove himself not a fool for trusting a fickled woman. Even before your father saddled you with a wife who could not love you, you second-guessed your right to the title. Your right to be viscount. Your place as Andrew's substitute."

Aidan's expression screwed up in a tight scowl.

"I am a surrogate for Andrew," he protested.

Hill spoke in adamant tones.

"No, you are not, and until you accept your rightful place as Viscount Lexford, you will live a miserable existence. A wife and children will give you no peace, my lord. You must learn to recognize your own worth and not depend on others to acclaim your significance."

As his friends rallied to his defense, something like culpability and like dishonor gnawed at Aidan's conscience. He certainly did not wish to think upon the possibility of what Swenton and Hill asserted.

"We may discuss my failings upon a future date," he said authoritatively. "For now, I am seeking suggestions of where next to look for the missing notes."

Hill cocked an ear toward the hum of those moving about below.

"It sounds as if services ended. I suggest we speak to those involved."

Swenton shrugged his agreement.

"Perhaps we will catch the pair before they concoct an alibi."

Aidan led the way to the main corridor. Mr. Payne returned to his post.

"Payne, do you know the whereabouts of Mr. Poley and Mrs. Babcock?"

Aidan knew it would be uncharacteristic of his valet and his housekeeper to keep company with the others on the staff.

"No, Sir. May I be of assistance instead?"

"Did not Mr. Poley and Mrs. Babcock join the others at church?" Hill asked.

"No, Sir. I saw neither this morning."

Aidan motioned Hill and Swenton to a nearby drawing room.

"This situation makes little sense," he said as he closed the door behind them. Aidan recognized they headed for unchartered waters.

"Neither Poley's or Mrs. Babcock's rooms appear as if the pair does not intend to return to his or her position. What does all this mean?"

"Evidently, we identified the two who admitted Jamot to your house," Swenton reasoned.

"But why?" Aidan ran his fingers through his hair. "And to where could they escape?"

"I have my suspicions," Hill ventured.

Swenton asked curiously, "Which are?"

"When I asked Miss Nelson the contents of the note the lady left me, she disclosed a secret, which she said I may share at my discretion. I think it is time," he said cautiously.

"Then spill it," Swenton encouraged.

Hill's eyebrow shot up in concern.

"Is this your wish, as well, my lord? If what I suspect is

true, your life will change forever, and not all changes will be welcomed. There will be no turning back once we set this plan in motion."

Aidan swallowed hard. Did he wish things to change? Could he not carve out a bit of happiness without turning the world onto its nose? A knowing look from Swenton said the baron expressed his sympathy.

"Tell me," Aidan said, his voice barely audible.

Hill nodded less than enthusiastically.

"While you were in Manchester, Miss Nelson discovered an opening in the vicinity of where you went into the water after your last encounter with Lady Susan's ghost."

"What type of opening?" Swenton asked.

Again, Hill eyed Aidan curiously, and Aidan shifted his weight uncomfortably. Was he supposed to hold prior knowledge of this 'opening'? His mind scrambled for an explanation.

"It is a tunnel in the rolling hills separating your property from that of Jonathan Rhodes. Before I returned to the house this morning, I examined the area to verify what Miss Nelson reported. The lady spoke the truth."

Aidan's lips thinned into a tight line.

"How do we know Miss Nelson was not aware of the tunnel long before that particular day?"

Hill glared at Aidan, and Aidan felt as if the headmaster at school called him forward. He prayed his friends would not recognize his vulnerability.

"Do not be such an arse."

Hill rarely spoke disrespectfully to Aidan, meaning Aidan riled the man with his assumption. "The woman acted unselfishly in all matters concerning your well being, and if you cannot see her goodness on your own, we should cease our maneuverings now and simply let things be."

Swenton reminded them both.

"We took the first step, Hill. Finish your tale."

Lucifer's expression reflecting an unwavering determination, the intensity in Hill's stare remained, but he grudgingly accepted Swenton's instructions.

"Miss Nelson worried whether news of the tunnel would bring you grief if your mind purposely blocked out its existence." Aidan said nothing, but he wondered if his memory buried another unpleasant recollection.

"The lady entered the tunnel with the intention of exploring its length, but instead she met a dark-skinned man."

Aidan's fear rose quickly.

"Jamot? Did he harm her?"

Hill shook his head in denial.

"I asked. Miss Nelson claimed Jamot released her when I called out her name."

"Why did Miss Nelson not speak to me of her encounter?" Aidan asked, his face set in taut lines.

The idea of Jamot accosting Miss Nelson bothered Aidan more than he cared to admit.

"I imagine the Baloch recognized the lady, and Miss Nelson likely feared her brother would discover her whereabouts. She confided the truth in the only means, which seemed reasonable to a woman hiding her identity. We must recall Miss Nelson placed herself in danger to bring you knowledge of the supposed hauntings. When you observe it for yourself, you will recognize how easy it would be for your ghost to disclose her presence in the cave's opening. Your ghost was as real as you assumed."

Aidan looked away in hopes of hiding his anxiety. *What were Miss Nelson's connections to this mystery?*

"We should see where the tunnel leads," Aidan said cautiously.

His decision set Hill in motion.

"I will secure several lanterns and the horses. You, Gentlemen, should bring the weapons."

With that, Hill exited.

Aidan braced his weight by catching the back of a chair.

"What have I done?" he murmured.

Swenton rested a hand on Aidan's shoulder.

"You, my friend, chose to reclaim your life, and I, for one, think it more than time. Wherever this adventure takes you, you are not alone in the madness. Hill and I are here, and I suspect Miss Nelson's heart is in your grasp."

Aidan said what he thought never to speak.

"The lady chose to spend the night with me before she departed."

His voice rose with desperation, and he swallowed hard to push the madness away.

"If Miss Nelson meant to leave me, why seek me out? Did the woman mean to drive me insane with questions?"

"I know little of the female mind, but a feminine confidant once explained that women do not reason as do men. They exist purely on emotions. If Miss Nelson chose you, it was because the lady meant to spend one night with the man she loves before escaping whatever demons chase her."

Aidan could not comprehend what Swenton purported. Everything about the woman said Aidan should walk away from her, but he was afraid he might never forget Mercy Nelson. He did not want to return to the man who barricaded the lonely pain within.

With a deep sigh of resignation, he said, "Let us finish this."

Twenty minutes later, they gathered outside the opening. Aidan permitted Lucifer and Swenton to lead the way. An unexplained panic sat heavy in his chest, and he could barely see two steps before him. The baron commented on how well the waterfall disguised the area, but Aidan experienced the sudden feeling he should remember the cave's presence.

It was a tight squeeze for Hill as the man moved from the small opening into the larger, but he was through in seconds, and Swenton followed. When it was Aidan's turn, he hesitated. In his mind the walls were moving. Compressing the space to one too thin for a child, let alone a man.

"Come," Swenton hissed.

He stared through the opening at Aidan.

Aidan made himself swallow. It was all a trick of his mind. He knew the reality, but it did not stop his heart from racing. He nodded curtly and stepped between the sandstone walls. There were worse ways to die, he reasoned. Being crushed by the earth would be relatively fast. He doddered and came close to tripping over his own feet.

The hills, which ran through his land, were part of a line of Bronze Age earthworks, quarried and mined for copper since the late seventeenth century. Surprisingly, an extensive area of lowland heath marked the summit of one of the southerly hills. In other places along the line, sandstone was extracted for building and sand used as a scouring agent.

When Aidan cleared the space, he expelled the breath he did not realize he held. Was it the walls or the fatalistic grimness pushing against his chest? Looking about the area to earn his bearings, he said, "What is next?"

Hill lifted his lantern higher.

"We should follow the passage. See where it takes us."

"It must have an outlet," Swenton insisted. "There is no way Jamot would allow himself to be trapped in a cavern without an escape."

Hill nodded his agreement.

"Stay close, and keep the lanterns high where we might see what lies ahead. I would not put it past the Baloch to include a few traps for unsuspecting souls."

They were moving along a gentle slope. At first, Aidan stumbled behind his friends, but with each step his resolve hardened. He would see this chaos to its conclusion. So, despite the drumming of his heart in his ears, Aidan permitted his Realm training to take control of his reactions. He searched the dark, narrow passages for clues.

They moved slowly through the channel. It was much longer than Aidan anticipated. He assumed it was a side shaft of a former copper mine. Water trickled through cracks in the wall, and it was cold, but Aidan experienced worse conditions in service to his country. In this instance, wailing half-dead soldiers did not surround him. Or did they?

Hill stopped suddenly, and he and Swenton nearly bumped against Hill's backside.

"What was that sound?" Aidan whispered anxiously.

They clustered together and shuttered their lights. They listened carefully: An odd whine could be heard somewhere in the distance.

"Could be a trapped animal," Swenton ventured in hushed tones.

"No animal I know makes a sobbing sound," Hill reasoned. "It is a person."

"And he is in difficulty." Aidan darted around Swenton.

His friend caught Aidan's arm to impede his progress.

"Easy, Hero," Swenton cautioned. "It could be a trap."

Aidan shook off the baron's hand. He let out a short, sarcastic laugh.

"Yes, someone set up a trap hoping we would stumble upon it. Be reasonable."

Hill stepped around Aidan. "I will lead."

Aidan scowled, "I do not care who leads."

Swenton chuckled. "That would be an anomaly."

"Someone lead," he growled through gritted teeth. Another soft wail drifted their way.

Hill opened his lamp to light the passage. He moved speedily, but carefully, through the darkness. The sobs grew louder, and their pace quickened.

Turning a corner, again Hill came up short. Aidan and Swenton framed Lucifer's shoulders. Before them, Mr. Poley crouched on the slate and sandstone floor. In his arms, he rocked Mrs. Babcock's body.

Aidan darted around Hill to kneel beside Mr. Poley.

"What happened?" he asked in concern.

"She is dead," Poley said on a catch. "What will I do without her?"

Aidan strained to check for a pulse on his housekeeper's neck. Finding none, he motioned Hill and Swenton close.

"Poley, you must tell me what occurred."

His valet looked wildly about him.

"I told Beatrice…we should attend services, but…she insisted…we should call on Sophia instead."

"Why would you call upon Mrs. Rhodes?" Aidan encouraged.

Confusion crossed the valet's countenance.

"Beatrice thought it time."

"Time for what?" Swenton prodded softly from beside the man while Hill eased the housekeeper's body from the valet's grasp.

Poley's chin dropped heavily onto his chest.

"To speak to Jonathan regarding…regarding Sophia's behavior."

Aidan wondered on the obvious familiarity of his servants with Susan's parents. He could not imagine the possibility. He experienced the sickening dread that his household staff assisted in Arlen Kimbolt's maneuverings.

Swenton noted Aidan's dismay.

"Mrs. Rhodes's behavior? Perhaps you should start at the beginning. Did you speak to Mr. Rhodes when you called upon the manor?"

Poley did not look up. Instead, the valet studied his empty hands. Sorrow deepened the lines of the man's face. The valet fought for composure. From his eye's corner, Aidan noted how Hill reverently wrapped Mrs. Babcock's body in the lady's cloak.

"Beatrice grew exceedingly concerned. We called upon our sister's husband."

Aidan attempted to stifle the word, but even he could hear the incredulity in his voice. "Sister!"

His heart lurched hard within his chest.

Poley's shoulders slumped in defeat, but he continued his

story. It was as if the man wished to free his conscience.

"Sophia. The youngest of the Poleys. Since our childhood, Beatrice was the matriarch of the family."

The valet paused awkwardly.

"Beatrice made the marriage between Rhodes and our Sophia. She arranged for our sister to know the respectability Beatrice could not. Merlin Babcock was a drunkard and a womanizer. We counted ourselves fortunate the day he passed out on the wharf and fell to his death into the icy waters of the Irish Sea. Afterwards, Beatrice moved us all to Cheshire. I began my time at Lexington Arms and eventually became the late viscount's manservant."

Swenton redirected the questioning, pressing for information.

"What occurred this morning?"

Poley raised his chin to gaze upon the baron. Aidan was certain the valet saw no one else.

"Beatrice called upon Jonathan. She thought our sister's husband permitted Sophia to fall deeper into despair and gave Sophia too much laudanum and other questionable medications, which Jonathan swears is the only means to control Sophia's fits of delusion."

"Sophia searches for Susan in my house?" Aidan suggested. He felt a sense of urgency.

Poley looked to Aidan as if seeing him for the first time.

"My sister's grief is great," he said simply.

"Your conversation with Mr. Rhodes did not go well?" Swenton proposed.

"Rhodes appeared at a lost for words, but we were encouraged," Poley returned his gaze to Swenton, "when Sophia joined us for breakfast."

The man dabbed at his eyes.

"Although a bit frail, Sophia appeared in good spirits. Beatrice and I returned to Lexington Arms with hopes of having our sister in our loving arms again. Yet, by the time we reached this point, Beatrice was doubled over in pain. Our Bea had trouble with her heart for the past few years, but this was more than heart trembles."

"Then you think Mrs. Babcock's heart gave way?" Swenton inquired.

Poley's shoulders stiffened.

"No, Sir. I believe someone poisoned Bea, and that someone was Sophia."

Chapter 20

AIDAN THOUGHT FOR A MOMENT he misheard his valet, but a quick glance to Swenton and Hill said his friends were as astounded as he. He softly assured Mr. Poley he would see to Mrs. Babcock's body before he motioned the others to the side. They huddled close in the shadows to speak in hushed tones. Meanwhile, Poley peeled away the wrapped cloak to hold his elder sister's hand.

"How should we proceed?" he asked.

Swenton followed Aidan's bewildered gaze.

"Needless to say, we know where this tunnel ends. It appears, we should seek out the magistrate; we should not act without the law."

It was a Realm policy not to respond to a crisis on a personal basis, but somehow this felt different.

"Mr. Poley did not actually admit Mrs. Rhodes is your ghost, but he revealed several incriminating facts. We should move him and the housekeeper's body to Lexington Arms and await the magistrate."

"I suppose I owe the pair that much," Aidan admitted.

A hint of insecurity darkened his expression.

Swenton continued, "We should determine if Poley knows

the whereabouts of Miss Nelson's letters, as well as what makes your valet believe Mrs. Rhodes murdered her sister, and why he and the housekeeper kept their counsel for so long."

"I want to know if Jonathan Rhodes housed the unknown lord, as well as Jamot in his home."

The baron frowned.

"Is it possible Susan's father has his hands in the opium ring?"

Again, Fate turned Aidan's world upside down.

"Poley spoke of the opiate-derived medications Rhodes provides his wife, but such pain encumbrances are common in many households," Aidan whispered.

The possibility of the connection between Susan's father and their investigation rocked Aidan's composure.

"Although I despise disturbing the happiness of the engagement party, we should send word to Pennington and Sir Carter."

Aidan watched Hill's countenance harden into a grim line with each new suggestion.

"Is there something you wish to share? You appear quite grave."

Hill hesitated, and that particular fact worried Aidan. His friend rarely withheld his opinion.

"*Grave* is an ironic word choice for I hold information, which will further complicate your life, and it is straight from the grave. I suffer, my lord. I am torn between doing what is correct and what will protect you. What I share goes beyond Mrs. Babcock's and Mr. Poley's secrets, but it will explain much of what occurred. The servants' secrets are also Lexington Arms' secrets."

"How can that be so?" Aidan asked in caution. "I know you well, Hill. You would never place me in danger."

He looked to Swenton for support.

Hill protested, "I never claimed you in danger, but you will suffer, nonetheless."

"If these secrets will free Lexford to claim his life," the baron insisted, "you must tell him, Hill. A friend would do nothing less."

Lucifer's eyes searched Aidan's countenance for a command, and Aidan wanted desperately to crawl back into bed and to start this day over, but with a deep steadying breath, Aidan said, "Tell me."

Hill sighed heavily before nodding his agreement.

"Mrs. Babcock was more than Lexington Arms' housekeeper. She was the late viscount's long time mistress."

"That is impossible," Aidan hissed. "My mother would never tolerate…"

Hill's words overrode Aidan's objection.

"Lady Cassandra wrote of her humiliation at the previous viscount's hands."

"When? When did my mother write of this degradation?" Aidan demanded.

Hill leaned forward to assure privacy.

"Lady Cassandra hid her diary in a false drawer in her escritoire. It was found with the renovations of the viscountess's suite. I hid the book in my quarters."

Aidan swayed in place.

"You read my mother's words?" he said through trembling lips.

Aidan could not read his friend's expression in the interior's dimness, but he recognized the familiarity of trust in Hill's tone.

His friend spoke in sadness.

"Aye, Sir."

Hill touched Aidan's shoulder in a comforting gesture, but Aidan knew no peace.

"There is one thing more you must know. When I said earlier you were born to be Viscount Lexford, I spoke the truth. Andrew was Beatrice Babcock's son. He was never meant for the viscountship."

Aidan was not certain the blackness rushing in had anything to do with the tunnel's lack of light.

"Why would my father and mother perpetrate a lie upon

me?" he said weakly.

His mind raced with the possibilities. Aidan shut his eyes to shore up his barriers, but he knew the dam well breached, and there was no turning back.

"You may read Lady Cassandra's confession to learn your mother's motivations," Hill confided, "but put simply, when the previous Lady Lexford did not conceive early on in the marriage, your father suggested a replacement. The viscount brought Mrs. Babcock to Lexington Arms before your parents' wedding, and she was with child. Many servants were dismissed so no one would know of the deception. Lady Cassandra was made to accept the falsehood, and Andrew became the heir. It was eight years before Aylene was born and ten before your birth. By then, no one could deny the lies they set in motion."

"Did Andrew know?" Aidan entreated.

Anger mixed with the churning in his gut. Could the untruths drive his brother to issue a foolish challenge over a woman for which Andrew did not affect?

"If Lord Andrew held such knowledge, Lady Cassandra never spoke of it."

Swenton glanced to the grieving valet before reminding them.

"This is beyond anything you faced previously, and we have much to untangle. Are you able to continue, Lexford?"

Aidan gave himself a good mental shake. He had much to absorb, but to find all the answers to the myriad of questions flooding his chest he knew he must take one step at a time.

"Please assume the lead."

Unable to respond on his own, Aidan would unquestioningly follow the baron and Hill. His mind raced with the scantily clad possibilities. Lucifer bent to lift Mrs. Babcock's body to him while Aidan looked on in dismay. He wished for the luxury of returning to Lexington Arms immediately to read his mother's journal. Perhaps then Aidan could comprehend what occurred so many years prior. He foolishly thought he should feel different; after all, if what Hill said was true, and Aidan held no doubt otherwise, he was the rightful viscount, but somehow his clothes seemed to fit him the same as they always did. Should not lightning strike, even in a tunnel? Like with a magic spell? Should not the world shift? Everything turned aright? He held the lantern higher so Hill could see his way; yet, Aidan could not seem to concentrate on the task at hand.

He dredged up an image of his late housekeeper, and his lips curled in distaste. Aidan could not fathom the woman as possessing anything but a sour expression. How could his father prefer Mrs. Babcock to Aidan's mother? Certainly, Lady Cassandra Kimbolt outshone Beatrice Babcock in beauty and grace.

"Damn!" he groused as he stumbled to a halt and then rushed to catch up to Hill's straining steps. Although Aidan followed dutifully behind the others, his thoughts remained on his father and Mrs. Babcock. An image of the two in a sweaty embrace caused the bile to clog Aidan's throat. The previous viscount likely shared a bed with the woman while his wife, Aidan's mother, rested alone in her quarters. Did Arlen Kimbolt bring Mrs. Babcock to the master's chamber while Lady Cassandra remained in the adjoining suite? The thought of the degradation his mother suffered caused Aidan to see red.

"Could you hold the lady while I fit through the space?"

Aidan looked up to find their group preparing to slip through the opening's entrance. Hill rested against the wall, his bundle held low against his middle. Swenton sent Poley through the opening first to wait on the other side of the waterfall.

Aidan's eyes darted to the narrow opening between the sandstone pillars; yet, he did not move to assist Hill. He shook his head adamantly in the negative. A blistering determination rose quickly.

"No!"

The word ricocheted off the tunnel walls.

"No," he said angrily. "I will not touch my father's whore."

He stiffened in open rejection.

Swenton swung around. Gingerly, the baron touched Aidan's arm to curtail Aidan's ire.

"You must hold your temper, Lexford. Do not play this hand too early," he cautioned.

"Do you not understand what that woman did to my mother?" Aidan hissed.

He pointed an accusatory finger at the housekeeper's body.

The baron backed Aidan up against the opposing wall.

"Now, listen to me. You have a right to despise what happened. You can own indignation. But it will not change a thing. Trust me, Lexford; I know scandal's foul tongue first hand. You must come to terms with actions put in place years before you were born or your anger will eat away your soul. Tell me what good it will do to make Hill's assertions known. You will ruin your good name for the vindictive pleasure of calling a dead woman a 'harlot.' Is it worth the shame you will bring to your threshold to label Mrs. Babcock as such? Will you have your servants and your tenants know your dishonor? And what of Aaron? If the child's father was a by-blow, what does that do to the boy's place in this world? Would you destroy an innocent's future?"

Aidan jammed his fingers into his hair. He felt begrudgingly cold.

"I cannot permit Aaron to inherit."

Swenton nodded his understanding.

"You are the child's uncle and guardian, which means you must protect the boy, even from yourself. See to Aaron's safety, but meanwhile, marry and produce your own heirs. No one needs to know Andrew's parentage."

Aidan stared into the baron's serious expression.

"You wish me to perpetuate another lie," he said in disbelief.

"No, Lexford."

Swenton's features twisted in mock amusement, and Aidan became uncomfortable with the intensity of the baron's gaze.

"I wish you to live a happy life, one that sings the praises of your viscountship."

With that bit of advice, the baron stepped away.

"I will take Mrs. Babcock, Hill. You did more than enough."

Swenton placed Mrs. Babcock over his shoulder, like a heavy sack of flour. Aidan watched as the baron worked his way carefully through the narrow opening.

"Are you coming?" Hill gestured toward the exit.

Aidan swallowed hard. Swenton knew much of the devastation of scandal upon a title. The baron's mother brought deceit to Swenton's door, but somehow the baron rose above the ballyhoo. Aidan thought of Aaron, the boy so like his father. Aidan could not in all conscience harm the child. Such a petty act would give Aidan no satisfaction. Permitting hurt and loss to coat every facet of the boy's life could not be part of Aidan's legacy. He made his feet take a few tentative steps.

"You go first," he said half-heartedly. "I will see to the lanterns."

Swenton sent Hill to retrieve the magistrate and the village physician. Aidan appreciated the way the baron took control of the situation. Aidan's mind could not concentrate on any one point for very long. He insisted upon Swenton using Valí to transport Mrs. Babcock's body the short distance to the house.

"Valí does not care for others to sit upon his back, but he will tolerate Mrs. Babcock's weight," he said as he held the horse's reins while his friend and Poley laid the housekeeper across the saddle and tied her body about the horse. Swenton presented Aidan an odd look, but despite the baron's earlier warnings, Aidan could not bring himself to touch the woman. The situation might require him to keep a tight lip, but Aidan would not grieve the housekeeper's passing.

As Swenton rode away with Valí on a lead string, Aidan and Poley began a slow trudge to Lexington Arms on foot. Aidan reminded himself not to permit his valet to know he learned of how Mrs. Babcock came to the manor. As an alternative, he focused on a subject most dear to him: Miss Nelson.

"Poley, I must know what became of the letters Mrs. Babcock recovered from Millie," Aidan said evenly.

The calm demeanor he managed to assume surprised him. *Thank Heaven for my Realm training,* Aidan thought.

The valet did not turn his head. Instead, Poley kept his eyes on Lexington Arms' chimney spouts, barely visible above the distant tree line. Aidan finally understood why his father tolerated Poley's dim-wittiness and the valet's singularity.

"Beatrice hid them under the stone hearth in her sitting room," the man said matter-of-factly.

Aidan hesitated before asking, "Did you read them?"

Poley paused, and Aidan patiently waited for the man's response. His man glanced to Aidan's home with a narrowed, speculative gaze.

At length, the valet said, "I did not, but my sister took the liberty to read Miss Purefoy's words; Beatrice apprised me of their contents."

"And?" Aidan encouraged.

"And Beatrice determined it was best to keep Miss Purefoy's letters from your notice. The lady departed, and that fact served Beatrice's purposes."

Aidan determinedly set his feet in motion again, and Poley fell in beside him. He purposely waited before asking his next question.

"Why would your sister desire Miss Purefoy's departure?"

The valet's shoulders rose in a protective slant.

"Beatrice spent the last thirty years protecting the viscountcy, and from the time of Miss Purefoy's arrival, Beatrice recognized the lady's perfidy for what it was. My sister's every thought was to protect Arlen Kimbolt's name."

Aidan quickly understood the housekeeper would possess intimate knowledge that Mr. Hill's deception held no basis. Mrs. Babcock would know Miss Purefoy could not be Arlen Kimbolt's by-blow.

Aidan bit back his reprimand. Mr. Poley would never

comprehend how Beatrice Babcock brought shame to the viscountship. The woman, obviously, captained the lives of her siblings and to a certain extent Aidan's life, as well. As the current viscount, the woman's loyalty should be to him, but Mrs. Babcock was a superb chess player, and they were all her pawns.

Cautiously, Aidan asked, "How was Miss Purefoy a threat to the Lexford title?"

Poley's long silence had Aidan thinking the man did not hear him.

At length, the valet said, "I loved my sister. Beatrice was the only one to see me as a competent man. I was never very strong, and with my small stature, I could not aspire to be a footman. But Beatrice made certain my shortcomings did not set my feet on the path to failure. She managed to protect both Sophia and me from the world's evils. When Lord Lexford bestowed a housekeeping position upon her, Beatrice convinced the late viscount to bring me along."

Like no housekeeping position of which Aidan was aware! Somehow, Aidan doubted Poley would recognize his eldest sister's shortcomings.

"I worked diligently to prove myself worthy of your father's trust. When Jonathan Rhodes took a liking to Sophia, Beatrice said we must divorce ourselves from a close relationship with our younger sister so Sophia might assume the role of the landed gentry. Beatrice even managed a dowry of a thousand pounds."

Aidan assumed his father provided the dowry. Likely as some form of blackmail. No woman of Mrs. Babcock's background could rally such funds. He remained silent to permit the valet his confession, but it took every ounce of control Aidan could muster.

"Beatrice adored Lord Andrew."

Aidan bit his tongue to stop the words begging to escape his lips.

"When your brother passed too early, Beatrice transferred her admiration to the child."

"Did you and Mrs. Babcock conspire to steal Master Aaron

away?" Aidan asked.

"Oh, no, my Lord!" Poley protested. "That was all Sophia's doing!"

The valet hesitated.

"You injured Sophia in your scuffle. She came to Bea's quarters afterwards. While you and the others saved the boy and Miss Purefoy, I drew attention away from the scene by going into the village. When everything was clear, Beatrice saw Sophia home. It was Rhodes's idea that I should claim a bad tooth."

"Did Mrs. Rhodes not realize she could not keep the boy from me?" Aidan said with a bit more terseness than he intended.

His valet blinked in surprise with the question–as if Aidan should know the answer.

"Sophia meant only to love her daughter's child. Aaron always called his grandmother, 'Mama.' She was quite distraught when she discovered Jonathan sent the boy away."

When the valet offered no more, Aidan ventured, "Did Mrs. Babcock wish to remove Miss Purefoy because of my attentions to the lady?"

Poley glanced to Aidan before saying,

"If you marry, your son would displace Lord Andrew's."

Aidan's fists clenched and unclenched. Those under his roof meant to sabotage his happiness. How long was it so? Did Mrs. Babcock pray for Aidan's early demise so no one would suspect her deceptions? Did the woman's hopes switch to Aaron when Andrew died so senselessly? What would happen to the title if Aidan met his death on the Continent before Andrew's demise? Would Mrs. Babcock and Jonathan Rhodes demanded the right to guide Aaron's youth? It was not uncommon for trusted servants to tend to a child's values and care while solicitors and men of business saw to a young heir's finances. Would the viscountcy survived their exploitation?

He and Swenton accompanied Squire Holton to Rhodes Hall. Jonathan Rhodes greeted them with a bit of caution.

"How kind of you to make a social call. Please sit. I will send for refreshments."

Although generally an easy-going man, when it came to his position as the local magistrate, Holton took his responsibilities seriously.

"Refreshments will not be necessary, Rhodes. We came on a matter of great importance."

Rhodes folded his hands across his lap.

"How may I be of service, Holton?"

Aidan examined Rhodes's countenance carefully. The man's voice might display his congeniality, but the slant of his shoulder and the twitch of his left eye said Susan's father hid something.

Holton pulled notes from his pocket. With Aidan and Swenton's guidance, the magistrate question Mr. Poley for over an hour regarding the man's belief that his youngest sister poisoned the elder of the siblings.

"We came on a complaint regarding an early morning visit by Mr. Poley and Mrs. Babcock."

"Why would two of the viscount's servants call upon my household unless Lord Lexford sent them on an errand?" Rhodes took the offensive.

Aidan would ordinarily pity the man, but not under these circumstances. A smart opponent knew when to attack and when to hold his ground.

"I assure you, Father Rhodes, I would never disturb *your* household." *Not the way your wife disturbed mine,* he thought.

"What are you saying?" Rhodes demanded indignantly before the accusations arrived. Perhaps Rhodes was wilier than Aidan first anticipated.

Aidan smiled with a smirk.

"We are well aware of the relationship between my servants and Mrs. Rhodes, as well as the reason for the Poleys' call upon your household this morning."

Rhodes did not respond for many minutes. Surprisingly,

Susan's father dropped his head in defeat.

"I spoken to you previously regarding Sophia's health," he said quietly.

"Did Mrs. Rhodes serve her siblings tea this morning?" Holton asked.

Rhodes looked up quickly.

"Why would you ask?"

"On her return to Lexington Arms, Mrs. Babcock collapsed," Swenton explained. "The lady passed."

Rhodes was on his feet immediately.

"You are saying Sophia purposely killed her sister!" he exclaimed. "Mrs. Rhodes does not possess the guile to execute such a foul act. I never heard of anything so foolish. My wife is barely knowledgeable of my existence."

Holton offered professional comfort.

"It is a charge of grave importance, Rhodes. The village physician assures me there is no doubt someone gave Mrs. Babcock arsenic. Whether it was enough to bring about her demise is the question. Despite your objection, as the local magistrate, I must speak to Mrs. Rhodes. I would prefer to do so in the comfort of your home rather than to transport your wife to the nearest gaol. Yet, either way, I mean to meet my duty."

Rhodes quickly assessed the situation. He begrudgingly rang for a servant to escort Holton to Mrs. Rhodes's sitting room and dispatched a maid to her mistress's quarters to inform Sophia Rhodes of the magistrate's presence. With Holton's exit, Rhodes turned his anger upon Aidan.

"I suppose the squire's sudden interest in my wife is at your hand. You mean to ruin my wife the way your father and brother ruined Susan." Rhodes pointed an angry finger at Aidan. "God! I wish never to know the Kimbolts!"

Aidan could say the same of the Rhodeses.

Rhodes's venom grew.

"You Kimbolts are all of the same ilk. A path of destruction wherever you go."

It was Aidan's turn to rant.

"I thought upon coming to Rhodes End to conceal part of what I know of your family's deceptions to protect the memory of those who went before, but I assure you, Father Rhodes, I want the bloody truth for a change!"

Rhodes's countenance flushed in anger.

"I suppose Poley told you of Arlen Kimbolt's interest in Susan. That brother of Sophia's could never keep his mouth tight. So, you mean to know it all do you."

Rhodes paced in agitation.

"Well, I tell you, it was none of my doing. It was Beatrice's idea. The seduction. The title. It was Beatrice's passion. She meant for one of her family to marry into the aristocracy. My wealth meant nothing without a title, and whatever Beatrice Babcock set as her goal became an absolute truth."

Aidan was thankful still to be seated for the air rushed from his lungs. Rhodes unknowingly opened the door to his family's deepest secrets. Aidan shot a quick glance to the baron. Aidan hoped he did not appear as bewildered as Swenton. He cleared his throat before saying what he prayed would make sense to Rhodes.

"My father's attentions drove Susan to destruction."

"My darling girl never recovered," Rhodes sobbed.

The man dejectedly returned to the chair he vacated earlier.

"Susan loved you, Kimbolt, but when you left, she had no one to protect her."

Aidan wanted to remind Rhodes it was a father's occupation to protect his only child.

"I wanted to make Susan happy."

Yet, Aidan no longer believed he loved Susan, not in the manner in which he once thought.

"I meant to marry your daughter, but arrangements were made for my service instead."

"Bea still held influence over your father. Arlen Kimbolt had no choice but to continue the lie he perpetrated upon the neighborhood. A second son is meant for the military."

Aidan's earlier fears of Mrs. Babcock wishing for Aidan's death resurfaced.

Rhodes closed his eyes before his tale continued.

"I should have put a stop to Beatrice's and Sophia's grand schemes, but I never was able to deny my wife anything she desires."

A long pause followed, and Aidan felt sympathy for Rhodes's plight. Susan's father was a very weak man.

"Bea came to the viscount's house before your father married Lady Cassandra. I knew nothing of the Poleys at the time, but from Sophia, I learned how Beatrice thought Arlen Kimbolt meant to end his engagement to Lady Cassandra and to marry Bea in your mother's place. Bea was with child when Arlen pronounced his vows to Lady Cassandra. The viscount brought his bride to her new house and placed his mistress beside her. According to Sophia, it nearly destroyed Beatrice not to claim the title."

Aidan thought of how his father's self-centered behavior destroyed Lady Cassandra Morrison, as well. Aidan sat spellbound. He wished to stop Rhodes's confession, but he knew this moment was the one for which he craved all his life.

"Arlen had a lusty appetite, and Beatrice kept him from Lady Cassandra's bed by presenting the viscount with a son. Your poor mother knew several losses early on, and Beatrice seized her opportunity to make her son the next viscount."

Aidan felt the anger again. His father permitted another woman to rob Aidan's mother of her rightful role as Viscountess Lexford and him his position as Arlen Kimbolt's heir.

"The late viscount berated Lady Cassandra for her inability to produce an heir and made the viscountess accept the changeover; Lexford proclaimed Andrew's birth as the legitimate one. The neighborhood thought it odd how Lady Lexford showed no signs of being enciente before the birth, but no one would speak out against the viscount."

Aidan shook with anger and misplaced guilt. His mother was too young to withstand the viscount's manipulations, but her actions nearly stripped Aidan of his birthright.

Rhodes paused again. This time he opened his eyes. The pain of the story showed a toll upon the man's countenance.

"Lexford adored the boy; but soon his eye left Beatrice, and he took up with a woman in London. While the viscount saw to his Parliamentary duties, Bea attempted to keep Lady Lexford in line. However, Cassandra Morrison was stronger than Beatrice anticipated. Lady Lexford visited her family's estate for an extended stay and returned to Cheshire with a new resolve. Your mother matured, and she fought for her husband's attentions. Lady Cassandra was more graceful and more beautiful than Beatrice Babcock could ever hope to be, and soon Kimbolt fell madly in love with his wife. It was late coming, but men also mature, and they learn what is important in a marriage," Rhodes reasoned.

The connection between Lord and Lady Lexford, which Susan's father described, was what Aidan observed in his childhood.

"With a renewal of Lexford's commitment to his wife, Lady Lexford delivered forth Aylene and later you. Beatrice watched her hopes dwindle. However, Andrew was proclaimed the rightful heir, and no one knew how to change what he set in motion. Arlen changed his will to give you the bulk of his fortune and all of his unentailed lands, leaving Andrew little more than the title."

Aidan wondered how Rhodes was privy to such intimate details of his father's will. Surely, Arlen Kimbolt did not tell his former mistress what he planned. Aidan could not imagine his father being so naïve. Perhaps, the housekeeper used her position to steal away his father's secrets.

"Shortly after your father's changing of his will, Arlen returned to London for important Parliamentary business. In his absence, first Aylene and then Lady Lexford turned ill and passed."

Rhodes turned his gaze upon Aidan.

"Do you realize you escaped something more dangerous than a contagious disease when you returned to your studies?"

Aidan's voice was heavy.

"What are you implying, Rhodes?"

"Think upon it. Why would both mother and daughter succumb to the disease and so quickly?"

Aidan's composure wilted. He shot a pleading glance to Swenton, and thankfully, the baron understood.

"Although it is not likely much can be done after all these years, but I will ask the squire to investigate the circumstances of Lady Cassandra's death in more detail. For now, perhaps, Rhodes, you will graciously return to your story of Lady Susan Lexford."

Aidan's shoulders remained tense, and he could not swallow properly, but he listened with all his being. Rhodes's voice took on the tones of an exhausted elderly man.

"When you showed an interest in Susan, I was most pleased to have my daughter so properly engaged, but Beatrice solicited Sophia's assistance for her own revenge against the late viscount. My sister in marriage discovered how poor the former Lord Lexford left Andrew, and she meant to reclaim her son's position. She would not have you placed above Andrew. In Beatrice's opinion, there was still time for Viscount Lexford to draw up another will. With Sophia's influence, Susan changed her affection from you to Andrew. The joining would serve two purposes: a Poley would finally marry into the aristocracy, and the situation would place Andrew in Arlen Kimbolt's good graces if your brother produced a child quickly."

"When Sophia approached me with the possible joining, I allowed my own aspirations for my daughter to override my good sense. Sophia and I came quickly to the conclusion that Arlen could live for many years yet, and who was to say Andrew might not predecease his father?"

Rhodes laughed ironically.

"It was as if we predicted the fall of the Kimbolts with our ambitions. Sophia and I planned to outmaneuver Beatrice and make Susan a viscountess much earlier by marrying her to Arlen instead of Andrew. Therefore, we placed Susan in Arlen Kimbolt's way so our daughter might claim her place as the viscount's new wife."

Aidan's stomach rolled, and the bile returned. He physically forced the bitter taste from his mouth. God! He could not imagine such twisted plotting! How would he ever tolerate seeing Susan with his father? Aidan would be perpetually estranged from his home.

"Sophia arranged for Lexford to dine regularly with us, and each time we would leave Arlen and Susan alone. By that point, you were away, and Susan had no one but her mother and me, and we turned our hearts from sensibility. We reasoned if Susan wed Lexford and bore him a son–a true heir–the viscount would send Andrew away, which would provide you assistance, as well."

"Did no one consider my presence?" Aidan said in bewilderment.

"Susan did. My daughter objected, but we convinced her that she was righting a wrong by permitting Arlen's attentions. But as for Sophia and me, we knew otherwise," Rhodes admitted honestly. "You were in war. It was conceivable you would never return."

"If you were aware my father willed me the bulk of his fortune," Aidan countered. "Why not permit Susan and me to marry? Your daughter would know a wealthy life and great connections."

"But not the title, and Sophia was as adamant as her sister in wanting someone in the family to claim a role in the aristocracy."

The extremes to which these people went to claim a part of the viscountcy amazed Aidan. He fought some of the most devious wrongdoers upon the Continent, but none could compare with the Poley family.

"Sophia met a man at one of Lexford's gatherings who knew a great deal about an opiate, which rendered those who took it unable to judge right from wrong. When next we hosted Lexford, my wife arranged a rendezvous between the viscount and Susan. She added a bit of the drug to several of their dishes. Between the opiate and the wine, neither the viscount nor Susan understood what overcame them. Sophia's barely veiled suggestions became a reality. Arlen Kimbolt succumbed to his baser instincts. He took our daughter over and over again during a two-day period and in this very room."

Aidan's hand came to his mouth, and he searched for a bit of air to clear his head. Poor Susan. Her mother constructed a plan to make Susan a viscountess, and Susan's father permitted a man to abuse her womanhood. How often did the pair walk by the closed doors to this sitting room and look the other way? Aidan's mind drew up an image of Susan's young body and his father's elderly one. The image sent his mind searching for a different reality, but none existed.

"It is not a pretty story, and I am not pleased with my role in it," Rhodes declared baldly.

Aidan caught the chair arm to keep from beating Rhodes to within an inch of his life.

"We thought Arlen would do right by Susan, but the viscount's heart remained with his late wife. He long since abandoned Beatrice no more than his housekeeper. Arlen let it be known far and wide how Lady Cassandra brought honor to the viscountship–an honor Beatrice Babcock could never achieve. My sister in marriage became the bitter woman you know today, but Bea's hopes sprang to life again when Arlen agreed to permit Andrew to marry Susan in his father's stead."

Oh, God! Aidan thought. *Could the tale be more twisted?*

"A quick marriage occurred. Andrew lodged only a few objections upon your part."

Aidan stifled the groan of despair resting on his lips. What could he say that was not a curse against all involved?

"I managed a sizeable dowry to assure my daughter would be the future viscountess, but the marriage was in immediate disarray. Andrew claimed his husbandly rights, and, naturally, was not pleased to discover Susan impure. He accused my daughter of losing her innocence to you, my lord. Before the household, Andrew announced he would have no part of his younger brother's leavings."

Aidan could sit no longer. He bolted toward the patio door and pulled the drape aside. He looked out upon the winter sun and wondered why the world appeared to go on without him.

"Continue," he said grudgingly, but he kept his back to the room.

Rhodes's tale was coming to an end; his voice held his weariness.

"Shortly after Andrew's exit, Susan discovered she was with child. Our daughter begged to return to her childhood home, but the viscount would have none of it. Lexford claimed Susan's desertion would play poorly against his family's name. Little did it matter that Andrew left his wife to live in the house with his father, a man she feared and despised."

Aidan's hands fisted and unfisted at his side.

Rhodes now rested his head in his hands. He spoke to the floor.

"Before we could right our daughter's world, Andrew met his Maker in a duel over a woman not half the lady our Susan was."

Aidan thought it more than ironic Rhodes turned his daughter into a whore, and yet Susan's parents termed her a lady.

"Your father ordered your return, but before you could save Susan, the viscount suffered from a weak heart. Just think if the viscount married Susan, all would be well. She would be the dowager viscountess and could marry where she wanted. Andrew, too, could know happiness. It was all Arlen's fault for not meeting his responsibilities to our daughter. Poor Susan accepted a man she once cherishede, but knew herself no longer worthy of calling 'husband.'"

Aidan turned at the sound of Swenton's baritone voice.

"Susan Kimbolt took her life because of the shame she carried, and your wife searches the halls of Lexington Arms for a daughter she lost long before the fire."

Rhodes nodded his agreement.

"I give Mrs. Rhodes laudanum so she might rest, but often her mind drives her from her bed."

Aidan caught the window frame as reality invaded.

"If Andrew claimed his husbandly privileges but once, then you are saying Aaron..."

He broke off, unable to verbalize the truth of the child's birth.

Rhodes cautiously met Aidan's eyes.

"I thought the child would provide Sophia comfort. The boy is the last remnant we possess of our daughter, but the boy's features are those of his father's. Every time Sophia looked upon the child, my wife was reminded of how she failed Susan."

Aidan's mouth had gone dry, but his lips managed to form the words he never thought to speak.

"Aaron is not my nephew–not Andrew's son. The boy is my brother."

Chapter 21

BY MID AFTERNOON of the third day, Mercy guided the let horse into the circle before Crandale Hall, Sir Lesley's seat. As they traveled since the trio departed the posting inn, the Baloch and Trent rode on either side of her. Exhausted from a lack of sleep, Mercy wearily slid to the ground when a groom caught the horse's reins.

They spent two nights upon the road, but unlike the six weeks she traveled alone, Mercy knew real danger and real fear while in the company of Trent. Mathias eyed her as if she were a thoroughbred whose spirits he meant to break. Surprisingly, Mercy found an ally of sorts in the one known as Jamot.

Trent stopped for the first evening at a seedy inn on a country road. The future baronet let a room for her on the top floor. It held nothing more than a small bed and table, but Mercy knew thanks to be free of the ill-fitting sidesaddle Trent purchased for her. Every muscle in her body ached from the strain of the ride and of the tautness of the unknown. She managed to dress for bed before a tap at her window brought her spinning around in fright. The Baloch stood precariously on a perch just below the window's sill.

"Permit me to enter," he said against the closed pane.

Mercy wrapped her robe closer about her. She shooed the man away.

"Leave me be," she hissed.

Jamot gave her a secretive smile.

"It is not as it appears."

Mercy rushed to the window to make certain it remained locked.

"If you do not leave, I shall scream for the innkeeper," she threatened.

"Who will open the door to Trent and the others," the Baloch insisted. "Now hurry before it is too late."

Mercy hesitated, but a heavy tread on the stairs told her Jamot was the least of her threats. She released the latch and shoved open the sash.

"Someone approaches," she whispered.

Jamot nodded before he lifted his weight through the opening and landed on silent feet. With a finger to his lips to indicate her silence, the Baloch moved across the floor to listen at the door.

Mercy's ears strained to hear what Jamot could hear. He caught the room's single chair and wedged it against the door at the same time as the wood rattled from a fist upon it. Mercy jumped when the pounding broke the silence.

"I brought your meal," Trent called from the other side. "Open the door."

Jamot whispered close to her ear.

"Stall him."

When the pounding began again, Jamot quickly shut and locked the window and drew the drape.

"I am preparing for night," Mercy called in what she hoped sounded of a sleepy drawl. "Please leave the tray outside. I will retrieve it shortly."

She knew surprise at how calm her voice sounded.

"The food is hot now," Trent insisted.

Mercy jumped again when the man jiggled the latch.

Thankfully, the chair did not permit the bolt to turn.

Mercy swallowed hard, but she countered, "I shall be thankful nonetheless for your kindness."

Mathias hit the door with his fist again.

"The innkeeper will be displeased."

Mercy pressed her weight against the door to slow Mathias's entry while Jamot rolled one of the towels from the table to stuff it under the bottom. The Baloch instructed her in a voice barely above a whisper.

"The cloth will preclude Trent from reading your shadow under the door and will prevent the wood from sliding easily if the future baronet manages to free the latch."

"Yet, the innkeeper shall be thrilled for the business," she answered Trent.

Mercy was extremely thankful for the Baloch's cunning.

"I will return for the tray," Trent grumbled.

She and Jamot leaned heavily against the door, ears plastered to the wood. Thankfully, Trent placed the tray pointedly on the floor and retreated.

Jamot spoke in soft tones.

"Trent will return. He earned his courage this evening. The future baronet sampled some of his own wares."

Mercy asked, "The opiates?"

During their long ride, she searched every memory she held of Mathias's interactions with Geoffrey, and she decided Mathias was more than a bungling heir to the baronetcy. The younger Trent was the mastermind behind the opium ring of which Mr. Hill spoke honestly. She wished she recognized the truth before she departed Lexington Arms.

Jamot nodded curtly.

"Do not judge, Miss Nelson. If you do, you will estimate me also, and, at the moment, I am your salvation."

Mercy blushed thoroughly.

"I only meant to know the truth," she confessed.

Jamot said no more on the subject. He released the chair

and the bolt. Quietly, he eased the door from its casement and retrieved the tray. Handing it to Mercy, the Baloch quickly closed the door again.

"We must do something to secure the opening. A chair will not be enough when Trent returns."

The Baloch was a conundrum. One minute he spoke as if he meant to have his way with her, and the next, he stood between her and Trent.

Mercy glanced about the small room.

"There is nothing but the bed," she reasoned.

The Baloch shrugged.

"Then we use the bed."

He strode to the dark wood piece and flipped the mattress from the frame. Then he placed his back to the wooden rectangle and shoved it across the floor to rest solidly against the door. The draping hung crookedly against the wall.

Mercy retrieved the blanket from the floor.

"What should we do with the bed linens?"

Jamot nodded to the poorly stuffed mattress.

"Make yourself a place before the hearth. We will wait for Trent's return."

"You mean to sleep in my room?" Mercy gasped.

The Baloch smirked.

"I could permit Trent to breach the opening."

Jamot withdrew a knife from a pouch at his side and placed it on the table.

"If you wish me to leave, you must simply say the word."

"Why?"

The word slipped out before Mercy could stifle it.

"Why are you protecting me?"

She was confused by his sudden empathy. After all, it was Jamot who suggested to Mathias that Mr. Hill likely aided in her escape.

Jamot shrugged noncommittally.

"I am not of the nature to believe a man proves himself by

overpowering those below him. If you ask if I will assist you in an escape from Sir Lesley, I will not. Despite his advanced years, the baronet will treat you kindly; yet, I will protect you from a man who means to make you his conquest."

And so he did. The Baloch slept on the floor under the bed frame and before the door while Mercy wrapped herself in a blanket to rest before the fire. Between Trent's three attempts to enter her room and her nervousness at Jamot's presence in her room, she slept but a few minutes. Now that she was at Crandale Hall, all for which Mercy could hope was her brother's interference, but that possibility was highly unlikely.

On the second day, their pace slowed so Trent could recover from his night of debauchery, but the man's many threats kept Mercy from enjoying the less punishing ride. Without her asking, the Baloch came to her room again on the second night, and despite a lack of attempts by Trent, Mercy again laid awake waiting for the pounding to begin.

Appearing quickly beside her. Mathias caught Mercy's elbow and directed her steps toward the house.

"You will treat my father well," he warned close to her ear. "I want the baronet busy with satisfying his new wife."

"And if I refuse?" Mercy ventured.

Trent tightened his grip on her arm. Likely, she would have marks where his fingers dug into her skin.

"If you refuse my father, then you will deal with me, and no bed before the door will keep me from your room."

Mercy swallowed the encroaching fear choking her throat. Trent knew the bed kept him from acting upon his impulses. Did he know the Baloch championed her safety? If he did, Jamot should be warned. It was the least she could do to repay the foreigner's kindness.

"Mathias!" Sir Lesley called when he appeared on the stairs. "I am pleased to see you…" The baronet halted his descent. "Miss Nelson?" he said in dismay. "We thought you in Nottingham." Sir Lesley's voice trembled.

She did not understand the reference to Nottingham, and so she waited for the scene to unfold. Mercy shifted her shoulders to stand taller.

"It has been a long time, Sir Lesley. In my absence, I knew the kindness of strangers." Without looking at Mathias, she said, "Mr. Trent graciously saw to my return to Lancashire. Now, if you will have someone escort me to Foresthill Hall, I will expect your call in the morning."

The baronet nodded his agreement.

"Of course, my dear."

Mathias stepped between her and his father.

"I thought, Sir, it might be better if Miss Nelson remained under our roof while I make new arrangements for your joining. Unfortunately, Baron Nelson departed for Dorset, and we cannot have our Miss Mercy staying at Foresthill without a proper staff to see to her needs. We will have the ceremony at week's beginning."

"So soon?" Mercy said before she could stop the words.

She noted the twinge of disappointment upon Sir Lesley's countenance, and Mercy felt guilty at causing the baronet additional pain, but she needed to stall for time to plan an escape.

Trent turned a triumphant smile upon her.

"Next week is not too soon; my father waited long enough to claim you as his wife."

Mercy said baldly, "You are assuming Sir Lesley still wishes the connection. After all, I was absent from Lancashire for over four months."

Her mind attempted to conjure up more excuses.

"And as to a speedy joining, we must wait for the banns to be called. I certainly cannot remain in my betrothed's house for three weeks. It would be unseemly."

Mathias caught her hand in his tight grip. To hide the pressure he put on Mercy's fingers–enough so to make her wince–he patted the back of her hand.

"Another calling of the banns will not be necessary."

"Another calling?" Mercy asked suspiciously.

Sir Lesley continued his descent.

"Yes, my dear," he said patiently. "It was always understood we would marry. After your departure, for several weeks, Baron Nelson neglected to inform me of your absence from his home. Only after the second call did I learn of your visiting a sick cousin in Nottingham."

So Geoffrey stalled the Trents in expectation of her return to Foresthill Hall. Likely her brother owed the baronet a hefty sum for the marriage settlements.

"I saw no reason to ask Wheaton not to speak the third call."

The baronet stood before Mercy to claim her other hand.

"But it has been more than three months for the ordinary license," she protested weakly.

Mercy's chances of escaping Crandale Hall grew weaker by the moment.

Mathias suggested to his father.

"Surely as Wheaton's living comes from your benevolence, something can be done. It is not as if the whole neighborhood does not know of your intention to marry Miss Nelson."

Again, Trent smiled warmly at Mercy, but she easily recognized the evil lurking behind the genial gaze.

Sir Lesley frowned.

"I would not wish to ask Mr. Wheaton to bend the church's tenets. Yet, for now, I am pleased to have you remain under my roof. Mathias, perhaps I could prevail upon you to see Miss Nelson to a room. Meanwhile, I will address a note to Foresthill to inform the baron of Mercy's unexpected return. Hopefully, Baron Nelson make an appearance in time for the nuptials."

"I will ferry the note to Foresthill Hall. I mean to examine a horse the baron plans to sell," Trent said in conniving joviality.

Sir Lesley good-naturedly chastised, "Your stable is overflowing now, Mathias."

"True, Father. But it will not hurt to look at what Nelson has to offer."

Mathias placed Mercy's hand upon his arm.

"Allow me to give you a tour of your new home. So as to avoid scandal, I will place a maid in your room at all times."

Mercy recognized the ruse: The maid would guard against any attempt Mercy would make to leave. In addition, a maid would keep her from pleading with Jamot to extend his benevolence. She truly was on her own.

Sir Lesley called from where he watched them climb the stairs.

"Yours is an excellent idea, Mathias. I want nothing to stain my future wife's reputation."

Mercy thought, *No Scandal. Nothing such as sleeping in a barn. Or working as a maid. Or eating near-rotten vegetables from an open field. Or living with Aidan Kimbolt.* The thought of the viscount brought a profound sadness. Mercy would never see Lord Lexford again, and her heart clenched from the pain of a world tilted sideways.

"You plan to hide in your quarters all day?" Hill asked as he strode into Aidan's chambers after nothing more than a sharp knock, which Aidan ignored. "Swenton is preparing to leave for London, and he wishes to say a proper farewell."

Aidan shrugged unrevealingly.

"The baron knows which is my door."

"Do not act as such," Hill cautioned.

"Behave how?" Aidan declared indignantly. "You mean, I pretend to be someone I am not? Something I am not?"

Aidan possessed no idea why he was acting so petulantly. Perhaps it was because he spent most of yesterday having his backside properly kicked by his past, and now it was his turn to do the kicking. After returning to Lexington Arms, Aidan retreated to his chambers to lick his wounds. His whole life was a farce.

While he was listening to Rhodes's tale of horror, Hill placed Lady Cassandra's diary upon Aidan's pillow; and Aidan read and reread each entry. Read of his mother's successes and failures and fears. He vividly recalled the pleasure of his mother's delight at his tutor bragging on Aidan's translations of Greek and Latin. On that day, he swore to keep the smile upon his mother's lips. Would Lady Cassandra be proud of the man he became?

When Aidan first heard of the lie his mother permitted, he knew anger and disgust, but upon thinking of how little rights a woman possessed in British society, he understood his mother's actions. He did not approve of what Lady Cassandra did, but he made peace with her situation. And once he read how his mother set her sights on restoring him to his rightful place, Aidan knew real admiration for the woman he called "Mother." Unlike most women, Lady Cassandra Lexford took the initiative to change her life. Very much like another young lady he came to admire of late.

Hill shook his head in denial.

"You do not believe the words you utter."

Hill picked up the clothes Aidan discarded last evening and draped them over the back of a chair.

"I will ask Mr. Payne to recommend one of the footmen to become your new valet."

Squire Holton took Poley into custody, along with Sophia Rhodes. The magistrate continued his investigation, but rumor and innuendo already spread through the neighborhood. People spoke of how Mrs. Rhodes purposely poisoned the Kimbolts' long-serving housekeeper. Aidan prayed nothing more incriminating than Sophia Rhodes's mental state would be listed as the cause. The prior connection between the Rhodeses and the Kimbolts could not be denied, and it would take more than just a bit of aristocratic arrogance to shush the gossip.

"Do as you please," Aidan said with lackluster. "That is what I plan to do. I plan to quit being the responsible one and to think of my own pleasures for a change. Perhaps I will ride with Swenton to London and engage myself a mistress."

"Riding to London makes sense," Hill said thoughtfully. "But not to find a mistress."

Aidan closed his eyes to the pain. Yesterday's events ripped him raw.

"For what would you have me look?"

Hill folded his arms across his chest.

"For a wife. For Miss Nelson."

Aidan sighed deeply.

"No one will wish to claim the connections I bring to the table," Aidan admitted. "I cannot turn Aaron into my father's by blow. There are too many secrets for a woman of Society to keep."

Hill scowled deeply.

"That statement is the biggest wagon full of cow manure I ever smelt. First, Miss Nelson is not like other Society women, and you know as well as I the lady would protect you with her last breath. And more importantly, you are in love with the woman."

"I do not know what love is," Aidan insisted.

Hill sat on the arm of one of the chairs.

"Do you recall the night you sent Lady Eleanor and Hannah out into the night to escape Louis Levering?"

Aidan remembered it well. It was the first time he felt the expectation of a future.

"Absolutely."

"In the dark, I assisted Lady Eleanor and her maid into that small hidden box under the wagon, but even though the night hid Hannah's sweet countenance, I fell in love with the girl. My lady wrapped my old callused hands between her two small ones, and she kissed my fingertips in gratitude. One of her tears fell upon the back of my hand, and I knew instantly I was meant to protect Hannah Tolliver from the world's evils. Tell me you do not feel the same for Miss Nelson. Tell me you do not grieve for her absence. Convince me your house could be a home again without the lady under your roof."

Aidan spoke his fears.

"What if Miss Nelson does not feel the same?"

Hill dug into his inside pocket.

"Read the lady's note and decide for yourself."

A quarter hour later, Aidan strode into the morning room.

"Mr. Payne, I will require a horse. I mean to ride into London with the baron."

The butler looked up from the plate he was preparing for Aidan.

"I believe, Sir, Mr. Hill previously saw to your horse and a small bag for traveling."

Aidan rolled his eyes in exasperation. He sometimes wished Lucifer Hill did not anticipate each of his decisions, and Aidan most definitely wished the man were not always so bloody correct. Upon Hill's earlier exit, Aidan broke the seal on Miss Nelson's letter and cautiously read the lady's words. Not so surprisingly, she confessed everything–her name, her reasons for leaving Lancashire, and her meeting of Jamot in the tunnel. But it was the poem from William Blake at the letter's end, which drove Aidan to take action.

Never seek to tell thy love,
Love that never can be;
For the gentle wind doth move
Silently, invisibly.
I told my love, I told my love,
I told her all my heart,
Trembling, cold, in ghastly fears.
Ah! she did depart!
Soon after she was gone from me,
A traveler came by,
Silently, invisibly:
He took her with a sigh.

With the poem, the lady spoke of freedom. First, of her freedom from her brother's rule–freedom to choose her own life. But more importantly, she meant to release him to know another. She would remain silent and invisible. Like the lady in the poem, Miss Nelson would turn to another, one she thought lesser than he.

The poem presented Aidan a promise. He reasoned only a woman in love would deny her own feelings in order for the man for whom she cared to know contentment. Then Miss Nelson signed the letter with the closing, "I claim this title once only–Your Mercy."

It was an exhilarating moment.

Hill appeared at the morning room door.

"The baron and I await you in the main corridor, my lord."

"I will finish my breakfast first, Mr. Hill."

Although Aidan had no appetite, he meant to make certain his friends waited. They manipulated him enough of late. With a smile, he took a large bite of the ham upon his plate.

They rode hard and long for three days, and Aidan had more than just a few sore muscles; but in another sixty miles, he would arrive in London. He meant to call immediately upon the boarding houses Hill recommended to Miss Nelson. More than a sennight passed since he last seen the lady, and Aidan ached to hold Mercy in his arms again.

They reined in before a small posting inn outside of Bedford to change horses. Aidan slid stiffly from the saddle.

"I will ascertain whether Miss Nelson boarded the London coach safely."

From Warwick, they traced the mail route, the one leading toward Nottingham and beyond from London. From a coaching agent some twenty miles north, they learned Miss Nelson would change coaches at this particular inn. Aidan did not look to his friends for affirmation; he realized they both sported knowing smirks.

Straightening his shoulders, he entered the darkened room. It smelt of stale ale and tobacco.

"Yes, Sir, may I be of assistance?"

Aidan's eyes slowly adjusted to the lack of light.

"I am asking after information on a young woman traveling

alone, some three days prior."

The innkeeper bowed a second time.

"Certainly, my lord. If'n you'd describe the lady I'd be pleased to be of service."

"Reddish blonde of head. Shoulder height. Dressed plainly. Fair of countenance."

The innkeeper nodded readily.

"Aye, Sir. I remember her. The lady waited some three hours for the coach from the North."

Aidan breathed easier. Miss Nelson could still experience difficulties, but he looked upon this information as a good sign.

"Then the lady continued her journey toward London?"

The innkeeper looked uncomfortably about the room.

"I fear not, my lord."

"Why ever not?" Aidan blustered.

"Lexford?"

Aidan turned at the sound of his name. "Lexford, is that you?"

Striding toward him with hand extended was Adam Lawrence, Lord Stafford, the future Earl of Greenwall. The viscount held similar acquaintances as Aidan, and he and Stafford shared more than one drink at White's. Godown had no use for the man for Stafford rivaled Godown in looks, and they often vied for the attentions of the same women, but Aidan always enjoyed the man's company. Stafford was intelligent and genial and always benevolent in his actions.

"Stafford, what brings you to this inn?"

Aidan willingly accepted the man's hand.

"Surely you did not take to riding the mail routes."

He and the viscount often bid on the same horses at Tattersall's. It was something else Aidan admired in the man: Stafford had an excellent eye for horseflesh.

"Monroe, Whitmore, Hetzer, and I meet every few months or so for a lengthy game of cards. Winner takes all. I mean to supplement the pitiful allowance Greenwall sees fit to present me."

Aidan was well aware of the ongoing feud between Stafford and his father. The earl meant to bring his son under control, but the viscount had other ideas.

"What if you lose?" Aidan asked with a wry grin.

Stafford looked over his shoulder to where Monroe downed another glass of ale.

"It will never happen."

"How long have you been here?" Aidan asked from curiosity.

Stafford rotated his neck to loosen the muscles.

"Nearly five days."

The innkeeper interrupted.

"His Lordship is looking for the girl. You know the one, my lord. The one Mr. Monroe took a liking to."

Aidan's heart slammed to a halt.

"He did what?" he said incredulously and shoved past Stafford, but the viscount caught Aidan's arm.

"Monroe never touched the girl," Stafford hissed. "I made certain she was safe."

Aidan's muscles remained tight, but he presented the viscount a sharp nod of gratitude.

"Did you see the lady board the coach? The innkeeper says she did not."

Stafford gestured Aidan toward a recessed area for privacy.

"The innkeeper speaks the truth. The girl left on horseback with two men."

Aidan's throat went dry.

"Two men? What can you tell me of them?"

"The taller of the two was a foreigner. Dark of skin and hair. Dangerous looking."

"Jamot!" Aidan's mind screamed.

He thought his knees might buckle under him. He should have given pursuit the night of the fire. Needless to say, the Baloch would attempt to strike back at Aidan by hurting Miss Nelson.

"Was the other a young gentleman with coal black hair?"

Stafford nodded his affirmation.

"I thought it odd that the girl waited so patiently for the coach and then departed in the opposite direction, but she did not indicate she required my assistance. Trent held her arm while the dark one arranged for fresh horses."

"Trent?"

It was a name with which Aidan was familiar. Swenton spoke of Miss Nelson's betrothed.

"Yes, Mathias Trent," Stafford confirmed. "The heir to Sir Lesley Trent. I only saw the future baronet a few times, but I have no high opinion of him. I thought to interfere, but I heard the lady call him 'Mathias,' and I knew they held a prior acquaintance."

Aidan sucked in a deep steadying breath.

"Thank you, Stafford. I should hurry," he said shakily. "My friends await."

Stafford's mouth set in a tight line.

"Do you require my assistance?"

Aidan shook his head.

"No. I must decide what I should do next."

The viscount whispered, "The girl? She was someone special in your life?"

Avoiding Stafford's measuring gaze, Aidan looked off.

"I thought it to be so, but if the lady departed with Trent, I likely erred."

Stafford lowered his voice.

"We do not know each other well, Lexford, but believe me when I say, I learned a bit about love and passion since that fiasco in Derbyshire at Pemberley several years back. If this girl is your ocean, your thunder, your rain, your mountains, your open door. If she is your everything, you would be a fool not to fight for her."

Chapter 22

MERCY STARED MOROSELY out the window. She was at Crandale Hall for five days. Tomorrow she would exchange vows with Sir Lesley. Mathias made certain Mercy had no opportunities to either to make her escape or to send a message to Geoffrey. Two maids kept Mercy company at all times. One slept outside her door, while the other slept within. She was unable to warn Jamot of Trent's knowing of the bed before the door. Although she held no doubt the foreigner would be a dangerous opponent, she still felt an obligation for the man's protection on the road.

The window looked out upon the house's main entrance, making an escape without being seen would be nearly impossible. Somehow, Trent convinced Mr. Wheaton to overlook the expiration of the ordinary license. She did not like to think upon what "inducements" Mathias offered the man. Hopefully, if Mr. Wheaton chose to break the church's laws, the cleric earned something more than the threat of bodily harm for his efforts. She supposed the dates changed on the necessary documents.

The first evening of her confinement, Mercy claimed exhaustion and dined in her room alone. The previous two evenings, she invited Sir Lesley to dine with her in her chamber's sitting room. She meant to avoid Mathias as often as possible. The baronet was a genial man, and if he were younger, Mercy might not consider this joining with such distaste. However, the thought of a man older than her father being her husband went against Mercy's sensibilities.

In addition to the agony of becoming Lady Trent, she now wondered how she and the baronet would be able to stop Mathias's manipulations. Mercy was quite certain Sir Lesley would not take kindly to her suggestion that Mathias was involved in illegal activities. She was very much on her own in this matter.

Aidan and Hill had set a course for Lancashire. The Bedford innkeeper had but two fresh horses, and so Swenton continued on to London as Stafford's guest in the viscount's carriage.

"Promise me you will tell no one of these events," Aidan pressed.

The baron earnestly studied Aidan's countenance.

"By your hand, Pennington, and likely Sir Carter, know of Jamot's presence in your home."

Swenton did not need to remind Aidan of what Aidan now regretted.

"I must, at a minimum, speak of our suspicions regarding Mathias Trent to Sir Carter."

Reluctantly, Aidan agreed.

"But nothing of Miss Nelson. Promise me, John. If I fail, I want no sympathy from our Realm brothers. I have had my fill of consideration."

Unwillingly, Swenton nodded his agreement.

"If you find Miss Nelson in time, take her to Linton Park. Even if the others are in London, Lord and Lady Linworth will welcome you to Linton Chapel. The place brought good fortune to the others, and you will likely require it after such a tumultuous time."

"I thought of Scotland. It is much quicker," Aidan objected.

The baron shook Aidan's hand in departure.

"Everyone will anticipate your going to Scotland. If anyone

means to stop you, your traveling in the opposite direction will fool your pursuers. As to the special license, in your stead, I will call at Doctors Commons tomorrow. Somehow I will convince the bishop to overlook the impropriety of your absence. When the special license is secured, I will have it carried to Linton Park by the Realm's fastest courier. Take Miss Nelson to Derbyshire and begin your life's journey in a proper church. It would please me to know you are among the fortunate ones."

The sound of Hill's approach brought Aidan from his musings. Even after two days of hard riding, Aidan still held doubts of his success.

"I secured rooms for the night. We should be in Chorley tomorrow."

Aidan glanced about the private room. He ate because he required the strength to carry on. He slept for the same reason, but with each mile they covered, he knew dread. What if he were too late or worse yet, what if he misjudged Miss Nelson's sentiments?

As if he read Aidan's thoughts, Hill assured, "We will arrive in time."

The sauce dripped from Aidan's fork. The utensil did not move from where he raised it to his lips.

"And what if we do not?"

Hill's eyebrow rose in stark disbelief.

"The lady is a fighter, my lord. Miss Nelson will not go easy."

Aidan jammed the fork into his mouth to accept the bite of meat and potato. In his mind, he chewed upon what Hill said. Miss Nelson was a fighter, but she meant to set Aidan free.

"I wish for an early start. I mean to be on Trent's doorstep at a most unsociable hour."

Aidan and Hill crouched low to watch the comings and goings of an obviously busy household.

"What do you suspect is so important?" Hill asked.

"I do not wish to think upon it," Aidan said dejectedly.

Hill started away.

"Stay here. I mean to ask."

Aidan caught his friend's arm.

"Trent may recognize you."

Hill smiled that wily grin Aidan knew so well.

"I do not intend to ask the baronet's son. That is not unless someone else cannot provide me an answer. You keep watch and save the heroics until we need them."

A few minutes later, Hill slipped into the open stable door. He glanced about, but no one appeared to be within. Cautiously, Lucifer edged along the line of open stalls. At length, he called out, "Anyone about?"

A moment of silence followed before an old man with thinning gray hair appeared from the tack room.

"May I hep you?"

Lucifer offered up an easy smile.

"Just lookin' for a bit of werk."

He used the dialect once common to his speech.

The man eyed Lucifer suspiciously.

"You been in the war?"

"Since '09 and Corunna."

Lucifer knew something of all the major battles. Lexford and the others taught him well.

"Been lookin' for steady werk since leavin' Belgium."

"You appear fit enough, but I'm 'fraid I kin offer you nothin' today. The baronet be gitten himself married. Twill be no hirin' for a week or more."

Hill shrugged regrettably.

"I don't be expectin' to remain in Lancashire a week, but I thank you for yer kindness."

He started toward the still open door.

"I hope yer new mistress be a kind one, and the baronet fills his house with children."

"Miss Nelson be a baron's sister and young enough to add

to Sir Lesley's family."

The man followed Hill toward the door.

Lucifer paused casually.

"You didn't say what time the nuptials be."

The old man took out a pocket watch.

"Less than a half hour."

Mercy with two maids in tow paced the small anteroom. She begged Sir Lesley to postpone the ceremony until Geoffrey could return to give her away, but the baronet answered each of her objections with "Mathias made arrangements for..." or "Mathias assures me..." Sir Lesley turned much of his life over to his son, which would prove a major mistake if Mercy could not convince the baronet of his son's duplicity.

When Mr. Wheaton spoke to her earlier, Mercy attempted to plead for his assistance, but the curate remained adamant that the ceremony was the baronet's wish.

"It is time, Miss," the maid known as Sally said from behind her. Mercy glanced down at the pale yellow dress Sir Lesley commissioned for her.

"Yellow," she grumbled. "It only goes to show how little my future husband knows of my preferences. I shall spend my life looking as if I am a wilted spring flower."

"I think the gown quite lovely, Ma'am," the maid assured.

Mercy rolled her eyes.

"But not for a woman of my coloring," she protested.

A light tap at the door indicated her options expired. Sir Lesley waited. Mercy grudgingly jammed the yellow bonnet upon her head and tied the too long ribbon in a flamboyant bow. She followed the maid from the room. With eyes dejectedly upon the floor, she walked toward her future.

Hill rushed to where Aidan waited.

"We have less than a half hour," he yelled as he mounted.

Aidan's heart jumped into action. They earlier scouted the

area and knew the location of the nearest church. Aidan whipped the horse's reins from side to side as he dug in his heels. *Please God,* he prayed with each pounding stride of his horse's hoofs. *Do not steal her away from me.*

He and Hill slowed their animals, as the small church grew larger with their approach.

"Damnation!" Hill growled as they reined in on the hill overlooking the chapel. "Trent is taking no chances."

Armed guards prowled the church grounds.

Aidan grinned.

"There are only ten or so, and I missed a bit of physical contact while I recovered from my injury."

Aidan extracted a gun from an inside pocket.

Hill shook his head in amusement.

"In that case, you can take the front. I will enter through the back."

Aidan's smile widened.

"Just the way I prefer it. Be wary, my friend."

"You too, Sir."

With that, they separated. Aidan made his way quickly down the hill. Crouched low, he half slid to the bottom and was charging the guards milling about before the church before they knew of his presence. The first one earned a small knife placed perfectly in the soft part of the man's throat while the second received an incapacitating blow across the back of his neck. The third a bullet to the knee.

The sound of gunshot brought Mercy's head up. Hope arrived. If there were trouble outside, perhaps she could escape in the melee.

"What is amiss?" Sir Lesley asked his eldest son.

"Likely nothing more than some fool cleaning his gun." Trent grumbled.

The baronet's heir strode toward the front of the church.

"Continue with the ceremony, Mr. Wheaton."

The curate's trembling lips began the customary reading.

"Dearly beloved…we are gathered…together here…in the sight of God…and in the face…of this company…"

***

Two more of the baronet's guards charged Aidan. He sidestepped, sending one flipping over his shoulder to land awkwardly upon his backside. The sound of bones breaking, said the man would not be moving soon, but to guarantee no renewal of the culprit's attack, Aidan stomped hard upon the man's chest. He turned to latch onto the second of the two. Like a bare knuckles champ, he hit the man squarely in the nose with several quick jabs. Blood poured from his attacker's nostrils. Aidan's next jab struck the man in the neck before shoving him to the ground.

"Move and I will kill you," he growled.

Finishing off the last of the guards, Aidan rushed to the church door. Jerking it open, he came face to face with the man who entered his house with Jamot.

***

"Which is an honest estate instituted by God…"

The noise outside told Mercy something more than a man cleaning his gun was amiss. She shot a glance to Sir Lesley's frowning countenance before making her decision to put a halt to the ceremony, even if it was only a temporary delay. With a fluttering hand to her cheek, Mercy pretended to swoon and dropped to the floor. Keeping her eyes closed, she waited for what would happen next.

***

Lucifer caught two of the men by their collars and slammed their heads together. Both sets of eyes went blank before he released them to kiss the ground. A third received an elbow to the neck before he slumped over. A solid blow to the man's back sent his attacker into the dirt.

Lucifer turned to meet the next assailant, but no one appeared. Two men scattered toward the hill without looking back. The sound of a single shot told him the viscount met a more established force, and Lucifer thought to rush to Lexford's side, but he knew his role in this mission. He was to reach and protect Miss Nelson. Therefore, he kicked at the locked door. Once. Twice. On the third attempt the door banged open. Rushing through the small storage room, Lucifer burst into the main church.

"Cease with the vows!" he shouted.

Gun pointing at the curate and an elderly gentleman, Lucifer planted his stance and waited for Lexford's appearance. As if on cue, the main door flew open to reveal the viscount. Unfortunately, another man waited also.

❧

One of the maids rushed to Mercy's side, but as far as Mercy could tell with her eyes closed, no one else thought to tend to her. Then a familiar voice called out, "Cease with the vows!" and Mercy's heart soared. Mr. Hill came for her. Was the viscount also present? She cautiously opened her eyes and pushed herself to her elbows.

Brandishing the gun, Mr. Hill sent the baronet and the curate, as well as the Sir Lesley's younger children, who huddled together in a corner, in retreat. Mercy took advantage of the distraction. She scrambled to her feet to reach Mr. Hill.

"Thank God, you arrived in time."

He shoved her behind him.

"Stay close," Hill cautioned.

"What is the meaning of this?"

Sir Lesley pushed past Mr. Wheaton to take a position of prominence.

When the main door flew open, Mercy prayed for her one particular miracle: Lord Lexford's appearance, but when she finally saw him after a fortnight of separation, all she could do was stare in bewilderment. He came.

"Aidan," she whispered as their eyes met.

The viscount also held a gun, and Mathias Trent raised his hands in surrender.

"Move!" Lord Lexford ordered, and Trent stepped away,

but not far enough for Mercy's comfort.

"Beware of Trent," Mercy warned Hill in hushed tones, and the gentle giant beside her tensed in response.

⁂

Aidan's eyes found her immediately. There she was in all her glory; his lips spoke her name before his heart closed about it, keeping it safely where it belonged.

"I will ask again," the older man said. "What is the meaning of this madness?"

Aidan ignored the baronet. He looked upon the woman he loved. Except for the color of her gown, which did her no justice, she was exquisite. He approached slowly, and Miss Nelson stepped beside Hill.

"I missed your company, my dear," Aidan said evenly.

The lady blushed from such open intimacies, but her eyes remained locked on his.

"And I you, my lord."

Sir Lesley demanded, "What is the meaning of this, Mercy?"

Aidan gave Miss Nelson a knowing look before saying,

"You meant, Sir Lesley, to force the lady into a marriage she would not have."

Sir Lesley looked about the room to analyze the situation.

"Who may you be, Sir?"

Aidan answered aristocratically,

"Lexford of Lexington Arms in Cheshire."

Sir Lesley offered an abbreviated bow.

"I assure you, my lord, Miss Nelson is my betrothed."

Aidan smiled easily. He loved it when others attempted to fool him.

"Even if that were true, Sir Lesley, a wedding could not occur today. Miss Nelson departed Lancashire in early November, and she resided with me since mid December. Four months would require another calling of the banns. An illegal marriage is beyond you, Sir."

Mathias Trent said from somewhere off Aidan's left

shoulder, "A second pronouncement of the banns occurred, my lord."

Aidan glared over his shoulder at the man. He hoped Trent did something to justify his taking his vengeance out on the man. He owed the future baronet for the fire and for invading his household.

"Yes, I fully comprehend fifteen days beginning on a Sunday would suffice to resolve the legality of exchanging of vows, but as you and Jamot were in my home less than a fortnight prior, and the lady's room was still warm from her presence during that intrusion, three callings could not occur."

Trent gestured wildly.

"You speak an untruth, my lord. I know no one named Jamot."

"Talpur," Miss Nelson said in explanation.

His mouth compressed. Time for a bit of honesty.

"You must never keep secrets from me again, my dear."

The lady shook her head in the affirmative before dropping their eyes. To Trent, Aidan said patricianly,

"Rahmut Talpur died nearly a year prior in the Cornish home of the Duke of Thornhill. Talpur kidnapped the Duke's daughter; the foreigner died at the hands of James Kerrington, the future Earl of Linworth. The man with whom you traveled is Murhad Jamot."

Trent's countenance relayed his surprise, and Aidan knew satisfaction.

"Then we will wait for another proper calling," Trent asserted. "Nothing changed: Miss Nelson remains my father's betrothed."

Aidan's lips twisted. He would complicate their lives further with one more fabrication.

"While she resided at Lexington Arms, Miss Nelson explained her brother's wishes were not hers. The lady chose elsewhere, Sir Lesley. Miss Nelson became my wife in early February. The marriage was consummated. There is the possibility

Lady Lexford carries my child."

Sir Lesley looked indignantly upon the lady.

"Is this true?"

Thankfully, Miss Nelson did not even blink. Aidan thought she would make an excellent spy.

"It is."

"But why would you not inform me of this aberration?" Sir Lesley demanded.

"My wife fled your son's threats and accusations. It was foolish of Lady Lexford not to trust me to protect her. Yet, with her brother's previous abuse, I can forgive her the lack of forethought. When Trent overtook Lady Lexford upon the London Road, I imagine my lady knew not how to divert Trent's desire to make you the happiest of men."

Aidan prayed he would not go to Hell for his many prevarications.

"Now, come, my dear." He extended his hand to Mercy. "It is time to return to Cheshire."

Aidan meant to have the lady safely in his arms.

Sir Lesley did not appear appeased by Aidan's explanation. While Trent reached suspiciously into a side pocket, the baronet raised a hand to still Mercy's steps.

"Why would you not say something when you arrived at Crandale Hall? You led me to believe you were in Nottingham?"

Miss Nelson looked upon the baronet with empathy.

"Both my brother and Mathias obviously misled you. When I arrived, you readily accepted the fact I should remain at Crandale. Would you believed me if I spoke out against your eldest son?" she challenged. "Should it not appear odd that I did not leave my quarters since my arrival? Or that the maids slept both inside and outside my door?"

"It was for propriety's sake," Sir Lesley protested weakly.

Miss Nelson shook her head in denial.

"It was so I could not escape."

She gestured toward Aidan.

"If you truly care for me, Sir Lesley, you would recognize I belong to this man. Even without the bonds of marriage, I would gladly remain with him forever."

Aidan understood what she wished him to know, but his mind was set. Once they were clear of this debacle, he meant to make Miss Nelson his wife.

"Lady Lexford does me honor," he said softly in response.

"Why did you not ask yourself how Mathias came upon me if I were truly in Nottingham?" she continued.

Sir Lesley looked accusingly upon his son.

"Speak to me of what Lord Lexford accuses. Were you in Cheshire a fortnight prior? Does your associate use an assumed name?"

Trent's shoulders shifted defiantly.

"While I saw to estate business I came across your wayward betrothed living with a man and pretending to be his relative. I simply applied a bit of persuasion to bring the lady home to you. I would not have you the subject of gossip."

"But you would have me marry another man's wife?" Sir Lesley charged.

Trent took several steps in his father's directions, and Aidan countered the movement. He watched the man carefully.

"Miss Nelson is not Lord Lexford's wife!" Trent argued. "She used the name Mary Purefoy and presented herself as His Lordship's cousin. There was no church ceremony!"

Sir Lesley's eyes narrowed.

"And how would you possess knowledge of these facts?"

"I tarried with your old associate, Jonathan Rhodes, while I was in Cheshire."

Aidan wondered if Rhodes had his hands in the opium trade invading Cheshire; it seemed he earned an answer to his question. The baronet's son confirmed Aidan's suspicions. At a minimum, Rhodes offered sanctuary to those involved. Aidan would use the information as a bargaining tool for secrecy on Rhodes's part.

"Rhodes's estate abuts Lord Lexford's and his late daughter

was the viscount's wife. Mr. Rhodes assures me what I say is true," Trent declared.

Aidan opposed Trent's self-assurance.

"Father Rhodes does not wish to think upon another replacing his daughter as viscountess, and as to Miss Nelson's use of another name, it was all prearranged by one of my longest acquaintances, the Marquis of Godown. The marquis took a liking to the baron and assisted in Geoffrey Nelson's rise to stability. Naturally, the baron sought the marquis's assistance in locating his sister once all of Nelson's resources proved futile."

Aidan noted another deep blush upon the lady's cheeks, but her expression did not change, a fact for which Aidan was grateful.

"The marquis and I served together upon the Continent, and Godown sought my involvement. When Miss Nelson's location became apparent to the marquis's hired investigators, Lord Godown sent Mr. Hill to retrieve the girl and to escort her to my home to protect Miss Nelson from difficult gossip. The name change and the supposed relationship hid her identity until she could be reunited with her family. Little did I anticipate the natural attraction. A special license assured our joining. The Archbishop spent an inordinate amount of time in Durham with the renovations."

It was a well-constructed tale. One furnishing too many details. If Sir Lesley had the training Aidan held, the man would know every word an invention. A person, who means to deceive, attempts to address every possibility. Such tale spinning leaves him open to those with intuitive attributes to identify the holes in the story, but Sir Lesley was not one of those with broader insights.

The baronet said, "I see. Then I beg your forgiveness, my lord, for my family's part in this disarray."

Aidan added for proper measure.

"Several of your men suffered injuries, and one will require a coffin. You should see to their comfort soon."

"I had no men outside," Sir Lesley insisted.

Hill said obstinately, "I am not accustomed to entering a church with a gun in my hand."

Again, Sir Lesley turned to his son.

"You did this? You took Lady Lexford captive? Placed guards about the church? Brought shame to my door?"

"I acted upon your behalf!" Trent persisted.

Aidan added for good measure, "It is my belief that your son had a hand in a fire at my home, as well as sponsoring someone taking a shot at Lady Lexford, wounding my wife in her shoulder. I know from my servant's lips that Trent purposely seduced Her Ladyship's maid to spy on her mistress."

Sir Lesley's ire rose quickly.

"I presented you too much freedom. Well, no more. I am not nearing my grave."

Aidan watched as Trent's self-possession took control of the man's reason.

"You are nothing move than a doting old man. I made the baronetcy solvent. We are rich, Father. Because of me, all of your children will find a place in Society. Bloody hell! There is even enough to see your by blows hold a respectable occupation."

Sir Lesley blustered, "Mathias, you will bide your tongue in the church. I will have no son of mine speaking thusly."

"I am no longer a child. I am a man," Trent hissed.

Miss Nelson foolishly said, "A man who deals in opiates."

Sir Lesley's countenance paled.

"Please tell me Lady Lexford speaks with an ill tongue? Have you made your fortune illegally?"

No answer came; instead a slight shift in Trent's position relayed the man's intent. Aidan acted from instinct. He shoved Sir Lesley from his path to wrap Mercy about the waist to drive her to the floor. From his eye's corner, he saw the flash of Hill's gun as his friend fired, and a bullet hissed past Aidan's ear. An elongated "No!" filled the air.

Aidan's weight knocked the air from her lungs, but she was safe. From above, people rushed to where he suspected Trent laid bleeding, but Aidan's attention rested solely on Mercy Nelson.

"Speak to me," he pleaded as he rolled to the side. Brushing the hair from the lady's cheeks, Aidan gently cupped her chin. "Speak to me," he said with a quick shake of Mercy's shoulders.

Chocolate eyes slowly opened to meet his. Although still a bit glazed over, they recognized him, and she smiled sweetly. It was a moment Aidan would remember forever.

"My lord," she whispered.

"Aidan," he insisted.

Her smile widened. "Aidan."

He kissed her with all the love in his heart. Mercy's arms wound about his neck, and Aidan deepened the kiss. Except for the clearing of a deep throat and the appearance of a scuffed boot near his head, he could remain as such forever.

"We should depart, my lord," Hill said seriously.

Aidan's body thought differently, but his good sense took hold.

"Can you stand upon your own?" he asked as he pushed himself to his feet and extended a hand in Mercy's direction. She nodded her agreement and accepted his hand.

"Present the curate with enough money to cover the damages and any funerals," Hill whispered. "We should move quickly."

Aidan glanced to where Sir Lesley and his family tended the wounded Mathias Trent.

"You are correct, as usual." Aidan dug ten pounds from his purse he kept hidden for emergencies and pressed it in the curate's hand before directing Mercy around the scene.

However, before they could clear the building, a dark figure entered from the church's nave.

"I see I am tardy in my duties to the bride," Jamot said with a smirk.

Aidan placed Mercy behind him.

"I wish no trouble today, but I am not opposed to finishing our business," he threatened.

"Our business dealt with those within your household who betrayed you. I suspect that information is no longer a bargaining coin to my benefit."

Aidan heard Hill cock the palm pistol his man carried. From beside him, Mercy said, "Let us pass, Jamot. Trent is finished, and he knows your identity. Because of your kindness to me on our journey, Lord Lexford will permit you to pass, but it must be over now."

Aidan watched the Baloch's expression soften.

"I prefer my women with hair of coal rather than of the sun, but you chose well, Lord Lexford. This one possesses a brave heart. Your children will know greatness."

With that proclamation, the Baloch bowed and turned toward the exit.

Aidan shook his head in disbelief, but he did not tarry. He caught Mercy's hand to drag her along behind him.

Racing to where the horses waited, Aidan lifted her to his saddle.

"You must ride with me today."

He straddled the seat behind her and settled Mercy upon his lap.

"You fit very well within my arms," he whispered in her ear as he turned the horse.

Her arms came about his waist, and she buried her face in the crook of Aidan's neck. He inhaled her as he kicked the horse's flanks.

"Being so speaks of home," she said softly.

Her breath warmed Aidan's neck. He agreed: She was his sun, his moon, his stars, his earth. His fears, his doubts, his triumphs, his everything.

"Where to, my lord," Hill called as he brought his horse alongside of Aidan's.

"Foresthill Hall." He grinned at his friend. "We require Baron Nelson's permission or else we ride toward Gretna Green."

Chapter 23

WITHIN A HALF HOUR, Aidan and Mr. Hill reined in before Foresthill Hall. A young groom Mercy did not recognize rushed forward to claim the horses. Mr. Hill dismounted first, and His Lordship lifted her to his friend's arms.

"Thank you, kind sir," Mercy teased as Hill set her upon her feet. She presented the man an exaggerated curtsy. "You, Sir, have my undying gratitude."

She launched herself into the man's arms.

"Who would think a guardian angel would sport a scruffy beard?" she whispered.

His Lordship cleared his throat.

"Either you release the lady or name your second, Hill," Lord Lexford said jovially.

Hill gently set her away from him.

"As you are my second for more years than I can recall, I will bend to your wishes, my lord."

Lord Lexford caught her hand and brought the back of it to his lips.

"If it is your wish, it is time we claim a future."

"More than anything, my lord, I wish to return to Lexington Arms as your viscountess."

The words brought tears to her eyes. A dream surely could not promise more.

His Lordship escorted her up the entrance steps to rap heavily upon the door. He replaced the bonnet upon her head.

"Whoever thought you should wear yellow for your wedding certainly never looked upon your beautiful countenance."

Mercy laughed self-deprecatingly.

"I fear, my lord, you must become accustomed to yellow as this is the only gown I own. My others remain at Crandale Hall, and Geoffrey may not permit me to claim my former ones."

Lexford said seductively, "I will purchase you better. You should wear silks and satin and velvet."

But Mercy had the distinct feeling the viscount's thoughts rested upon her sans clothing.

The door opened to a familiar face.

"Mr. Soames," she squealed.

It was a lifetime ago since she departed this house, Mercy nearly forgot why she made her escape.

"Glory to God!" the elderly butler exclaimed. "Miss Mercy came home."

He opened the door wider.

"Please come in from the cold. The baron will be most anxious to see you. He grieved with your disappearance, Miss."

"Except for the loss of Sir Lesley's connections, I had no idea Geoffrey might care," Mercy admitted.

Mr. Soames glanced about to secure privacy.

"The baron no longer requires Sir Lesley's influence. The Marquis of Godown assumed control of the estate," Soames whispered. "Conditions are much improved."

Mercy turned to Aidan.

"You spoke the truth of the marquis's interest in Geoffrey. Why did you not tell me before?"

The viscount leaned close to whisper, "Because, my dear, you guarded your identity until recently."

He tweaked her nose for good measure, and Mercy blushed

thoroughly.

Mr. Soames accepted Mercy's cloak.

"Your sister set her husband to tending to the baron's financial papers."

Mercy caught the man's hand.

"Grace? Grace is alive?"

Soames gently patted the back of Mercy's hand.

"Oh, yes, Miss. Miss Grace is the Marquise of Godown."

Mercy felt the walls swoon. She prayed for Grace's safety. Daily she said the words aloud, but she feared for the worst. Somehow, God recognized her heart. Swirls of colored lights clouded her vision, and Mercy's insides went icy cold. When she swayed, Lord Lexford caught her under her legs to lift her to him. She heard him order Soames to show him a place where he might place her down, and then it all went black.

Despite all signs to the contrary, Aidan always assumed Miss Nelson knew of her sister's conquest, but her reaction proved otherwise. From the butler, she learned Grace Crowden lived. Now, it would be Aidan's responsibility to inform her of the marquise's disappearance.

"Mercy," he whispered. "Mercy, Darling, wake up."

Slowly, her eyes opened, and Aidan breathed easier.

"My lord?" she said sweetly.

He carefully lifted her to a seated position.

"Do you know your whereabouts?" Aidan asked encouragingly.

She gave her head a gentle shake before answering,

"In my brother's home."

Before they could say more, a young man strode through the door.

"Mercy! Praise God! You returned to us."

Despite Aidan reaching for her to protect Mercy, the man scooped her from the sofa to embrace her. The man caught Mercy's chin and lifted it to look upon her countenance.

"You look well; I feared the worst."

He kissed Mercy's forehead. Then he glanced to where Aidan and Hill looked on.

"And who did you bring us?"

Mercy blushed, and Aidan smiled at her innocent embarrassment.

"Lord Lexford, may I present my brother, Baron Nelson. Geoffrey, it is my great pleasure to bring you the acquaintance of Aidan Kimbolt, Viscount Lexford of Lexington Arms in Cheshire, and his close associate, Mr. Henry Hill."

The baron held his sister's hand, but he offered a proper bow.

"Welcome to Foresthill Hall. May I send for refreshments? I cannot thank you enough for returning my sister to us."

"You misinterpreted our presence in your home, Nelson," Aidan warned. "Your sister graciously accepted my proposal. You and I have business to address."

Swinging his gaze to his sister, Nelson's smile filled with pride.

"A viscountess, Mercy? You did well, my dear."

"Perhaps, you have a place where we might speak privately, Nelson. Urgency is of import," Aidan suggested.

"Absolutely, we can use my study," Nelson said suspiciously.

"Hill, would you make arrangements for a carriage?" Aidan instructed.

He did not wish to ride all the way to Derbyshire with Mercy seated upon his lap. Moreover, nearly six days in the saddle marked their tolls on his body.

"Certainly, my lord."

Hill started for the door, but the baron called him back.

"I possess a small carriage you are welcome to use if you are so inclined, Lexford. If we are to be brothers, it is the least I can do."

Mercy said in disbelief, "A second carriage?"

Her brother cleared his throat.

"It is more economical," he explained.

"I will call in at the stable, my lord," Hill assured.

Aidan nodded his agreement, and his friend made his exit.

To Mercy Lexford said, "My dear, perhaps you have several gowns you wish to reclaim while I speak to your brother."

She laughed up at him with sparkling eyes.

"I will find a more appropriate gown, my lord."

She went on tiptoes to kiss her brother.

"Thank you, Geoffrey. I heard heartening words of your new constancy. I am pleased to see you looking well and set on making our father proud."

The negotiations with her brother went better than Aidan anticipated. Obviously, the strict hand Godown placed on Nelson's shoulder made a difference, and Aidan would assist the marquis once Aidan married Mercy.

"Miss Nelson knows nothing of what transpired between the marquis and her elder sister. If you hold no objections," Aidan suggested, "I will explain the complications Lady Godown experienced in her marriage."

Nelson shook his head sadly.

"My part in my sisters' woes brings me grief."

Aidan took sympathy on the man.

"I am certain Miss Nelson would be pleased if you would attend the wedding, as would my associates. My friends and I are family in action rather than by blood."

"Thank you, Lexford. It would be an honor to know such esteemed company. Before I follow you to Derbyshire, I will call upon Sir Lesley to assure him I was never away from my estate."

Aidan shared the few details he learned from Miss Nelson during their short ride from the church.

"I will also discreetly inform the baronet of his son's involvement in illegal activities. Hopefully, Mathias Trent survived his injury."

Aidan smiled knowingly.

"I assure you, Nelson, Mr. Hill is extremely accurate with an assortment of weapons. He shot Trent in the leg to prevent the baronet's son from making a speedy escape."

The baron paled.

"It is another of my personal failures in participating in Trent's maneuverings," he admitted.

Aidan could add sugar to his response, but he knew Nelson had much to learn.

"It is only because of Godown's great admiration for his wife that you are not sitting in a cell in London. Never forget the immense gift you were given and to whom you owe your allegiance."

Nelson chuckled ironically.

"For many weeks, I cursed Lord Godown to the heavens, but slowly life returned to my body and my estate. The marquis plays a heavy hand, but he does not cheat in repaying his debts."

It was not necessary for the baron to speak the words written in the man's eyes.

"You are fortunate to claim the marquis as a brother," Aidan cautioned.

The baron nodded his understanding,

"I am well aware of Lord Godown's vast influence."

Nelson reached into his desk drawer.

"I was saving this for Mercy's return."

Aidan accepted the locket.

"Is this the one Miss Nelson lost to the Foyles?"

A smile uncurled, reaching the baron's mouth.

"She told you of her adventures? That is good."

Intense sadness crossed the man's countenance.

"That means my sister trusts you."

Aidan heard the unspoken phrase, *More than she did me.*

"Mr. Soames attended a local fair and came across this piece. He sent for me, and I claimed it stolen. After all, images of my parents are easily recognizable in the neighborhood. The

Foyles would not say where or when they met Mercy, but finding this piece provided me the hope of her success. She should wear it on her wedding day. I hope you will share it with her on your journey to Derbyshire."

"I will indeed, Nelson. Your sister will be ecstatic to have it in her possession again, but would you not prefer to return it to Mercy yourself?"

"No, it is better if it comes from you. I was the reason she lost it. I would prefer my sister concentrate on the happiness of knowing our mother's presence at her wedding than the chaotic world Mercy escaped and survived."

Aidan surreptitiously watched Mercy as she readjusted her bonnet's ribbon. He pretended to look out the coach's window, but his eyes could not get enough of the lady's countenance. He did not think it possible to feel complete contentment and lust at the same time, but he did. The hope of spring rested in that delightful dimple he had yet to explore properly.

"You look quite fetching, my dear," he said invitingly.

As if she read his thoughts, she blushed.

"So does my maid," she teased. "I presented her with an equaling fetching yellow gown and bonnet."

Aidan's lips twitched in amusement. She would truly be a perfect match for him.

"That gesture is most generous of you; however, I hope you warned the girl not to wear the gown where Sir Lesley might see it. I cannot imagine the baronet would be pleased to know you thought so little of the frock."

"Until the past week, I always thought Sir Lesley conniving and manipulative, but the baronet was as much a victim as was I," Mercy said seriously. "I felt empathy for his lost of face."

Aidan was not so sympathetic. The baronet permitted his son too much swagger. When Aidan thought on how close he came to losing Miss Nelson, a shiver of cold ran up his spine. If he did not knock Mercy to the ground, the bullet, which sped past

Aidan's ear, would lodge in her heart. Aidan meant to see Mathias Trent fully punished for the man's many crimes.

"I asked your brother to join us in Derbyshire."

"Is Derby our destination, my lord?"

Aidan chuckled in irony.

"I suppose we should discuss our journey in more detail. The mad rush to reach you in time precipitated my speedy negotiations with your brother."

Every part of Aidan's body ached to forget this conversation and just know the lady intimately again, but he meant to begin their marriage in complete honesty.

"I am honored by your devotion to my safety, my lord," Mercy said tentatively, "but did the mad rush, as you term it, also precipitate an omission of a proper proposal?"

Although her voice held a quiver of nervousness lacing her words, Miss Nelson's eyes spoke a challenge.

Aidan swallowed the bubble of happiness threatening to escape. The lady would bring a hoydenish mix of elegance to his life.

"I would think my 'mad rush' would be declaration enough of my affections," he countered.

The lady's chin rose in customary defiance.

"Even so, a girl would prefer to be asked. A man should not take a woman for granted, my lord."

"They are merely words, Miss Nelson," Aidan teased.

As he spoke, he shifted from the rear-facing seat to sit beside her.

"And I doubt you would refuse my hand."

She petulantly looked away.

"Do you consider yourself such a great catch, Lord Lexford? My, I never realized your vanity."

Aidan caught her chin to turn it in his direction.

"You of all people know I possess no call for either vanity or pride. My historic family is shaken to its core, but what I offer is my true regard for you. For your loyalty. Your creativity and your boldness. Your beautiful smile and your expressive eyes. I wish to spend my life with you by my side. You would do me a great honor, if you would accept my hand in marriage."

A single tear ran down her cheek.

"That was so beautiful," the lady said with a sigh of admiration. "I shall remember the moment forever."

Aidan's brow rose in curiosity.

"Was that a *yes*?'

She launched herself in Aidan's arms.

"Most assuredly, it is a *yes*. I was never happier."

She offered her mouth, and Aidan took great pleasure in tasting her again. She pressed her body to him, and heat rose quickly. Her eyes fluttered closed; her lips parted, and their tongues began a passionate dance. It pleased him to know he taught her to kiss so keenly. He sank into the kiss, pulling her to him.

As his lust grew, with great difficulty, Aidan set her from him. He gasped for breath, but it was the best he felt since those carefree childhood days of playing with Aylene in his mother's chambers. It was as if the shadows, which haunted him forever, disappeared in the mid day sun.

"We should...we should wait...wait for the vows," he stammered. When she frowned, he added, "I want us to come to the marriage bed with all our secrets in the open. During your absence from Lexington Arms many details of my life were revealed. I must tell you all, and we must set a new path. There are secrets, which would destroy Aaron and the viscountship."

Aidan gazed at her intently, awaiting her response.

"I would do whatever is necessary to protect Master Aaron. The boy is quite dear to me. I would be honored and grateful to have a say in the boy's future. Without us to stand in his stead, the world would have the child suffer for his parents' sins."

Aidan returned to the backward-facing seat.

"Then we should have at it."

For the next half hour Aidan told her of how Mrs. Babcock's death hurried his learning the truth. Like peeling away the layers of an onion, Aidan placed his family history at Mercy's feet.

"When we marry, we must continue the ruse. You are still my cousin, and I am the second son of Arlen Kimbolt. Aaron is my nephew and first in line as the heir until we produce legitimate heirs to the title. When we exit this coach, those are the parameters of our lives."

Aidan felt nothing but awkwardness in discussing his family with her. He hoped Mercy understood how much he required her to place her trust in him–how often he prayed for someone to accept him as he was. No feigned cordiality. No being everyone's friend. Simply recognizing him: Aidan Kimbolt, a man of eight and twenty, who meant to bring fame to his family's name as a breeder of fine horses. As a man of great passions.

Reeling from his revelations, Miss Nelson sat stunned for several seconds. She twisted her hands together.

"I have a confession, my lord. I discovered Lady Cassandra's diary, but I feared what was within would bring you grief. I asked Mr. Hill to destroy it. Can you forgive me?"

Aidan's eyes narrowed.

"Is this your answer to my revelations? A plea for forgiveness?"

There went that little flip of doubt in his chest again.

This time, it was she who moved to sit on the bench beside him. She met his gaze and answered with complete sincerity.

"Did you truly think I would deny you, my lord? Do you not understand, Aidan? I love you most dearly. So dearly my only concern is I disappointed you."

"You love me?"

He blinked in surprise.

"Surely, you realize I could not have..." Mercy blushed thoroughly. She paused as though seeking strength. "You wish to know if I can live within the strictures you describe. As I assisted in creating the myth, I assure you I am your servant. I see no impediment. You were born to be the viscount, and you will define the title. We will think of Andrew as your brother and Aaron as your nephew. The boy will make a great cousin for our children."

Again a flush rose to her cheeks.

"We will play our roles so well no one will question our children's rights to the title."

Aidan pulled her close and held Mercy to him.

"I loved you from the first moment I held your hand," he whispered against her hair, and Aidan meant it.

He kissed her slowly and quite thoroughly. A future was finally within reach.

Inhaling her essence, Aidan set her away for a second time.

"I have one last confession. This one will bring you grief, but you must learn it before we arrive in Derbyshire."

Her bottom lip trembled, but she said, "Then tell me quick."

Aidan cleared his throat.

"Until today, I thought you aware of your sister's good fortune in marrying Lord Godown. It was my failure in not understanding how desperate were your circumstances."

Mercy said softly, "I should have trusted you with my identity. Geoffrey taught me to fear my choices."

"You learned of Lady Godown's survival," he began.

"Oh, yes," she said anxiously. "Please say after we marry we may call upon my sister. It would be the greatest of gifts, my lord."

Aidan caught her hand.

"If I could give you your sister's company, I would readily agree."

Aidan hesitated, very serious.

"Do you not recall my speaking of the marquis and the attacks upon his being?"

Aidan did not pause to give Mercy time to answer. His remark was meant only to prompt her memory.

"The marquis and his wife argued. Lord Godown chose to send the marquise to one of his lesser properties to await the birth of a child."

Her eyes closed in despair, and Aidan could feel the tension break over him. Tears pricked at her lashes.

"Grace is to be a mother? To be with child and to be banished from her home…oh, my poor Grace!"

Mercy pleaded, "Do you know of this property? May we journey there to bring Grace comfort? My sister should not face motherhood alone."

Aidan's thumb stroked a line across her wrist, and Aidan did not meet her eyes.

"The story is quite complicated, but know your sister is not in Devon. She assisted the marquis in rescuing his aunts from the man you knew as Lord Spectre, but before Godown could dispense with Spectre and see to his elderly aunts' well beings, your sister left her husband to find shelter for her and her child."

Mercy's expression displayed her confusion.

"Your tale does not articulate the truth of Grace. My sister would be a devoted wife and mother," she asserted. "Speak to me of Grace's sin. What would cause the marquis to send her away?"

Aidan was uncomfortable discussing Godown's personal life.

"Spectre, whose real name is Benjamin Talbot, orchestrated several attacks upon Godown's life. The marquis knew of your sister's acquaintance with the man. Circumstances indicated Lady Godown conspired against her husband. More importantly, Godown feared the child was not his."

Tears crept down Mercy's cheeks.

"Oh, my darling Grace! How could the marquis ever doubt her? Grace would never perpetrate such a lie!"

"The evidence spoke of your sister's connection to Spectre," Aidan admitted. "Even I questioned her involvement." A long silence followed. "For what it is worth, Lord Godown grieves for his wife's absence. He searches for her everywhere."

"The marquis deserves any pain he knows," Miss Nelson said with a snit. "I briefly held kind thoughts regarding Lord Godown's assistance with Geoffrey, but not if his doing so was at Grace's detriment. Do you not understand, my lord? Being with child will prevent Grace from earning a living. How will she and the babe survive?"

"I assure you, Lord Godown will never stop searching for his wife. Despite their contentious beginning, Godown adores his marquise. I witnessed the marquis's affection written upon his face. Before I returned to Lexington Arms to discover you under my roof, I was quite jealous of Godown's transformation," he confessed.

Mercy's tears flowed easily.

"May we assist Lord Godown in his search? Keep whatever you offered in the marriage settlements for my pin money and use it to find Grace. I require nothing new. I shall gladly make due with the gowns I possess at Lexington Arms. My sister is more important. Promise me it will be so, my lord."

"There is no need for your plea, my dear. I will gladly make the offer to Godown. A man knows his obligations."

She kissed Aidan's knuckles.

"My family will never be easy, my lord. If you wish to withdraw, I would understand."

They both knew the 'not exactly comfortable,' and never simple, ways of a fractured family.

Aidan gathered her to him.

"Even if I did not hold you in great affection, there is the possibility of your carrying my child. We are bound to each other in spirit. The vows are only for the public announcement of that bond. A piece of paper cannot demand love or fidelity. Only trust and faith and affection can keep two together as one."

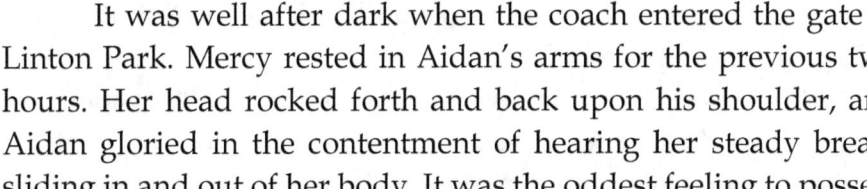

It was well after dark when the coach entered the gate of Linton Park. Mercy rested in Aidan's arms for the previous two hours. Her head rocked forth and back upon his shoulder, and Aidan gloried in the contentment of hearing her steady breath sliding in and out of her body. It was the oddest feeling to possess someone who returned his affection. Foolish as it sounded he wished to climb the gables of Linton Park and shout of his happiness.

"You must wake, my dear," he said as he shook her lightly. As Mercy's eyes batted open and close, Aidan kissed her tenderly.

When he released her, she sighed deeply, and the knowledge she affected him as much as he did her went a long way in satisfying Aidan's hunger for his betrothed.

"Where are we?" she said sleepily.

Aidan smiled as he straightened his waistcoat and carvat.

"We will be at Linton Park in a matter of minutes."

"Oh, my!"

Mercy slid to the other bench and began to rearrange her clothing.

"What will your friends think of me? I am so disheveled."

She tucked strands of hair into her chignon.

Aidan smiled easily at her.

"The only one you must please is seated in this carriage, and I believe you beyond beautiful."

As the carriage rolled into the circle before the house, the manor's door swung wide to reveal James Kerrington standing in the muted light of a lantern. The viscount's presence surprised Aidan for he knew the Worthings attended the dowager duchess's engagement party. They must have departed London immediately following the party's conclusion. Aidan thought he would be required to plead with the Earl and Countess of Linworth for permission to use the Linton Chapel for his nuptials. Now, he supposed Worthing would extend his best wishes. When Swenton joined the viscount on the main stoop, Aidan breathed easier. His friend did not fail him.

The carriage rolled to a stop, and Aidan slid across the seat to loosen the door's latch.

"It is you," Worthing declared as he pulled open the coach's door. "Ole Taylor recognized Lucifer in the seat, but the gatekeeper did not know the carriage."

Worthing glanced toward an obviously nervous Mercy.

"I see you were successful in your quest."

"Did you expect anything less," Aidan said a bit tersely.

He was not in the mood for the "Captain's" jesting.

"Assist the lady from the carriage, Worthing, and then I will make the proper introductions."

Worthing chuckled in easy companionship.

"As you wish, my lord."

The viscount set down the steps and then extended his hand to Mercy.

"Please accept the hand of a stranger, Miss," he teased.

Aidan's lady rose to the challenge, and in that moment, Aidan knew she won over the viscount.

"As I possess my most loyal knight at my side, I shall venture into the unknown, my lord."

She gracefully placed her hand in Kerrington's to debark.

Aidan followed close behind her, and he overheard Worthing whisper, "I am handier with both a sword and a gun than is your deserving knight, my dear."

Mercy smiled up at the viscount.

"Yet, my knight's heart is true, my lord, and yours belongs to another."

Worthing barked out a laugh.

"You will do quite nicely for Lord Lexford; welcome to the family."

Aidan cleared his throat menacingly.

"Please release my betrothed, Worthing."

The viscount held tightly to Mercy's hand.

"I must think on your request, my lord. You see, I am in a quandary. I hold a beautiful woman's hand, and I was considering kissing the back of it."

Aidan said through gritted teeth.

"I would prefer you did not, my lord."

Worthing turned to Aidan and smiled widely.

"And I would prefer you did not kiss my wife," Worthing taunted.

Even in the dark shadows, Aidan was certain all could

observe his embarrassment.

"When did you discover this particular fact?"

Worthing brought Mercy closer to his side.

"Ella keeps no secrets from me," Worthing said seriously. "At least, not for very long. And that is my advice to you. Before you join your lives, commit to each other completely. Only then, will you know true happiness."

With that, Worthing handed off Mercy's hand to Aidan.

Aidan's brows tightened together before he slid his arm about her waist.

"A hard lesson," he said solemnly.

Worthing bowed.

"The only kind to which you ever adhered. Now, introduce me to your lady so we may retreat from the cold. The others await you inside."

"What others?" Aidan said suspiciously.

Worthing shook his head in disbelief.

"Only a fool would think we would permit you to open your life to your lady, and we would not be witnesses. All are within, excluding Fowler. The Duchess is suffering with the child she carries, but know the duke played his part. When Swenton attempted to claim a license in your name, the bishop denied the request. It took the considerable sway of a duke, a marquis, an earl, two viscounts, a baron, and a baronet to convince him."

Aidan questioned, "Two viscounts?"

The idea of his friends' devotion shook Aidan's composure.

"Lord Stafford joined our quest," Worthing explained. "The viscount signed the license as if he were you. The man is quite daring."

Aidan chuckled,

"Although Godown would not agree, I often thought Stafford would make a good agent." He brought the back of Mercy's hand to his lips. "As Viscount Worthing suggests, we should meet our wedding guests, my dear."

They stepped into a whirlwind. His friends and their ladies greeted them. Aidan could not recall a time when he smiled so much. Miss Nelson remained by his side throughout, and he was drunk with excitement. Swenton explained in more detail how he recruited the others to pressure the bishop into signing off on a special license.

"When the Bishop entered the room to discover a gaggle of aristocrats seeking his understanding, the man quickly changed his mind."

"A gaggle?" they questioned in unison.

Swenton smiled easily.

"How else should I have described an unorganized group dealing with a pompous cleric? In military terms, a 'gaggle' is a group on a mission, which is exactly what we were."

After another round of laughter, Worthing related the tale of Lord and Lady Godown's reuniting. Tears misted Mercy's eyes when Lord Worthing announced the expected arrival of the marquis's carriage on the morrow.

"Oh, Aidan!" Mercy clutched at his hand. "Grace will be with me when I marry!"

"The marquis knew nothing of his wife's return when he appeared at Doctors' Commons to support Swenton's application in your name. Needless to say, he did not join us for a hearty meal and drink after our success. The marquis and Viscount Stafford conducted their usual posturing, while Thornhill took great pleasure in siding with Stafford. I thought after the duke won his duchess and the marquis Lady Godown that such foolishness would die out."

Aidan said sagaciously, "When Godown learns the lessons of family, he will no longer need to claim prominence. Some hold on to their vanity as protection for bruised pride."

Worthing nodded his agreement. "It is a generous lesson." As if Worthing could not deny Lady Eleanor, the viscount reached for his wife's hand, lacing their fingers together.

"Does my sister not know of our joining?" Mercy pleaded.

"Grace knows," Lady Worthing assured. "When James disclosed Lord Lexford's plans to marry at Linton Park, I sent word to the marquise. She welcomed my interruption of her reunion with Lord Godown. The Godowns will arrive tomorrow; have no fear."

Epilogue

"DEARLY BELOVED," Doctor Perry's voice rang out across the chapel. Four months passed since the vicar had pronounced Aidan's vows, and Aidan never was happier. He glanced to his wife, and her fingers wrapped about his arm. Reflexively, Aidan's muscle tightened. From where her hand rested at the crook of his elbow, heat radiated down his arm to his fingertips. His obsession with the woman grew, and Aidan generously surrendered to the heat that always sizzled between them.

Mercy's other hand surreptitiously rested on her lap-splayed across her abdomen. Just this morning, she shared her hopes of being with child. His lady swore Aidan to secrecy, at least, until they were certain, but Aidan wished to climb to the highest church spire and shout to the world of his good fortune.

Good fortune, he thought ironically. Until recently, those were two words rarely associated with his life. When he and Mercy returned to Lexington Arms, their farce took on a second life. The neighborhood rejoiced at his marrying his "cousin." When those within the village learned he and Mercy meant to welcome Aaron as part of their family, they received great praise for their benevolence. Within a month of their return to Cheshire, they successfully hosted a house full of aristocrats for a weeklong party. The presence of so many excellent examples of the socially elite, recognizing Aidan and Mercy as equals, went a long way in defining Aidan's viscountcy. Each of his friends arrived on Lexington Arms' doorstep with one mission: naming Aidan's reign as Viscount Lexford as a successful one.

He pensioned off Mr. Poley and Mr. Payne, the former for the obvious reason and the latter because the butler was aware of Mrs. Babcock's relationship with Arlen Kimbolt. Aidan wished no remnants of his family's shame under his root.

With Pennington's assistance, Aidan saw Sophia Rhodes placed in a facility for those suffering from hallucinations. The lady's husband reluctantly agreed to sell his estate to Aidan and to leave the area; Aidan's knowledge of Rhodes's connection to the Trents was the proper leverage to drive the man from the neighborhood. Aidan wanted nothing to cloud his marriage.

Authorities captured Mathias Trent along the Scottish coastline. Sir Lesley foolishly financed a scheme to save his eldest son and now faced resettlement charges.

Aidan glanced about the church. They were all in attendance–the Realm–even Aristotle Pennington. All came to witness the joining of Henry Lucifer Hill to Hannah Louise Tolliver. A room full of aristocrats honoring a common man and a lady's maid.

Hill returned with Aidan to Lexington Arms to assist with the turmoil they left behind while they raced off to rescue Mercy. When Rhodes abandoned his estate, Aidan attempted to thrust it upon his friend.

"I would be pleased to call you neighbor," he said.

Needless to say, Hill laughed in that self-deprecating way the man always used to remind Aidan they were not of the same social class.

"I extend my gratitude, my lord, but I mean to make Hannah my wife, and my lady would refuse such a grand home. Something simpler with land for farming would suit me well."

And so, Aidan found a farm some fifteen miles south of

Manchester–larger than Hill would chose for himself, but Aidan convinced Hill it was an excellent purchase.

"Large enough to fill the halls with children of your own," Aidan baldly suggested when Hill protested.

Doctor Perry continued, "Those whom God hath joined together let no man put asunder. Forasmuch as Henry and Hannah consented together in hold wedlock, and witnessed the same before God and this company and thereto give and pledge their troth, each to the other, and declare the same by giving and receiving a Ring, and by joining hands; I pronounce that they are Man and Wife. In the Name of the Father, and of the Son, and of the Holy Ghost. Amen."

After the vicar's blessing, Hill and his bride turned to face their guests. Aidan enjoyed the lopsided smile upon his friend's countenance. Behind where he and Mercy sat, he heard Lady Worthing sniffle into her linen.

"Hannah has been with me since I was a young girl," she said for the hundredth time.

Aidan chuckled when James Kerrington soothed his wife's woes.

"Yet, we wish Hannah the best, my dear."

As Lucifer and Hannah disappeared into the holding room to sign the church's ledger, Aidan rose to follow the others to the wedding breakfast.

"Godown," he called as the marquis stepped into the aisle. "When do you return to Staffordshire?"

"I mean to depart as soon as I give my best regards to the bride and Hill."

Mercy teased, "Missing my sister, Lord Godown?"

With Lady Godown's encouragement, Aidan's wife quickly forgave the marquis's earlier misunderstandings.

Godown brought Mercy's gloved hand to his lips, and even though Aidan knew the marquis meant nothing by the gesture, a bead of jealousy slipped down his spine.

"You speak the truth, Lady Lexford." The marquis winked

at Mercy. "Your sister possesses many charms, as do you, Sister Dear."

Aidan recovered his wife's hand.

"And you are wild about your son," Aidan reminded the marquis.

"The child is perfection, Lexford." Godown's smile grew. "And, yes, I am in great need of both my wife and the boy."

"I have a gift for Baby Renard," Mercy shared. "I will fetch it when we return to the house. And you must ferry my love to Grace."

"Your brother journey to Staffordshire to keep Lady Godown company in my absence. You will be pleased to know within another year, two at the most, the baron's estate will be solvent again."

Mercy's eyes sparkled with happiness, and Aidan thought her the most magnificent creature he ever knew.

"Did you hear, Aidan? Geoffrey will soon be restored."

"Yes, Dear. The marquis has been quite clever. Now come along. I wish private words with Hill before the man becomes too enamored with his wife."

Godown laughed easily.

"We each realize that is not a possibility."

It took Aidan longer than he expected to isolate Hill. At length, a moment arrived, and he whisked Lucifer into a nearby drawing room while Lady Worthing assisted Hannah with a change of clothing before her departure.

"I will only require a moment," Aidan assured his friend when Lucifer protested leaving Hannah's side.

"I did not predict a farewell, my lord," Lucifer said in amusement. "We will only be a two hours' ride in separation."

The man's happiness erased ten years from Hill's countenance. His friend's eyes danced with light-hearted delight.

"I am designated by the others to present you with a small gift," Aidan began.

Hill interrupted, "There is no need, my lord," Lucifer protested. "You and the others gave me my life. If you did nothing more, it would be enough. Instead, you opened your home to me–gave me your companionship–treated me as an equal. You took a struggling soul and showed him the gift of learning–of seeing the world. Through you, I met Hannah. I possess more than ten men over."

Aidan swallowed hard. From Hill, Aidan learned compassion and reasoning. Hill brought Mercy into Aidan's life–restored Aidan's faith in others. Aidan owed the man everything.

"Men, such as those with whom we served, do not speak easily of their respect and their loyalty. Yet, there are means to name their fidelity."

Aidan reached for a rolled paper resting upon a side table.

"This represents such devotion from those with whom you served."

Hill cautiously accepted the scroll and unfurled the page. Aidan watched as Hill first swayed in place and then his Adam's apple worked hard to breathe.

"It is too…too much, my lord."

"It was by consensus," Aidan said with determination. "The men celebrating your nuptials mean to offer their gratitude, Lucifer. Surely you can find it in you to be gracious in your acceptance."

"I served because it was my personal vow," Hill protested. "I never meant to seek a reward."

"Neither did any of us, Lucifer," Aidan assured, "and it is not a reward. Your Realm brothers offer you their hands in friendship. Do not slap them away because of your stubborn nature."

Hill's eyes returned to the paper.

"Be reasonable," Aidan pressed. "It is too late in the summer to plant, and without a harvest, you could lose everything before you begin. This way, you will possess time to prepare the land."

"How do I repay the men's loyalty?" Hill asked honestly.

"By being a success," Aidan said simply. "Prove their confidence was well placed."

Hill extended his hand in acceptance, but Aidan pulled the man into a male embrace.

"My home will appear empty until your return. Lady Lexford and I mean to have you visit often."

Hill nodded sharply as he stepped away.

"I should return to the gathering."

As Lucifer slipped from the room, Mercy entered seconds later.

"How did Mr. Hill react?" she asked as she slid into Aidan's loose embrace.

He rested his chin on the top of his wife's head.

"Very much as predicted, but Mr. Hill did not rip the deed to shreds," he said.

He inhaled the lilac scent as she rested her cheek against his chest. Such moments went a long way in soothing Aidan's troubled soul. It was in a similar embrace that a major piece of his lost memory returned. Evidently, he found his mother's diary and read the truth of Andrew's parentage before he traveled to Manchester to court Cashémere Aldridge. With his appearance at Chesterfield Manor, he meant to win the lady's agreement and to place his father's exploitations firmly in the past.

When Aidan shared this new reality with Mercy, his wife shed tears of sorrow for his painful discovery, as well as tears of joy at their finding each other.

"If you were successful, my lord," she said as he dabbed away her tears with his linen, "we would both possess very different lives."

Aidan assured her through a slow seduction that he would face it all again for the pleasure of knowing her as his wife.

"One need only to look upon my countenance to realize I found perfection in my life."

Mercy chuckled as she snuggled closer. They spent a month in London enjoying the accolades of the *haut ton*. He danced with her and escorted Mercy shopping on Bond Street. While there, Aidan set connections in place for Miss Chadwick's entrance in the design field by finding the girl a position in a prestigious shop, as well as proper lodging. Miss Chadwick's first commission was the renovations at Fugol Hall for the marquis's heir. Lord and Lady Godown adored the nursery for Aaron. Contentedly, his wife nibbled along Aidan's chin line, and he adored every seductive gesture.

"What should we expect when Mr. Hill discovers you stocked his barns and his house for the winter?" she asked on a rasp.

Aidan smiled widely as he gathered her closer.

"Until your news this morning," he kissed the column of his wife's neck, "I thought a journey to China and back might provide Mr. Hill's indignity time to subside," Aidan said teasingly.

"And now?" Her voice held the huskiness he relished hearing.

He paused to kiss her tenderly.

"Now," Aidan said distractedly. "Now, I will…" Kiss. "Will need…" Kiss. "Need to…" Kiss. "Need to hire…" Kiss. "Extra guards…" Longer kiss. "To protect the estate. Mr. Hill will bring his protests to my door."

Aidan's mouth found his wife's in a feast. It was how Aidan enjoyed knowing his wife. How he began each day and ended each night. The air became thick and close. His blood pumped savagely, always on fire with need for her.

Mercy clung to him, her fingers tight against his lapels. She placed a hand against his cheek. He breathed through the simmering connection that buzzed through his body. One hand traced light circles on the back of his wife's neck. His hands cupped her hips and edged her closer. Aidan's erection throbbed for release, but the scuff of a foot in the hall invaded his desire-filled mind. He broke the kiss and shielded her against him as he looked up to see Thornhill with a smirk of amusement on his lips.

"It appears, Lexford, it is my turn to find you in a

compromising situation," the duke taunted.

Aidan said through gritted teeth, "You are a prat, Duke. What do you wish of me?"

The duke's silly grin widened.

"I meant to find Sir Carter. A friend is in need of the baronet's special talents."

Instinctively, Aidan asked, "What friend? May we not all be of service?"

Thornhill shook off the offer.

"Sir Carter holds the administrative power to save Mrs. Warren."

Aidan kept Mercy's countenance hidden, but he loosened his grip on her.

"Mrs. Warren?" he asked curiously.

Thornhill gestured to Mercy.

"It is a long, complicated story. I will share it a bit later. For now, my lord, enjoy your life."

With a quick bow and a lazy salute, the duke withdrew, closing the door behind him.

Aidan glanced at his wife. He expected to discover her embarrassment. Instead, Mercy tugged at her bottom lip to stifle her giggles. As awkward as the moment was, Aidan, too, began to chuckle.

"Next time, remind me to close and lock the door."

She buried her face once again, but her shoulders shook with glee. Nervous laughter peppered her speech.

"I assumed once I…once I married…the opportunity…to be the source…of gossip…would dissipate."

His jacket muffled the words, but Aidan understood her sentiment.

"I cannot promise it will be the last time others may observe the full extent of my regard for you," he said softly against her ear.

His wife rose on her tiptoes to kiss his chin. Her eyes became luminous.

"I certainly should hope not," she pronounced baldly. "But

for now, I suppose I will suggest we wait until later."

Aidan's fingers caressed the softness of her cheek.

"*Later* is such a morbid term," he teased.

Since the day Mercy Nelson appeared on his doorstep, Aidan's time as a loner disappeared. His wife invaded every inch of Aidan's soul: The lost boy deep inside him found.

"How often do I use the word *later*?" his wife taunted, and her eyes darkened in that delightful way that signaled her desire. "Especially with you."

Her breath hitched, and Aidan could not wipe the smile from his lips. He tasted her, knowing the pleasure of the warmth of her mouth. She clung brazenly to him, and Aidan celebrated love.

"I would adore you even if you would choose to use the word all the time."

And with that, he kissed her again.

"You, Mercy Kimbolt, are the answer to all my questions. At length, after a lifetime of searching, I found exactly where I belong–in the arms of a spirited wood sprite."

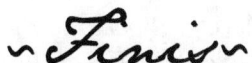

Finis

"Teach me to feel another's woe, to hide the fault I see, that mercy I to others show, that mercy show to me."
- Alexander Pope

Other Novels by Regina Jeffers

Jane Austen-Inspired Novels:

Darcy's Passions: Pride and Prejudice Retold Through His Eyes
Darcy's Temptation: A Pride and Prejudice Sequel
Captain Wentworth's Persuasion: Jane Austen's Classic Retold Through His Eyes
Vampire Darcy's Desire: A Pride and Prejudice Paranormal Adventure
The Phantom of Pemberley: A Pride and Prejudice Mystery
Christmas at Pemberley: A Pride and Prejudice Holiday Sequel
The Disappearance of Georgiana Darcy: A Pride and Prejudice Mystery
The Mysterious Death of Mr. Darcy: A Pride and Prejudice Mystery
The Prosecution of Mr. Darcy's Cousin: A Pride and Prejudice Mystery
"The Pemberley Ball" (a short story in *The Road to Pemberley* anthology)
Honor and Hope: A Contemporary Pride and Prejudice

Regency and Contemporary Romances:

The Scandal of Lady Eleanor – Book 1 of the Realm Series (aka A Touch of Scandal)
A Touch of Velvet – Book 2 of the Realm Series
A Touch of Cashémere – Book 3 of the Realm Series
A Touch of Grace – Book 4 of the Realm Series
A Touch of Mercy – Book 5 of the Realm Series
A Touch of Love – Book 6 of the Realm Series
A Touch of Honor – Book 7 of the Realm Series
His: Two Regency Novellas (includes "His American Heartsong," a Realm series novella, and "His Irish Eve," a sequel to *The Phantom of Pemberley*)
The First Wives' Club – Book 1 of the First Wives' Trilogy
Second Chances: The Courtship Wars

Coming Soon...

Angel Comes to the Devil's Keep
The Earl Finds His Comfort
Elizabeth Bennet's Deception: A Pride and Prejudice Vagary
Elizabeth Bennet's Independence: A Pride and Prejudice Vagary
Mr. Darcy's Bargain: A Pride and Prejudice Vagary

A Touch of Love

LUCINDA STOOD on the busy street corner for a quarter hour, attempting to shore up her nerves. She carefully read the social register for the past few weeks, waiting for the return of the Duke of Thornhill to his London townhouse. A single line of type reported Brantley Fowler's presence at Briar House, and Lucinda wasted no time in sending a note around, requesting an audience with the duke. Thornhill responded immediately, setting the date and time.

Self-consciously, she checked Matthew's pocket watch for the time. She regularly carried her late husband's watch in her reticule. It was one of the few items she kept to mark her days as Matthew Warren's wife.

"Time," she murmured.

Matthew never found the time to speak the truth, Lucinda thought bitterly. As she set her shoulders to cross the street, she wondered how Thornhill would take to Lucinda's report of his old friend. *I possess no choice,* she assured her rapid pulse.

She sidestepped a fresh pile of horse dung while dodging a young gentleman's poorly driven curricle to step upon the curb before Briar House. It was a magnificent house: plenty of windows to permit the light and warmth of even a weak sun, as well as beautiful columns giving the exterior the look of a Roman theatre. Briar House spoke of the Fowlers' place in Society. Her breath hitched, and Lucinda chastised herself for the very feminine desire to break into tears again. Her eyes swept the townhouse's façade. Splendor she would never know.

With a deep steadying breath, she entered the gate and ascended the few steps to release the knocker. In less than a minute, the door swung wide to reveal the duke's very proper butler.

"Yes, Miss?"

Lucinda swallowed hard to clear his throat.

"I am Mrs. Warren. His Grace is expecting me."

The butler's eyebrow rose as he peered behind her to look for her maid, but it was more than a year since Lucinda could afford help of any kind. She pretended not to notice the servant's disapproval.

"This way, Mrs. Warren," the butler said diplomatically.

Lucinda politely followed the man up the stairs and along an elaborately decorated passage. She attended the Come Out ball for Thornhill's sister, Lady Eleanor Fowler, and his cousin, Miss Velvet Aldridge in this very house. Now, Miss Aldridge was Brantley Fowler's duchess, and by all accounts the man's one true love. Yet, on that one evening, Lucinda received the duke's attentions, and although she was a bit uncomfortable with Thornhill's sudden adoration, the evening remained one of Lucinda's favorite memories. A man of worth revered her intelligence and her good sense. A man found her attractive, something Matthew never did.

The butler tapped on an already open door.

"Your Grace. Mrs. Warren to speak to you."

The man stepped aside, and Lucinda entered a very masculine study. Dark wood panels spoke of a strong mind and an unqualified determination, both of which could easily describe the Duke of Thornhill.

The duke rose to greet her. His light brown hair was peppered with strands of gold. It was unstylishly long and tied back with a leather strap. Eyes of darkest chocolate glittered with genuine welcome, and Lucinda breathed a bit easier.

"Thank you, Mr. Horace. If you will ask Cook to send in tea."

"Certainly, Your Grace."

Brantley Fowler caught Lucinda's hand and brought it to his lips.

"I was pleased to hear from you," he said easily, "but I admit you piqued my interest."

Lucinda always liked the young lord. The future duke spent but two months in the same company as did Lucinda's late husband; and during the brief interval, Fowler and Matthew renewed their university friendship. She was proud to say the young lord always treated her with respect. She was the daughter of the third son of an earl, and the future duke accepted her as his equal socially. In fact, once when Matthew found fault with the meal Lucinda managed on the few supplies available, it was Brantley Fowler who took up her defense.

"I appreciate your seeing me on such short notice, Your Grace."

The duke led her to a nearby settee before assuming the seat across from where Lucinda sat.

"I beg your forgiveness for my bold gesture."

The duke frowned.

"I would hope you would view me as an ally, Lucinda."

His ready familiarity eased her tension.

The butler returned with the tray.

"Mrs. Warren will serve, Horace."

"As you wish, Your Grace."

The butler closed the door upon his exit.

Lucinda dutifully took up the service. This cup would be a treat for her. Her meager funds did not stretch to expensive tea.

"My sister Eleanor's husband, Lord Worthing, declares he spent seven years of service to his country without a decent cup of tea."

The duke's words were as if Thornhill could read her mind,

and he meant to set her at ease.

Lucinda nodded her understanding.

"Even on English soil," she said as a means to define her purpose in coming to Briar House, "many cannot afford the weak mix with which we suffered on the Continent. The military's idea of tea is less than inspiring, but it would be welcome in many English households."

A long pause kept Thornhill silent. The air was thick with nerves and unspoken truths. At length, the duke asked, "Are you among those who cannot afford such luxuries?"

Lucinda always prided herself on her frankness. She came to beg Thornhill for his support, and the duke deserved the truth, as she knew it.

"I am, Your Grace," she said more calmly than she felt.

Setting his cup aside, the duke sat forward bracing his arms along his thighs. He cocked his head as if seeing her for the first time, and Lucinda fought the urge to squirm under the man's close scrutiny.

"When last we met, you spoke of a small settlement from your mother and, of course, your widow's pension. Had I known…" he said with concern.

Lucinda cut off the duke's offer.

"I am not your responsibility, Your Grace, and a pity call was not my purpose this day."

He jammed his knuckles into the side of his leg. The duke held a reputation for rescuing "damsels in distress." It was one of the reasons Lucinda sought his assistance.

"But what of your parents? Or of the Warrens?"

Lucinda cleared her throat and hoped her voice did not betray the chaos rushing through her veins.

"My mother passed some five months after my marriage to Matthew. The Colonel lost his life in Belgium."

She could not hide the grief, which tugged heavily at her heart. Losing her father came close to sending Lucinda over the edge, both figuratively and literally.

"I would prefer not to seek the assistance of the Earl of Charleton. The Colonel and Uncle William were often at odds. I would not wish to claim the role of poor dependent."

Lucinda did not think her father's oldest brother would take kindly to the situation in which she now found herself.

"And the Warrens?" the duke prompted.

His words caused Lucinda's heart to stutter. Every time she thought of Matthew's betrayal she wanted to curse the heavens.

She schooled her expression. Matthew's parents turned from her after their son's death. At the time, Lucinda did not understand the reasons the Warrens placed distance between them. Matthew's parents pledged their only child to Lucinda when she and Matthew were but babes, and the Thornbys gloried in the connection. She felt the shame for her parents' hopes. Although she could not say she loved Matthew Warren, she always held her husband in great affection; they were friends for as long as she could recall.

"Father Warren indicated I am no longer welcome at Coltman Hall."

The duke's mouth formed a thin line of disapproval.

"I once thought Warren's parents perfect in every way," he confessed.

Lucinda thought, *Perfect in their outward displays, but greatly lacking in essentials.*

"If you hold no objections, Your Grace, I would care to speak to the reasons for my calling upon you."

"By all means." The duke leaned back into the chair's cushions. "I am your servant."

The nerves she had tamped down roared to life again. A thousand frightening scenarios flitted through her brain. Purposefully, Lucinda took another sip of the tea. It really was quite lovely to taste the bitter leaves. Setting the cup on the tray, she caught Fowler's gaze and held it.

"Some three months past, I was presented a most difficult situation. I opened the door to my let rooms to find a small boy setting upon the threshold. There were no adults about and upon investigation, no one knew of how the child came to waiting outside my quarters."

"Was there no identification?" Thornhill inquired earnestly.

Lucinda set her shoulders in a stiff slant. She dreaded what was to come, but the duke would accept nothing less than the absolute facts.

"Only a note pinned to the child's jacket."

When the duke did not respond, she continued.

"The note announced the child to be Matthew's. By his wife, a woman Mr. Warren married in '09, some two years before he returned to Devon for the pronouncing of our vows."

Lucinda kept part of the truth as her own special torment. She did not tell him the complete facts of the child's mother.

The duke appeared perplexed.

"How may that be so? You are telling me, Matthew Warren took another without his parents' knowledge?"

Lucinda asked herself that very question repeatedly.

"I would hope the Warrens did not knowingly foist a sham of a marriage upon me." She forced the tremble from her words.

The duke was up and pacing.

"I heard of such perfidy, but I would never place Matthew Warren among those who would practice such duplicity. The extent of this falsehood is of the gravest debasement."

"The boy was conceived after our joining," Lucinda said softly.

She would not permit the duke to observe how the thought of her husband with another woman ripped Lucinda's heart from her chest; yet, she cried her last tear for the soul of a dishonorable man.

Thornhill dejectedly returned to his seat.

"This is all too much." With a heavy sigh, he asked, "Where is the child now?"

Lucinda glanced to the sun streaming through one of the windows. There was only one small window in her rooms, and she sorely missed the air upon her countenance. *Too many years of following drum,* she thought.

"Today, young Simon is with my landlady. The child is staying with me."

Again, she withheld an important fact that would likely color everything with a black stroke.

The duke set forward again.

"You took it upon yourself to care for the offspring of your husband's betrayal?" he asked incredulously. "You must realize, Mrs. Warren, that your raising this child within your home will bring you nothing but ostracism. You are opening yourself to public humiliation when this situation becomes common knowledge."

Lucinda fought back the tears stinging her lashes.

"The child holds the right to know the touch of love. I could not turn the boy out on the streets, but it is Simon's presence, which brings me to your door. The child complicated my life in ways I could not anticipate. If Matthew married another before speaking his vows to me, I am not his widow, and my only source of income for the boy and me vanisheds into a foggy London sky. I require someone to discover the truth of the note's claim. I can easily voice a myriad of questions, but I possess no resources to discover the answers."

About the Author

Regina Jeffers, a public classroom teacher for thirty-nine years, considers herself a Jane Austen enthusiast. She is the author of several Austen-inspired novels, including *Darcy's Passions, Darcy's Temptation, Vampire Darcy's Desire, Captain Wentworth's Persuasion, The Phantom of Pemberley, Christmas at Pemberley, The Disappearance of Georgiana Darcy, Honor and Hope,* and *The Mysterious Death of Mr. Darcy.* She also writes Regency romances: *The Scandal of Lady Eleanor, A Touch of Velvet, A Touch of Cashémere, A Touch of Grace,* and *The First Wives' Club.* A Smithsonian presenter, a Time Warner Star Teacher and Martha Holden Jennings Scholar, Jeffers often serves as a consultant in language arts and media literacy. Currently living outside Charlotte, North Carolina, she spends her time with her writing, gardening, and her adorable grandchildren.

Website www.rjeffers.com

Blogs http://reginajeffers.wordpress.com
http://austenvariations.com
http://englishhistoryauthors.blogspot.com/

Twitter – @reginajeffers
Facebook – Regina Jeffers
(Books available from Amazon, Barnes & Noble, Books-a-Million, Kobo, Joseph Beth, Regency Solutions, Pegasus Books, Black Opal Books, and Ulysses Press.)

www.ingramcontent.com/pod-product-compliance
Lightning Source LLC
Chambersburg PA
CBHW070346260626
47161CB00001B/31